Caribbean Crush

Not So Nice Guy*

Scoring Wilder*

The Beach (novella)

The Beau & the Belle*

The Fortunate Ones

The Foxe & the Hound*

The Trouble with Quarterbacks*

Three Strikes and You're Mine*

To Have and To Hate*

With This Heart

Available Titles within a Series

Heart Series

The Duet*

The Design*

Allure Series

The Allure of Dean Harper*

The Allure of Julian Lefray*

Summer Games Series

The Summer Games: Settling the Score*

The Summer Games: Out of Bounds

*Romantic comedies

Caribbean Crush

R.S. GREY

 Montlake

Text copyright © 2024 by R.S. Grey Books, LLC
All rights reserved.

Published by Montlake, Seattle

www.apub.com

Amazon, the Amazon logo, and Montlake are trademarks of Amazon.com, Inc., or its affiliates.

ISBN-13: 9781662517648 (paperback)
ISBN-13: 9781662517655 (digital)

Cover design by Hang Le
Cover image: © New Africa, © klyaksun, © Macrovector, © Lana Brow / Shutterstock

Printed in the United States of America

Caribbean Crush

Chapter One
CASEY

I squeeze my eyes shut as I white-knuckle the metal railing with both hands. *Oh dear god.* I've really done it now. I've flown too close to the sun. It serves me right for being such a liar, liar, pants on fire.

I feel a slight rocking underfoot that shouldn't be there. It's in direct contrast to everything I read online.

It's just like being on land!

You won't notice a thing!

These new ships are practically floating cities!

The sway is so gentle I could almost miss it, but not now, not with my eyes closed and my other senses dulled. It's a perpetual reminder of where I've found myself: adrift.

My erratic heart is going crazy in my chest. My knees bend as I grip tighter to the rail.

I never thought I'd be standing on the balcony of a suite on board a luxury cruise liner about to set sail around the Caribbean.

I can't force my eyes to peel open. The sun bears down on me, adding fire to the stifling moist heat. How do people live like this? Fort Lauderdale might as well be the devil's butt crack for how sweltering it is down here. The seagulls caw overhead. The briny sea breeze whirls and lifts my hair so it dances around my shoulders. The boat's horn rumbles a low, long blare—a triumphant send-off that has me nearly doubling over.

Is it too late to jump and swim ashore? Surely, I could make it. I'm not *that* far up.

I peek my eyes open to check, and the heady height almost makes me lose my breakfast. I *am* that far up.

It's going to be okay. Don't panic. Ignore the impending doom creeping in from all sides. The impostor syndrome chirping in the back of your mind isn't real. You belong here!

And I do.

I *do* belong here. I'm an intrepid reporter. A legitimate journalist with a press badge and *real* credentials. I didn't steal any of it! A sprightly blonde attendant willingly handed me a press packet when she showed me to my suite an hour ago. It had my name on it and everything. Printed in black and white.

I, Casey Hughes, have a job to do.

I work at *Bon Voyage*, a travel magazine that boasts more than five million readers and another few million online subscribers. I've worked there for six years, ever since I graduated from college with a degree in journalism. I have a very fancy, very chichi title. Here it is. Gird your loins. I'm a . . . *drum roll* . . . fact-checker. I know what you're thinking— *That can't possibly be a real job.* Well, it is. On my email signature, it reads, Casey Hughes, fact-checker.

But that's not my end goal.

This isn't the career I've always longed for. I didn't stand up at my kindergarten graduation—after the boy who picked astronaut and the girl who couldn't choose between veterinarian and Barbie—and tell the crowd that I longed to be a glorified grunt worker.

I've always wanted to work in travel journalism. My initial longing to see far-off places stems not from inspiring college lectures but from TV shows like *The Price Is Right* and *Wheel of Fortune*. In the afternoons, after school, my grandmother and I would sit on the couch together, watching Bob Barker and Pat Sajak woo contestants and audiences alike with the promise of luxurious vacation prizes. Jamaica, South Africa, England—it didn't matter.

"Oh, Italy!" my grandmother would exclaim. "I've *always* wanted to go there!" Then she'd turn to me with an imploring look in her eyes. "Promise me, when you're older, you'll go off somewhere exotic and tell me all about it! I want to know *everything.*"

And I would nod and agree and promise to do just that. Her desire to see the world became my desire.

Unfortunately, I haven't quite worked out how to make that happen yet. I have no money to travel, and I haven't worked my way up to my dream job yet. As a fact-checker, I get tasked with lowly assignments a monkey could do and get paid shit all to do it. My paycheck can be counted in pennies.

Now what is a fact-checker doing aboard a luxurious cruise ship?

Oh, simple.

I've committed a crime, and it's only a matter of time before I'm found out.

It's why I'm panicking. Why I'm squeezing my eyes shut again as I try those slow, drawn-out breathing exercises pregnant women do while trying to endure a painful contraction in the delivery room. *Heee heee hoooo.*

My crime is mild, though the person (er . . . *man*) involved likely won't see it that way.

Well . . . maybe he will. It's hard to know—

"Blimey. Everything okay over there?"

My eyes fly open, and my head whips around as I search for the voice.

I look up to the balcony above mine, but there's no one leaning over trying to talk to me. Then I check the balcony below mine to find it's empty too. I look to the left . . . and just when I start to worry the voice was in my head—that on top of everything else, I'm now hallucinating posh British accents—I turn to the right and see her. My neighbor, one balcony over.

She smiles like she's a little wary of me. That's fair. I can't imagine what I look like right now. There's no telling what this humidity has done to my already unruly hair.

It doesn't seem to have affected her the same way, though. Her glossy blonde strands look to be at her beck and call. She's likely just come from a salon, where they've added a little curl to her blowout, making it shiny and neat.

"You look a little peaked." She tilts her head, studying me. "Are you seasick?"

"Uh, yeah . . . ," I mutter, deciding that's the best route forward. It'd be too complicated to get her up to speed on everything else. We'd be out here all morning. I'd get a sunburn.

"I have some Dramamine. Hold on."

She disappears into her suite before I can tell her there's no need. It won't cure my real ailment.

I lean over and call out to her ("Uh . . . lady?")—trying to get her attention, to no avail—then I jump out of my skin when there's a knock on my suite's door.

"It's me!" she says on the other side.

"What . . . ?"

Do I just—

Let her in?

I look around as if someone's going to give me the answer.

In normal life, I would never let a veritable stranger into my home, but cruise ships don't abide by standard rules. This ship doesn't function like an apartment building so much as a jail or, better yet, an insane asylum. I've heard cruise mates bond fast, that relationships form overnight. Everything takes on a heightened importance. Maybe because we'll all be a little dehydrated (from the heat) and a little drunk (from the free booze).

The woman knocks again, and I'm forced to abandon the balcony. I rush to the door, with the intention of accepting whatever she's offering and then quickly shooing her away so I can continue my downward spiral. The Lamaze breathing did seem to be helping slightly . . .

Instead, once I open the door, she waltzes past me like I've invited her in. A waft of her floral perfume tickles my nose as she slips across the foyer. She peruses the place, getting the lay of the land, dipping her head around the corner into the bedroom. I'm left speechless, staring back and forth between her and the open door leading back out into the ship's hallway.

I know I'm emitting heavy doses of kindly-get-the-hell-out vibes, but she's unbothered. She sets the small box of medicine beside the espresso machine on the long buffet and continues her perusal of my suite, with a whistle of appreciation.

"So then we've all got fancy digs. I was wondering about that. I think every suite on this floor is as big as an entire London flat. What do we need with a sitting room all to ourselves? And that balcony could host a whole bloody football team!" She whirls around to face me again. "Have you taken a look at your vanity in the little changing room outside the loo? *All La Mer products.*" Her green eyes widen with excitement. "Full-sized ones too. Not those dinky travel samples. I've already nicked mine and stowed them. With any luck, the cleaners will take pity on me and gift me replacements."

I look to my bedroom door. The sleek paneling, the crystal knob.

"I had no idea," I tell her. "I haven't made it that far yet."

I sound dumbstruck, or maybe just dumb. I'm still playing catch-up.

When I arrived at the dock this morning, I was a half hour late, and it took me another twenty minutes in the blazing heat to find where exactly I was supposed to board the ship.

"This entrance is for staff only."

"Provisions unload here, dear; you need to head back that way."

"Oh, sorry, you've gone too far."

I was already sweating and anxious when I found the short line of invited press waiting to be checked in. Of course it annoyed me further that everyone else seemed to look as though they belonged. No nervous newbies in the bunch, just a bunch of old classmates and friends. Yay! Men clapped each other on the shoulders. Women smiled with ease. At the top of the gangway—just as a bead of sweat rolled down my chest beneath my bra—I was greeted by a dozen uniformed staff all in a line. A cheery blonde woman promptly stepped forward to greet me by name.

She introduced herself as Ingrid, and she explained she would serve as my butler for the duration of our ten-day cruise.

"Now, Ms. Hughes, if you'll follow me, I'll lead the way to your suite." Ingrid's accent was clipped and formal with a hint of what I suspected to be Scandinavian roots. "Jacques here will take care of your luggage."

Already, a strong hand was lifting my duffel bag and suitcases away from me. Panic spiked my blood. "Oh! My laptop's in there!"

Ingrid smiled in understanding. "Jacques will be along shortly. Have no fear."

It's a rich-person thing to lose sight of your valuable belongings. I can't easily afford to replace my laptop, so, therefore, I don't make a habit of parting with it very often. Still, it felt silly to argue with her in front of everyone, so I swallowed down my resignation and handed off my bags to the capable-looking Jacques before allowing Ingrid to lead me on board.

On the way to my suite, I barely had time to register the over-whelming opulence of the ship. Ingrid was walking too fast. I'd take note of a painting—*Could that really be a Picasso?*—or a gargantuan crystal chandelier that seemed to be levitating midair, and then we'd curve around another corner or wind up another flight of stairs, making our way to deck seven. We talked on the way—well, *she* talked. She let me know how excited she was about her new position on board *Aurelia* and that she was a mom of two teenage boys, and when I seemed shocked by that, she whispered her age. I couldn't believe it. She looked so young!

This immediately put me in her good graces. "I avoid the sun at all costs," she explained with a wink.

Outside room 602, she scanned a thin silver key card and pushed open the door to allow me to walk in before her.

My jaw dropped, and I blacked out a little as she droned on about the suite's accommodations: "innovative curved windows surround the living areas, giving the effect of indoor-outdoor living"; "one of the largest balconies on board"; "separate bedroom and bathroom"; "walk-in shower and whirlpool bath"; "writing desk"; "complimentary laundry, pressing, and wet cleaning."

And what about dry *cleaning?* I almost asked, just to poke fun at the absurdity.

I just stood there, unmoving, trying to find the breath that had suddenly vacated my lungs.

She wasn't even done yet. She was explaining the Wi-Fi access to me when I cut her off.

"Are you sure you have it right?" I asked her with a funny little laugh. "This room is probably for dignitaries or . . . or presidents. Have you mixed me up with a celebrity or something?"

People sometimes think I look like a mixture of Emma Watson and Emilia Clarke. It's the catlike curve of my blue eyes and my pronounced cheekbones. They want to belong on a more notable face. Maybe Ingrid was confused.

I expected her to smack herself on the forehead and apologize for the blunder before shoving me belowdecks, to a cramped cabin stuffed between the boiler room and the communal toilet. I'd get a squeaky cot and a scratchy blanket.

Instead, she grinned. "These are your accommodations for the duration of your stay on board *Aurelia*, Ms. Hughes. Jacques will be up shortly with your bags. If you should need anything at all, please don't hesitate to contact me. There's a button beside the phone in the living room as well as one on the nightstand in your bedroom. Think of it as a butler's bell. Just press it, and I'll be here in the blink of an eye."

She walked over to the long console table in the foyer and started to neatly arrange items from inside the folder she brought along with her. "Here is your key card along with your press packet. Inside, you'll find a badge and detailed itinerary, map of the ship, and most importantly, your emergency protocols. You can access the muster drill on your suite's television. It needs to be viewed within the next hour, prior to our departure."

She turned then, smiling at me. "I know you're probably anxious to take a look around. A guided tour of the boat will take place this afternoon. We'll meet on deck nine in the observation lounge. Mr. Woodmont will be there along with the captain."

She noticed my startled reaction at the mention of Mr. Woodmont, and she beamed with pride. "*Yes.* It will be so exciting. I'm sure you're all eager to get a moment with him. I know I shouldn't be gossiping, but he truly is as handsome as everyone claims him to be."

I swallowed down that bit of news and stayed completely silent. I didn't want to encourage the topic of Mr. Woodmont for one more second.

"I'll leave you to it. I know you must be anxious to freshen up."

What gave me away? The stink lines coming off me? The dried sweat on my face?

She shut the door behind her, and that's when the doom and gloom set in, the reality of where I was and what I'd done to get here.

The British stranger in my suite points back to the Dramamine, forcing me back to my uncomfortable present.

"I thought about just tossing it over to you, but my aim is shite, and I didn't want to lose all my pills. Here. Take two. Or three. I doubt you can overdose on something like this. It's probably just B_{12} and beeswax or something. Do you know?"

The chemical makeup of Dramamine?

No, I'm afraid not.

I swallow down a pill and then pass her back the box with a thanks, scrutinizing her now that she's made herself at home in my suite.

"Who—who are you?" I ask with a curious lilt.

The girl laughs and tosses her shiny tresses over her shoulder. "Sienna Thompson. British lifestyle blogger." She eyes me skeptically. "You really don't know?"

I cringe with guilt. "Should I?"

She laughs. "Oh my god, how stuck up did I just sound? 'You really don't know,'" she mimics herself. "I'm so embarrassed! It's just that . . . yeah, I've got quite a large social media following. A bit like the *it* girl of London. I'm so used to getting recognized everywhere I go." She rolls her eyes. "See? There I go again, sounding like a right idiot. How stuck up can one person be? I'm working on it, I swear."

I can't help but smile. She might be a tiny bit full of herself, but it's clear she's not a total snob. "I feel bad. I'm sure you are really popular. I'm just not on social media all that much. Kind of late to the game."

Sienna's pretty green eyes narrow with suspicion. "What are you doing on board, then? I thought this was a brand trip for media and influencers. A huge push to get the word out on social media."

"Well, I'm a journalist."

My voice wavers a little as I say it, and I feel like a phony. Am I allowed to call myself a journalist if I've never *actually* been published and don't *actually* get paid to write?

Don't ask my title. Dear god, please don't make me cop to being a fact-checker. I only just regained the ability to breathe without an ache in my stomach.

Her sleek eyebrows waggle. "A journalist? Fancy that. I bet you've got a lot of brains, then. Not that you need them with a face like that. Shame you aren't on social media. You'd build quite the following in no time. You're practically wasting away behind the screen."

I bristle at her derogatory assessment of my chosen field.

"Working as a travel journalist has always been my dream."

It's only after I finish saying this that I realize she was trying to pay me a compliment of sorts.

She smiles, unperturbed by my harsh tone. "Well, good for you, then! You're doing it. What did you say your name was? Maybe I've caught one of your articles online somewhere."

I don't have the heart to tell her she definitely has not.

She'd need to have private access to my laptop to find all the articles I've written over the years. The ones that *have* never—likely *will* never—see the light of day.

"Casey Hughes."

She nods. "American?"

"From White Plains, near New York City."

"Very cool. Right near the Statue of Liberty?"

That's like asking if her flat abuts Buckingham Palace, but I just nod. "Sure, yeah."

She tilts her head, giving me a quick once-over. "Well, listen, I think we've lucked out here. These ten days will be loads more fun if I have someone to pal around with. What do you say?"

A friend.

I would absolutely love to have someone by my side for this trip, but I feel like I won't live up to Sienna's expectations. She's dressed in this fancy coordinating silk set. The cami is sexy yet demure—meant to look a little like lingerie—and the shorts take inspiration from men's tailored trousers. It's the kind of thing I'd pass in Zara and wonder who the hell could pull it off. *Sienna, that's who.*

I'm sure her entire wardrobe has been carefully curated. Her appearance as a whole, really. You would never say her beauty is effortless, but all the effort she's put in is definitely paying off. She's so gorgeous I bet men fawn all over her.

I don't want her to feel stuck with me just because I'm the first person she's chatted with on the boat. "I'm sure there'll be other social media influencers here. People you might know. Girls a little more glamorous—"

10

She won't even let me finish. "*More glamorous?* Do you not own a mirror? You're as glamorous as they come, Casey Hughes." Her green eyes belatedly glance over my outfit replete with wrinkles and ambiguous travel stains. (*Ketchup or blood? Who knows!*) "Well, not exactly right this minute, per se. You aren't planning on wearing that for the afternoon's festivities, are you?"

"No, of course not."

I say it like it's laughable, but I actually *had* planned to wear this sundress all day. Now that's obviously not an option. Good thing I packed heavy. I didn't want to be without choices on this trip.

As if it's settled, she says, "Good. Well, why don't you unpack and get ready, and I'll do the same."

I find I'm all out of excuses, and more than that, I want to accept her kindness. I'll need it. "Okay, sure. *Yes.* That sounds great."

I even tack on a genuine smile. Already, I feel my worry starting to dissipate now that I'll have someone by my side as confident and carefree as Sienna.

"We can meet out in the hallway at a quarter to one and walk to the meet and greet together. I don't want to be late! I cannot *wait* to meet Phillip Woodmont."

There he is again.

Phillip Woodmont.

The man of the hour.

The person who's going to take me to task for my crime.

My old friend . . . *of sorts.*

Chapter Two
CASEY

Oh, look at that; I'm panicking again.

I think it's my new normal at this point.

Sienna did say to meet her out in the hall at a quarter to one, didn't she?

I'm starting to doubt myself.

I've been out here stalling for close to ten minutes, and I'm worried that if I don't start heading toward the observation lounge now, I'm going to be late. I don't even want to check my watch. It'll only make my nerves more frayed.

This is what I get for trying to make a friend!

I should have just remained a lone wolf.

A door opens down the hall, drawing my attention. An older man steps out onto the plush carpet in the hallway. Like me, he's wearing a press badge. It's pinned over the left breast pocket of his dinner jacket. I study his profile, trying to decipher if I know him. There will be some serious talent on this trip. Journalists and photographers I've looked up to since I was in college.

He's got a little heft to him. Tall and broad. Very little of his white hair is left, and deep, hard-earned wrinkles surround his eyes.

He looks my way and nods in greeting once he sees my press badge. "Lincoln O'Neal. *Nat Geo.*"

My eyes widen in awe.

Jesus. That's how I know him! He's a famous photojournalist!

Say something, you nitwit.

"Casey Hughes. *Bon Voyage.*"

I tack on a little salute that feels charming in the moment but leaves us both a little confused as to how to proceed. Fortunately, he has the sense to carry on as if it never happened.

"Heading up?" he asks, indicating toward the bank of elevators at the end of the hall.

I smile weakly. "Um . . . yes. In a moment."

"Right, then. See you."

He turns on his heel and leaves.

No!

I just lost out on a chance to chat with Lincoln O'Neal! I would have *loved* to pick his brain about his work. Not to mention, a moment with someone as influential as him could change the entire trajectory of my career. I could have endeared myself to him. We could have chatted and exchanged business cards. At which point, he would have seen my title and laughed. Dammit. Fine. Maybe it wouldn't have been all that helpful, but as it is . . . I'll never know.

With a new font of courage and annoyance churning inside me, I turn back to Sienna's door and give it three loud knocks. I was too chicken to do it before when I first came out into the hall, but it's now or never. I can't wait around for her all day.

"Sienna?" I lean in and speak loudly against the suite's door. "Are you almost ready?"

"Coming!" she shouts back in a chipper tone.

That's followed up with an audible groan like she just smacked into something, and then she shouts again. "*Coming!*"

A moment later, the door swings open, and I see Sienna hopping on one foot, trying to keep her balance as she slips on her second high heel. She's grimacing apologetically. "I know I'm late. Sorry. *Sorry.* A tale as old as time. I couldn't decide what to wear."

The number of outfits strewn about her living room is proof of that. I can't imagine what her bedroom in London looks like. The place must be a disaster.

She notices my judgment. "Ignore all that."

"I'm impressed, actually. How many suitcases did you bring?"

The amount of clothes in her suite could fill a department store.

"Only four. Big ones." She laughs. "I'm horrendous when it comes to packing light for trips. I like options!"

She finishes with her high heel, then whirls around to grab a dainty Chanel bag from the table near the door. "I'm ready. Let's go!"

Out in the hall, on the way to the elevator, she gives me a drawn-out appraisal.

"Sheesh. Absolutely knew you had it in you. A total knockout. Spin, let me see the back."

"It's nothing fancy."

I'm wearing a pale-blue wrap dress that ties just above my left hip and hugs me in all the right places. The soft material falls a smidge too high above my knees, and though it's not *exactly* work attire, it's the best I could do. I had a hard time figuring out what to pack for this trip. I don't have a closet chock-full of pantsuits and blazers. I mostly work remotely for *Bon Voyage*, and when I do have to commute to Manhattan for our once-monthly all-staff meeting, anything goes. Jeans, caftans, concert T-shirts. In fact, putting *too* much effort into your look makes you seem like a try hard (according to people more fashionable than me).

When I was given this assignment on board *Aurelia*, I knew my wardrobe needed a serious facelift. Pajama bottoms from high school and stretched-out Old Navy V-necks would not suffice. I strategically purchased a few nice dresses, but I couldn't afford to blow it out. I don't have enough fancy clothes to carry me through the entire trip, so I'll have to pick and choose and strategize—and talk to Ingrid about the cleaning services she mentioned.

To jazz up my blue dress for this afternoon, I added a pair of diamond studs (courtesy of my late grandmother) and a pair of nude secondhand Manolo Blahniks that I had fixed up and made to look as good as new. I'll be wearing them on repeat for the ten-day cruise. I've pulled my hair up into a high ponytail with neat wavy curls, and my makeup is clean and fresh.

As Sienna and I step into the elevator, I feel ready to take on the battle ahead of me.

Well . . . right up until we actually arrive at the observation lounge, located at the top of the ship on deck nine. It's a spacious, open room lined with expansive windows highlighting the view of the ocean and faraway horizon. A dozen separate seating vignettes—intimate tables surrounded by inviting armchairs—surround a midcentury bar.

The design aesthetic of the ship continues in here. A lot of monochromatic layering of tone on tone—beige, gray, silver, and white contrast against dark wood and sumptuous brown leather. It's like the whole place was inspired by James Bond. Or rather, one of his rich nemeses. From the ornate light fixtures to the neatly arranged throw pillows—it's clear the owners have spared no expense.

The room is already brimming with people mingling and chatting, but thankfully, it looks like we're not late. Or at least no one has started giving a presentation yet or anything. We slip into the room, and Sienna leads me straight to the bar.

"What should we drink? Wait. Let's start with lemon-drop shots. Something to loosen us up a bit." She leans in closer, lowering her voice. "Doesn't this place feel a bit stuffy to you? I expected a few more people our age."

"What about that group over there?"

I nod toward a group of women sitting in plush leather chairs near us, all around our age, stylish, and *gorgeous*. Each one of them is done up fancier than the next. Huge statement earrings, feathers, clinking bracelets, glitz and glam on a scale that has me rethinking everything I packed.

Sienna peers over her shoulder at them, grumbles, then looks away with a shake of her head. "Bella, Jenna, Avery. I can't stand them. They're influencers like me. I used to get on with them before I realized how horrible they all are. I mean absolutely *savage*. They'll steal a brand partnership right out from underneath you if you aren't careful."

She waves the bartender over and orders our shots.

"Right, so they're off the table. What about them? They look fun."

She follows my gaze to the group of men I'm nodding toward. They have to be the oldest among us. One of them is dozing off in his chair.

Sienna bursts out laughing and nudges me with her shoulder. "I knew we'd get on."

Our lemon shots arrive sporting rims caked in sugar crystals and curlicue lemon rinds. They almost look too cute to drink.

Sienna picks hers up and meets my gaze with a mischievous smile. "To new mates."

I smile and clink my glass with hers. "To new mates."

Just before I tip it back, I add, "Why does this feel so ominous?"

She laughs and shakes her head after downing her shot. "Don't worry. This'll be the easiest ten days of work ever. Now, should we mingle? Or take pics? I need to get some content. Help a girl out?"

I expect her to shove her phone in my hand while she poses, directing my every move, trying for the best lighting, best angle. I can see it now. I'll be playing the part of her begrudging Instagram husband for the remainder of our trip. But instead, she turns the tables on me. With her camera in selfie mode, she presses her face up against mine so that we're cheek to cheek and smiles for the camera. I can't help but do the same.

We look cute.

Better than cute, actually.

Our features complement each other. My rich brown hair seems all the more alluring next to her bright-blonde shade, and though my eyes are deep blue while hers are pale green, we're both tan and happy and smiling. We look beautiful and carefree. We could be an advertisement for summer.

Well, false advertising.

I'm anything but carefree.

Now that I'm here, it's time to rip off the Band-Aid. I have to find Phillip Woodmont.

Sienna turns her attention to her phone and starts typing a million miles a minute. "What's your handle? I'll tag you."

"I don't have one."

Her wide eyes fly up to me. "Oh wow. You really weren't kidding about not being on social media. How do you survive?"

"I manage . . . *somehow*."

I'm distracted. Already, I'm looking around the room, searching for Phillip. I'd prefer to avoid him at all costs, but I don't have the luxury. Not if I want to complete my assignment for *Bon Voyage*.

To earn my exclusive ticket aboard *Aurelia's* maiden voyage, I've been tasked with writing a comprehensive review of the ship and all its offered amenities. I'll need to create teasers and sidebars, bite-size content they can share online and in the magazine. Most importantly of all, though, the real reason *I'm* specifically here on the ship is because *Bon Voyage* wants an exclusive interview with Phillip Woodmont himself.

And I promised I could get it.

That was my big bad crime.

I completely lied at the all-staff meeting last month. It sort of just happened. I was in the back of the room, leaning up against the wall, trying to keep my personal life together while I tuned out the people around me. My phone was buzzing in my pocket, but I was too scared to check it. No one good had called me in months. Every time I answered, it was a new problem. My life had become so complicated that I was relieved every time an unknown number turned out to be a good old-fashioned scam call; a Nigerian prince asking me to wire him money was the least of my problems since my grandmother had passed away.

I'd been so focused on my phone's incessant vibrating, counting the rings, that I'd missed the first half of the discussion about *Aurelia*.

Gwen Levis, my boss and the editor in chief at *Bon Voyage*, sat at the head of the conference table with her oat milk latte and her Hermès scarf knotted around her neck, her cool white-blonde bob and her vintage glasses. She started giving details about the trip, and it seemed like a done deal that the assignment would be handed off to Gabriel Rousteing, the most seasoned writer at *Bon Voyage* and a bit of a celebrity within our niche world of travel journalism.

I held back an eye roll. What did Gabriel need with another illustrious assignment? He wasn't at the meeting! He wasn't even in the country! He was in Dubai, covering a food-and-wine festival and partying with Bono. I mean, honestly . . .

I was bitter about it, already starting my private pity party, when Gwen mentioned the possibility of trying something slightly different and moving beyond our standard coverage of the cruise. She wanted an exclusive with Phillip Woodmont.

The moment she said the name, it felt like someone sent a thousand volts of electricity through me. Phillip Woodmont?

It couldn't be.

She answered my question for me.

"Phillip is heir to one of the United States' oldest shipping dynasties. He moves in exclusive social circles, and he's notoriously tight lipped when it comes to speaking to the press. It's why most of you have never even heard of him. I'm desperate to change that. Our readers would devour an exclusive. I want to cover—"

"The man behind the mast."

She looked up, confused about who'd spoken. Fair, given the fact that I don't think I'd said a single word in the last thirty consecutive all-staff meetings. I might as well have been part of the wallpaper, an inanimate object people confused for furniture. *Oh, sorry, Casey, didn't mean to set my coffee down on you.*

"What was that?" Gwen asked, curious.

The people standing on either side of me scrammed, saving themselves.

I cleared my throat and tried to be brave. "I said, 'the man behind the mast.'"

Gwen's lip quirked. "Cute. Yes."

Just that the slight upturn of her lip was enough to send me to cloud nine. When had I ever once received her approval?

She gave me a succinct once-over. "Cassie?"

"Casey," I clarified before adding with a little chuckle, "Or Cassie, whatever works."

I hated myself a little in that moment. Not "or Cassie"! Cassie was not my name!

She looked to her assistant, and I could sense she was about to move on to the next agenda item. I felt my window of opportunity closing. My phone would start vibrating again; my insurmountable problems would continue to pile up. I'd return to my small cubicle in the darkest corner of the third floor, check my email, and find all sorts of busywork that had shit-all to do with writing. After I left the office for the day, I'd go back to my late grandmother's house and continue packing up her things, stuffing the remnants of her life into tattered cardboard boxes.

"I know him," I blurted.

WHAT?

Instead of backtracking, I doubled down. "I know Phillip Woodmont."

Gwen's pencil-thin eyebrow quirked with interest. "How?"

"We were . . . classmates, sort of. It's an interesting story."

I'd never had her focus like I had in that moment. My knees almost buckled under the weight of her expectations and piercing gaze. "Meet me in my office after the meeting. We'll chat."

Now, I take a step away from the bar and crane my neck to see over the crowd. There are at least fifty to sixty invited guests in the observation lounge, all sporting press badges, all vying for each other's attention. I'd like to mix and mingle, eventually. Right now, though, I'm on a mission.

"Where are you off to?" Sienna asks when I step away from her with a purpose.

"I need to hunt down Phillip Woodmont. I have to get an interview with him for work, and I'd like to make a good impression *early*."

"Well, you're heading in the wrong direction." She reroutes me, turning my shoulders so I'm facing the right way.

"He's just there, the bloke in the blue suit."

She aims me toward a cluster of men talking in a semicircle. Only one of them is wearing a blue suit, and he cannot be Phillip. A laugh spills out of me. Not because the sight of him is funny. Oh no. It's the opposite of funny. It's toe curling. Fever inducing. *Trouble.*

I'm struck by the sight of the boy I used to know.

Intimidating, strong, tall, handsome—unfortunately, he's all these things and more.

He has dark-brown hair that's been styled in that perfect way: tousled a bit up top and neat on the sides. There's a little wave to it, which has the effect of making him that much more tantalizing. There are two deep-set dimples bookending his lips and another on his chin. A hint of a five-o'clock shadow.

Dammit. Dammit. Dammit.

Despite the few photos I saw of him online during my research, I was holding out hope he'd somehow remained the pip-squeak with braces, a man who wouldn't throw me off. This assignment was going to be hard enough before, when I assumed Phillip would be spindly and awkward.

The man in front of me—the one I still can't quite believe exists— gives off the air of someone absolutely assured that everyone in the room would willingly bow at his feet.

He's an all-American prince in a cobalt blue suit.

"Jesus, he's good looking. Do you reckon he's single?" Sienna asks, staring at him from by my side.

"No idea."

Why would his relationship status matter to me? That's not what I'm concerned with, well, unless it pertains to my interview. I'd love to know about his personal life . . . for the story. That's it.

Sienna glances over to me. "Well, go on, then."

All of a sudden, I find it hard to move my feet. It's like I've accidentally stepped in a patch of superglue. "I don't think I can do it."

"You can! Be brave. He *wants* to chat. Why else would he have invited press on board?"

She makes a good point.

Giving in to these nerves is silly. Beyond the fact that *he's* invited *us* on board, there's absolutely no way he will recognize me. I'm worrying over nothing. We knew each other briefly, years ago. I look like any other journalist. In fact, compared to the glitzy glam of some of the influencers in the room, I could be a veritable wallflower, easily forgettable. I'll use that to my advantage.

"Okay, I'm going."

"Yes, go!"

She pats me on the shoulder, and I adjust my clutch beneath my arm.

I start to walk on unsteady legs across the parquet floor in the center of the room, not because it's the fastest route to get to him but because it's the path of least resistance. Everyone's hanging around the periphery of the room or mingling at the tables. The center of the room, for some reason, has turned into no-man's-land.

I'm alone there, dead center and midstep, when Phillip strides purposefully to the edge of the parquet floor before us all as if he'd like to address the room. He doesn't need to hush the small crowd as he slides his black-framed glasses off his face and folds them in his strong, tanned hand. We're rendered mute at the sheer sight of him. This is not the boy I remember from my time at Fairview Prep.

I freeze, unsure of how to proceed. I should scoot back and join the others, but just like before, my legs feel like jelly, all thanks to this man.

Phillip looks out toward the crowd, his gaze sweeping across the amassed group waiting with bated breath to hear what he's about to say. He could read through his grocery list, and we would all lean in, wanting more.

When his gaze passes over me, I swear I can feel it like a feather across my skin. My stomach squeezes tight with anticipation, but he doesn't stall, doesn't linger at all. I'm barely there.

I ignore the initial pang of rejection because this is what I wanted! *Anonymity is better!*

Though to intrigue a man like him, to catch his attention—*god, what would that be like?*

I need to edge back into the crowd, but it feels disrespectful, like shuffling around during the playing of the national anthem. Everyone is stock still, and I don't want to draw attention to myself, but I also don't want to hover alone in the center of the room any longer either . . .

Quickly, with my breath sucked in, I scurry back to the line of people, scooting in alongside a group and blending in with the crowd just as Phillip smiles out at us.

"Good afternoon, everyone. I'm Phillip Woodmont, group president at Woodmont Overseas International." His voice is just deep enough to command respect. You could hear a pin drop in the room as he continues, "It's a pleasure to stand before you all today, on board *Aurelia*, a ship that for many years was considered a hopeless pipe dream. For those who are unfamiliar with Woodmont Overseas, we're a transportation and logistics company facilitating services between international and domestic ports. But more than that, my father, Captain Nathaniel Woodmont, built this business on a genuine passion for the sea and an unwavering commitment to serving people and communities."

He's clearly an experienced orator. There's no rush to his words, no wobble in his voice. If I were speaking in front of this group, my hands would be shaking so badly I'd have to hide them behind my back.

"When I was first brought on in the company, I knew my focus would be on our cruise lines. Though they functioned well and proved lucrative enough, the fact remained that they were lagging behind our company mission to protect the seas we claimed to covet. Cruise ships, in general, are notoriously high producers of black carbon and are disproportionately bad for the environment, even compared to bulk carriers and oil tankers. As part of the leadership team, I felt a sense of obligation to bring them into the twenty-first century. I saw it as a black-and-white problem. Innovate or die. We have to be bold. No more polluting our oceans in the name of leisure travel. This world is moving so fast, baby steps won't suffice. The cruise industry can do better, and at Woodmont, we have. *Aurelia* is our pride and joy—proof of what can be. Most other major players in the cruise industry have promised carbon neutrality by 2050." His jaw tenses as he shakes his head. His passion is pervasive, infecting us all. "At Woodmont, we don't feel that's good enough. *Aurelia* features a closed glass façade, urban gardening areas, and drone landing pads. We rely on harvested wave energy, solar power, fuel cells, and wind energy to eliminate the need for fossil fuels. More than that, we've made it clear we're willing to share these technologies with our competitors in the hopes that in the coming years, we can *all* become greener. Rather than innovating and bolting closed the door behind us, we've paved the way for others to come with us. Hand in hand."

Throughout his speech, he's worn a fierce expression so compellingly handsome that I've found I've somehow gone too long without blinking. Now, though, the tension in his features eases. A hint of a smile plays across his lips as he continues, "I know many of you might be worried that with these new changes, we've prioritized efficiency and economy over guest experience, but I assure you, that's not the case. With the help of Biron Design Group, *Aurelia* boasts luxury accommodations on a scale that could rival any five-star hotel the globe over." He presents the woman standing at his left. She's wearing a black pantsuit and a statement necklace that looks like a piece of modern art, along with a warm, welcoming smile. Her black hair is trimmed in a face-framing pixie cut that accentuates her high cheekbones. "I'll allow Ms. Patel, our head of interiors, to walk you through a tour of the vessel before we convene here again for cocktails and light bites. Ms. Patel . . ."

She steps forward and invites us all to join her.

Everyone else follows after her right away, eager for a good spot during the tour, but I take advantage of the opportunity laid before me. Phillip is momentarily alone, a king without his royal entourage. I doubt I have long. If I hope to get a private word with him this afternoon, this will likely be my only opportunity. It's a stroke of luck I seize upon quickly, weaving through bodies, beelining straight for Phillip, ignoring the bite of pain as someone accidentally steps on my toes. They apologize, but I throw my own "Sorry!" over my shoulder without breaking stride. Phillip doesn't see me until I'm upon him, cutting straight into his path, forcing him to stop abruptly before he runs into me.

We're close. Too close. I'm inches away from his broad chest, and I have to tip my head back to get a good look at him. With a timid laugh of apology, I take a half step back.

His expression doesn't soften. It's as if I'm still breaking some kind of social code merely by existing. And I guess I am. Marching over to him was a little uncouth even for me, but there's no room for social courtesies in journalism. Not if you want to get the story.

I really booked it over here. I'm breathing slightly harder than normal. Also I'm meant to do something. I've stalled him; I don't want it to be in vain.

"Hello, Mr. Woodmont," I blurt. "I'm Casey Hughes from *Bon Voyage* magazine. It's a pleasure to be here, meeting you."

I stretch out a confident hand, hoping to make the best introduction, or technically *re*introduction I possibly can. My smile couldn't be wider. My eyes shine with hope and opportunity.

His wonderfully spiced cologne is distracting, but then so is everything else about him, specifically his size. He's not overly bullish or anything, not like a hulking beast. Rather, he's tall and broad shouldered, and he has a sort of lean stealth to him, a layer of muscle merely hinted at beneath his well-cut suit.

My, my, someone really had a growth spurt . . .

I think I used to be a half inch taller than him.

He's more intimidating than ever at this proximity, and it's hard to force a swallow as my hand hangs limply between us. It becomes clear to me, a moment too late, that he isn't going to accept my hand. He never even contemplated it.

My cheeks burn with embarrassment as he looks me over slowly. His scowl gentles to something more like an amused smile. There's a joke he's enjoying, and his expression says it's at my expense.

He peruses my dress, my shoes, my body with a lackadaisical indifference. When his piercing blue eyes finally deign to meet mine, my stomach squeezes tight. Dread chills me to the bone. I'm surprised I don't shiver.

He tucks his hands into his suit-pants pockets—the final nail in the handshake coffin—and then replies with a confident air of indifference. "No introduction needed. I remember you, Ms. Hughes."

His eyes cut past me in dismissal, and I want to shrink away and hide, but I can't. I have to stick this out, painful as it may be.

"*O-of course.* Right. You do?" My voice lilts a little with surprise. "I'm flattered, actually. I remember you, but I wasn't sure, given your success . . ." I'm stammering now, making a fool of myself. "I mean to say, I'm sure you meet so many people in your line of work. So many people eager to make your acquaintance."

Yes! Flatter him! Stroke his ego into submission!

"I do meet a lot of people." His eyes recapture mine, and I feel like I'm staring straight into the barrel of a sniper rifle. "Fortunately, I'm good at remembering the assholes."

Assholes!

WHAT?

He tries to take a step around me, but I'm faster. After all, I'm the one with something to lose here. My job is on the line.

My laugh is forced and fake. My hand touches his bicep, and he looks down at it as if he'd like to cut it off at the wrist.

Oh my god, this is going horribly.

"Eighth grade was a really long time ago." When it looks like he's about to cut me off, I rush on. "But you have every right to be angry with me after everything that happened. I'm not proud of my actions back then. But look at you! You've clearly won. Made a real name for yourself. I was hoping to hear more about that, actually. My editor in chief at *Bon Voyage* thinks our readers would love an exclusive with you, getting to know *the man behind the mast*, so to say."

I hope my witty wordplay will seduce him into compliance, and to my credit, he does smile.

Then he replies simply, as if it doesn't pain him at all to say "No."

I'm so stunned I don't even think to stop him again as he curves around me and starts to head toward the set of double doors leading into the hallway where the tour has begun. Ms. Patel's out there chattering away, and I should be at the front of that group, taking dutiful notes, asking questions about every last detail. Instead, I twist around to face him, dumbstruck.

It's not out of the question that he doesn't have time for an interview, but any polite person would understand you can't just blurt out no. You offer some kind of platitude like *I'll have my people contact your people* or *Let me check my schedule*, with both parties knowing that really means *I'm not interested*. But the fact that he just outright turned me down is worrisome for too many reasons to count.

"Is that a 'no, but try me again another time'?" I ask, sounding hopeful.

At this point, I'm a fighter getting up after yet another knockout. He's got to be thinking *Christ, when will this girl quit?*

He shakes his head, not even bothering to turn back. "That's a 'no, be glad I'm letting you stay on the ship.'"

Panic seizes me.

"You're kidding."

"Not in the least."

Oh god. This is worse than I could have imagined. I hurry to catch him, curving around him, cutting off his path yet again. This is going *way* off the rails. I should cut my losses and regroup, form a proper strategy with a step-by-step game plan to smooth things over. Instead, I ask, "Is this *really* about something that happened between us in *middle school?*"

Oops.

Now why did my tone have to sound so judgmental just then? I'm trying to smooth feathers, not ruffle them!

"Don't make it sound so trivial. It's not. You showing up on this ship, needing something from me is proof that karma never loses an address."

Oh, he's *really* enjoying this.

"It was nothing! Seriously! *Come on.*"

"It was eighth-grade district finals, and you cheated."

I throw up my hands, waving them to encompass the whole observation lounge and the lap of luxury we've found ourselves in. "*What does that matter now?* Look at where you are!"

He doesn't glance around the room. He doesn't need to. His attention is on me for one last searing second before he states plainly and simply, in terms any dummy would understand, "No interview, Ms. Hughes, and that's final."

Chapter Three
CASEY

Unlike most schools where you have to watch out for the jocks with Y chromosomes, Fairview Prep was a matriarchal society lorded over by the queen bee herself: Shelby Carothers. She had an endless font of meanness in her. Her anger issues might not have been so bad on their own, but she was also the daughter of an ex-NBA player and thus a good foot taller than the entire student body. On a good day, my head crested her hip bone. She could have tossed me around like a rag doll if she had the inclination to do so. Her meaty fists could have closed over my windpipe and snuffed out my life in mere seconds. It would have happened eventually, I'm sure, if I hadn't ingratiated myself to her from the start. I was a scholarship student at Fairview Prep. The lowest rung on the social ladder. However, I had something Shelby desperately needed: a brain full of useless trivia facts and not much going on in the way of a social life.

Fairview Prep was filled with so many bright young minds that even the bullies making fun of the nerds were nerds themselves. Everyone knew Shelby loved her beloved quiz-bowl team, and everyone also knew that Nicole Sanders had recently quit due to Shelby's tyrannical leadership style. And now they needed a fourth player to round out the team.

When our paths crossed, the day Shelby's vicious brown eyes landed on me and mischief sparked, I knew if I wanted to walk away with all body parts intact, I had mere seconds to act.

"I can join your quiz-bowl team. I'll do it! You need me!"

The words had barely left my lips by the time Shelby had grabbed ahold of my collar and started to twist.

Already, my life was starting to flash before my eyes. I was too young to die! I'd never tried sushi! I didn't know what it felt like to be kissed! I had a half-eaten Hershey's bar stashed in the side table next to my bed!

Then she narrowed her eyes, weighing my offer like an ancient Roman emperor trying to decide my fate with the flick of a thumb. Up, I'd live. Down, I'd get thrown to the lions.

"Fine. We'll start now."

At lunch, Shelby invited me to eat at her table, and I could not refuse her offer. The universe reminded me of that as I trailed behind her, passing pitiable Hillary Vickers, who was standing at her locker with sopping wet hair and a soggy uniform, evidence of a prelunch swirly. She trembled as Shelby and her cronies passed by—expecting more brutality—then her eyes fell on me, and I thought I'd see pity, maybe even fear on my behalf. Instead, her eyes narrowed in confusion. Her lips parted as she tried to make sense of what she was seeing. Shelby wasn't dragging me behind her. There were no threats. It looked like I was following her willingly. And I suppose in a sense, I was. Standing in Shelby's shadow was the safest place to be at Fairview Prep. Becoming one of her minions was wrong on a moral level, sure, but I couldn't get bogged down by lofty concepts like ethics. I didn't have the luxury. It was about survival more than anything else. Hillary Vickers had a rich mommy and daddy who could nurse her wounds and buy her a new uniform and ease her suffering with endless therapy sessions. I had a chain-smoking grandmother who worked two jobs and thought beat-up shoes from Goodwill were a splurge for my back-to-school attire. In other words, I had no choice.

Before I joined, Fairview Prep's middle school quiz-bowl team was mediocre at best, but in my eighth-grade year, we were unstoppable. Partly because Shelby made us practice three nights a week, and partly because I had a preternatural talent for quick buzz-ins. I mean, not to brag, but even Alex Trebek would have sat up and taken notice of my nimble thumbs.

Still, Shelby would stand at my side during practice. "Faster! *Faster!*"

Her mom would knock on the basement door. "Yoo-hoo! Anyone want some Cheetos Puffs?"

"*Not now, Mom!*"

There was only one other team as good as ours, and it was our all-male private school counterpart, Hillandale Academy.

And guess who went to Hillandale?

Phillip Woodmont.

He was the shining star on the Hillandale team, quick on the draw with his buzzer, just like I was.

I actually remember the first time I ever laid eyes on him. It was on a Saturday afternoon—a time when other kids our age were out riding their bikes, lounging aimlessly in front of the television, enjoying their lives. It was tournament day, which meant my grandmother had dropped me off on the curb of some randomly assigned public school, and I was left to rot there for eight to ten hours. The tournament experience consisted of quick bursts of action thickly sandwiched between hours of downtime.

I'm sure I'd tried to bring a book or something, but there was no way Shelby was having that. We were seated on a cold tile floor, trying to get far enough away from the bathrooms so that we didn't have to listen to every single flush but near enough to the auditorium so that we'd know when it was our turn to duke it out in front of a crowd brimming over with tens of fans.

Shelby was forcing us to endure round after round of last-minute warm-up questions when I looked up and saw the Hillandale boys making their way toward us.

There were four in total—each one drastically different in size, so much so that it was like seeing a giraffe and a mouse in the same posse. To say they were good looking would have been a stretch. None of us were turning heads. We were middle school quiz-bowl participants. *Hello*, there wasn't a good haircut or a stylish article of clothing in the entire vicinity.

Still, though, I thought Phillip was . . . cute. Maybe the way his braces glinted off the light was really attractive to my midpubescent brain. Maybe his starched uniform and the way it hung off his slim shoulders really called to me.

Whatever it was, something about Phillip compelled me to smile and wave at him as his team walked by us. Phillip caught my wave and stared down at me like I'd just sprouted a second head. His look of consternation was my first hint that I might have messed up.

The second hint came when Shelby grabbed my hand and forcibly yanked it down. "What are you doing?" she hissed. "We aren't friends with the enemy!"

I paid for that wave.

My buzz-in thumb was arthritic by the time I made it home that evening, and I'd had my head chewed off for losing to Hillandale. Never mind that Shelby herself had cost us the win, wrongly answering three *easy* questions.

What followed after that day was a tension-filled quiz-bowl season that saw us neck and neck in the standings with Hillandale. We'd perpetually swap first and second place with them depending on the week.

As far as Shelby knew, the most interaction I had with Phillip was onstage when we'd stand across from each other, posed behind our respective tables, buzzers in hand, facing off in a way that felt deeply, life-alteringly serious, but was, in fact, *not*.

However, the truth is Phillip and I formed an illicit friendship that Shelby never found out about. On tournament days, I liked to eat lunch as far away from Shelby and the crew as I could get, which usually meant finding a weathered bench outside, facing an all-but-empty school parking lot. I'd repeated this same routine a few times up until one day, while I was working through a turkey sandwich my grandmother had packed me, when, out of the corner of my eye, I caught sight of someone approaching my bench, and I looked up to see Phillip standing there. He'd taken off his blazer and rolled up his white shirtsleeves. He looked shy. His eyes didn't quite meet mine when he pointed to the opposite end of the bench and asked if he could sit.

I jolted into action, quickly shoving aside my bag to clear a space for him. "Of course, yeah."

He sat, and though it was clear he meant to join me—there were plenty of other empty benches outside he could have claimed—we didn't immediately rush into conversation. Deep in the throes of middle school, we were still sprucing up our social skills. Seasoned conversationalists? Not even close. We were all but silent as Phillip unloaded his lunch. I carefully appraised his decadent spread: warm pasta, fluffy garlic bread, proper silverware. The sight of his expensive name-brand soda convinced me to push my Dr. Cola off to the side of the bench, out of view.

"Turkey?" he asked, referring to my sandwich.

I held it up. "Yeah, with provolone."

It gave me great pride to proclaim I was eating a type of cheese one step up from childish American.

"My favorite," Phillip said with a small smile.

His blue eyes were so kind behind his glasses that I couldn't help but match his smile with one of my own as I pointed at his food. "Your lunch looks good too. I love garlic bread."

His dark brows shot up. "Oh! Want some?"

He was already holding out a slice for me to take, and in return, I offered him the other half of my sandwich. Though he was perfectly willing to give me some of his pasta, I was too embarrassed to accept it. I didn't want to make a fool of myself slurping spaghetti in his presence, but we did go halfsies on my chips and his brownie.

I can't even recall what we discussed that day. Our respective schools? Our current classes? Our interest in quiz-bowl trivia? The only thing that lingers now is the warm feeling I had while sitting there with him, indulging my little crush and hoping that maybe he felt the same way about me.

From that day on, Phillip would always seek me out during lunch on tournament days, and though we became friends, I never dared to tell him that I thought he was cute or hinted that I would have liked us to move beyond that. I mean, talk about a wasted opportunity. All those unsupervised hours! We could have been making out in public school bathrooms, making out under public school bleachers, making out in public, period. But instead, we were playing adversaries. Shelby kept a tight leash on me and the rest of our team, ensuring there was no possible way I was going to cross enemy lines, and she scared me enough that I wasn't even tempted to try to see Phillip outside of our secret lunches. There'd be other boys down the road, surely. Right then, staying on Shelby's good side was all that mattered to me.

I didn't care all that much about the quiz-bowl team, but I did care about keeping Shelby happy, and at the end of our season, when we were at district finals and only one team could advance on to compete at regionals, she wasn't going to stand idly by and let fate decide for us.

"We're going to sabotage them."

I still remember the three of us—her minions—looking at her like she was talking complete gibberish.

"What do you mean, sabotage them?" I asked.

She looked around, worried for a second, before leveling her gaze on me. Her eyes felt like two sharp daggers. "Keep your voice down, idiot. You want us to get caught?"

Well . . . it didn't seem like the worst thing in the world. We'd only be held responsible for *attempted* sabotage, not the real thing. The tournament organizers would threaten to call our parents; we'd be released from the competition, forced to take the *L*, and then we'd get to go home early. It kind of sounded nice when I thought about it . . .

Shelby pulled a small plastic tub of peanut butter out of her bag.

With a villainous smile, she informed us that Jake, one of the key players on Hillandale's team, had a severe peanut allergy.

I remember gasping in horror. "You could kill him!"

"Oh, *relax*," she said with an exaggerated eye roll. "Fine, if you're too much of a pansy for that, I also brought some laxative stuff my mom uses sometimes."

She went digging in her bag for it.

"That's still horrible."

"It's just going to make him poop his pants. Big deal."

I didn't like any of it. Cheating was bad enough but poisoning someone! I wanted nothing to do with it.

My other teammates—Lindsey and Anika—remained silent. Shelby had tortured them into submission. They knew better than to speak up. I was too useful to her to suffer the same fate, but my insubordination that day went one step too far for her.

Shelby shoved the bottle of liquid laxative into my hand. "You're going to do it."

I tried to push it back to her. "No. I'm not."

"Do it," she bit out with venomous rage. "*Or else.*"

Lindsey started sniffling then, obviously scared of Shelby's threat. "Just do it, Casey! Stop arguing with her."

I snorted because this was all absolutely ludicrous. "Do whatever you want to me, but I'm not poisoning someone. It's stupid."

I crossed my arms—case closed.

Shelby's mouth curved into a smile. "No, you don't understand. It's not what I'll do to *you*. It's what I'll do to poor Lindsey here." She dropped a hand onto Lindsey's shoulder and squeezed. "You wouldn't want her suffering because of you, would you?"

Diabolical.

Obviously *now*, as an adult, I see that Shelby was an actual psychopath in need of serious help. I should have immediately run to an authority figure and ratted her out, but I was thirteen and naive enough to think that Shelby really did hold all the power in the world.

I yanked the laxative bottle out of her hand as if I was going to play her game. I wasn't. I just needed Shelby to *think* I was a willing participant in her stupid plan so she'd leave Lindsey alone. There was no chance in hell I was going to physically harm someone for the sake of a *quiz bowl*. Get real.

It took me all of ten minutes to come up with a new plan. One that didn't involve forcing Jake to drink a bottle of medicated sludge without him realizing (which, by the way, was *never* going to work). My new plan was still wrong, and I fully expected to get in trouble for it. I was damaging public property, but I reasoned that at least this way, no one would get hurt.

All it took was a pair of scissors I found in the school's art room. The auditorium was empty when I walked in with them concealed in my hand. We weren't due to take the stage for another thirty minutes. There was no one acting as security, no one lingering around. The quiz-bowl organization could barely get volunteers to conduct the tournament itself, for god's sake. Most of the time, they were an overworked and underpaid collection of teachers who were solely in it for the free Subway sandwiches the organization provided. Not one of them was trying to linger in here on their off time.

Up on the stage, there were two long rectangular tables on which rested four buzzers each, connected to the floor outlet by long black rubber cords. I walked to Hillandale's assigned table, picked up the buzzer Jake usually used, trailed my hand down the long cord a few inches, and then quickly made a tiny cut in the rubber so small that no one would notice it unless they knew to look for it.

Then I spent the next thirty minutes worrying over what I'd done. I had sizable pit stains on my red polo shirt by the time our school was called to take the stage for competition. A mediocre round of applause greeted us as Shelby shoved me out from behind the curtain. The Hillandale boys were already at their table, poised and ready to take us on. I worked up the courage to look over at them, trying not to be too conspicuous about it. I didn't want to give myself away, but my nerves slipped free of my tight control the moment I realized the setup was all wrong. They'd switched around their assigned spots. Jake wasn't in the middle. He was at the helm now. Phillip had swapped places with him, making it so he and I stood directly across from each other when I took my position and picked up my buzzer.

Shelby growled in annoyance under her breath and then spun around to face me.

"Jake is here. *Why?*"

Earlier, I'd assured her I'd gone through with the plan, which wasn't a lie. I did go through with the plan, just not *her* plan.

"Trust me," I whispered with a small shake of my head.

We were already drawing attention to ourselves. Shelby needed to cool it if she didn't want to blow our cover.

I adjusted my shirt and listened halfheartedly as the moderators ran through the rules and then introduced us each by name. There couldn't have been more than five people in the crowd. One guy in the back was the janitor waiting for us to clear the room so he could finish his job for the day.

"Contestants, please pick up your buzzers. The first round is about to begin."

My hand shook so fiercely that I doubted I'd be able to buzz in. My stomach squeezed with anxiety, tightening into a knot so tight that I could barely look up from my table, not even at the seated row of moderators.

"Question number one. The first civilizations arose around 3500 BC in this region known as the land between the riv—"

I buzzed in before he could even finish.

The moderator nodded my way. "Fairview Prep."

"Mesopotamia," I answered confidently.

"Correct."

My teammates hooped and hollered, jostling me with their congratulations. It only made me feel worse. I shouldn't have been on fire that first round, but I was, so much so that there was no chance for Phillip to realize what I'd done to his buzzer. Once I finally worked up the nerve to peer over at him from beneath my lashes, I was surprised he didn't look angry. On the contrary, his eyebrows were tugged together as he studied me, impressed and intrigued.

I glanced away quickly and gulped, focusing all my attention on the moderators for the second round: English literature.

"In this novel, a character protects his sister Georgiana and plans to marry Catherine de Bourgh's daughter."

Their team buzzed in faster than we did.

"Hillandale."

"*Pride and Prejudice*," Jake answered.

"Correct."

"In this novel, Cardinal Richelieu's plan is thwarted by d'Artagnan and a small group of swordsmen."

Shelby and I buzzed in at the same time.

"Fairview Prep."

Shelby nodded for me to take it.

"*The Three Musketeers*," I answered.

Murmurs grew louder at Hillandale's table, drawing stares from everyone in the auditorium except for me. I couldn't trust my face to remain neutral if I looked over and saw them inspecting the cut in the cord. I would give myself away in an instant.

The arguing grew louder.

I could barely make out Phillip saying "This isn't right." And by then, my palms were so slick I could barely get a decent grip on my buzzer. The granola bar I'd eaten a few hours earlier was churning in my gurgling cauldron of a stomach.

The moderator began the next question, but Phillip interrupted him.

"There's an issue with my buzzer!" he called out. "It's been broken this whole time!"

Well, there it was: the beginning of the end.

I could see my bleak future play out before my eyes. The police would be called; they'd investigate and see the cut in the cord. An experienced detective would know just how I'd achieved it. He'd sweep the art-room scissors for fingerprints, find mine on them, and then I'd get thrown into the clink. I could kiss my future goodbye. Adios, middle school; *hello, juvie.*

The moderators paused the questions. There was chatter and chaos. I stayed perfectly still, keeping my attention down, my eyes on my feet. While Phillip tried to explain the issue to the moderators, a bead of sweat rolled down my forehead. Shelby hissed at me to "Keep it together." She knew if we were pulled into separate rooms for questioning, I'd crack like an egg within the first five minutes.

Eventually, exasperated that they weren't taking him seriously, Phillip circled around his team's table and tried to walk over to the edge of the stage in an effort to speak to the moderators one on one, but he never made it there. In horrifying slow motion, I watched his feet tangle with his buzzer's cord, and then he tumbled forward and face-planted down onto the stage, hard enough to crack his glasses. As if to add insult to injury, when he pressed up off his hands, blood dribbled from his nose.

I didn't even think before I rushed to help him up, ignoring Shelby's scornful gaze and growl of agitation as I left my post.

When I reached Phillip, my hand wrapped around his bicep, and I tried to tug him up. He looked at me, dazed and embarrassed.

"I'm *so* sorry. I didn't mean—" Then I winced and shut up, realizing my contrite words were all but proclaiming my guilt.

It was too late to rewind, though. Phillip was nothing if not astute. His expression changed in an instant, closing off with hardened betrayal. He put two and two together easily enough. He knew his cord had been cut. He knew he'd been sabotaged. And right then, as I leaned over him, he deduced somehow that I was the catalyst to his demise, the source of this embarrassing middle school moment that would apparently bury deep into his psyche forever.

He shook off my grip and stood to leave the stage, presumably to find a bathroom so he could clean up.

When Phillip returned a few minutes later with toilet paper shoved up both nostrils to stem the blood flow, the competition picked up right where it had left off. There would be no investigation, no police presence. There would barely be a pause. These tired moderators (the ones who were *volunteering* their time) were unwilling to hear Hillandale's continued arguments and were most certainly uninterested in a makeup match. Even if they were game to redo the first few rounds, the auditorium was promised to the chess club starting at 4:00 p.m. We had to clear out soon, no matter what.

They did acknowledge Phillip's buzzer was broken and gave him a spare one, but it didn't matter. We had a solid lead, and after the last round, Hillandale had no hope of catching us. We finished on top and progressed to regionals.

The moment the competition ended, I booked it offstage and out of the auditorium, running like I was headed for a getaway car in the form of my grandmother's beat-up 1998 Pontiac Grand Prix.

I yanked open her passenger's side door, tossed my backpack inside, and jumped in, slamming the door closed behind me like an afterthought.

"Drive!" I shouted at her.

With all the speed of sap drip, drip, dripping from a tree, my grandmother turned her head to look at me and cocked a haughty white brow. "Girl, I'm not sure who you think you're talking to with that tone, but it ain't me."

Then she stubbed out her cigarette, took her sweet time fiddling with the radio until she settled on a song, and pulled away from the curb slow and steady. My knees were bouncing up and down as we edged out of the parking lot. I didn't look back to see if Phillip was coming after me. I held my breath through that entire drive home.

My grandmother killed the engine after we'd pulled into our driveway, but she didn't get out. She tapped a red nail on the gear shift, waiting.

Eventually, she asked, "Something you want to tell me?"

I thought about it for all of half a second before deciding I'd be taking this particular transgression to my grave. "No."

"Right, then, let's get inside," she said, no hint of judgment. "I'm about to start supper."

I never knew if Phillip lodged an official complaint with the quiz-bowl organization or if he tried to take the issue any higher. All I know is that I couldn't sleep for a week after I cut that cord, because I was so scared that the consequences of my actions were going to come back to bite me in the ass. I never did tell my grandmother what I'd done, and the shame and weight of my lie ate away at me. It might have continued on like that forever if karma hadn't stepped in.

On the day of the regionals competition, Shelby came down with a terrible stomach bug. She couldn't even make it out of the bathroom. Our team had to forfeit our match, and that was the end of my middle school quiz-bowl career.

The case grew cold. No quiz-bowl moderator ever came knocking on my door. There was never a warrant out for my arrest.

I made peace with my mistake and moved on from it, deciding that everything worked out the way it was meant to.

Except now of course I realize I was wrong.

Karma isn't finished with me yet, and Phillip seems intent on getting his due.

Chapter Four

PHILLIP

The sun shines brightly overhead. There's not a single cloud in the sky as *Aurelia* slices through the water with calm efficiency. I look around the bridge, and I can't help but think of all the naysayers. How many times was I told that this wasn't possible? That the technology wasn't up to snuff? That if only I could wait another five or ten years, I would have no issue constructing a ship run solely on renewables.

I can't help the satisfied smile from creeping across my face before I take a small sip of my celebratory Macallan. I should be a gentleman about it, but truthfully, given the option, I'd love to rub everyone's noses in this success.

I did it, *assholes*.

I stand beside the captain on the bridge as we cruise away from port. We'll reach Key West tomorrow, our first stop of many on this maiden voyage. Though I've grown up on boats and yachts, my captaining experience lies mostly with sailboats, nothing of this caliber. I enjoy watching Captain Neal at work. He makes it all seem easy, and he damn well should. He's the best in the business, and he's getting paid a staggering amount of money to captain this vessel.

My phone vibrates in my pocket, and I check to confirm it's another email from the ship's chief engineer. We've been in constant communication. With so many new energy systems in use, I can't take any chances. I've doubled the engineering staff on board, outpacing maritime requirements so that there will be no shortage of hands on deck should we need them.

I've requested hourly reports from the chief engineer. The last few have confirmed that all systems are functioning just as we'd hoped.

I breathe a small sigh of relief.

On this first day especially, it feels like there's a lot on the line. If there's one thing I know about technology, it loves to fail. I can't allow it. There are too many influential people on board. Too many reporters and journalists and photographers who would love the pleasure of writing a scathing review, detailing every instance of failure on our part.

If I hear one more joke about another *notorious* ship's maiden voyage in comparison to ours, I'll throw the joker overboard. Better yet, I'll order someone else to do it for me.

I pocket my phone again and tune in to the conversation taking place behind me. While all our other invited guests are with Ms. Patel enjoying an exhaustive tour of the ship, including the technical areas usually off limits to anyone outside of the crew, we've granted Arthur Burton, a lead reporter from *The Times* in London, an exclusive interview. Our first of many on this trip.

I try not to let that thought sour my mood.

This moment is cause for celebration.

Besides, Tyson Ackres has it. There was no way I was taking this trip without him. As my closest friend and business partner, Tyson knows he has to be the sunshine to my rain, the smiling, cheery face to my otherwise doom and gloom.

I listen as Tyson gives Arthur a tour of the bridge. Just like everything else on this ship, our command center is pushing boundaries. Tyson explains how we've employed sensors, cameras, and artificial intelligence to help analyze data for millisecond-by-millisecond situational analysis. Thermal imaging, GPS, AWIPS, radar, sonar, ECDIS, lidar—we have an almost unlimited amount of data the crew on board can utilize to their advantage.

"So is the eventual goal to replace manned crews all together?" the reporter asks.

Captain Neal snorts under his breath. We all knew his question was coming. It's what everyone wants to know. How is technology going to hurt us? Why should we be scared?

I look over my shoulder to see Tyson is taking the question like a champ. Better than I would, certainly. All the media training in the world can't change my personality. Tyson is smooth and cheerful; he can hide his real opinions behind a shiny veneer. It's why he's better with the press than I am.

He flashes a practiced smile as he shakes his head. "While that could *theoretically* be possible, we're choosing to look at technology as a friend, not a foe. Remote fleet command centers have been whispered about for years, but we aren't out to take jobs. We simply want to make failures obsolete. We want to ensure that Captain Neal and his team have every resource at their disposal."

The reporter jots something down in his notebook, apparently satisfied with Tyson's response. Then like a homing missile, he turns his attention on me. I have no doubt he's been hungry for my input since we began. While Tyson is the president of the cruise division for Woodmont Overseas International and, therefore, extremely important and in the know about all matters of this ship, for reporters, he's lacking one crucial thing: the Woodmont name.

"Mr. Woodmont, you must be incredibly proud."

"I am."

He takes a purposeful step toward me. "Tell me about it. The trials and tribulations it took to get here."

A proverbial microphone has just been thrust into my face.

I knock back the last of my Macallan—not wanting any of it wasted on this charade—and then I give him the robotic answer our PR team carefully reviewed and approved weeks ago.

For trials and tribulations, speak only about technological issues and theoretical red tape; make the engineers and staff at Woodmont Overseas seem like the heroes and leave real names and people out of it. It doesn't serve us to piss off legislators, even if a few of them deserve to be thrown under the bus for their attempts to derail innovation. The few with nefarious ties to big oil and gas are on the tip of my tongue, but I refrain from deviating from the script, and Tyson winks at me over the reporter's shoulder.

He knows how hard this is for me.

I'd rather do just about anything than talk to the press. I'm a private person by nature. I don't enjoy the limelight, and I've succeeded in building a life largely outside the sphere of public opinion.

Arthur's good at his job. His questions are succinct and to the point. He hits all the talking points I expect him to. None of the questions come out of left field, and when I think he's about to wrap it up and move on—perfect timing, considering Ms. Patel should be finishing her tour soon—he pivots.

"Now concerning your family and friends. They must be—"

I talk over him quickly. You have to do that with reporters. Like snakes, it doesn't work to let them wriggle about. It's best to cut them off at the head. "No."

Tyson laughs. "You have to give them something, Phillip."

Whose side is he on? The prick.

My gaze cuts back to Arthur, and I make sure my words are curt and clear. "My priority is Woodmont Overseas. I have no social life to speak of. I'm dedicated to my career, and outside of that . . . there's nothing else to say."

"It's rumored that you and Vivienne Chén—"

"*There's nothing else to say.*"

Unbothered, Arthur slides his pen and notebook back into his leather bag. He's a veteran reporter, and he knows not to take my *no* personally. With a smile, he nods first to Tyson and then to me. "It was a pleasure talking to you, gentlemen. I look forward to chatting more over the coming days."

An attendant near the door of the bridge steps forward, seamlessly inviting Arthur to follow her so she can connect him with the tail end of Ms. Patel's tour.

"Thank you," he replies. "I'd appreciate that."

The moment the door closes behind him and we're left in peace, Captain Neal curses in his notorious Scottish brogue. "Christ, they're like leeches. *Worse.* And we've got a whole boat of 'em." He shivers like something's crawling up his spine.

Tyson laughs. "You two make them out as monsters. They're harmless if you just feed them properly." He points an accusatory finger at me. "*You* don't make it easier on yourself, Phillip, playing the cloak-and-dagger shit. You make it seem like you're more mysterious than you are."

"I *am* mysterious," I say, barely able to get it out without a laugh.

Tyson shakes his head, and I point a finger right back at him. "Why should I care about your opinion? They don't ask *you* about *your* personal life. Jesus, if they only knew."

Tyson smooths a hand down his tweed sports coat, not the least bit offended. The cocky bastard. If there are two things I know about Tyson Ackres—and I know *many*, considering we've been friends going on a decade—he likes to dress sharply and flirt with women.

The list of women in his contacts could rival Casanova's.

Sadly for them, he's no longer on the market. For the last three months, he's been a one-woman man. I've never seen him so caught up in someone, and most shocking of all, he wasn't hooked by an attention-seeking socialite or some status-hungry model—it was a working mom of two, named Samara. Tyson was on a work flight from Moscow to London four months ago when he struck up a conversation with a shy flight attendant. The way he tells it, she was eager to do her job and get out of his sight. *He* was eager to get to know her better. Eventually, he wore down her defenses. When they got to London and he learned that they both had one night together in the city, he begged her to give him a chance. Despite her initial reservations, she agreed to a date.

I think she could really be it for him. Shocking as it seems.

"Does Samara know about your past?" I ask now, trying to needle him like he's been needling me.

He shrugs. "She does. I've been honest with her. And by the way, you don't have to say it like that. I was single, and I dated around. I never cheated. I never acted like a heartless womanizer."

He's being honest there, at least.

"Speaking of women," he continues, "who was the enchanting brunette I saw you speaking to earlier in the observation lounge? The one chasing you down."

"No one."

"So you don't deny she was enchanting?"

"*Enchanting*? Who talks like that?"

"Can you two hens bicker somewhere else?" Captain Neal grumbles.

Tyson can't help but smile.

But I'm not smiling.

I bristle at the reminder of Casey.

Casey Hughes.

Jesus, talk about a blast from the past. I haven't thought about her in years. *Longer.* I mean, I'm surprised I even recognized her. But I did, immediately. There was no lag time for my brain, no stalling as I ran through a mental Rolodex of contacts. Even all grown up, styled, and made up in a way that barely resembled the middle schooler I used to know, I pinpointed her immediately—the girl I ate lunch with a handful of times. My long-forgotten quiz-bowl crush.

Back then, I really liked her. She was smart and nice and beautiful. Of course that was all a front. Though there was no way to prove it at the time, I know she sabotaged me all those years ago. After the quiz-bowl district finals, while I was squinting through my shattered glasses, she fled from the stage like she was guilty of murder. Meanwhile, I went home a sore loser with a broken nose. *I had to have surgery!* And while she wasn't exactly the direct cause of that, at the time, I couldn't help but pin all the blame on her. After all, if she were innocent, she would have stayed to check on me. She would have acted like a friend. We *were* friends, or so I thought.

Funny.

"There's nothing interesting to tell you," I reply with a shrug. "She's a reporter."

"Ah, so it was a work issue that had her running you down like that? I didn't hear what you two were talking about, but it seemed heated. I figured you two must know each other."

I look away, narrowing my eyes as if inspecting a blip on the horizon. "In a way, we do. Our paths crossed a long time ago."

When I look back at him, it's just in time to see him unfurl a gotcha grin. He's barking up the wrong tree.

I roll my eyes. "Not like that."

He should know better. I don't leave a trail of discarded women in my wake. I've always been serious about relationships, in it for the long haul. Just ask Vivienne.

"She's beautiful."

I hum as if the thought hadn't even occurred to me.

It had, obviously. It felt like a gut punch to see her again, but for some reason, I find myself wanting to play this situation close to my chest. I have no idea why. Tyson wouldn't care if I found Casey attractive; in fact, he'd be relieved to hear it.

I guess I still feel a certain loyalty to Vivienne even though she and I are no longer in a relationship, as of a month ago.

Tyson would tell me it's time to move on.

He *has* told me that, plenty.

I'm just not quite there yet.

I'm still certain that this thing with Vivienne will resolve itself. She's the type of woman I need by my side. I understand she doesn't quite see that, and for now, I'm fine with tabling the issue. I have enough on my plate. My sole focus is on making sure the maiden voyage of *Aurelia* is a success. I want the best media coverage possible.

"So then what was she after?"

"She wanted to interview me, and I declined."

He hums like he finds this particularly interesting.

I feel like I have no choice but to defend myself. "Every minute of my time during this cruise is accounted for. I think I'll be giving enough of myself as it is."

"Ah . . . and so you were telling her that—turning down an interview request with someone you invited on the ship *for interviews*—while actively checking her out?"

Instead of engaging, I turn my head to the side and address the captain. "Captain Neal, remind me of the maritime laws for murder in international waters?"

"Christ," he curses. "Don't bring me into this."

Chapter Five
CASEY

Well . . . that went badly. I'm kind of shocked, actually. I supposed there could be some awkwardness between us if Phillip *happened* to remember who I was, but I was able to delude myself into thinking that was impossible. With everything he's done since we last met—all the places he's traveled, all the people he's met—a lowly eighth-grade girl surely pales in comparison.

Well, lesson learned.

He not only remembers me, but he's also still angry with me. Oh, I wish I'd never sabotaged his team!

I'm summarizing all this into a neat little paragraph in a Word document. It's not what I'm supposed to be working on. My fingers should be flying a mile a minute on all sorts of exciting descriptions about my tour of *Aurelia*. I'm supposed to outline the various spa packages and the dining experiences—everything I just learned, everything that could fly out of my brain if I don't carefully jot it down. I should *not* be fixating on my encounter with Phillip Woodmont.

What is Aurelia *compared to its owner?*

Its enigmatic, haughty, ARROGANT owner.

Phillip Woodmont is just as proud and spiteful as you would expect for someone in his position. I can't get over how much he's changed. Oh sure, he's handsome. Aren't they always? His good looks are probably a gift from the devil in exchange for the souls of a thousand suffering children or something equally horrible. How blasé. How CLICHÉ to be handsome when you also rule the world.

His suit was custom. His neat black glasses were probably designer too. His watch was expensive and heavy and actually very ostentatious. I can't believe he has the nerve to walk around with something worth that much casually draped across his wrist when there are starving people in the world!

What else . . . ?

What else!

His hair! Oh god, the money he probably spends on haircuts.

The vanity of it all.

The blinking cursor taunts me. An entire blank page waiting to be filled with every detail of the tour I just completed with Ms. Patel. Instead, I can only focus on Phillip.

Dammit.

I push away from the desk in my suite and look around at all the pristine furnishings—luxurious jewel tones on the lamps and light fixtures, compelling artworks, subtle wallpaper, inviting furniture, and lots of natural light pouring in through the large windows.

My bags are still packed and sitting neatly by the door. I didn't have time to unload everything before heading to the observation lounge earlier this afternoon. For one fleeting second, I contemplate leaving, but I can't. I also contemplate working around my promise to Gwen. I could save face and give up on the interview with Phillip and just turn in a detailed report of my time aboard *Aurelia*. It's tempting to throw in the towel, cobble together the last scraps of my dignity, and leave the Phillip issue well enough alone.

He doesn't want to give me an interview. In any other circumstance, I'd accept that.

But not now.

The stakes are too high.

Everything—and I mean *everything*—rides on this assignment.

There are no two ways to slice it: my life is currently . . . in shambles.

Up until last year, I lived with my grandmother. We'd always been a team. My parents were what we in the *biz* call degenerates. It was my grandmother who raised me, who took on the role of mom, dad, uncle, aunt, sister—you name it. She's all I had. The strongest woman I've ever known.

When cancer came calling a few years ago, I wouldn't even entertain the idea that she'd succumb to it. We're talking about a lady who at sixty years old signed up to coach my Little League team when no one else would do it. A lady who once made a mechanic start crying when he tried to swindle her into getting unnecessary work done to her Pontiac Grand Prix. A lady so caustic and sassy, everyone in our town knew not to cross her. I mean, the cojones on the woman were something else.

Still, after the cancer diagnosis, I felt like it was prudent for me to move back in with her to help out. The arrangement worked well for the both of us, actually. I'd just graduated from college and was drowning in student loans while trying to make it as a fledgling journalist. Even after I got the job with *Bon Voyage*, I stayed with her because I wanted to be there to drive her to appointments, to hold her hand on the bad days. Whenever she grumbled about it, I told her it was *me* who needed *her*. It wasn't even a lie. My pittance of a salary is not nearly enough to afford a decent apartment along with all of life's other necessities.

For a good long stretch, we were making do. It seemed like we could really pull this off. She'd get better, I'd get a promotion, and we'd eventually laugh about the hard times that were well and truly behind us. This delusion was so strong that when she got the diagnosis that her lung cancer had started to spread, I didn't even balk. Never mind that she'd spent the better part of fifty years sucking cigarettes down to the filter. I figured cancer would get the message and scurry off to find some other more hospitable host.

The chemo and radiation didn't do the trick, though. The rail-thin end, the way she wheezed in each breath—I wouldn't wish it on my worst enemy.

I remember the last time I broke down in front of her while she lay mostly helpless in her hospital bed, heavy, grief-laden tears pouring down my cheeks as she gripped my hand and pursed her lips at me. Jean Hughes did not abide tears. Not then, not ever. She pulled me down to her with a strength I didn't realize she still had. Her fingers tightened around mine, and she reassured me, "You're gonna make it, kid. Okay? You've got sunshine in you, you know that? You don't ever let anyone snuff it out."

Her death last year was bad enough on its own. Becoming an orphan when you're a young adult is a bitter pill to swallow. No one really feels all that bad for you because you're not a kid anymore, but it doesn't negate the fact that you're really on your own now. No safety net to speak of. No emotional support system.

Then came the money issues.

Guess who was the first to come knocking after my grandmother passed away. I'll save you some time here. It wasn't a kind stranger. Not a valiant white knight. Sadly, I was fresh out of rich relatives wanting to play my benefactor.

No, the person knocking on my door and calling my cell phone incessantly, the one sending letter after letter was none other than Steve Buchanan, your friendly debt collector.

Now, let me clarify something for anybody as dumb as me. My grandmother may have died, but her mountain of credit card bills and medical debt were alive and kickin'. Oh, and wouldn't you know? Grandma hadn't paid her taxes in over a decade. Good going, Jean.

"Okay, well. How much does her estate owe?" I asked him when I finally gained the courage to take one of his calls. The question is absolutely hysterical when I think back on it, because it shows the state of mind I was in at the time. I thought there was a way out. *Oh, shoot. A couple grand? Let me see what I can do.*

The actual figure—the one I still can't think about without wincing—came later, after Steve asked if I was sitting down, and he assured me he would do everything he could to help me out. *Helping me out* actually meant seizing my grandmother's house and all her possessions, ha, ha, ha! Steve, you're so silly!

So yeah, I've definitely been navigating a rough patch lately.

As of two weeks ago, I said goodbye to my childhood home, moved all my earthly possessions into a storage unit in White Plains, and started to halfheartedly search for an apartment while living out of a hotel room.

When Gwen spoke about this assignment during our staff meeting, I hadn't been in the right frame of mind. *Clearly.* I regret sticking my neck out and lying about my relationship with Phillip, but it's too late to turn back now. There's nothing to lose—no real place to call home, no family, no boyfriend, a job I hate . . . my hope of having a future career as a successful journalist and making my grandmother proud is all I have left, and it hinges on getting this damn interview.

Phillip probably assumes he can run me off with a halfhearted rejection, but he's dead wrong, and he's about to find that out the hard way.

Tonight's welcome dinner is in two hours.

I spend the next thirty minutes unpacking and settling in, taking full advantage of the place I'll call home for the next ten days. I spread out my things in the bathroom, organizing my moisturizer and face wash on the black marble countertop along with all my cosmetics.

Then I shower and carefully blow out my hair before moving on to my makeup. My grandmother spent thirty years behind the Chanel cosmetics counter at Saks Fifth Avenue in New York City. She never left our house without a full face of makeup, a fresh set of curls, and two strategically placed spritzes of Chanel N°5. Though I protested at the time, I'm grateful she taught me well.

The natural, subtle makeup I've worn all day? Gone.

A touch of bronzer and the right swipe of a warm-pink blush melds perfectly with my tanned complexion.

I achieve a soft golden smoky eye with ease. I layer honey-brown tones and then tap on a little shimmer so that my blue eyes don't just pop, they *punch*.

My full lips are stained a strawberry red.

When I step back and turn my chin from side to side, inspecting every detail, a zing of excitement races through me.

Am I trying to seduce Phillip?

Absolutely not.

I just want to stop him dead in his tracks. I want him to feel the same way I did when I saw him in that suit this afternoon.

News flash, you aren't the only one who grew up.

I don't even hesitate before I grab a flashy gold dress from my closet and slip it on. It's short and fitted, with a structured bodice and a draped silk skirt. It's one of the dresses I splurged on for the trip, and I'd planned to pull it out a little later on in the voyage, but tonight's the night.

My shoes are a lace-up pair of gold heels.

I can practically hear my grandmother's hearty round of applause.

Eat 'em up, Sunshine.

When I knock on Sienna's door so we can walk to dinner together, she swings it open, and her jaw practically comes unhinged. Her reaction is exactly as I'd hoped.

"Well done, Casey." She circles around me, getting a view of every angle. "Trying to steal the hearts of every man on board?"

Just one.

But no. That's not right. I don't want Phillip's heart. I want his soul in glossy magazine print. My name on the byline.

Sienna's gone all out for dinner too. She's gorgeous in a bright-aquamarine dress with beaded embellishments that look like abstract tropical birds. Her blonde hair is slicked back and knotted at the nape of her neck.

She takes a silly video of the two of us as we head toward the elevator, instructing me to blow a kiss right at her camera.

I'm grateful for the levity she brings. I haven't had a friend like Sienna in a long time. I had good girlfriends in college, but after we graduated, their lives continued while mine stalled so I could move back in with my grandmother. They have relationships, marriages, even children now. I don't. We've kept in touch as best as possible, but it gets to a point where you start ignoring people's calls and texts, knowing all you have to tell them is more of the same: my grandmother is still dead; yes, I'm still working for *Bon Voyage*, no promotion in sight; no, I haven't gone on any dates; in fact, I haven't even *thought* about going on a date in ages.

I've been avoiding filling my friends in on the worst of what's transpired over the last few weeks. If they knew about my grandmother's house getting seized, I know they'd offer to take me in, but I can't seem to bring myself to stoop to that. It's embarrassing that they've all done it—created the lives they always wanted—while I'm still at the starting line, worse off than ever before.

Sienna's a good distraction, fun and carefree. The perfect companion on a cruise like this. With her by my side, the reality that awaits me back in White Plains feels a million miles away.

Just before we head into the dining room to join the others for a predinner cocktail, I tug on Sienna's arm.

"Thanks for teaming up with me. It's better with you here."

It's true. I can't imagine having to walk into events solo. I'd be even more intimidated than I already am.

She assesses me thoughtfully. "Seriously, same. Fate knew what it was doing by putting our suites side by side." As we step inside the dining room, she takes a glass of champagne from a passing waiter, hands it to me, and then takes another for herself with a thank you and a smile. "Now tell me, how'd the chat go earlier with Phillip? Have you secured your interview?"

"Not exactly."

The declaration is followed by a heavy gulp of champagne.

She frowns, waiting for me to elaborate.

"He told me no, flat out."

Her brows tug together in confusion. "But isn't that the point of all of this? Why are we here if not to chat with him?"

"I suppose he wants everyone's focus to be on *Aurelia*, not him. Though I think his rejection is more personal than that."

She frowns. "How so? Did you put your foot in your mouth earlier? Bad first impressions can always be undone. I swear it."

I take another sip of champagne, and for the first time, I let my gaze rove around the room. It's already packed with the other invited guests. I'm among royalty. I see an older woman I recognize as an editor from *Vogue*. There are journalists here from *Bon Appétit*, *Condé Nast Traveler*, and *Travel + Leisure* amid a slew of other boutique magazines. Then there are all the freelance content creators like Sienna. The room is packed with influential people, and Phillip stands at the center of it all, holding court.

He's changed into a sharply fitted black suit that he's paired with a gold tie.

It gives me endless pleasure to see the tie is almost the same shade as my dress. If we were a couple, it would look like we'd planned it.

Good looking doesn't cut it with him. A travesty, when you think about it. It's one thing to go up against a formidable man, and another to have to endure a collection of panty-melting features that make you suck in a sharp breath every time you see them. Absolutely, cruelly unfair. He's arrogantly old-money handsome, drowning in good genes so that even if he had a long, thick scar down his face, he'd still somehow pull it off. He could chip a tooth, grow a third ear, anything. Women would still sigh and say, *God, he's good looking*.

He's talking to the same man I saw in his company earlier—tall, Black, handsome, well dressed. They're two peas in a pod. I recognize him now because, along with unpacking and getting ready for dinner, I combed over the Woodmont Overseas International website again. It was a failure on my part that I didn't take the time to memorize every single member of the executive board before today. I can chalk it up to a hard few weeks, but it still makes me feel like a novice journalist.

The man beside Phillip is Tyson Ackres, Phillip's business partner, and from what little information I could glean online, his good friend. Phillip is a *supremely* private person, but it doesn't mean there's nothing to be found about him online. I came across a few tidbits about Tyson, a few photos of Phillip alongside a pretty woman—Vivienne Chén, his longtime girlfriend. Though rumor is they recently split.

When I interview him, I'll be sure to ask about it.

Sienna sees me looking at Phillip. Whatever expression I'm wearing must be pathetic enough that it makes her take action. Champagne flute still in hand, she nods toward Phillip's group. "Follow me."

"Wait. *Why?*"

My question goes unanswered as I trail after her. Surely, she knows what she's doing. She seems extremely confident.

"Sienna," I hiss quietly. "It's not so easy to explain. This situation between me and him. It's silly . . . but it's complicated."

"Well, we're about to *un*complicate it."

Oh, Jesus, she doesn't get it.

We're already across the room, beelining straight for them. Phillip hasn't seen us yet, so it's a surprise to him and to me when Sienna turns to me suddenly, laughing as she accidentally (on purpose) stumbles back into Tyson.

There's a gasp of surprise, a perfectly contrite apology.

"Oh gosh, sorry. *Sorry.* I'm such a knob. Did I spill anyone's drinks?"

Tyson smiles—no doubt charmed by Sienna's British accent—and shakes his head. "All good here. Phillip?"

"She didn't touch me," he replies a tad too brusquely, looking at me rather than Sienna.

He holds my gaze for a painful second; then he looks away, not even bothering with a once-over. If someone asked him the color of my dress, I doubt he could even guess.

Thank god Sienna's here to cut the tension. "Casey and I were just chatting, and I wasn't looking where I was going. *Ugh*. Apologies, truly. I'm Sienna Thompson. I recognize you, Phillip. Thanks, by the way, for the invitation to come aboard! And sorry, I don't think we've formally been introduced yet?"

Tyson smiles politely and extends his hand, first to Sienna and then to me. "Tyson Ackres. Pleasure to meet you, Sienna and . . . ?"

His warm brown eyes turn to me in invitation.

"Casey Hughes," I supply. "From *Bon Voyage*."

He grins. "Excellent. We're happy to have you both on board."

"*We're* the lucky ones!" Sienna gushes. "Our suites are insane."

Tyson chuckles. "Where did they put you two?"

Sienna looks to me for backup, but she doesn't need it. "We're on deck eight. I think we've got master suites; that's what Ms. Patel called them. Though I could be confused. Premium suites, signature suites, silver suites, who knows—the ones with the huge balconies and loads of windows. Forget my flat in London; I'll never want to leave this boat!"

"The suites on deck eight are something special. Are you happy with your accommodations as well, Ms. Hughes?"

Tyson's question jars me out of my staring contest with my champagne glass.

I look up. "Yes. *Very*. Thank you."

"And have you enjoyed your first day on board?"

What a loaded question.

I can't help but glance at Phillip, though he's looking away, his features pensive, his jaw tightly clenched.

I hate how difficult he's making this.

"I think it could have been *much* better if your friend agreed to let me interview him."

The words tumble out on their own accord, but I'm not upset about it. I have nothing to lose, remember? Better to have it out now, with witnesses.

Phillip turns slowly, leveling me with a gaze that's meant to shrink and cow and bend. I stand tall.

"I thought I made myself perfectly clear this afternoon, Ms. Hughes."

My eyes narrow like I'm pondering some great mystery. "I've never known someone to go through the trouble to amass a collection of journalists on board a boat and then deny them the thing they've been hired to do. Is it a power trip or some other game you're playing?"

"Write about the boat, Ms. Hughes."

His tone is a biting warning I blow right past.

"I'd rather write about *you*. Scratch that. *My boss* would rather I write about you." I lift a shoulder, feigning indifference. "I couldn't care one way or another."

Tyson's booming laugh jars me into the realization that I've stooped too low. Phillip's dragged me down to his level. An apology is on the tip of my tongue, but Tyson speaks first.

"Sienna, I was about to go over and chat with Ms. Patel for a moment. Care to join me?"

"Oh sure! I actually have a few questions for her," Sienna says, clearly eager to leave me all alone with Phillip.

The moment Tyson leads Sienna away, Phillip steps closer to me, emphasizing our size difference. My heels don't cut it. My makeup and dress barely feel like armor anymore. I can smell his spiced cologne. The heady scent binds around me, tethering me to him like a rope.

His scalding blue eyes practically sear me. "I find your obstinance incredibly annoying."

"And I find your rudeness ridiculously unprofessional. Have you treated every journalist here the way you've treated me?"

"Absolutely not. I've been nothing but respectful to them."

I can't help but laugh at how rude he is! "Is this all because of what happened when we were barely teenagers? Because I do actually regret it."

"So you admit you did tamper with the cord?"

I restrain an eye roll. I'm not against apologizing to him. I would have led with that straight away the first moment I saw him if I thought there was a chance he remembered me. But since then, we seem to have gotten off on the wrong foot. This tension between us seems to make it hard for me to say the right thing.

"Yes. *I'm sorry.* Is that what you want to hear?"

He shrugs coolly. "Maybe before. Now, though, it's done. I've made up my mind, and I've always been stubborn."

"And proud."

He doesn't even deny it.

"This is my career we're talking about here. Not some juvenile trivia game!"

He doesn't respond to this, and I'm left to take a deep breath and regroup, to try to salvage as much of this exchange as I possibly can.

"What am I supposed to do?" I ask, softening my voice, trying to appeal to the humanity that must exist deep down inside him.

"Oh, all right. I'll help." For a second, hope flares inside me like a flame. He leans in, taunting me like a fish on a line. "Here's what you're going to do. When we get to the next port, you're going to take your pencil and notepad. Got it? Make sure you have your phone or recorder, too, whatever it is you journalists like to use for interviews. You're going to tuck everything into your bag—all your belongings, actually—and head toward deck five and disembark. If you promise to never bother me again, I'll even pay for your flight home."

I wish I could bring my high heel down onto his foot, *hard.* "I'm not leaving."

His tone is smug and final. "You won't win."

I unfurl a teasing smile. "I suppose all I can do is *try.*"

Then I tip back the last of my champagne—aware of his focus on my berry-stained lips—before I force the empty glass into his hand, turn on my heel, and walk away.

God, it's satisfying.

I feel his gaze pinned on me like it's a real tangible thing. A cuff around my neck. A belt around my waist.

I'm buzzing with energy, though I don't fully understand the private smile that unfurls across my lips.

He didn't agree to an interview, so why do I feel like I just won?

Chapter Six
CASEY

It's the second day of our cruise, and Key West, Florida, is our first port of call. I can see the gorgeous turquoise water just outside my window, but I've yet to make it out of bed. My printed itinerary lists an entire day's worth of activities I can pick and choose from: gastronomical experiences, workout classes, painting lessons. I could have disembarked the ship at 7:00 a.m. for yoga on the beach, but it's already 8:45. I don't normally sleep in past 8:00, but I went to bed *way* too late last night. Sienna and I were up to no good. It started at dinner. They seated us side by side—clear across the room from Phillip.

In the dining hall, they'd arranged and decorated two long banquet tables. Phillip's place card was at the head of the first table. Mine was at the foot of the opposite table. We might as well have been on two different continents. It can't be a coincidence. He undoubtedly had me moved on purpose. *The nerve.*

Sienna spent the entirety of dinner wearing down my resistance so I'd spill all the details about my past with Phillip. She wouldn't accept god's honest truth: nothing all that interesting.

"The tension! I swear it's like you personally offended him and his entire family."

"It's nothing like that."

"Then what is it?"

"Later," I said, aware that the other guests near us were trying to eavesdrop on our conversation.

We ended up back in Sienna's suite after dinner, sipping our way through a bottle of champagne we'd ordered up, and once we'd drained that dry, we moved on to cocktails. She taught me some TikTok dance, and we filmed it together. We watched it back a dozen times, laughing harder every time until, eventually, I had to wipe tears out of my eyes. I did finally fill her in on my silly situation with Phillip—all of it. It's hilarious that out of everyone in my life, she's the first person to hear the whole sordid truth. That I'm a wanted woman. A criminal on the loose! *Hah.*

"He's holding a grudge from when you were *children*?"

She couldn't believe that was all.

"*Exactly!*"

She laughed. "No. No. There has to be more to it. Things you're leaving off."

"There's not. That's the whole thing. My grandmother drove me home after the competition. We didn't even make it to regionals. End of story. I never saw Phillip again until yesterday."

"He acts really torn up about you."

I scrunched my nose, not really seeing it. I mean, sure, I rankled him; that much was obvious.

Beyond that . . . who knew? With all the champagne in my system, I couldn't really think too hard on the subject.

Now, still, I'm not exactly all here. I have a pounding headache to show for last night, and I feel guilty for not setting my alarm for earlier. I should have been up and at 'em, early birding the hell out of this assignment. With a deep let's-get-this-over-with sigh, I thrust myself out of bed, moan through the first few steps to the bathroom, and—not bothering with a cup—I stick my head right under the faucet and drink.

Once I've felt around the counter for some Advil, I toss two back, drink more water, and dare a quick glance in the mirror.

Good, not great.

We'll take it.

My next item on the agenda is to shoot off a quick email to Gwen and the team.

> All good on board *Aurelia*! First day was jam-packed
> with activities. No chance for one-on-one with Phillip,
> but I can send a summary of the day and my tour of
> the boat.

Gwen's reply comes while I'm still sitting at the suite's desk: No need for trivial updates. Just send over bits of your interview with Phillip when you have it so we know what we're working with. Also, Mark is going to send a few articles for you to fact-check.

I groan and let my head fall forward into my hands. It feels good to dig the heels of my hands into my tired eyes, waking them up.

I want to crawl back into bed and doze for another few hours, but I can't. I can't. I CAN'T.

I leap up from my chair and head into the bathroom to wash my face and get ready for the day. I've missed yoga, but there's still a lot on my agenda. Starting at 11:00 a.m., small groups can disembark and link up with local tour guides to explore the beaches and Old Town, and I will absolutely be among them. I have big plans to soak in as much vitamin D as possible. Gobs of it. I want to come back on board the ship nicely bronzed. I dress in a bikini layered beneath a sundress. I hide the hint of dark circles under my eyes with some concealer and dab on a bit of blush and a few swipes of mascara, and by the time I leave my suite, I look fresh as a daisy.

I have a bag with my phone, ID, a small camera, notebook, tennis shoes—anything I might need when I'm off the boat for the day.

When I'm out in the hall, I consider knocking on Sienna's door, but if I were her, I'd want to be left alone. She isn't in the same position as I am. We talked about her job last night, the freedom it affords her. Sure, she has to produce content and post it. She has a schedule she adheres to for brand deadlines, and there's the occasional conference call with her manager—but her day-to-day is mostly dictated by her own whims. She doesn't have a boss in the same way I do. She can sleep in for as long as she wants.

She has the dream setup, as far as I'm concerned, and it's not so much about the fact that she doesn't need an alarm clock, it's the fact that the world is her oyster. Last night, I was more than a little envious listening to her travel schedule of all the places she's seen. I probably didn't do a great job of hiding it (thanks, Mr. Champagne).

For the first time since boarding the ship, I have to be brave and head down to the common areas on my own. Without Sienna by my side, I almost feel naked. At least I know right where to go. They're serving breakfast in the main dining room until 10:30 a.m., so I head there to get a little something to eat, preferably something carb heavy and sugary. I'd kill for coffee too. I could have made a cup in my suite, but something tells me *Aurelia's* crew knows how to whip up something a little more delicious than an espresso shot.

Thanks to Ms. Patel's tour yesterday, I have no trouble navigating the ship. Decks one through three are the lowest decks and are meant for staff only. Decks nine and ten have the observation lounge and library. Decks six, seven, and eight mainly house suites and small cabins. The real action is on deck five. There's the reception desk, a salon, a spa, a high-end boutique, and a pool. Deck four has the food. There's a fancy French restaurant called La Dame, which is run by a Michelin Star chef and only open for dinner; a semicasual Italian restaurant called Roma, open for lunch and dinner; and the main dining room, which serves every meal. It's beautiful inside. They've carried the neutral-gray and cool-silver tones into the room and added deep-teal fabric on the chairs for a pop of color. It's a large space, able to host almost every guest on board all at once, but they've designed it to give the illusion that it's much more intimate. No austere cafeteria here.

Walls jut out from the perimeter of the room to create private nooks for certain exclusive tables. It's not enough privacy, however, because I see Phillip immediately upon entering. He's at a back table, his attention on his phone.

I can't believe he's alone.

A smiling host informs me that the dining room is open seating. I can sit at any table I like, and I nod and move along, already certain of where I'm heading.

I have no choice.

I have to take full advantage.

Sink or swim, Sunshine.

Phillip doesn't look up from his phone until I'm tugging out the chair across from him.

Bold doesn't cut it. This is downright insane.

The waiter is there before Phillip can comprehend what I'm doing.

"Would you like to start with a coffee or tea? We have a full range of coffee options on the back of the menu if you'd like to glance over it."

"A latte please, with a splash of vanilla," I say at the same time Phillip cuts in.

"Bring it in a to-go cup. She won't be staying."

The waiter doesn't even bother to check this with me before he hurries away, eager to do Phillip's bidding.

Phillip's gaze tries to flay me open. "I don't recall inviting you to sit."

My smile doesn't waver.

I'm not so bad mannered that I don't realize I've broken quite a few social cues here. It's just that with Phillip Woodmont, civility and politeness will get me nowhere. In fact, normal human social cues hold no weight with him at all.

I tip my head to the side, playing dumb. "Are you usually this rude so early in the morning?"

"No."

"*Ooh la la*. Special treatment, then? I'm flattered. Humor me, though, considering my Advil hasn't kicked in and my head is aching. The caffeine should help, but until then, let's play nice."

"There's a slew of open tables. Pick any of them. Nurse your headache *there*."

I pick up the napkin sitting on my plate—artfully arranged to look like an origami bird. "How delightful."

His eyes narrow on me. He's obviously perplexed. It's clear that he's used to a certain way of life (i.e., he speaks and the world listens). He's probably forgotten what insubordination feels like. It'll be my pleasure to remind him.

Whatever searing comment he's thinking now as he studies my face, he contains it. A pity. I'd love to know what he thinks about me. He might have grown up into a man who holds all the power, but I'm no shrinking violet.

At least . . . I didn't think I was.

Sitting here across from Phillip has my cheeks flushing, my hand slightly unsteady as I smooth my napkin across my lap.

I swallow past my nerves. "I promise I won't take up too much of your time."

I reach down into my purse to grab my phone. It's only a swipe and a click, and then I have my trusty recording app open. I slide my phone across the table set with crystal stemware and a gardenia floating in a bowl of water. Its fragrance almost masks his cologne.

"You mind?"

"Actually, I do," he says haughtily.

"Righto."

I expected this, obviously. I reach forward and make a show of stabbing my phone screen with my index finger to pause the recording. Hopefully, it sends a clear message that I'm a team player. We can do this his way.

"There, now. It's just us."

His eyes pointedly sweep across the diners filling the tables behind ours, contradicting me. Fine. We aren't absolutely alone, but there's no one at the table directly adjacent to ours, and with all the chatter and clinking silverware, our conversation is relatively private. This wouldn't be my first choice of an interview location, sure, but it'll have to do. The odds of getting Phillip to agree to . . . well, *anything* are slim to none. For all I know, this is the last time I'll see him for the entire voyage. I have an idea that, given the choice, he'd happily throw me overboard.

"I'm not giving you an interview."

"Fine . . . no interview *this morning.*" I sound light and chipper. My sweet smile says I'm not bothered in the least. "That's perfectly okay. I still think it'd be prudent to get the basics out of the way, though—our location, your physical appearance . . . details I might forget later."

The curl of his lips tells me he finds this particularly amusing. As if I could possibly forget the way he looks.

Right. So he knows he's attractive. How maddening.

I expect another roadblock here. I mean, with how rude he's been so far, it wouldn't be all that far fetched to imagine him picking up my phone and tossing it clear across the room. Or better yet, over the side of the ship.

He remains mum, though, tucking into his breakfast with all the practiced grace of a man used to fine dining. No confusion over forks for this guy. He's ordered an omelet and breakfast potatoes that look to be seasoned and cooked to perfection. My stomach growls, and I ignore it. The waiter hasn't come back yet with my to-go latte.

Maybe it's wishful thinking on my part, but I get the impression Phillip isn't sure what he wants to do with me. After all, he'd only have to lift a finger, and security would be all too happy to haul me out of here.

The fact that he's letting me sit here is a small victory in itself.

I should build upon it.

Unfortunately, it's not how I'm wired.

Something in me just wants to needle him. Always. It's too tempting. The stuffy boardroom appearance. The sharpness in his elegant features. I want to ruffle his feathers, wrinkle his shirt, make him laugh.

I press record again and lean down, speaking directly into my phone.

"It's Monday, a little past nine. I'm sitting across from Phillip Woodmont, who seems to be in a surly mood this morning."

He exhales a small grunt and reaches for his coffee. Black. No room for cream or sugar in his overflowing cup.

"We're on board *Aurelia*. Ship details to follow. Phillip—"

His eyes cut into me.

"Er . . . Mr. Woodmont will sit for an interview another time."

"No, I won't."

Spurred on by his obstinance, I start talking like I would if he weren't listening. "His suit looks designer. I have no doubt he employs a stylist. The watch on his wrist, while beautiful, could probably feed a bevy of orphans. Would his wealth be better spent on charity? More on that later. His appearance . . ."

My mouth goes dry. I refuse to gift him the truth about his face and all the annoying beauty it contains, so I move right along to his head of thick dark-brown hair.

"Well, it's clear he went for the billionaire hair-plug special. Perhaps he got a referral from Elon Musk?"

Phillip reaches forward and pauses the recording with a deft finger. "This is my natural hair."

I restart the recording, leaning down and lowering my voice even further, teasing. "He seems particularly defensive of his hairline. Investigate further."

At this point, he's lost the battle with his smile, and though I should be ticking a tally beside my name for having succeeded, I can do nothing but stare, a little slack jawed as if I've just had the wind knocked out of me. Phillip was handsome enough sporting a frown and furrowed brow, but it pales in comparison to the absolute devastation his smile wreaks on me.

An oversight I can't repeat because he sees it—the momentary lapse in my defenses. The effect he has on me.

Dammit.

I'm sitting on the edge of my seat, waiting for his return blow, when a voice speaks behind me.

"I thought you were going to save me a seat this morning."

I turn to see Phillip's friend Tyson aiming a charming smile my way. He's dressed just as nicely as Phillip, and I feel slightly out of my element in my sundress and bikini. Silly me for dressing for a tropical vacation when I should have slipped into my finest pantsuit.

"She sat down without asking first," Phillip says rudely. "Here, let me tip her out of it for you."

He stands up as if to act on his words, and I find myself gripping ahold of the cushion. *Childish* doesn't begin to cover how we're acting. It seems we've reverted right back to middle school.

"Phillip, let her keep her seat. Look, here's another one coming."

A uniformed waiter is hurrying over with a chair for Tyson. He sets it down at our table, and then behind him, two more waiters arrive with a charger, coordinating china, silverware, and a crystal glass. The whole production is so coordinated it's like they've practiced a thousand times. They might have.

"Will you be having coffee this morning, Mr. Ackres?" one of them asks.

"Yes, please. Fill it up so high you're scared it'll spill over. Better yet, just leave me the pot."

The waiter's head dips in a reverent nod before he rushes off. The original waiter comes back with my latte—in a to-go cup, the lid placed to the side—and asks me and Tyson what we would like to order.

I hadn't even gotten a chance to look at the menu. I didn't think I was going to make it this far. I half expect Phillip to cut in and tell them not to bother with food, that I'll be dining elsewhere.

"Are you a vegetarian, Ms. Hughes?" Tyson asks, trying to smooth down the tension radiating off his friend.

"No."

He nods in confirmation, then turns to address the waiter. "Then we'll each take the sunrise omelet. Potatoes and fruit on the side, please."

"*Pancakes*," I whisper.

He chuckles. "And a side of pancakes for both of us. Lots of syrup." I smile at him, and he smiles back. He's so welcoming and friendly.

The happy mood is cut short, of course, the moment my gaze shifts back to Phillip. He's such a black cloud—all that frustration evident in his furrowed brow.

"Seems you won't be getting rid of me quite so easily this morning."

"Don't push your luck."

I look to Tyson. "Do you see what I have to deal with? I've been nothing but kind this morning, I assure you. *He's* the problem."

Tyson's clearly amused as he replies, "He explained the circumstances to me. Apparently, there's bad blood between you two."

"'Fraid so. Think you could broker peace?"

He puffs out an exhausted sigh. "I'm not *that* good, I'm afraid. Phillip is a much better negotiator."

I tilt my head at Phillip. "*Truly*? I have a hard time believing that."

"Drink your latte, Ms. Hughes," Phillip says by way of ending the discussion.

Like a good girl, I pick up my latte with its intricate foamed-milk design—I swear it's a tiny version of *Aurelia, absurd*—and I take a long, pointed sip, holding eye contact with Phillip while I do it. There, now I've done what you asked. You can't be mad about that.

I don't know why I've found myself here, going up against a man positively dripping with power. I'm awfully confident for a person who has no arsenal to speak of, no ally, just a lowly fact-checker title and nothing to lose, I suppose.

Phillip's gaze never wavers. He watches me lift the mug to my lips, and then his gaze drops to my throat as I swallow. I lick the bit of foam from the corner of my mouth and brush my lips together. It's the most mundane thing—just a sip of coffee—and yet for some reason, I find it's turned into something so heated that my body hums with excitement. I recognize what it is: innate, obvious attraction. *Oh fuck.* It's so, *so* inconvenient to feel that zing. The sort that feels inevitable and deep. The kind of thing that digs its talons into you.

It's one thing to acknowledge that Phillip is objectively handsome. Poll the US population and everyone would agree: he's a grade *A* hottie. Attraction is different, though. *Chemical.*

Tyson clears his throat.

I set my latte back on the table.

"Tell me what I should do to win him over," I say, talking to Tyson, though I'm looking at Phillip.

"I doubt you can," Tyson replies truthfully.

My brow arches.

"Ah. 'My good opinion once lost is lost forever,'" I say, quoting from Jane Austen.

Phillip's mouth quirks like he wants to smile. "Exactly. And don't you forget it."

Tyson barks out a laugh. "Easy there, Phillip. She's our invited guest, remember?"

I give him a gloating, devilish smile. "Yes. See? As your invited guest, I'm untouchable. *And don't you forget it.*"

The air crackles as Phillip's eyes darken. I was absentmindedly stroking the side of my to-go cup, but I yank my hand back and stuff it beneath the table.

The tightness in my belly almost hurts.

That ache of desire is so foreign to me.

I realize what I've done a second too late. I came over here with a clear goal: persuade Phillip to give me an interview. Instead, I let him goad me and drag me down to a position I can't afford to be in (quite literally). Now that I know how easily he strips me of my self-control, my filter, my manners, I'll have to be more careful with him in the future.

I open my mouth, preparing to offer a proverbial white flag by way of apology, but Phillip drains the last of his coffee and then scoots his chair back, standing so that I'm forced to acknowledge his intimidating size. I feel diminutive sitting in my chair across from him.

"Off already?" Tyson asks.

"I need to check in with Devin."

"Ah, let me know if there's any trouble."

Phillip nods, casts me a quick glance, and says, "Ms. Hughes, enjoy your breakfast."

When he walks away, I have to make a concerted effort not to let my gaze follow him through the dining room. I want to watch him, but I focus on my latte and take a heavy gulp.

Tyson's attention is on me. I'm aware he's studying me, but I'm too chicken to call him out for it.

I puff out a heavy sigh. "Well, that went horribly . . ."

He shrugs cavalierly. "Eh. Don't sweat it."

Don't sweat it? Impossible. I'll be replaying our encounter on repeat the rest of the day. I'll be dissecting every word, beating myself up for not playing my part better. I could have kissed his ass, really cranked up the charm. Instead, I was too focused on trying to get in some verbal jabs.

"You don't have to eat with me. I understand I've put you in an awkward position."

He can't keep the smile off his face. "You have? This has been one of the best meals I've had in a while. Well . . . certainly the most entertaining."

"*Entertaining.*" I snort. "I should apologize to him."

He balks. "Apologize? Absolutely not."

"I was rude."

His expression turns steely. "So was he."

"Yes, but *I* need *him.* Not the other way around."

He frowns, considering this for a moment; then he casts the thought away with a shake of his head. "I'm not so certain of that."

On the heels of this little veiled comment, the waiter arrives with our food.

"*Oh my god.*"

Our side of pancakes was misinterpreted. In addition to our omelets, we're both presented with a stack of six pancakes, each one the size of my head. Syrup drips provocatively over the sides, and butter melts in a way that has my mouth watering as they set the plate down in front of me.

Tyson's eyes widen. "Well, damn."

I laugh. "Eat up."

It should be slightly awkward to eat alone with Tyson, but he's so adept at carrying on conversation. He asks me how long I've worked at *Bon Voyage*, where I live, what I think of *Aurelia*.

In return, I ask about his position with Woodmont Overseas International, his time with the company, and eventually, his relationship with Phillip.

Tyson knows what I'm doing, of course. He hasn't forgotten I'm here as a journalist first and foremost. He doesn't shut me down, though. Either he's trying to make up for Phillip's harshness or he sees the benefit in throwing me a bone.

"Phillip and I are extremely close. We started working together when we were in our early twenties, and he let me live with him while I was looking for an apartment in New York City." He gets a faraway look as he considers something. "That would have been seven or eight years ago, now. God, we were kids."

"Single?"

He laughs. "Yes. We were both single at the time."

"Was he a good roommate?"

"Course. I mean, his apartment takes up an entire city block. It's not like we were on top of each other or anything. There was a cleaning service, private chef. All the usual pitfalls of having a roommate didn't even come up."

"So you two have been friends and coworkers for a while. That must get difficult at times?"

He mulls this over as he cuts into his pancakes. "Not really. Phillip's extremely intense about work. So long as you do your job well, he gives you a wide berth."

"Is he your direct superior?"

"Not technically, but with the Woodmont name, in a way, he's everyone's direct superior. The only people above him in the company are his father and uncle, and it's no small secret that—with their approval—he'll succeed them both when the time comes."

"Do you think that's good for the company?"

"It's essential. No one could run Woodmont Overseas like Phillip can."

"So he's generally liked among staff?"

Tyson chuckles. "Think of it this way. You know the way Brits idolize Princess Diana? That's how people at Woodmont Overseas feel about Phillip. He gives everything he has to the company. He cares about every member of staff, from the janitorial department to the chairman on the board, and they feel it."

"So then professionally, he's damn near perfect. What about his personal life?"

Tyson shakes his head, giving me a daring look. "*That*, Ms. Hughes, is something you'll have to ask him."

Chapter Seven

PHILLIP

My stride is punishing as I storm away from the dining room. My fists flex, then relax only to immediately flex again, over and over, at my sides as I keep a maddening pace. I don't bother with the elevators. I take the stairs up to my suite on deck eight. I'm early for my meeting with Devin. I didn't need to leave the dining room for another ten minutes. Getting away from that table—from Casey—felt paramount.

I'm angry I got so carried away, angry over the situation with Casey. I've never, in all my career, dealt with a journalist like her, a *person* like her, even. In my social circles, everyone is polite—at least to your face. I'm not used to open hostility, and her outward fire draws me in until I say too much, cross the line. I did it last night and again this morning. I can't remember the last time I was so rude.

When she took a seat across from me at breakfast, I couldn't believe it.

No one, and I mean *no one*, at Woodmont Overseas would dare to do such a thing. I'm shocked she did. I've made myself clear. It's not like I've minced my words with her. *No interview* means *no interview*—it doesn't mean *try harder to persuade me*. It won't happen.

It's not just personal at this point; it's protocol.

I grew up in a deeply private family. The Woodmont name doesn't grace gossip websites or tabloids. Discretion is key.

It's not hard to keep out of the spotlight either. I've done it my entire life. Every so often, my publicist will receive the odd interview request. *Life, People, Forbes*—they've all tried to profile me at one point or another. Every time, I've declined. It's for the best. I value my private life. It's the one normal thing I have. The wealth I grew up with can sour your soul. Seeking public adoration on top of it would be a recipe for disaster.

My phone buzzes, and I look down, relieved. Anything would be a good distraction from my current thoughts. A text from Vivienne lights up the screen.

I'm shocked, to say the least. We haven't been in communication lately. I've seen her out occasionally. We were at the same gala a few weeks back, and I had thought it would be horrible to have to see her like that, out in public, not on my arm. It was . . . fine. Of course I could never admit that to her. It would only prove her point further.

Her text pertains to my work with *Aurelia*.

VIVIENNE: Sending you a huge congratulations, Phillip! I saw a segment about the Aurelia on the Today show this morning. Such a wonderful achievement. I'm so proud.

I don't even know what to reply, so I stick with a simple thank you.

My ex-girlfriend was perfect for me in every way. Vivienne Chén is studious, business oriented, and strong willed. Her intelligence amazed me on a daily basis, perpetually keeping me on my toes. A graduate of Stanford Law, a Fulbright scholar, and now a global strategist for Yves Saint Laurent—she can carry her own in any crowd. I saw her as my future wife, the mother of my children, until we were eating dinner a few months ago and she asked me, out of the blue, if I was happy in our relationship. If I was happy, specifically, with her.

I thought it was a trivial question.

What is happiness next to satisfaction, contentment, pride? Love is an amorphous blob, impossible to pin down from one moment to the next, elusive, and silly.

"Happy? Yes. Sure," I'd replied confidently.

Then I returned to my steak, assuming the conversation was over.

"Phillip."

Her tone said *Be serious.*

I thought I had been.

Still, I set down my cutlery and looked up. Her slender eyebrows were pinched together. Her lips turned down in frustration. It made my stomach sink.

She'd leaned in, straightening, then restraightening the linen napkin on her lap. "I worry we don't bring out the best in each other," she spoke softly, almost like she barely had the nerve.

I'd audibly balked.

Was she kidding? Since meeting her, I'd perfected my drop shot in tennis. I'd expanded my love of good wine and literature. We completed the Sunday crossword, worked out routinely and efficiently. Went to bed on time.

With Vivienne by my side, my life was orderly and efficient. I was so deeply rooted in my comfort zone, surely it meant we were supposed to be together.

"We're bad influences on one another," she emphasized, like we were two drug addicts caught in a vicious cycle. Like after our caprese salads, I was going to suggest a bump in the bathroom. "We barely talk anymore."

So what if Vivienne and I shared a comfortable quiet life together? We would occasionally discuss news articles at dinner, things we'd read in *The Times* that morning. What else were we supposed to do? Muse about life? *Laugh?*

Then she took it one step further by asking "Do you love me?"

I didn't know what to say to that.

Now, of course, I realize my response should have been *Yes. Madly.*

That's what most people want to hear, I imagine. Instead, I reached across the table to take her hand so I could ask "What is this really about?"

She moved out that night in what will go down as the world's most docile breakup. Not a tear was shed. No screaming. A preschool teacher would have praised us for using our indoor voices as we pragmatically discussed how best to divide up our stuff.

"You can have the air fryer," I offered, which I thought was pretty big of me, considering how often I used it to reheat leftover pizza.

"All right," she said, pushing it into her pile.

"And the espresso machine?" I asked.

"It's yours. I gave up coffee weeks ago. I swapped to tea to help with my insomnia."

Had she?

At the time, I didn't understand why she was uprooting our life together for no good reason. It's not as if she was desperate for the next steps, a proposal or children or something, and I was acting as a roadblock. I figured we would get there eventually. I want all of that. We never fought, barely disagreed. She was so easygoing and seemed to want everything I wanted.

I'm still not wholly convinced we've done the right thing.

I regret not fighting harder for her, not saying something that compelled her to stay and give me a chance.

For the last year, I've imagined a future with Vivienne by my side. Now I'm storming down a hall, angry over a conversation with a woman I barely know. Casey is nothing like Vivienne. Of that much, I'm certain.

Chapter Eight
CASEY

I've never seen water as crystal clear as the ocean surrounding the dock in Key West. It's a tropical paradise, so irresistibly inviting, especially with the late-morning sun bearing down from overhead. I'm almost tempted to shuck off my shoes, toss my bag aside, and take a quick dip. Unfortunately, I'm on the clock.

We're waiting on the dock for the rest of our group to arrive so we can start our tour of Old Town. There's a local tour guide, a guy about my age with shaggy brown hair and intricate tattoos along his right arm. He's a total beach bum, but he pulls it off well. Not my usual type, per se, but I still blush a little when he gives me a quick once-over as we go around the circle and introduce ourselves.

He does a head count as he walks around the group, finding an excuse to stop right beside me. *Smooth.*

"What did you say your name was again?"

"Casey," I say, smiling.

"Ricardo."

I accept his handshake and find it refreshing that he seems eager to be in my company. It's a far cry from Phillip, that's for sure.

"Been to the Keys before?"

The way he asks the question, it's dripping with innuendo.

"Never."

He grins, flashing a white smile. "You're in for a treat."

"I'm here! I've arrived!" singsongs a familiar British accent. "Call off the search party!"

It's Sienna, strolling toward our group without a care in the world. She's wearing a thin crochet dress that reveals a neon-green bikini underneath. Whereas I'm trying to skirt the line between paradise chic and business casual, she's able to go full-on vacation mode, and the difference is glaring. She looks gorgeous.

I half expect Ricardo to realize his mistake in chatting me up first and push me off the dock in an attempt to get to her, but he only gives her a smile and a nod. "Our last arrival."

"Hello, everyone! *Apologies.* I got turned around on the boat."

That's probably a huge lie. If she's anything like me, she's nursing a killer hangover and wishing she could lie in bed all day. I'm actually feeling better, though. Breakfast helped.

Ricardo introduces himself to Sienna and then directs us over to the curb where another tour guide gives us a wave. "Now that we're all together, we can set off. We have two three-row golf carts, big enough for our entire group if we split in two. Joseph will drive the second golf cart, but we'll be making all the same stops and largely staying together."

Sienna sidles up next to me, mouthing a complaint about her head aching. I can't help but laugh, thinking back on our night.

As we all head toward the golf carts, she asks if I've eaten. "I didn't manage to snag anything on my way down here."

I open my bag and tip it toward her so she can peer in. There's a to-go box from the dining room, sitting on top of all my stuff. "I brought you food."

Her jaw drops. "You're joking."

I take out the small container and hand it over to her. "It's a few pastries. They're probably a little smashed, but they were delicious. Here."

"Oh my god, where have you been all my life?" She cracks the lid and laughs. "Christ. There's enough here to feed an army."

"Casey?"

Ricardo tries to get my attention, and I look over to see he's waving me toward his golf cart. "There's room up here."

He's indicating the seat beside him.

Sienna titters under her breath. "Ah, a little vacation romance brewing? My, my. You work fast."

"Don't even go there."

"He's cute. What's wrong with him?" she asks, taking a huge bite of a croissant.

"I'm working," I say as if we both weren't three sheets to the wind and acting like fools in her suite last night.

"Oh, please. This is hardly a stuffy boardroom. Who cares if you live a little? Surely, that's better for your writing anyway. Getting the inside scoop from letting Ricardo get inside—"

I cut her off by clearing my throat. "Noted."

I accept the seat beside Ricardo, and Sienna hops in right behind me in the second row. While Ricardo drives us around Old Town, pointing out the sights, Sienna wastes no time at all in prying into his personal life.

I've got the gist. He's lived on the Keys his whole life. He works part time at a bar by Sunset Pier. No girlfriend.

"You don't have to keep humoring her," I tell him while we're stopped at the Key West Lighthouse. Sienna and I listened to Ricardo's spiel about it. It is as interesting as an old lighthouse could be, but the rest of the group is still roaming the grounds, taking their sweet time. Sienna and I sit in the golf cart, wanting the shade. "She's about to ask you if you have a 401(k) . . . when you last had a dental checkup, that sort of thing."

Sienna leans forward, not even denying it. "Yes, actually, those are both good questions. Let's see your teeth."

Ricardo laughs. "I don't mind. Swear. You two should come out tonight."

"*Out?* Where?" Sienna asks with a mouthful of pastry.

"I'll be bartending. Free drinks . . . dancing. It'll be a good time."

"And they say romance is dead!" Sienna jokes.

"Ricardo?" A guy in our group waves to get his attention. "Who did you say built this lighthouse again?"

Ricardo hops out to answer his question.

Sienna moans quietly. "Who cares about some shitty lighthouse? Can't we go to the beach already? It's sweltering. I feel like I'm sweating out every ounce of alcohol we consumed last night."

"Maybe that's not a bad thing . . ."

"I don't know. At this point, I feel like I could lick my arm and come away tasting tequila."

The thought makes me laugh.

"I had breakfast with Tyson, sort of by accident."

"Oh, really?"

Her brow arches. I remember him carting her off yesterday to give Phillip and me a moment to talk by ourselves. I wonder if there was more to it.

"So . . . what do you think of him?"

I expect her to go gaga over how handsome he is—styled, groomed, charming. All of the above.

She holds up her hand. "Save it. He's not single."

I'm more than a little surprised. "How do you know?"

She shrugs and crosses her arms, squinting over at the lighthouse. "I looked him up last night in my drunken stupor. He has an Instagram account. He doesn't post much, but when he does, it's all pictures of the same woman with these nauseatingly sweet captions. The whole account is like an homage to her. The lucky cow."

"Oh well. Ricardo's nice."

"He's interested in *you*," she points out, shifting her gaze to me with a waggle of her brows.

"Well, I bet he has friends," I say with a teasing wink. Surely there's more just like him. Sexy locals.

"*True*. All the better for me. I need a proper lay."

"*Same*, but it's kind of hard to get things going on a vacation like this. We leave Key West in the morning, so it's now or never with men like Ricardo. I've never had a one-night stand," I admit, recognizing the truth of my earlier suspicions about cruise ship relationships. Sienna and I have known each other for barely twenty-four hours, and already, I'm spilling secrets to her. We're on friendship warp speed.

"I have, twice." She scrunches her nose in distaste. "They were just okay. Sort of not worth the trouble of having to sneak off in the morning all awkward and guilty. Still, I have mates that *swear* by them. I'm willing to give it another go." Her expression turns wicked with glee. "Maybe we should both live a little on this trip. *Explore our options*."

I shrug, mulling it over. "Could be interesting."

With everything else in my life quite literally in the gutter, I don't see any issue with letting loose and having fun with a guy. Distracting myself for a few hours sounds perfect. No strings attached. No need to fill him in on my sad little life.

She claps. "Okay, so it's settled. We're going to sow our wild oats." She leans closer, perusing our tour group. "I'm afraid to say, but outside of Ricardo, we've managed to get the oldest and crustiest of the bunch. I mean, where are the *hunks*? Ignoring this sad lot, who would be your pick for a one-night stand out of everyone we've met so far? Ricardo?"

Her eyes spark with the idea that there's something brewing between me and our tour guide. Unfortunately, *Phillip*, not Ricardo, is the first man to come to mind. The realization startles me like I've just had a bucket of cold water poured over my head.

I remember the spark we shared at breakfast. My stomach curls in on itself as I think back on the way he watched me from across the table. There was no shy glance, just a bold, arrogant perusal. A look that said *I own the place. Literally.* I've never experienced a man like him. Not on a date, definitely not in bed. I've always gone for quiet, studious boys, mostly due to ease of access. The guys in my journalism classes in college were not exactly the most intimidating creatures on Earth. And after college, the guys I dated were much the same. Most recently, I went out with an associate editor at *Bon Voyage* for a few weeks before it petered out partly due to lack of chemistry but mostly due to bad timing. It was around the same time my grandmother was at her sickest, and the guy wasn't looking to hold someone's hand through that amount of intense grief. I don't blame him for ending things. In fact, looking back, it was for the best. My feelings for him were lukewarm. We would have probably dated for a few months and then gone our separate ways anyway.

Since then . . . well, there's been a veritable drought. It's kind of complicated to piece together a dating life while I'm living out of a suitcase, like *Hey, baby, want to come back to my place? Yeah, it's the Motel 6 just off the highway* . . .

I suppose I would make it work if the right man came along, though.

Someone like Phillip.

My heart races with startling clarity.

Though he's absolutely, ludicrously wrong for me, I'm still intrigued by him. I'm convinced a one-night stand with him would be *incredibly* hot. All that angsty tension. *Jesus.*

I'm aware of the flush creeping up my neck, and I feel like an absolute pervert fantasizing about the one man who should be completely off limits. Not only does Phillip hate me, but he's also the subject of my work assignment. It's not outlined in the company handbook—which I've *definitely* read all of and didn't just skim through on my first day on the job—but it seems pretty obvious that it would jeopardize my integrity as a journalist.

I realize Sienna's watching me, still waiting for my choice for a one-night stand. I smile and shrug.

"Ricardo, I guess."

She nods approvingly, turning to look at him as he goes about his tour guide duties. "Yeah. He's a great option. Fit and tan. I might go for that cute photographer from Spain. Did you see him at dinner last night? The one a few seats down from me? God, he was sexy. There's the language barrier to contend with, but I took Spanish for two terms, so we'll have no problem working it out. How do you say 'Let's el bono'?"

A laugh bursts out of me, and we draw the attention of everyone in our group.

Whoops.

Our blisteringly hot tour of Old Town lasts another two hours. I take notes as best as possible, but outside of the hour we spent at Hemingway's house, it wasn't all that noteworthy. People come to Key West for the beaches, not a roundabout tour of an old cemetery. By the time Ricardo pulls the golf cart up to the beach, Sienna and I are melting like two Popsicles left out on hot asphalt.

"Oh, thank god," I sigh quietly.

Sienna wipes sweat from her brow and leaps off the golf cart before it's even come to a full stop.

"So help me, I'm going to drown myself in that water. *Look at it!* It's so blue."

She takes my hand and starts tugging me onto the sand so that I'm half running, half stumbling after her. My bag slips off my shoulder, and I have to secure it before everything falls out.

"Slow down!"

Ricardo races after us, laughing. "I was supposed to tell you guys, there's a picnic set up for you all. That tent right over there."

I look to where he's pointing, and my jaw drops.

"Well done, *Aurelia*," Sienna says with an impressed tone.

A few yards from where we stand, closer to the water's edge, there's a large-scale blue-and-white-striped tent under which sits a long banquet table set low to the ground. Around it, throw blankets and pillows have been arranged by careful hands. A bartender serves cocktails in carved-out pineapples, and there's another table overflowing with charcuterie.

"This could be someone's wedding," Sienna notes, already reaching for her phone so she can take pictures for social media.

She's right. There are floral arrangements set out everywhere and morning glory vines twist around the tent poles. Everything is so beautifully done that it's hard to believe it's just for a beach picnic.

"Good afternoon," a kind voice greets us, and we turn to find a crew member smiling at us.

I recognize her from the welcome reception in the observation lounge. She has pale-blonde hair and piercing blue eyes that seem to leap out at you. Shannon, her metal name tag reads.

"Would either of you care for a cocktail?" she asks.

"*Absolument*," Sienna teases in French, all too happy to skip off to the bar.

Shannon looks to me, and I smile. "I'm all set for now."

My stomach feels a little off after I've been baking in the heat all day. Ricardo wasn't the best driver behind the wheel of the golf cart either. My insides feel like slush, and I'd rather not tempt fate by adding alcohol to the mix. Shannon points toward the water.

"If you're interested, we've arranged surf lessons."

Now *that* sounds fun.

I'll take any excuse to slip out of this sundress and get in the water.

"I'm game," I say excitedly.

"You can stow your things over there with the attendant for safekeeping and then head down to the water."

I see a row of surfboards set up in the sand, six of them lined up one after another. Though we're early to the beach—most of *Aurelia's* guests have yet to arrive—two of the surfboards are already being claimed. One by a girl I don't immediately recognize and one by Sienna's Spanish lover (or *soon-to-be* lover, that is). I claim the surfboard beside him after slipping out of my sundress and applying a quick spritz of sunblock.

I'm eager to help facilitate a wingwoman situation, so I introduce myself with a little wave.

"Hi, Casey Hughes, *Bon Voyage*."

Sienna's man turns to me with an easygoing smile. "Javier Mendez, freelance mostly."

Oh, his accent is heavenly. Sienna's going to melt.

"Pleasure to meet you," I say before turning to the girl.

I realize she's one of the influencers Sienna told me about yesterday, the ones she wanted to steer clear of. I can see why. My welcoming smile is met by a sour expression.

"*Avery,*" the girl says with a snooty tone. And that's all, no last name, no job title. It's like she's on par with Beyoncé or Madonna. One name, and we should damn well know it.

I can't help myself. "And what do you do, Avery? Are you a writer?"

She gives a little pitying laugh, like she feels sorry for me that I don't already know the answer to my own question. "I'm in digital marketing."

I scrunch my nose like I'm confused. "So you're in advertising? Client side or . . . ?"

"No," she says more sternly now, her cool gaze slipping to Javier for a moment like she's worried about his opinion of her. Oh. *Oh.* Maybe that's why she's giving me the cold shoulder. I wonder if I've interrupted something she had going with Javier. "I'm an influencer."

"Like Sienna," I say, pointing over to where my new friend stands at the bar. Javier follows my finger just in time to see Sienna laugh with the bartender and then look over at me. She wiggles her pineapple cocktail beside her head, pointing to the drink and mouthing, "*It's huge!*"

I laugh and peer over to see Javier inspecting her from head to toe. For the moment, he's forgotten that Avery and I exist. I have a hard time suppressing my satisfied smirk.

"I recognize her," Javier says.

"Oh yeah?" I say, wanting to press the subject.

"We run in the same circles," Avery says quickly, trying to remain relevant.

"She didn't mention that," I say before deciding it's probably time to reel it in. I've done my job. I've ensured that Javier's aware of Sienna. There's no need to rub Avery's nose in it. "So . . . have either of you surfed before?"

Today will be my first time attempting it. Bold, considering I'll have an audience watching me make a fool of myself. More guests arrive by the minute. Other tours are wrapping up, and everyone's converging on the beach. The last few surfboards fill up, and our instructor starts the lesson.

It will come as a shock to no one that a girl who grew up surrounded by books and nowhere *near* a beach (unless you count the less-than-pristine beaches in the greater NYC area) isn't all that great at surfing. I try my hardest. The instructor walks me through the motions—paddle hard, plant your feet, pop up, keep your knees bent, and stretch your arms out by your sides for balance as if you're walking a tightrope. Logistically, I understand it. Physically, my limbs won't cooperate. I tip over into the water time and time again, crashing through the waves, plunging under the refreshing blue surface. I don't even mind. It feels good to get soaked, though the competitive spark in me grows annoyed that I can't quite figure it out. Somehow, Avery's even worse. She takes up most of the instructor's time, but Javier sticks close by me, trying to help coach me as best as possible. He's a natural, though he's admitted to surfing a lot.

We sit side by side on our surfboards bobbing in the water, waiting for our turns.

"Last time I surfed, I was in Hawaii. The waves were massive."

He arcs his hand up over his head to emphasize his point, and I laugh.

"Sounds awesome. Were you there for work?"

"Yeah, I covered the Kapalua Wine & Food Festival for *The Times*."

I'm immediately envious. "So how does freelancing work for you? Do you choose your destinations or do publications post assignments?"

He shimmies his hand from side to side. "Both. This trip was last minute. I'm filling in for a friend. I was in Bolivia last week."

My jaw drops. "You're kidding."

He smiles and shakes his head.

"I can't imagine. I'm not even close to getting there. This assignment is a first for me. I'm usually behind a desk at *Bon Voyage*."

"You'll get there," he reassures me with a sympathetic smile.

Yeah, hopefully sooner rather than later.

"So do you travel alone mostly?"

He doesn't understand my intent when he replies, "Yes. No assistants."

"Right, *but* what about a girlfriend? Or are you married?"

He looks at me anew, like he's trying to feel me out. I nod my head toward the beach, trying to help him catch on. "Sienna was wondering . . ."

Realization dawns, and excitement sparks in his dark-brown eyes. "Ah. No girlfriend. No wife."

"I'll be sure to pass that on," I say with a cheeky smile before our instructor calls my name to let me know I'm up next.

"Oh gosh. Here goes nothing . . ."

It's my last turn before our surf lessons end, and I'm hopeful I'll finally succeed. Even Avery somehow managed to accomplish something *resembling* surfing in her last attempt. Antsy to catch a wave, I paddle through the water as fast as I can. The instructor shouts, "Now!" And I shoot to my feet and squeal with glee when I find my balance. Adrenaline spikes my blood. My heart hammers, and my smile is impossibly wide as I become one with the water—Moana has nothing on me—then it's over in the blink of an eye. I lose my footing, and with a sound something akin to *whooaohshit*, I go crashing into the surf in a tangle of limbs. I doubt I was standing up on the surfboard for more than a few measly seconds—worse than Avery—but when I swim up and break through the surface, I still hear loud cheering.

I whip my hair back and look toward the shore to see Sienna whistling loudly. "Well done, Casey! Look at you! You're a pro!"

I laugh and grab for my board so I can drag it behind me as I start walking the last few yards to shore. Now, one entire pineapple cocktail in, she continues making me blush with comments about my *Baywatch* body.

"*Is that Pam Anderson?*"

Never mind that I look nothing like Pamela Anderson save for my chest area (which I know damn well is awesome). Sienna is being funny, but she's starting to draw attention. I'm about to slice my hand across my throat and tell her to knock it off when I'm suddenly overwhelmed by a sharp sting on my left calf. My step falters as I wince in pain. I hiss and start leaping as fast as I can through the water, wanting *out* of it immediately. The pain only intensifies as I make it up to the sand, barely keeping ahold of the surfboard. The moment I can, I drop the board with a loud thunk and look down.

I clench my teeth, expecting a huge gash or gnarly wound given the intensity of the pain, but there's only a mild red rash starting to bloom, stretching a few inches along my calf. A jellyfish sting, most likely.

"Are you okay? What happened?"

I stiffen in surprise. I would have expected Sienna to be the first to reach me. She was nearest to me a moment ago, but there's no mistaking that voice.

I didn't realize Phillip had even joined us for the beach picnic, and now I'm wincing for an entirely different reason—mainly over what a fool I made of myself over the last hour. He probably loved watching me tumble off my surfboard time and time again. Get this man a bag of popcorn and an ice-cold Coke. He could have sat and watched me fail for hours on end, I'm sure.

I mostly manage to wipe the surprise off my face before I look up and meet his gaze.

I'm expecting cool indifference, silly considering he went through the trouble of coming all the way over here to check on me. It wouldn't make sense for him to rush down here just to rub it in my face. We might not see eye to eye, exactly, but I don't get the sense that Phillip is downright cruel or anything. Just . . . difficult. Difficult in an annoying way that somehow intrigues me *and infuriates me* all at once. Try and tell that to a shrink.

"I'm all good. Just a jellyfish sting, most likely. It's—"

A jab of pain has me clenching my teeth, but it's fleeting. Already, the throbbing is starting to ebb.

"Key West is filled with moon jellyfish; that's probably what you encountered. Let me see."

He's bending down already, crouching low enough so that he's eye level with my butt. Just great. "Your left calf?" he asks, gently touching my leg just below my knee so he can turn it slightly and get a good look at the developing rash.

His fingers on me are barely there, whisper soft, and still my heart is *thundering*.

I clear my throat before giving him a nod, which he doesn't see.

"*Yes?*" he asks, baring his impatience. I take back my earlier musings about his cruelty.

"Yes," I say with a little bite in my tone.

He runs his thumb along the perimeter of the rash. It doesn't hurt one bit. I can't even feel the jellyfish sting anymore. Not now that he's doing that. "I'll drive you back to the ship so our medic can take a look at you."

"That's not necessary."

His dark eyes look up, displeased with me and my arguments. "I'm not absolutely certain it was a moon jellyfish. Did you happen to see anything in the water?"

"No."

I leave out the part about me not seeing anything because I was already leaping and jumping around like an idiot.

"So then we'll proceed with caution. I'd rather not take any chances."

He turns his attention to my calf again, and then he slowly draws his gaze upward, behind my knee and inner thigh . . . higher. I know he's checking for any other stings, but it feels intensely hot. So hot, in fact, that I can't help but mentally throw water on the fire kindling low in my belly.

"Now don't be silly and miss out on a perfectly good opportunity to get me off your ship for good. You'd love any excuse to send me packing. No need to go to the trouble of fixing me up first."

There's an answering spark in his gaze when he looks up at my face, and then he holds my attention captive as he slowly rises to his feet. Once he's back to his full, intimidating height, he leans in, though barely enough to make it noticeable.

"I would relish the opportunity to send you off, of course. Still, I don't like the idea of you getting in harm's way. Have I given the impression that I would?"

His brow furrows as if he's genuinely concerned that I have the wrong idea of him. Oh, just great. Wonderful. Just when I've concluded that he's bombastically entitled and rude, he has to go and show his kind side. Where am I supposed to file that away? I refuse to start a Reasons-Phillip-Isn't-So-Bad list. Not that it matters. I've already subconsciously begun to compile reasons in my mind. Foremost on that list would be his good looks. Don't tell him I said that, though.

"No," I say with blushing cheeks. I feel childish for insinuating otherwise.

"I want to be cautious, but there's only the minor sting on your calf."

My chin lifts infinitesimally. "It didn't *feel* minor while it was happening."

"Only two, maybe three inches . . ."

"More like five *at least*."

He smiles, and our eyes lock. There's a fleeting moment of lightness—the promise of more teasing banter—before I regain my good sense and look away.

"Can you walk over to that golf cart on your own?" he asks, pointing over to where we parked earlier.

"Of course." I bend down to undo the Velcro strap around my ankle; then I stand. "Where can I put my surfboard?"

"I'll have someone collect it. Don't worry about it."

He drops his hand to my lower back, presumably to direct me toward the row of waiting golf carts. Warm, large, possessive—that's how his hand feels before I step out of his grasp. I doubt he realized what he was doing, touching me in that way. It might not have been an issue if I were in normal clothes, but I'm still wearing my bikini, and it was too much to have his hand on my bare skin so close to the top of my bikini bottoms. Having him touch my leg was bad enough . . .

"Casey!" Sienna cuts in front of us, reaching out for my hand to squeeze it. "Are you okay? What happened?"

I tilt my leg out so she can see the rash on my calf, and she sucks in a sharp breath as if she's never seen anything worse.

"Just a tiny sting. It's really not that bad." I look up at Phillip as if wanting his opinion; then upon realizing that, I frown and turn back to Sienna.

"I'm so sorry." She grimaces and lets go of my hand. "I bet it's painful."

"It's fine, promise. I'm just going to head back to the ship to get it looked at."

"Smart. We're so early on. Barely one destination in! Best to get it checked out so you can be on the mend." She steps closer and lowers her voice. "I was hoping we'd still manage to go out on the town tonight with Ricardo, but if . . ."

"I'll keep you posted," I promise. "I bet I'll be good as new in no time."

She grins. "Want me to come with?"

"No. *Stay.* Go enjoy the rest of the picnic. I'll knock on your door later."

She doesn't look convinced, and I'm actually touched that she'd be willing to forfeit all the fun of the afternoon to be by my side, considering we only met yesterday. "Are you sure?"

"Positive."

Phillip touches my shoulder in an effort to get us going again. I slip off to collect my things, and then we walk the last leg of the journey back to where the golf carts are parked. He points to the black one nearest us.

"This is Ricardo's cart," I note, like it matters.

"Ricardo?"

"My tour guide for the day." When he doesn't say anything, I tack on, "He was nice. Is he employed through your company?"

"We hire local vendors at all the ports. It ensures a more authentic experience for our guests. We try to ensure they've really got the lay of the land."

When we're beside the cart, I drop my bag on the seat and rifle through it for my sundress. I feel Phillip's gaze on me, watching me as I unfold it and slip it on. I adjust it at my waist and look up just as he looks away.

"Are you ready?" he asks, a tight set to his jaw.

"I'm happy to drive myself."

He ignores this and takes the seat behind the wheel. I have no choice but to slide in next to him. All day, I sat beside Ricardo as he drove us around, but it didn't feel like this. There's half a foot of space between Phillip's thigh and my leg, and it's like I've just been slid into a furnace. It doesn't help that we're alone.

"For the record, I don't think this is necessary."

He doesn't take his eyes off the road. "I do."

"And what you say goes?"

"Usually," he says, not even bothering to conceal the beginnings of a cheeky smile. He likes his lot in life, that's for sure.

"Except when pesky little journalists come knocking?"

He throws his head back with a laugh. "Exactly, Ms. Hughes. Exactly."

"I'm hardly the first person to give it to you straight, I'm sure. Tyson seems to have an open, honest relationship with you."

His gaze seers me, though I don't get the sense that there's much anger behind it, just curiosity. "Did you enjoy picking his brain at breakfast? Trying to gain information on me?"

"I did, actually. All of the social prowess you lack, Tyson seems to have in spades."

"*Watch it.*"

"Or what? You won't give me an interview? That's already off the table. It seems like there's nothing left to do but to needle you, and it just so happens that I enjoy it immensely."

"Are you always so difficult?"

"*Pfft.* Never. At work? I'm a wallflower."

"Impossible."

I nod to prove my point. "I barely say two words. When I make it into the office, I'm stuffed in a tiny cubicle."

He turns a corner, and a car veers slightly into our lane. With lightning-fast reflexes, Phillip reaches out to band his arm in front of me, a human seat belt. Though it wasn't necessary. He barely had to swerve.

He hisses a curse under his breath and takes ahold of the steering wheel with both hands before asking, "And how are you with your friends? The ringleader?"

It's hard not to bristle at the word *friends*. "I'm a lone wolf these days."

We could leave it at that. We're venturing into personal territory, and he's the one who'd rather keep things surface level between us. Instead, he studies me out of the corner of his eye, as if this reply doesn't quite sit right with him. "Why?" he presses.

"It just sort of happened that way. Just . . . the phase of life I'm in." I could put the kibosh on this entire conversation, but instead, I make a conscious decision to proceed with caution, to open up in a way that might be reciprocated down the line. "My friends are mostly settled, married, expecting children. Meanwhile, I'm not. More than that, I've found myself in a tricky spot, not that you'd understand." I can't fight the urge to roll my eyes. Envy bleeds into my tone. "You couldn't even imagine my life at the moment, living out of hotels."

His brow furrows as he tries to keep up. "Because you travel so much for work?"

Now *I'm* the one laughing. "Oh, I wish it were because of that. No, I'm not moaning about too many exciting travel assignments. I'm currently homeless, I guess, for lack of a better word."

He rears back like the declaration alarms him. Likely, he's never encountered anyone in my position. His friends likely have multiple homes. Their only issue? Deciding which one to stay in. *Saint-Tropez for the summer? No, we absolutely must go to Saint Barts.*

"Don't worry," I say, tacking on an easygoing smile. "I'm not destitute. No sleeping in my car or anything. I've been hotel hopping and all that. Just . . . I'm currently between places, and all my stuff is in storage. And actually, it's not the worst thing ever. I'm just trying to figure out where I go from here, careerwise, *lifewise*. Don't let it depress you. I only brought it up to say that it can be a little isolating. Anyway, you asked if I was always so difficult, and the answer is no, plain and simple. You bring out this side of me."

"A privilege," he teases.

I look away and smile as we slip through the streets of Old Town. We'll be back at the dock in a few minutes.

I think I've managed to mostly gloss over the most personal details, throwing in enough fluff to distract him from the actual issues at hand (i.e., the fact that I have no tether, no one in my life who loves me— yeesh, it's sad to say it like that), but still, when I glance back, I see him looking at me with an indiscernible expression that almost makes me shiver. It's like he's trying to look for something I'm not willing to give. It's almost unsettling. Provocative at the very least.

"I told you, it's really not *that* bad."

Maybe I shouldn't have said anything at all.

With a frown, he asks, "Where will you go after these ten days at sea?"

"Back to New York, I guess . . . though now that you're bringing it up, I'm not absolutely sure. Most everyone works remotely at *Bon Voyage*. I could stay in a shitty hotel *anywhere*, I suppose."

I smile at the idea. It's tempting, for sure.

"There's no family to tie you to the area? No relationship?"

"Neither."

"I'm sorry to hear that."

"About the relationship? Who cares. About my family? Yes, well, that's the straw I pulled, so there's no sense in dwelling on it. Are you going to get me to this medic or not?"

We pull up to the dock, and he turns off the golf cart. Before I can reach for my bag, he has it in hand. He looks over at me and waits until I finally meet his gaze. *Oh dear . . .*

"If you're in dire straits—"

"I'm not," I say with a heavy eye roll. "I'm merely young and wild and free. Stop feeling sorry for me."

"I'm not."

"You're looking at me like I'm a poor orphan you found living under some freeway overpass."

He flinches and reconfigures his features, wiping the pity away and replacing it with a void of indifference.

"Let's go." With that, he starts striding down the dock, still holding my bag.

"You don't have to stomp off like that." I hurry after him, wincing over my stinging calf. "I'm not as tall as you are—I can't keep that pace even if I break into a run. Are you in that much of a hurry to be rid of me?"

He slows down. "So this hotel thing—"

This again?

"You really can't drop it, can you?" I shake my head before muttering under my breath, "I never should have told you."

"Where were you before?"

"A house. My grandmother's house. She died. There, you've found my deepest, darkest wound. Feel better?"

"No. When did she die?"

"None of your business," I say with an icy tone.

I try and yank my bag away from him to prove my point—that I don't need him for anything, not even to carry my stuff—but he doesn't let go. In fact, he holds it up out of reach like we're in grade school. Though he was definitely not tall enough to do this back then. The nerve.

"And why don't you just get an apartment?"

"I don't want one," I say bluntly. In the following silence, I realize he's forcefully unveiled a little nugget of truth.

I've been looking at apartments in White Plains for the last two weeks, and there were some decent contenders, but I managed to find fault with every single one of them. One apartment complex didn't have any vacancies for another month. Another one only had apartments on the fourth floor with a dingy view. Yet another had so little natural light the whole place felt like a dungeon. Even the last one I looked at, what should have been the Goldilocks apartment, left me wanting more. It was a cute one-bedroom, slightly under budget, in a good neighborhood with a park view. I couldn't find a single fault, and yet when the leasing agent asked if I wanted to proceed, I said no, flat out. I looked online the next day to find it was no longer available. Relief was the only thing I felt.

I realize now, in this unlikely moment with Phillip, that I don't want an apartment back home. I don't want to move on as if my grandmother never existed. I don't want to simply trudge through and save face. I don't want . . . any of it.

"Let me walk you to the clinic," Phillip says, his voice gentle as if he's realized he's struck a nerve. He lowers the bag within reach, and I yank it away from him before turning on my heel.

"No need. I can find it myself."

Chapter Nine

CASEY

It was harsh the way I left Phillip on the dock—a sort of don't-kill-the-messenger situation where he got all the blowback from my newly realized quarter-life crisis. I didn't like how deep he was delving, and so I stormed away in a huff. I'm already sorry for it. I looked for him after I left the clinic yesterday. After only an hour, I was as good as new thanks to a paste of baking soda and seawater the doctor applied to my calf. When I left, I was given clear instructions to take a hot shower and apply an ice pack if the pain worsened, though it never did.

I went to dinner in the dining hall, ready to offer Phillip an apology and a thank-you for carting me back to the boat, but he never showed. Or at least, I never saw him.

I carried my disappointment all the way back to my suite, where Sienna and I went to debate having our big night out.

Ricardo had asked us to meet him at his bar so he could show us some of Key West's nightlife, but it was a quarter to nine, and neither of us was making the moves to get ready. In fact, Sienna was splayed out on the couch in my living room.

"It's not that Ricardo isn't nice . . . ," I started.

"No, I know. I feel bad that we can't phone him and offer an apology. It's just I can't manage to move a single muscle. *Not one.*" She strained to pick up her arm as if to prove her point and then, with a groan, let it drop back onto the couch beside her. Apparently, after I left the beach picnic, she got talked into playing a few rounds of beach volleyball. Sienna admitted she isn't very good at the sport—or rather *any* sport—but Javier was playing, and so she forced herself to "give it a go."

"I have aches in places I didn't know could ache." She forced herself up onto her side.

"But was it worth it? Did you get to talk to Javier?"

She grinned. "Oh yes. I have no idea what you told him when you two were out surfing, but he seemed to get the idea that I fancied him."

"You do—"

"Yes, but he doesn't need to know that!" She sounded exasperated.

"*Well?*" Guilt washes over me. "Did I completely ruin it or what?"

"No. Nothing's been ruined," she says, and I let out a relieved sigh. "I actually need to thank you. I feel like my usual MO is to make men squirm. Does she, doesn't she? That whole game, but Javier cut straight through all that nonsense. Apparently, he feels the same way. We've arranged to have a drink tomorrow night after that show in the theater we're all meant to go to."

"A *date?*"

"Yes. A proper date. All thanks to you. Now hand me that bottle of Nurofen, will you? I'll barely be able to stand up here in a second."

On our third day on board, we left the Keys and started toward Turks and Caicos. With no port to explore, the crew planned an entire day of activities for us, starting with morning yoga, which Sienna skipped in favor of wallowing in bed ("Do you think I can manage a sun salutation right now? I can barely crawl to the loo!"), followed by a poolside lunch, and a ladies' spa afternoon.

I'm having the best day. I enjoyed yoga almost as much as I'm enjoying hanging by the pool and working on my tan. I did manage to work a few hours, laptop open on my sun lounger. I typed up all the key points from the previous day, including my encounters with Phillip. It's not that I suddenly think he'll change his mind and give me the interview, but it's better to get metaphorical pen on paper while everything's fresh in my mind. It's no coincidence that I can manage to type up pages upon *pages* of content about him, many more than I can compared to . . . say . . . the food offerings in the dining hall. It's much more fun to wax poetic about Phillip's jawline than it is to describe a sashimi roll.

Before I head to the spa, I shoot off an email to Gwen with another day's worth of updates, pointedly leaving out the information about Phillip.

Her response is much the same as it was the day before.

This is fine, Casey, but truly we need that interview!!!

Three exclamation marks seem like three too many. I'm doing everything I can. I've looked for Phillip all day, and he wasn't in the dining hall, neither was he at yoga or up by the pool. I'm not going to stoop so low as to hunt him down in his suite. I'm really enjoying my time on board *Aurelia*, and I'd rather not be hauled off by security just yet.

When the sun's too hot to manage and I've done just about as much swimming as I can handle in one day, I venture down to the spa to join the others for our complimentary treatments. Yes, *complimentary*! This job. I can't even handle it. Getting paid to get a massage? Yes, please! I can't believe I've been toiling away fact-checking while other journalists were living it up like this!

Sienna's waiting for me outside the spa, and she does a double take when she sees me.

"God, look at you. A sun goddess. Now I regret not joining you down by the pool even more. No work-around, though. I had videos I needed to edit and post, and I phoned my parents." She waves her hand. "They worry about me with all the travel. Silly, I know, but I'm their only daughter."

"Well, lucky for you, we still have six more days on board to soak up some sun. How are you feeling?"

She frowns for a moment, confused. Then her eyebrows shoot up. "Oh, after yesterday? Still sore a bit, but it's nothing a good masseuse can't work out."

She shimmies her shoulders as she says this, and then she links her arm with mine and tugs me into the spa.

Now, I've been in *lots* of spas in my life. *Dozens.* At least.

Okay, truth, I've never been in one, ever.

If ole Jean Hughes was feeling like treating herself (and me), we'd get manicures at a salon that would run a two-for-one special on Wednesdays, down the road from her old house. Only catch? We had to use the same color, and my grandmother always picked. I rocked fire-engine red nails until high school.

But even if I were a frequent flyer at spas, I have a feeling this one would still take the cake. We enter a foyer with plush carpet, serene shimmery wallpaper, and a round table almost completely covered by a cascading floral arrangement tucked beneath a dripping chandelier; tranquil music plays quietly in the background. Two attendants greet us with glasses of fresh lemon-infused water and then direct us to where we can stow our items and change into custom-designed Hermès terry cloth robes (which we get to *keep*).

They were smart to space us out throughout the day so it's not a huge group filing in at once. I'm one of six, and the two attendants who come to collect us from the changing room—Brigitta and Ana—explain that we'll each be able to choose three services from the spa's overflowing offerings, which include things like seaweed wraps, HydraFacials, massages. As if all that wasn't enough, we'll then be whisked over to the salon for our choice of hair and makeup treatments.

I feel like a princess being pampered before a royal ball.

I start with a facial, and next I opt for a full-body citrus wrap, and then finally a decadent massage. I am so relaxed by the time my session is over, my worries don't even exist. They've left my body.

I'm merely a vessel for lemon water and facials. Thank god for Sienna, though. She's the one who had the sense to recommend we get our hair and makeup done at the salon, so we're ready for the show.

"That way, we don't have to worry about doing it ourselves. God, it's such a treat not having to blow-dry all this hair."

"Good call."

I sit in the salon chair while some heavily accented blond man named Viktor—*I think he's Russian, maybe?*—inventories all the things wrong with my hair. I didn't see it before, but I certainly understand *exactly* what he means once he's done with his diatribe. What was I *thinking*, keeping it this length? And no layers? How was it supposed to breathe? *My god.* I'm as offended as he is. Get the scissors!

He does his thing, working flawlessly and efficiently. I'm stunned with the end result. He's cut my hair; I know he has, and yet, somehow, it looks longer and fuller than ever. *How did he . . . who is he . . .*

"Flawless," he tells me, and I glow under his admiration. I've known him for forty-five minutes, and I'd trust this man with my life.

When I stand up to move to the makeup chair, he shouts at me not to slouch, and I straighten my back immediately lest I accidentally piss him off.

"He's a bit scary, isn't he?" Sienna whispers.

I just shake my head, worried he might somehow have ultrasonic hearing.

"He's a creative genius. Don't question it."

After everything is said and done, once the last stroke of mascara has been applied to lengthen my lashes and my cheeks have been dusted with a shimmery pink blush, I've never felt prettier in all my life. I stand in my suite, in a slinky gold cocktail dress that Sienna's let me borrow, and I almost, very nearly tear up. It's the thought of my grandmother never seeing me like this—looking so grown up and glamorous, that is.

I suppose I dressed up nice for my high school prom and the occasional date or two, but it was nothing like how I look tonight. I never quite looked this stunning. *Yes. I'm allowed to think it,* I tell myself. Now that there's no one else to say it for me. I deserve to hear it, if only here, in the quiet of my suite. I'm allowed to feel like pure sunshine in this gold dress. My legs go on forever in my coordinating sky-high heels, and though they'll absolutely ruin my feet, tear them to bits most likely, there's no choice. They *have* to be worn. I've never seen a more tempting pair of shoes. There's a demure strap over my toes and another midway up my foot; then instead of a traditional buckle around my ankle, there's a long thin snake-shaped spiral that winds up my lower calf. God, they look expensive. They're Sienna's as well. Some London brand I've never heard of.

"You take them. They're yours. They were gifted to me, and they're a half size too small, and I don't know *what* I was thinking packing them for the trip. I suppose I was hopeful they'd work out, and now they have, *on you.*"

"You're like my fairy godmother."

"Oh, yuck, wasn't she old? I'd like to be Cinderella's sexy friend, the one who has a tryst with Prince Charming's brother instead."

My stomach is filled with nerves and not much else as we make our way to deck four. The performance starts in fifteen minutes, and I meant to grab a bite to eat in my suite before meeting Sienna, but I didn't get the chance. They gave us little snacks and things at the spa earlier—cucumber sandwiches, fancy French cheeses, a sampling of smoothies, but looking back, it equated to about seventeen calories, certainly not enough to take the place of dinner.

Outside the theater's entrance, there's a cocktail bar. Sienna shoots me a look like *Should we?* I shake my head adamantly. *We shouldn't.* But then she responds with a look that says *C'mon, what do we have to lose?* I roll my eyes. *For me? Not much. Just my last lifeline.* She crosses her arms and purses her lips.

In the end, we take our seats in the middle of the theater, each with a glass of champagne.

"Do not let me guzzle this down," I say just before my lips come into contact with the most effervescent, bubbly, delicious champagne I've ever tasted. It's gone in two seconds flat. "Right, well, don't let me guzzle down my *second* glass."

"Good evening, Ms. Hughes. Ms. Thompson."

Sienna whirls around with a big smile. "Oh, *hello*, you two!"

I turn to greet Tyson, genuinely happy to see him for the first time since yesterday morning until I notice his friend behind him. Phillip is devastatingly handsome, as always. In a fitted black suit, sans tie, with the top two buttons undone at his collar—my mouth goes dry. I freak out. Look away. Then I realize after the fact that I forgot to greet him. Whatever happened yesterday on that golf cart doesn't warrant me completely ignoring him, but what do I do now? Turn back and laugh? Offer a smile? I can't. I'm glued to my spot, my heart thundering in my chest.

They fill the two seats behind us, talking to Sienna while I review the program like my life depends on memorizing every word of it. Somehow, they arranged it so Phillip is directly behind me, though it should have been Tyson.

Sienna and Tyson act like two chatterboxes, carrying on so easily, though Phillip is as quiet as I am.

Eventually, though, he leans forward, breaking the awkwardness with a greeting that sends goose bumps down my arms.

"Ms. Hughes."

I smirk before turning gently to look over my shoulder, just enough to get him in view without having to spin all the way around in my seat. It's easier now to look at him knowing what to expect. My heart rate only barely picks up. His hair is combed smoothly, dark and gleaming like it's still damp from a recent shower. His jaw is clean shaven. His cologne is subtle but there, tingeing the air with a spice that has me wanting to lean closer.

I brace myself before I meet his gaze, proud that I manage to do it so confidently. You'd never know my hands were fisted in my lap. My heels bouncing against the floor.

"Surely, we're on a first-name basis by now? I can't go around calling you Mr. Woodmont."

"Casey," he amends with humor in his gaze.

My name rolls off his tongue, and it's like he just said the most taboo thing my ears have ever heard—that's how swiftly my body reacts.

He looks me over as if after only three days of being together, he can already tell the subtle differences in my appearance tonight. He can't see much of my slinky gold dress, but the rest of me still captures his interest. My golden eye makeup, my striking red lips.

"I see the ladies' spa afternoon treated you well."

"It did. You've employed wonderful people. Brigitta, Ana—oh my god, *Viktor*. They're very good at what they do. I'd spend my entire ten days in the spa if I could."

He smiles, pleased with my compliments of his staff. It's clear he takes pride in the crew on board *Aurelia*, and I have no doubt they're compensated well for all their hard work. Every staff member I've encountered seems eager and grateful for their position with Woodmont Overseas.

"Did you have a hand in hiring them?"

"I review every last employee file, from the captain down to the most junior crew member."

"Nothing gets by you."

"*Nothing.*"

I don't know if he realizes his gaze is lingering on my lips. I brush them together and then offer one last smile before turning back. A lyrical song is beginning to play as the lights dim. The heavy black curtains rise as a group of dancers take the stage. I realize quickly that this is a modern dance performance rather than a traditional ballet or opera. Each dancer wears elaborate costumes and heavy makeup—transforming them into various wild animals found deep in the jungle. A tiger, a cheetah, a green shimmering snake. I'm transfixed by their movements; the passion and pageantry of the show are almost enough to take my mind off the man sitting behind me.

Throughout the performance, I feel his attention on me as if I were one of the dancers on stage. Having him directly behind me makes it so I can't fully relax in my seat. It's like I have one of these jungle predators at my back. At any moment, he'll strike, and I have to be ready. I sit pin straight, my gaze focused intently on the stage. I don't want to be seen talking or disrupting the performance, not while he's there ready to grade me on my decorum.

My hair is down and curled by *his* expert stylist in the salon. I feel it slip over the back of the chair. I shiver, and Sienna sees.

"Want my coat?" she whispers quietly.

I shake my head and keep my attention up onstage.

Phillip shifts in his seat, and I hold my breath.

I'm not some big dummy who doesn't understand the nuances of sexual attraction. It's very obvious that I'm painfully attracted to Phillip. Though becoming aware of that and deciding what to do about it are two different things. I've established that it's inappropriate to feel this way. I could land in hot water with Gwen if I pursued Phillip in that way—though would I really? Gwen's never been all that prudish. If I were able to secure an interview with Phillip by any means possible, would she even care? In fact, she might be a little impressed by my willingness to go the extra mile. Or perhaps that's just the champagne talking. They've passed around more. I'm on the last sip of my second glass, and I know I'm going down a dangerous path, but my hand keeps lifting the glass to my mouth despite the dull warnings in the back of my mind.

The performance is magical and captivating. I try to remember as much of it as possible so I can jot down notes when I get back to my suite, though truly, my mind is mostly preoccupied with Phillip. I've made my mind up about what I'll do. It's absolutely insane. My grandmother would get such a kick out of it. She'd hoot with laughter and cheer me on, especially if she knew the depth of my loneliness in the last year. The shell of a person I've become since her death. No wild nights. No romantic dates. Just life in its most basic form: rise, work, eat, exercise some, watch a few minutes of television, scroll online, lie awake until at some point my brain takes pity on me and lets me sleep. Each day is an exact replica of the day before. A carbon copy of boredom that's become the status quo. I wonder if I should get a third glass of champagne.

I find Phillip in the observation lounge after the performance. It's where everyone has gathered for more drinks. He's speaking to Tyson and the captain, a booming, loud Scottish man with flaming-red hair. It's wild of me to waltz right up to them and ask Phillip for a moment of his time, but as I've said, there's nothing to lose. I'm at rock bottom. On the floor of the ocean. It's me and all those weird blind fish slithering around in the depths with nowhere to go but *up*.

"Phillip, could I steal you away?"

All three men turn to me, surprise evident on their faces.

Phillip doesn't agree right away, and his silence has me almost wanting to flee, but I'm here. I've done the hard thing, so I lift my chin and wait him out.

It's Captain Neal who puts me out of my misery first. His thick red eyebrows shoot up, and he bellows a laugh. "You can steal *me* away, lass."

He even holds his wrists together out in front of him as if begging to be led away in handcuffs.

Phillip shakes his head and steps forward, a private smile concealed as he dips his head for a moment. When his blue eyes lock with mine again, he motions for me to go ahead of him. I'm tempted to lead him to a quiet corner of the room, somewhere we won't be overheard, but even that won't do. We need absolute privacy for this conversation.

I loop past Sienna at the bar, glad to see she's perched beside Javier, twisting a martini olive around the rim of her glass while she listens to him talk. Her chin is propped on her hand as she leans closer, completely enamored. I wonder if that's customary for her or if he might be something special, unique in a way that Phillip is for me.

I'm surprised he doesn't protest when I leave the room completely and walk out into the hall. It's as deserted as I'd hoped it'd be. All the guests gathered in the observation lounge are deep in conversation or gambling at one of the tables set up in the back corner. The night is young, and I doubt anyone will bother us for the next few minutes. At least, I hope not.

Beside a small table tucked into a shallow alcove, I stop and turn, watching as Phillip reaches me. He carries a thick crystal glass holding the last remnants of a rich-amber liquor. He finishes it off before setting it down on the table, crossing his arms, and leaning ever so casually against the wall, obviously waiting for me to speak.

"I appreciate your time," I say, hating how formal I sound. Aren't we past this?

His lip curls in a deliciously wicked smile. "Care to tell me what this is about?"

His gaze falls to my wringing hands, and I immediately pull them apart. Thinking I might look as relaxed as he does, I try to lean against the table. But when it catches my weight, it teeters, and I blanch and reach out for a vase of flowers sitting on top before it topples over.

With an ever-encroaching flush creeping up my neck, I decide to just have out with it.

"All right, let's cut to the chase. I'm prepared to offer you an exchange."

Good. I managed to sound confident.

He doesn't even balk, which is slightly disappointing. I'd hoped to catch him off guard.

"An exchange would require interest from both parties," he says, nearly sounding bored. "You have nothing I want."

"Sure about that?"

His icy-blue eyes seem to carry a question.

I arch a brow and sweep my hand down my body like I'm an all-you-can-eat buffet open for business. Still, he seems to have a hard time piecing things together. Maybe he isn't regularly offered sex in this way. Admittedly, I'm a novice at it, too, but subtlety has no place here. I'll clearly have to spell it out.

"I'm offering an exchange of *favors*. Mine will be of the sexual kind. If that wasn't obvious already . . ."

Chapter Ten
CASEY

Phillip doesn't say a word, but I can tell he wants to laugh at my proposition.

Dammit. That's what I get for being cutesy rather than sexy. I wish I could snap my fingers and create some luscious curves. The kind guys go gaga for. I settle for arching my back a little, accentuating my nice, full C-cup chest.

Phillip notices. Oh yes. His eyes widen just enough to let me know that he's not immune to my advances. I watch his Adam's apple bob before he narrows his eyes and asks shrewdly, "You'll sell your body for a story?"

I cross my arms and reject his judgment with a bored tone. "When you put it like that, it sounds crass, but yes, I suppose so."

He advances on me then with a dark look. Apparently, the time for conversation is over. This is happening. He's going to pounce.

My arms drop back down to my sides. My lips part in anticipation.

"You're going to show me how badly you want that exclusive, Casey?"

Oh, *how dirty*.

I didn't think ole Mr. Quiz Bowl had it in him.

"*Yes.*"

There's no tripping over that word; it spills out of me like I've been waiting to say it for days. His eyes spark with mischief, and that little muscle in his jaw works as he clenches it, approaching me confidently as I hold my ground despite my shaking knees.

I'm frozen in surprise. I didn't think we'd get here this fast. I thought there'd be a bit more give-and-take, some convincing on my part, but his blue eyes challenge me to uphold my promise.

"Show me what you're willing to do, Casey. Make me believe it."

Oh my god.

I try not to panic.

It's happening! IT'S HAPPENING!

Right, but . . . does he want me to do something *here*? In the hall? It's one thing to talk a big game and another to actually go through with it in public like this. It's a sort of dare, I realize. He doesn't seem bothered by our current location, and so I damn well don't care either. *Hah.* I peer around the corner to find the coast is clear, and by the time I look back at Phillip, my mind is absolutely made up. I'm going to kiss Phillip, and if it's a disaster, then let it be a disaster. At least I will have *done* something worthy of regret. At least I won't have to sit in that uncomfortable state of wondering *what if* for one more day. I look at his mouth, at the luscious color, at the slight fullness and pout. He has lovely lips. That doesn't seem like a compliment you can give a man, but he deserves to hear it. I'm too shy to tell him, though, so I'll just have to show him. I sidle up to him, and after taking a moment to gather my bravery, I slide my hands up the front of his suit jacket—over his broad chest—until they come to a stop at the lapels. I look up, waiting for him to call it, to laugh or shake his head, to give some indication that I've pushed things too far. When he just stares down at me in silence, I take it as a green light.

With one final quivering breath, I rise up and lean ever so gently against him before pressing my lips to his.

It's a kiss, but it's one sided. *I'm* kissing him. *I'm* leading the charge with soft lips and gentle teasing.

For so long, he makes me work for it. His hands move to rest on my hips, but that's it. There's barely any possession there. He could be holding on to a stair rail, for god's sake. He doesn't lean in; he doesn't make a sound. His lips move only in accordance with mine, and it pisses me off. I press closer and part my lips so my tongue can dart out for a lick. I make a tiny sound of longing—a desperate plea, more like—and it's as though I've just shocked him with a defibrillator and brought him back to life. *Now* he moves; *now* his fingers dig into my dress. Something hot flutters in my belly as we kiss hungrily, devouring each other. God, now it's good. Everything I wanted it to be. We kiss, and we kiss, and I start to slip away from that deserted hallway. I'm nothing beyond a racing heart, a tightly wound belly. His hands slide over my backside as my own sink into his hair. Ownership—that's what we're playing at. Our lower bodies mold together, and without warning, he whirls me around so that my front is flush against the wall, my arms down by my side, caged in by his hard body. *Holy* . . . As my mouth is torn away from his, I swallow a squeal, our heavy breaths mingling as our faces stay close together.

He bends low and nuzzles the side of my neck. "That's good, but it's not enough."

The arrogant bastard.

My nails scrape down the front of his thighs. "What do you want, then?"

"Truly?" he asks, tipping his head back to meet my eyes. "Nothing will convince me. You shouldn't bother."

I shouldn't bother?

He has me pressed up against this wall like he's about to take me here and now. I can feel how hard he is, pressed right against my backside. I roll my hips to prove my point, and I succeed in provoking a low groan from him.

"You're putty in my hands," I goad with a triumphant smile.

He kisses the side of my neck, stealing my glee and replacing it with red-hot wanting.

If he meant to make it quick, he doesn't succeed. We're dragged right back down to a place full of feelings and baser needs. His body presses up against mine, and we grind on each other, trying to sate our growing desire. My hands band around his thighs, and I feel his muscles shift. His body is so full of strength, but his kisses are slow, mesmerizing, explorative . . . He's no brute. He's sensual in a way I wasn't expecting, wasn't prepared for. When was the last time a man kissed me like this?

Oh, right . . . *never.*

I turn and push him off me, suddenly needing air. Only the second I do, I want him back. I fist his jacket and tug him closer again. I'm about to lock our lips together when he turns his face to the side and strings kisses down my neck instead. It feels like a teasing rejection, more of this addictive game.

"Should I show you how it's really done, Casey? Show you what I would do if I were in your position? If I were trying to convince someone in this way . . ." His teeth barely scrape across my skin, and my eyes flutter closed as my head tips back to give him better access. "I'd be sure to make them think my entire heart was in it."

For the first time, he moves one of his large hands so that it's just at the hem of my short dress. *Do it, please,* I plead in my head. Then his thumb caresses the inside of my thigh as he slides his hand up under my dress, bunching it enough so he can easily trace my panties, right at the spot where my pelvis meets my thigh. Then he runs his finger up and down, right along the edge, but he never slips a finger beneath the silk. A whimper leaves me, louder than I'd intended. I try to press my lips together, but it's no use. Phillip has already heard me.

"I'd be sure to make it feel like they were mine, *totally.*"

His fingers brush me on top of the silk, right over that tight bundle of nerves, and I shudder. "Your plan, sweetheart . . . it's not working."

Somewhere deep in the recesses of my mind, I know that he's mocking me, that I should call him an arrogant bastard, push him away, and storm off in a huff. Oh, that would be good. Someone should really do that! Not me, though. No. I'm seeing this through.

At this point, I'm panting and desperate. We'd have to hit an iceberg before I forfeit my night with this man. "Take me back to your room."

"I'm not giving you an interview," he murmurs against my skin, lifting up to recapture my mouth in a long, searing kiss as his fingers continue to work me up.

"Then we should stop."

He makes a move to pull back, and I growl at him. Actually growl! Damn my traitorous mouth!

"Don't listen to me; I don't know what I'm saying!"

His eyes sweep down the length of me; then he looks me square in the eyes as he takes his hand out from between my legs. "The interview isn't happening." There's a stern edge to his voice that turns me to absolute goop.

"Fine." He thinks I care about the interview right now? "Take me back to your room."

He laughs like I'm kidding. *Oh ho, buddy boy. I'm not joking in the least.*

"One night," he tells me.

I roll my eyes, like *obviously.*

I step forward and drop my hand to the front of his suit pants. He hisses in a sharp breath as I rub him, revealing just how badly he wants this. I'm not alone here.

His hand reaches out to grip my wrist and still me, but somewhere along the way, he loses the will. I smile as he captures my hand and tugs me from my spot. I nearly get whiplash, he's moving so fast.

I laugh. "Where are we going?"

Already, he has me halfway down the hall. We're not going toward the central bank of elevators. We stop in front of a discreet door built into a paneled wall, and he keys a four-digit code into a small pad before tugging the handle and revealing an austere staircase clearly meant for staff and crew.

Racing down three flights has my heart pounding.

Phillip has no issue, though. "Should I carry you?"

"Stuff it. I'm in sky-high heels."

He laughs and slows down a bit until we make it to deck six. We slip out of the crew door and into the central hallway. I haven't explored deck six yet beyond our tour on the first day, and it doesn't look like I'm about to get a chance to do it now either. Phillip's on a mission, his fingers laced through mine. He stops to kiss me for a moment.

"It's not too late to turn back," he murmurs against my lips. "Now. Later. You have to be honest with me."

"Okay, you want honesty?" I fist the lapels of his jacket. "*Honestly* . . . if you don't take me into your suite now, I'm going to pounce on you right here in the hallway."

Too direct? Oh well. He kisses me once more, and then we proceed until we make it all the way down to the last door at the end of the hall, the one removed from all the others, with its own private lobby, for god's sake. As soon as he touches the door handle, it opens. Either it was already unlocked or it recognized the key in his wallet, or perhaps there's a sensor in his watch. At the moment, I don't care one way or another. The door opens into his suite, and I take it in—absolutely *not* shocked to find it's a floating palace.

I point toward the dining table . . . the one that can comfortably seat twelve. "Understated, I see . . ."

He smiles at my sarcasm. "It's not mine. I'm merely using it for the next few days. It's the presidential suite. It needed to be . . . presidential."

"I thought *mine* was the presidential suite," I mumble; then I turn to see a geometrical abstract painting hung in the living room, done in primary colors with stark black lines. "*Jesus.*" I turn to him. "Is that an original Mondrian?"

He looks it over and shrugs. "Are we here to discuss art or . . . ?"

"Oh, right. Very to the point. Well then, strip if you're in such a rush."

He laughs and walks toward me, only stopping when his dress shoes touch the tips of mine. He doesn't touch me at all, save for the hand he slowly lifts so he can cup my chin and tilt it up gently, angling our mouths so they're only a few inches apart.

"I'm sorry. I'm rude."

My brow furrows. "You aren't rude."

"It is a Mondrian."

My jaw drops, and he leans in to press a kiss to my cheek. "Now, should I undress you here?"

I smile. "Show me the rest of the suite."

He groans. "*Casey.*"

I feel almost lightheaded with power knowing he wants this as badly as I do.

"I'm not giving you a tour. There are a few powder rooms, a living room, dining room . . . guest bedroom . . . main bedroom . . . who fucking cares." His hands slip around the back of my dress until he finds the zipper, which he slowly works down my back while he speaks.

I don't stop him. I hold perfectly still until the material gapes open.

He steps closer as he gathers the two shoulder straps of my dress and pulls them down. The material gathers at my waist, and then he pushes it until it pools on the floor at my feet.

"Step out."

I do, listening to the click of my high heels on the marble floor.

Only when he has me completely sans dress does he step back to look at me.

I'm flush with nerves, hyperaware of the rise and fall of my chest, of my quaking stomach. I want to band my arms across my belly, to cover up in some way, but the moment his eyes fall across my skin, I can't. I want him looking. I feed off of the way his eyes darken and narrow as he takes in my panties and bra. They're the palest pink, almost sheer.

That muscle tenses in his jaw, and I dip my head and bite down on my lower lip to keep from outright gloating.

"This is insanity."

My gaze rises to meet his in question. "Sleeping together?"

He nearly smirks. "You think we'll sleep?"

My mouth goes dry as he takes me in, lazily drawing his gaze down my chest, my stomach, my hips, that private spot between my thighs. "I've never done this," I blurt.

His eyes grow wide in fear. "Sex?"

I nearly snort. "Sex, of course. The one-night stand thing . . ." I shake my head. "No."

"Right. Well . . . I'm not really the type either."

"Shocking."

His blue eyes pierce mine.

"Is it?" he presses, wanting my full assessment of his character.

"No," I amend.

I feel bad for throwing out such a capricious comment. It's not true. Just because he carries the money and title doesn't mean Phillip falls in line with the playboy stereotype. He seems too thoughtful. There is Vivienne, though. Do I ask about her now? Confirm that the rumors about their recent split are true? It seems like such a heavy topic to bring up, but I'd rather not accidentally become the other woman simply because I didn't want to ask a tough question.

"Just to confirm . . . you *are* single, aren't you?"

He looks offended. "Of course. Aren't you?"

My eyes widen. "Yes. I just . . . wanted to be clear."

"I wouldn't be here otherwise," he confirms.

I lift my chin. "Good."

"And we're clear on the interview?"

His tone is sharp and unyielding, like he's speaking in a boardroom.

I roll my eyes. "Oh my god. Yes. *Mr. Woodmont*, I'm aware you won't be giving me an interview. *Enough.* I'm not here to persuade you. I want—"

His lips twist into a gloating smile when my sentence hitches. "You want *what*, Casey?"

I can't say it.

I'm not used to having conversations like this. My previous bedroom encounters included a lot of lights-out fumbling. Let's just say I've never stood on board a luxury cruise liner, inside a presidential suite, in nothing but a revealing bra and silk panties. This is uncharted territory, and Phillip can see that plain as day. He knows, of the two of us, he has the upper hand. That should make me nervous, but instead, it turns me on. This imbalance between us, down to our current state of dress . . .

He slowly slides off his suit jacket, moving to place it over a chair before rolling up his shirtsleeves. That's it. That's as far as he undresses before he looks at me, holds my gaze, and asks with a wicked gleam, "Should I fuck you?"

My mouth falls open. "*God*, Phillip."

That word from his lips. The raw nature of it compared to his prim and proper exterior. The juxtaposition catches me off guard, makes my heart race.

"Let's be honest. This is . . ."

I cut him off. "The sexiest thing *ever*."

He grins and strolls over to reward me with a soul-searing kiss that's over too soon. I'm leaning into him as he pulls away. "I appreciate your honesty."

"And I'd appreciate if you'd lose some of these clothes. I'm nearly naked here."

"Nearly naked and entirely naked are two different things."

"Ha ha ha."

I toy with the buttons on his shirt until the top three are undone. I spread it open to find his chest is toned and tan. He's all man with a smattering of dark hair. Just enough to prove to me how far we've come from when we first knew each other as kids. He doesn't stop me, so I grow bolder, undoing the rest of the buttons and pushing his shirt off his shoulders. His arms are sinewy muscle, hard and strong. The sight of him takes my breath away, and I'm careful to keep my gaze pinned on his chest rather than his face. He knows so much already, why offer even more?

His hand circles my neck, his thumb just over my throat. I swallow, and his hand tightens. There's no threat there; he's not choking me. It feels different somehow. Sexy in a way that has me trembling. His mouth lands on mine as his other hand returns between my legs. He rubs me back and forth over my panties, working me up, and I let him—standing stock still, a puppet on a string.

I close my eyes and think of what we must look like standing together in the middle of his suite. Me in my high heels and not much else. Him in his midnight-black pants, his dark hair ruffled from my fingers. Everything else about him? *Perfect.*

His fingers slip inside my panties, and I whimper. He must feel the vibration of it in my throat. His body is cloaking mine, heating me from head to toe. I feel as if I'm about to go off like a firecracker as I spread my legs slightly, my high-heeled feet sliding across the marble. Every ounce of energy is focused between my legs. I'd sag if he weren't propping me up with his body, his hand around my neck. He sinks his fingers into me, stretching me, and I gasp.

I want . . .

That's just it, *I want.* Everything. Suddenly.

I want him with a fierceness that scares me.

He murmurs the most descriptive things, tempting, erotic words falling against the shell of my ear as his fingers continue to sink in and out of me and his thumb rubs expert circles.

The orgasm slams into me so quickly, out of nowhere. I grip his arms, shuddering as the moment stretches on. My breath arrests in my chest as tingles spread from the center of my legs, up my spine. He makes a growling sound of satisfaction, dragging his fingers in and out until he's eked every bit of pleasure from me that he possibly can. At least for this first time . . .

He withdraws his fingers and steps back, composed, sedate almost.

I have no doubt that I look the exact opposite, hot and tingling from the high of my orgasm; I feel like my skin is electrified.

His eyes rove over me as he whispers a muted "*Fuck.*"

I don't even think, I reach behind me and undo my bra clasp. The silk eases off my hot skin, and I let it fall slowly to the ground. I watch him swallow . . . processing . . . desire so evident in his gaze I wonder if he's even bothering to try to hide it.

I'm not.

He pounces on me suddenly, backing me up to the couch until I think he's about to prop me up onto the back of it. Instead, he turns me around, cups the back of my neck, and slowly pushes me over. The sight makes him groan. With a sexy ferocity, his hand grips my hips, and then he gathers my panties up on both sides, revealing my ass. I'm fully on display. Almost uncomfortably so, but he makes me feel so sexy, at his mercy and yet somehow still in control. He twists the material until it bites into my skin, and at the same time, he rocks into me, grinding his hard length against me.

"I feel possessed," he admits, doing it again so that I shiver, the tendrils of a second orgasm already reaching out for me.

I'd assumed we'd make it to the bedroom, and maybe eventually, we will, but first? Phillip takes me against the back of the couch. He pushes down my panties, unzips his pants, fists his length, and unrolls a condom. I shimmy my hips, impatient, needy. He stretches me once more with his fingers, ensuring I'm ready, and then I feel him sink into me—all that heat pouring inside me until my elbows buckle and I fall over.

"Are you okay?" he whispers.

I nod reassuringly.

"I don't want to hurt you," he says while slowly pulling out of me only to thrust back in roughly.

God.

Why is it like this? How could he possibly understand this part of me so well?

"Casey," he murmurs, caressing my hair, forcing me to turn my head to the side so he can see me. "Tell me to go slower. To go easy on you."

He wants me to push back, but I won't. I'd rather swallow my tongue.

"I—like it," I say, my voice lilting up just as he thrusts in all the way to the hilt.

It's magic, pure and simple.

I don't overthink it; I don't try and reconcile whether it's proper or good for Phillip to be taking me in this way. I just feel it, enjoy it. I tease him and let the whimpers fall from my lips as the tightness in me starts to wind up like a band about to snap.

My toes are tingling as he picks up his pace. It's maddening, but nothing I can't handle. My hands bite into the back of the couch as I lean over even more. And I know without asking that Phillip loves the new arch in my back, the way my body drapes over for him.

I feel him in ways that I know will haunt me, but I don't struggle against the burn. I let him tug my hair, fist it in his hand. Then he touches me between my legs, whispering those dark words again. Telling me what a good girl I am, how much he likes me like this, bending over the back of his couch, letting him have me in this way.

I let him take, and then he gives me everything in return—a second orgasm that has me crying out so loud I'm almost ashamed, but he feeds off my cries, tumbling into his own release, shuddering and pulsing so roughly it's almost like *I'm* hurting *him.*

My name falls from his lips, and when it's finally over, when I can focus again, I realize he's propping me up, cradling me against his body now, holding me in a tight embrace.

"Tell me you're okay," he says, withdrawing and turning me around, holding my cheeks.

"I'm fine," I say, almost laughing.

Does he think he hurt me?

He didn't. Far from it.

He's the one who looks shaken from the experience. He kisses me again, and then like a child who's had a first lick of ice cream, who's desperate for more, he asks, "How long do I get to keep you?"

Chapter Eleven

PHILLIP

I tip my head back against my chair and close my eyes, feeling the sea breeze ruffle my hair. I came out onto my balcony hoping the fresh air would give me clarity of thought. I inhale deeply, though it ends up sounding more like a heavy groan. *Christ.* I sit up and reach for my coffee cup on the low table in front of me, but I cut my sip short once I realize my drink has gone cold, *again.* Twice now, I've made a cappuccino only to set it down and forget about it as my mind wanders back to last night.

I can't seem to stop fantasizing about her.

Casey's body was extraordinary, and not just the obviously tempting parts—*everything.* Her intoxicating smile as she tried to hide her face against my pillow. The soft trace of her fingers down my back. The little tattoo on her hip. It's so small I didn't notice it at first. Not until I was stringing kisses down her stomach, pushing her back on the bed. We'd showered and ordered room service. She was tucked into a white terry cloth robe, and I couldn't hold myself off her. The whole evening felt like a frenzy. I wanted her again and again, endlessly. At the time, she held a french fry midway in her mouth when I started to push her back flat onto the bed so I could part her robe.

She'd laughed and tried to push me away, but it was so halfhearted that it didn't deter me in the least. God, she smelled good. She'd used my soap, but it smelled different on her skin, heady and tempting.

I kissed her stomach, and she strung her fingers through my damp hair with a familiarity that sent a shiver through me.

"What are you doing? I'm trying to eat here," she complained.

"So am I."

"*Phillip!*"

I laughed at her reaction. It was so easy to rile her up, to make her skin flush pink and hot.

That's when I caught sight of her tattoo. A tiny outline of a sun on her hip, so small you wouldn't see it even if she wore a bikini.

"A sun?"

"Sunshine, a nickname."

I arched a brow. "From a previous boyfriend?"

"Yes," she said with a mischievous look in her eyes. "A bulky biker named Stan. Watch out, he's going to come for you now that we've slept together."

I kissed her tattoo and then traced it with my finger. She couldn't stay still while I did it, so I did it again. "I'll take him on, no problem."

She smiled. "He'll tear you apart limb by limb."

"Oh no."

"It was nice knowing you, though. The sex has been . . ." She stuck out her bottom lip and tilted her head back and forth like she was only mildly impressed. "Decent."

I knew she was teasing me, and yet my pride still sat up and took notice. "Decent?"

"Eh, the couch thing was nice, and that little session in the shower was sort of exciting . . ."

"*Casey.*"

She feigned guilt. "Oh no, have I hurt your feelings? It's not *your* fault. I've just had some really wonderful lovers. Experienced. Really limber. *Big.* I mean, you're impressive and all . . . but—"

I yanked her down so she fell flat, pinned to the center of the bed. Our room service got shoved aside and forgotten. For all I knew, it was spilled on the floor.

She squirmed back, playfully trying to get away from me before I latched my hands onto her ankles and pulled her toward me. Her robe splayed open as I held her down, coming over her so our eyes locked for a moment. Her gaze shone with longing. I knew she was right there with me—feeling this.

I worked the tie open on her robe as she laughed.

"Phillip!"

"Should I tease you the way you've been teasing me?" She was laughing, but the moment I slid her thighs apart, her breathing hitched.

"Don't you dare."

"All that talk about past lovers . . . I bet you can't name a single one who turned you on like this."

I thought she'd have some witty retort, but she went silent as I slid down her body, stringing kisses down her stomach, passing over her tattoo again, claiming it. Past boyfriend, my ass.

I settled myself between her thighs, making myself right at home as she writhed and moaned. I licked her, and she arched off the bed, begging for more.

I'm turned on now, alone on my balcony, thinking back on it.

"Jesus," I hiss under my breath.

I'm a schoolboy.

When Casey left sometime after 2:00 a.m., insistent that she wanted to go back to her suite to sleep, I walked her back and kissed her goodbye and stood aside as she shut her door, using it like a heavy axe, hoping it would cleave the magic that had spun around us over the last few hours. It didn't work, and I'm annoyed that my feelings for her have carried over into today. I slept like shit after she left, tossing and turning, indecision keeping me awake. A part of me wanted to go knock on her door and continue where we'd left off. The other part of me won out, though. Barely. I might not have chased after her, but I've yet to get up and shower, or dress. I can't seem to get my shit together today.

I'm surprised by the guilt gnawing at me.

I made it perfectly clear last night that I had no intention of giving Casey an interview, and though I thought that would be enough to clear my conscience, it wasn't. Everything we did was hot and consensual, yes, but there's no doubt that feelings could get twisted. More than that, I was in a position of power over Casey last night. She needs something from me. It was a game, and now that game is over. It has to be.

Vivienne is my future. I haven't relinquished hope that she and I will work out in the end. She'll come to her senses and beg for me to come back. I'll put on a show like I'm really debating it, but I will go back in the end. She and I belong together in a way Casey and I never will. Vivienne and Casey are polar opposites, down to their very core. Their work, their lifestyles, their personalities—Vivienne is exactly like me. She thinks four or five steps ahead, always. She leaves nothing up to chance. Casey scares me—her authenticity, her vulnerability . . . all of it. The simple fact that she doesn't have a place to live right now, that she's okay with stowing her things in a storage unit and hopping from hotel to hotel rather than immediately signing a new lease and getting her life in order. I would have had a plan in place *weeks* ago. I'd know exactly what to do and how I was going to do it. Yet she seems perfectly fine with her circumstances. Enough to board a cruise for two weeks!

It drives me insane just thinking about it. What is she going to do when she gets home? How long does she plan to keep this up?

I'm a fixer, and I want to fix this situation for her, but I can't. She's not my problem. She's . . . nothing to me.

As guilt languishes inside me, I stand and head to my computer back inside my suite. I want to right this wrong. I want to be done with Casey. I feel a quiver in my stomach. Something close to panic rises up inside me.

I never once felt this with Vivienne, and that's how I know it's wrong—last night was a mistake. The peace Vivienne brings to my life could never exist with Casey. That much I know.

It's not hard to find Casey's email. There's a master list of everyone currently on board *Aurelia*, their full names, phone numbers, addresses. I realize now that Casey listed *Bon Voyage's* address rather than her own, and I feel a fresh wave of anger and annoyance over the fact that I can't solve her problems.

I want to be able to cleanly walk away from this situation with Casey. To do that, I'll have to relent. The task at hand isn't something I'm comfortable with, but well . . . what choice do I have?

It takes me thirty minutes to compile answers to a list of ten popular interview questions. I expand on all of them, giving her as much as I can so she has a lot to work with. I veer toward discussing my business and leave most of my personal life out of it. I know she won't like that, but it'll have to do. It's far more than any other journalist has gleaned from me in years. Hopefully, it'll suffice.

I stall when I go to attach the interview answers to the email only because I'm not sure what to add in the body of the email, how to address her, what to say after last night. I don't want to be overly formal, and yet I don't want to put anything in writing that could jeopardize her career.

In the end, I leave the body of the email completely blank and hit send.

Chapter Twelve

CASEY

I'm so happy; it's like someone has filled me with stuffed animal fluff. I can't stop smiling. I woke up thinking of last night, and I smiled and rolled over to shove my face into my pillow, which is absolutely ridiculous considering I was the only person in my bedroom. *Who do I think I am hiding from?* I didn't expect to feel this way. No guilt, no shame. I might be a one-night stand kind of girl. I mean, last night was . . . *something else.*

Quickly, I roll back over and hold up my covers to give myself a once-over. No bruises, no teeth marks, nothing to prove I did what I did, but there is an exquisite little ache *there*. I laugh again, blush *again*.

Phillip did this to me.

I should thank him when I see him.

Though no, that's not possible.

We'll have to keep things professional. I don't want word spreading on the cruise that I've, well . . . spread my legs for the boss on board. How cliché. How perfectly expected for the lowly reporter to go to bed with the powerful businessman who holds her future in the palm of his hand. Only Phillip made it abundantly clear that he wasn't going to be furthering my career in any way, and I was okay with that. I am.

Last night was wholly separate from my assignment with *Bon Voyage*. It was just a passionate night of fun. A perfect one-night stand. I highly recommend it!

Today, when I speak to Phillip, it'll be like we've reverted back to before—I still need an interview; he doesn't want to give it to me . . . and so the world turns.

I suppose it would be okay if I told Sienna about last night. I mean, I have to tell *someone*. I can't just keep this fluff inside me. I'm liable to explode from happiness.

I get out of bed with plans to brew two coffees and take them over to Sienna's suite, right after I check my email. Old habit. I know you're supposed to start your day with meditation and lemon water and some kind of self-help tome titled *Forty Easy Ways to Improve Your Life*, but well, I like what I like, and lemon water ain't it. I enjoy shoving an electronic screen in front of my still mostly closed eyeballs while huddling under the warmth of my bedding. Now *that's* living.

There's the usual junk mail, an inquiry from a leasing agent about an apartment I'm definitely not taking, and then an unexpected email from Phillip with a subject line that reads Interview Questions.

I'm stunned, to say the least. I click it, expecting to read a droll paragraph filled with bullet points where he reiterates for the umpteenth time that he is definitely not, under no circumstances, giving me an interview, just in case I got things twisted last night. No big deal. It's nothing I haven't dealt with in the last three days. Instead, I find absolutely nothing in the body of the email, just an attachment at the bottom. I download the Word document and open it, with my thumbnail between my teeth and my stomach in knots. There are paragraphs upon paragraphs, answers to questions that he's organized himself. I'm shocked beyond belief to see that he's taken the time to do this—the one thing he said he'd never do.

He's given me an interview, of sorts.

Why?

Because of last night?

I'm relieved to have it. Of course I am. My career hinges on this interview, and now that he's given me these answers, that's one less thing on my to-do list. However—and this is a *big* however—there's also a large part of me that's annoyed this email was sent on the heels of our one-night stand. Whether he intended to or not, he's tainted last night. Does he think I expected this? That deep down, I was in his suite on the off chance something like this could happen? I wasn't. I'm not all that cunning. Need I remind anyone of my very bad middle school quiz-bowl sabotage plan that involved a pair of safety scissors?

I don't have what it takes for seduction on that scale. I barely had what it took for the one-night stand, and I thought I pulled it off pretty beautifully. I mean, we really went for it. That session by the couch, another in the shower, *god* . . . when he took me on his bed, I saw stars. I left rather than sleep beside him because it just felt right. Easier that way. I got to wake up in my own bed; there was no bumbling or confusion, no send-offs that would have made it all seem boring and awkward.

This changes everything.

All that fluff? It's lumpy and deflated now.

I don't scurry off to Sienna's room with news of last night. I make a single cup of coffee and take it to my desk so I can get to work. I haven't even looked outside, but I know we're in Turks and Caicos now after cruising all day yesterday. I want to be outside, enjoying paradise, but instead, I'm stuck at my desk for the better part of the morning while I rework Phillip's answers into something that resembles a proper sit-down interview. In the end, he's given me nearly three thousand words. By my count, that's three thousand more words than anyone else has about him.

I email Gwen an in-depth outline and barely manage to push back from the desk when I hear a knock at my door.

"Yoo-hoo! That's enough work in there. Come on now, we're about to go out on a hike, and I'm *not* going by myself."

I laugh as I walk over to fling open the door.

Sienna's dressed and ready to go, looking like Hiker Barbie. She has her hair pulled back in two French braids, a subtle bit of makeup. She's wearing a coordinating set of yoga pants and a tank top, as well as a little backpack filled with water and snacks.

"And plasters; well, you call them Band-Aids," she tells me proudly. "In case these boots give me a blister. I meant to break them in, but where the hell am I going to go on a hike in the middle of London? Anyway, come on, get dressed; you can't stay cooped up in here all day, even under the guise of work."

"I really *was* working." I toss the words over my shoulder as I walk into my bedroom to get dressed. I brought plenty of workout clothes with me, so I rifle through them in the closet until I find a pale-blue tank top, sports bra, and running shorts.

"Oh yes?" she calls from the other room. "And what about in the middle of the night when I heard you banging around in the hallway, trying to find your key card? Were you *working* then too?"

I yank my pajama top off over my head. "I didn't think I was being that loud."

"A herd of wildebeests would have been quieter! So tell me, where were you?"

"Can't say!" I walk into the bathroom to brush my teeth and apply some tinted sunscreen and ChapStick.

I don't know why I'm suddenly feeling coy. Though I haven't known her long, I know in my gut that I can trust Sienna. It's not about that. I just feel suddenly protective about my night with Phillip. Putting words to those feelings will only decay the fragile magic at play.

"*Ooh la la*, now I have to know. Actually, it's funny. I saw you leave the observation lounge last night right alongside Phillip, and then it was the weirdest thing . . . neither one of you reappeared the rest of the night! Coincidence?"

"Purely!"

I take a cue from Sienna and braid my hair off my face.

When I walk back into the living room, ready to go, I find Sienna wearing a gloating little smile. "You, my dear, aren't fooling anyone. Spill the beans and spill them fast because we're due down for this hike in five minutes, and I doubt you'll chatter on about it in front of other people."

"There's nothing to tell," I say with a shrug.

She groans in agony. "Don't be this way! I thought we were real mates."

"We are," I say, getting my phone and essentials so I can stow them in a little backpack. I grab a bottled water from the minifridge and turn to see that Sienna hasn't dropped the issue, not even a little bit.

"Fine."

I tell her everything—well, the CliffsNotes version of everything—in record time.

"He was that good?"

"Phenomenal."

Her brows shoot up and her jaw drops. "Best you've ever had?"

I chew on my bottom lip before admitting, a little sadly, "Yes."

"Blimey. I wasn't sure he had it in him. Sometimes, the real handsome ones are so lazy about it, like they don't even need to work all that hard. *You*-should-be-glad-to-be-with-*them* sort of thing."

"No," I chuckle, recalling a few of the highlights. "It wasn't like that at all."

"*Well, well, well* . . . and so now?" Her eyes alight with the possibilities. "Are you going to meet up again today for another clandestine boning session?"

A laugh bursts out of me. "Now, *nothing*."

"*Nothing?*"

I head for my door, and she's forced to follow me, otherwise we'll be late for this hike.

I shrug. "We agreed it was a one-night thing."

She groans. "Ugh. And so? That was probably *before* you both realized how good it would be. What's the harm in extending the tryst a little bit, you know, just finishing out the cruise?"

I wrinkle my nose. "Just seems complicated."

"God, are you always this sensible?"

Am I sensible?

Or a coward?

To me, it feels like the safer option to leave last night in the past, especially after his email this morning. I wish I knew his motives. I can't believe he didn't include anything along with the attachment, no hint or clue as to how he's feeling. I hope he's not regretting last night.

I'd like to see him face to face this morning. That would help me understand where things stand between us. It's wishful thinking that he'd join the hike—he's a busy man—but I'm still slightly disappointed when we meet up with the group and I find he's not among the dozen people ready and willing to trek through a forest.

Sienna's disappointed, too, because Javier is not here either. She's frowning as we load onto the bus that's going to transport us from the cruise ship to the national park.

Javier has apparently signed up for a cooking class with *Aurelia's* head chef.

"I invited him to join us, but he didn't want to swap out his itinerary last minute. Said it would look unprofessional, like anyone would care."

We sit together in a row of seats near the back, and then I lean in to ask, "Are things heating up between you two?"

She very nearly blushes, something I didn't think I'd ever see from Sienna. "He kissed me last night. Just a quick peck outside my suite when he walked me back, but it was quite nice. *He's* nice. I think that's our problem. He might look like the type that's real suave . . . the kind of guy who'd pull you into dark corners and have his wicked way with you, but he says he wants to take things slow! *Hello*, we've only got the rest of the cruise to get something going, and then he's flying back to España, and I'm going back to Bristol for my gran's eightieth birthday—not like I can skip that! I love her, and well, she'd probably cut me out of the will if I flaked. She's spiteful like that, the witch."

I can't help but smile at Sienna's colorful assessment.

"Well, why don't *you* make a move?"

She rears back in her seat. "*Me?*"

She acts like it's physically impossible.

"Yes." I laugh, knocking my shoulder into hers. "*You* figure something out. Some way to push things forward."

"That's—"

"Brilliant. You're welcome."

She feigns annoyance. "Fine. Okay. Let's strategize on the hike."

We end up not strategizing at all. The hike is so strenuous and intense that we manage very little conversation outside of a lot of huffing and puffing.

"I'm in shape!" Sienna swears.

I thought I was too. I mean, I'm not one of those people who's constantly training for some half marathon where you have to crawl your way through mud and dodge barbed wire, but I get out a lot; I bike and jog and generally stay active.

Our issue is that the first half of the hike is all uphill, and the path is steep and muddy. Also the tour guide must be trying to wrap up his workday early or something because his pace is brutal. Sienna asks to stop for a water break, and he tells her no! "The view is really better if we stop up ahead."

Up ahead means going another two miles!

We trail behind the others by a lot, so much so that the group has to stop a few times to ensure we haven't collapsed out of sheer exhaustion. No one's happy with us. We hear the grumbles.

"I thought we were going to take a leisurely walk through the forest," I admit to Sienna quietly so the others can't hear.

"I bought these boots mostly for show!" Sienna admits.

Our route is beautiful, don't get me wrong. The forest is lush and overflowing with tropical plants and flowers. We catch breathtaking views of the surrounding water and islands, but those views last all of thirty seconds as we're constantly ordered to "Keep up!" and "Pick up the pace, girls!"

I have half a mind to pop a squat and let them go on without me, but I'm worried I'd be lost here forever. The route isn't completely intuitive. A few times, the tour guide has had to quite literally hack through overgrowth with a machete. I mean, we're really off the beaten path here, folks. I try to think of how I'll word my review of this hike for my write-up and mostly come away with three simple words: *Don't do it.*

We can do nothing but groan in exhaustion by the time we make it back onto the bus.

We're barely sitting up. Sienna's splayed out like a starfish, airing out all her bits and bobs, she says.

"I'm so knackered I might never get up again," she groans.

"Why did we do this to ourselves?"

"We should have booked another spa day! I could be lazing with cucumbers over my eyes! Listening to Enya!"

Turns out, it was our own fault. Neither of us read the fine print before we signed up for the *extreme cardio hike* specifically *not for amateurs.* If I have one rule in life, it's that *extreme* and *cardio* should never belong in the same sentence. The group waiting outside the bus in the morning, sporting spandex and toned butts, should have been a dead giveaway that we were out of our element, but I just thought people were really getting into the hiking spirit! They might as well have been Navy SEALs sporting CamelBak hydration packs, marathon jerseys, and sweat bandannas. I thought my practical Nikes—the pair classified under *walking shoes* online—would cut it. They're so muddy that you can barely see the logo anymore.

We did it, though. We made it to the end of the hike and took photos in front of the waterfall while I propped myself on Sienna for support and she held gauze to her scraped knee.

I think we sweat out most of the liquid in our bodies, but that doesn't matter now. We're finished, and we're gloating and delusional, riding high on endorphins and a *little* bit of dehydration psychosis.

"Was it *really* that hard?"

"You know what? Looking back, it wasn't so bad. I could have gone a bit longer."

"I'd totally do it again!"

We're still doing it now while we walk into the dining hall for dinner. Of course Sienna has a slight limp from a strained muscle in her thigh and a bandage on her knee, and I'm still wincing with every step I take—but we damn well deserve to brag!

I'm a full-fledged hiking aficionado, thank you very much.

Is there a special section where we should sit with the other ultrafit people eager to tear into a high-protein, low-carb dinner?

Sienna and I are laughing about this—poking fun at ourselves—when I glance across the dining hall and see Phillip. He's sitting at a table with Arthur Burton and Tyson. I'm a half step behind Sienna, and she doesn't notice that I freeze in place. I was looking for Phillip, though the moment I see him, I short-circuit as if surprised I actually succeeded.

He kills the laughter on my lips. The sight of him is a physical reminder of everything that happened last night—tangling together, naked in his sheets. I was going to pretend and act as if nothing all that serious even happened. It was just sex, and it was supposed to be casual, but then nothing about Phillip is casual. I should have known it wasn't possible to keep him at a distance.

He looks up, and our gazes clash. I feel his eyes on me like a caress. I look away quickly—flushed with embarrassment—then realizing how silly that is, I glance back up and smile. We can be cordial to each other, friendly even, can't we? He's still looking at me, the ghost of a smile playing across his handsome face. Suddenly it all seems so intimate. Those lips were pressed between my thighs last night. *Oh my god.* A thousand riotous butterflies take flight in my stomach, a complication I wasn't expecting. I had hoped I sated something last night. Though as my heart thunders in my chest and a tantalizing warmth spreads over me, a sinking feeling starts to creep up inside me—a worry I was hoping to avoid. There's been a shift, and we both notice it. Something feels markedly different between us, like the air is tinged with secret longing. I realize now that last night doesn't exist in the past; it lives here and now, a breathing thing that grows between us.

Sienna says my name. She's wondering if I like the table she picked. "It's great," I say, barely looking at it. "Could I sit on this side?"

Before she's even responded, I tug out the chair that puts my back to Phillip. I feel relieved the moment he's behind me, out of sight.

Sienna takes the seat across from me, looks up, and smiles. "Oh, now I see. Playing hard to get? I doubt there's any need. He's still looking this way, you know . . ." Her expression shifts as she catches his eye and offers a little wave.

I want to hiss at her to stop, but why? She can wave to Phillip, and I can peruse my menu as if I'm not even bothered.

"I wish I'd thought ahead and let you borrow something from my closet." She frowns at my blue flowy sundress like it doesn't live up to her exacting standards. "I have this little black number that would have him swallowing his tongue."

"I don't want that, remember? It's over." I concentrate on the menu, willing myself to believe my own words as I read over the entrées. *Hmm. Pasta or steak tonight?* I'm starving after our hike.

"*Pfft.* It's *over?*" She leans in close. "So if he cornered you and asked for one more night, another little romp in his suite, you'd say no?"

I nod forcefully before pointing at the top corner of the menu. "This seafood pasta sounds good."

"Oh," Sienna says, and I realize she's not responding to my comment; she's looking over at Phillip's table still, her brow furrowed in confusion—or is it annoyance?

I can't help but follow my curiosity. I glance over my shoulder and see that two of the bloggers Sienna warned me about on my first day—Jenna and Avery—have come to join Phillip and his friends at his table. In fact, Avery takes the empty seat directly beside Phillip; then she leans in and touches his shoulder, speaking low and saying something with a playful smile. She might as well be waving a neon sign that reads **PICK ME! PICK ME!**

"I'm sure he didn't invite them to sit," Sienna assures me, and I hate that she's trying to protect my feelings. "They're the type of women who feel as though they belong anywhere. Especially Avery. God, look at those extensions in her hair. Who does she think she's fooling? That's like four times the amount of hair on a normal human head."

I desperately want to rise above it all, to compartmentalize last night from the here and now. Acid churns in my stomach, though, that painful bite of jealousy. I have such a tenuous grasp on Phillip. He owes me nothing in the same way I owe him nothing. The interview he sent is proof of that. If he chooses to spend his evening entertaining those two women, I have no say in it. I can only control myself, and I absolutely refuse to sit here wallowing over something that's not that big of a deal. So what, they're eating dinner together? Why should I care?

I flag down a passing waiter. "Two champagnes please."

"Heavy pours," Sienna adds, gesturing for emphasis.

When he leaves, I lean across the table toward Sienna. "Listen, our night out in Key West got curtailed because of the jellyfish sting . . . let's go out tonight instead! I bet there's a ton of nightlife around here."

"They said we have to be back on board by ten p.m."

"*So?* It's only a little after seven. Let's eat fast and then go live a little. We'll be back, no problem."

Sienna's lips split into a wide smile. "All right. You're on."

The waiter brings around our champagne, and I order the seafood pasta.

"Same for me," Sienna adds.

After scarfing down our food, I don't give Phillip another glance as we hurry out of the dining hall. We end up walking off the ship directly into a shopping and dining district full of bars and clubs crammed along a street, one after another. There's not much real dancing happening yet since it's still early, but the places are packed, and Sienna and I are just happy to be a small part of it.

The first bar has two open stools for us, and we strike up a conversation with a couple nearby who live on Grand Turk full time. Though they're wearing loose linen and flip-flops, their accent gives them away as being nonislanders, at least by birth. When I ask about it, they explain they retired early and left their lives in Canada in favor of operating a surf shop on the island. They proudly proclaim that they could never go back to the brutal winters now that they've fully acclimated to life on the island.

They end up buying Sienna and me each a beer, probably thinking they owe it to us for listening while they droned on, but I would have chatted with them all night, quite happy to pick their brains about such a huge life change. *How did you know it was right, and weren't you scared about the future? Of all the ways you could fail?*

It's on the tip of my tongue to ask them, but then Sienna hears music blaring one bar over, and she pulls me off my stool, forcing me to keep up with her as she dashes out the door.

Inside, her eyes go wide with wonder. "I knew this place would be a riot. Oh, look, it's packed to the gills, and some of these men are absolutely divine. Let's have a look, shall we? Just a quick loop around the room, and if someone catches our eye, well . . . we're both single, aren't we?"

I laugh as she shimmies to the music. "What about Javier?"

"What about him?" she says with a tone of haughty indifference, though she's not fooling anybody. "He could have me if he wanted, but he's nowhere to be found, is he?"

"So then we find Javier 2.0."

She grins. "Precisely."

There's a coconut drink at this bar that everyone's ordering. A kitschy cocktail with a little paper umbrella and enough liquor to knock out a horse. It's so sweet I can barely down the first few sips. Sienna pulls a face and winces.

"It's pure sugar!"

Not to brag, but as we drink and dance and join forces with other little clusters of travelers, I don't bring up Phillip even *once*. Oh sure, I think about him nearly every second we're out on the town. I torture myself with thoughts of what he could be doing with Avery. Bending her over that same couch? Showing her that lovely little trick in the shower? Inspecting *her* hip for little grandmother-inspired sun tattoos?

Well, good riddance.

Sienna commends me for letting my hair down and having fun. She doesn't bring up Javier either, and we're both good sports about understanding that it's vital—this front we're putting on cannot be questioned or else it might collapse like a poorly constructed house of cards. We are playing two carefree girls out on the town, dammit.

Every half hour or so, one of us suddenly panics and asks for the time.

"Oh, thank god, it's only eight thirty . . ."

"Relax, it's only nine fifteen."

By the time we really *do* need to book it back to the boat, we don't want to leave.

"The party's only just getting going. I could tell that place was going to get wild," Sienna says as we're walking back on the dock. "Could you see them pushing the tables to the side of the room and clearing the floor in front of the speakers? *Ugh*. I wanted to dance so badly." She sweeps her hair up. "Just lose myself in music!"

"I'll put music on in my suite and order us up a bottle, how's that?"

She gasps and reaches over to grab my arm with both of her hands. "Brilliant! *Yes*! I am a first-rate DJ. Ask any of my flatmates from uni."

She shakes me like I might not believe her. "Okay, all right." I laugh. "You can prove it once we get there. Now if only we could find the boat . . ."

We've been on the dock for the better part of ten minutes. We walked straight here from the bar, and I thought we took the same route as earlier. Down past the restaurant with the huge marlin on the front door, past a little conch shack, that man on the corner playing drums, and voilà, the ship should have appeared before my very eyes.

There are boats at the dock—other cruise ships, even—just not ours.

"That's not funny," she warns.

"I'm not trying to be funny. Was our ship docked there?" I point over to the left. "I could have sworn it was." I'm starting to get a little worried. I don't want to have to explain to Gwen why I had to expense a plane ticket from Grand Turk to Puerto Plata because I missed boarding and had to fly to meet up with the cruise ship. "What time do you have?"

I don't even really have alcohol to blame for the fact that we're lost. I could barely down more than a few sips of the coconut cocktail at the bar, and the nice couple bought me that beer close to two hours ago. I'm mostly sober now. Sober and lo—

"Do you two need help?"

"Oh!" Sienna squeals and whirls around, her hand clutching her chest. "Lord, you scared the bejesus out of me!"

It's dark out, sure, but the dock is well lit. It's not *that* eerie, especially with how many people are out walking around. Sienna's reaction was a little over the top, and it makes the men chuckle. The sound makes my spine stiffen.

I hardly want to turn around, but it would be extremely weird to totally ignore him. I don't let my cowardice win out. I turn around to face Tyson and Phillip with a confident smile in place.

I hate that I check behind them to confirm they're alone—sans Avery and Jenna—and I blatantly ignore the surge of triumphant relief when I see it's just the two of them.

"Help, you said?" Sienna says, coming to her senses first. "Please. Yes. God. You two are like angels. We're absolutely *smashingly* lost. Have we got the right dock? It is this one, isn't it?"

Tyson laughs and points behind us. "Right dock. Just need to go down a few more yards."

Phillip and I haven't said a word yet, though we have acknowledged each other in that private way, his eyes on me, seemingly full of questions.

Where have you been, and who've you been with, and why haven't I seen you all day?

I tip my head and study him. He's so handsome in his blue button-down, his sleeves rolled up to reveal his tanned forearms. Blue is his color, though I could say that about *any* color, really. I love the way he looks in black and brown, gray, white . . .

Tonight, he's swapped out his suit pants and slacks for charcoal gray shorts. He's still dressed nicely—you know how you can just tell sometimes when clothes are well made and tailored? But the overall takeaway is still casual and sexy. I like that his hair is slightly mussed up from the breeze. Not that perfectly combed look he so clearly prefers. And it's nice to see a bit of his chest too.

"We're happy to walk you two back to the ship," Tyson says, interrupting my in-depth perusal of Phillip. It's like I was trying to catalog every inch of him for scientific purposes. Maybe I had more of that coconut drink than I thought . . .

"No need—" I say at the same time that Sienna cuts in effusively.

"That would be wonderful! *Thank you.*"

Then she smoothly takes her position beside Tyson, and they walk along so that Phillip and I are left behind them, stuck with no other option than to acknowledge each other out loud. To speak.

"Ahem."

He mimics me with a throat clearing of his own. Our eyes meet, we laugh, look away.

I contribute by offering, "Nice night, don't you think?"

"Oh yeah. The weather has been great."

It's like we're both in on the same inside joke—the hilarity of our situation is not lost on either of us.

"Been wandering around?" I ask, trying to keep the conversation going. I finally see *Aurelia* up ahead. We really weren't that far off. I think we could have found it *eventually*.

Phillip angles his head back up the path. "Just popped into my favorite bar on the island. Had to visit it while we were here for the day. I live in fear that it'll change. New owners and all that . . ."

"Was it like you remembered?"

He smiles and looks sidelong at me. "Exactly the same, down to the signed dollar bills pinned on the wall. What about you?" he asks, his eyes lighting on my dress.

It's the same one I've had on all night, and I recall the way Sienna dismissed it at dinner, but it seems Phillip likes it well enough. I see the way his gaze stalls on my legs. The dress *is* a little short.

"Sounds like we had similar nights. Our place was packed to the gills. One of those restaurants that turns into a dance club at the stroke of nine. It was only *just* starting to get really loud and fun. I didn't want to leave, but I was worried we'd miss the boat."

He checks his watch, the one I teased him about my second morning on board. "You still have ten minutes."

"Ten minutes of aimless wandering if you and Tyson hadn't come along."

"I would have stalled them if you hadn't shown up," he says like it's a solemn swear.

I puff out a disbelieving breath. "Uh-huh. I'll bet."

"Our manifest is updated electronically every time a guest boards or disembarks the ship. If you weren't accounted for, there's no way I would have gone on without you."

I lay a hand over my heart like I'm really touched. "So that's my special treatment after last night? Along with the interview questions, I guess. Why'd you do that, by the way? I told you that's not why I was there. There was no angle. No secret hope. I expected to be back at square one with you."

He drags a hand through his hair, his brow furrowing for a moment before he shakes his head. "I know your intentions were the same as mine. Pure, that is. Well, as pure as your intentions can be when there's a woman like you draped across the back of my couch . . ."

"*Phillip!*"

He grins like he enjoys teasing me before he goes on. "I just . . . it felt like the right thing to do."

That doesn't quite answer my question. I should drop it. We seem to have somehow eased through the worst of the awkwardness and come out the other side.

But . . . I just can't help myself.

"Do you regret it?" I ask quietly, almost immediately wishing I hadn't. What made me say it? I'm not at all prepared for the consequences if he does regret it. Oh my god, I'll need therapy! Years of it!

"Not at all."

His answer is swift and clear. His stern determination is extremely appreciated.

"Good. Neither do I. I enjoyed myself. There's nothing more to it."

"Exactly."

"God, look at us behaving like adults." I bump my shoulder against his—or at least I attempt to. My timing is slightly off. I lean over as he's taking a step, so that I miss him and lose my footing. His reflexes are fast, though, and he has his hands on my shoulders, righting me before I take a tumble.

He chuckles as he asks if I'm okay.

I don't reply.

My reaction to his touch is immediate and overpowering. I go still as his hands squeeze my biceps, and then he slowly drags his palms down my arms. It's so gentle, and in another circumstance, it could be misconstrued as mere politeness—him just wanting to make sure I'm secure on my own two feet again—but then ever so quickly, his fingers lace with mine. He tightens his grip, holding me as our eyes lock. A fissure of want slices through me. Another kiss, another night. I'm desperate for them.

And then he drops my hands and steps back, cleaving the moment. The distance is important. Necessary. I take his lead and go so far as to hurry up and catch Sienna so that the four of us can walk together. It's safer that way. No confusion over intentions. No need to feel embarrassed if he maybe saw one emotion too many on my face.

I almost believe I've gotten away with it. Succeeded in enjoying a one-night stand with a handsome man *and* fulfilling my work assignment, but this idea comes crashing down when I see the email from Gwen Levis waiting for me back in my suite.

> This is not nearly enough. It's stale. Where's the commentary? The personal touch? I feel like I could find these answers with a simple Google search. Did you sit down with him? Go through your interview notes again. Delve deeper, Casey.

> This won't do.

Chapter Thirteen

CASEY

My mouse hovers over the blue send button at the bottom of my email; I'm stalling because I'm too chicken to press it. I lean back and cross my arms, staring at my computer screen, trying to figure out if I'm a bad person.

It's Thursday, late afternoon—my fifth day on board *Aurelia*—and I haven't left my suite all day. I've been chugging coffee on an empty stomach. I ordered up breakfast earlier, but I only managed to pick at it. I'm not hungry at all. The pancakes and eggs sit cold on their tray behind me.

Sienna came calling a little while ago, asking if I wanted to go down to the pool, but I begged off, saying I had to work. And I do. I've been working all morning. We're docked in Puerto Plata, and I doubt I'll get to venture off the boat even once today. Outside, the sky is a cheery blue, but it doesn't seem to have any effect on me.

Gwen's email last night did this to me. It was the catalyst for the downward spiral I'm currently enduring with clenched teeth. Her critique of my work felt especially harsh. I stayed up late last night, rereading what I sent her, disappointed to find that she was right in her assessment. What did I expect she'd say when I delivered Phillip's canned responses to those ridiculous questions?

I went to bed and woke up this morning feeling as though I was failing at the very last important thing left in my life. What do I have outside of my work? At the moment, nothing really.

Over the last few years, my life has been chiseled down to a single goal: make it as a travel journalist, which will get me promoted and allow me to leave my small life behind. It's why I'm on this cruise. It's why I've put in the hours at *Bon Voyage*, working a menial job I can't stand.

So then why am I not going for it?

Why am I not giving this assignment everything I have?

The answer is obvious. I've prioritized Phillip's feelings over my own career goals. I've tried to have my cake and eat it too.

Ask any noteworthy journalist if they've ever had to *slightly* trample on the feelings and wishes of others for the betterment of a story, and they'll snort in your face. Of course they have. Gwen didn't ask me for a puff piece. She wants real and interesting. I've given her neither.

So . . . I spent the better part of last night and this morning rewriting my special-interest piece about Phillip. Gwen called my first draft stale; she wanted me to delve deeper, so I did. Though at first, I had to force it a bit. I'm a travel journalist at heart, but fortunately, from my first day on this cruise, I've found it incredibly easy to write about Phillip. It's really no challenge at all to describe his demeanor and humanity after spending the last few days witnessing it firsthand. Most of what I wrote is rooted in facts. I included snippets of my conversation with Tyson at that breakfast, as well as my own experiences with Phillip, excluding our bedroom activities, that is. I could have stopped there. Maybe I should have. However . . . I also conjectured about his failed relationship with Vivienne and the difficulty he must face as the successor of such a large company. I delved into his personality, the tight control he seems to exact over his life—from the way he dresses to the way he carries himself. I spoke of his past, what little I know of it, and

I tried to expand him from a two-dimensional businessman into the complex human he is.

When I finished, I read it back with a twisted sense of dread. From a journalist's perspective, I thought I'd done it, woven the pieces of the man together to give the reader the full picture of him. As a friend, a—a lover . . . well, it feels exploitive to write about Phillip in this way without his consent. He's been so tight lipped about everything; even the interview answers he sent were restrained and polished . . . bland, for lack of a better word.

I sit here now, wondering what's right and wrong, wondering what my grandmother would tell me to do. I picture my future after this cruise, the one where I tell Gwen point blank that I can't give her what she needs. I fail and slink right back to my old job. I suck it up, find a lonely apartment, start paying rent, and continue living the way I have been, forever and forever.

Then I think of how this article could change my life if Gwen really likes it, if she thinks my writing is worth investing in, if other publications catch wind of the story and it really gets picked up. This could be life changing, I'm sure of it.

So whether or not it's the polite or nice thing to do, after I read through my new exposé about Phillip for the twentieth time, I send it to Gwen.

I also send it to Phillip.

It's a bold move on my part, especially considering I have no idea what his reaction will be (spoiler, it won't be pleasant), but it's the least I can do. Over the coming days and weeks, if Gwen approves the story, someone from *Bon Voyage* will reach out to Phillip's team for approval and input. He'll read what I've written about him *eventually*. It feels important that it at least come directly from me first so that he can prepare himself now rather than later.

I sit back on my couch, my hands shaking from adrenaline.

If I made a mistake, well . . . there's no going back now.

I stare at my inbox almost as if I expect them both to reply to me right away, but nothing happens. I refresh once and then again; there are no new emails.

After a few minutes, I close my laptop and look around. I'm itching to get out of this suite. I could try to hunt down Sienna at the pool, but I'm too scared to wander around the ship. I'd rather not cross paths with Phillip just yet. Better to give him a chance to read the article . . . a moment to cool down if he needs it.

Instead, I take a book out onto my balcony. I have every intention of reclining back on one of the loungers and losing myself in my book, but instead, I lean against the rail and stare out at Puerto Plata, the tiny slice of the Dominican Republic that stretches out in front of me. It's midafternoon. I've missed the planned excursions for the day, but nothing's stopping me from doing a little bit of exploring on my own. I barely think it before I'm already acting, throwing on a dress and comfortable sandals, grabbing my purse and wallet, sunglasses and sun hat.

I race through the halls of the cruise ship, hurrying toward the gangplank. I'm scared I'll bump into Phillip, but the moment my feet touch solid ground again, I breathe easy. The cruise port is right in the heart of the city. Freight and cargo are getting unloaded; taxis whiz past; music comes from every direction; and people are *everywhere*: sitting outside clustered together on plastic chairs, playing cards; walking along the sidewalks; riding bicycles and motorcycles, sometimes piling an entire family onto a single bike. The city is eclectic, and once you bypass the overtly touristy parts—the pink street and the umbrella street—you see the real lives of the locals. I walk past old, sagging buildings in need of a fresh coat of paint, mismatched architecture, grocery stores, and laundromats. There's color everywhere as if the city has a personal vendetta against painting things white or gray or beige. The beauty of Puerto Plata is evident everywhere, highlighted most prominently by the huge mountain that serves as the city's backdrop, looming over the squat one- or two-story buildings. The mountain is part of the Isabel de Torres National Park, and I find out by asking a few nice locals (who help me with my cobbled-together Spanish) that I can take a cable car to the very top.

I rush in that direction, wanting to stay on foot rather than hop in a taxi. I'm documenting everything, snapping photos with my phone, trying to absorb every last detail. Gwen hasn't seemed all that interested in my review of the trip so far, but I'm hoping I can change that. I want to prove to her that this interview is a stepping stone to bigger and better things. I'll write up a review of Puerto Plata and send it along anyway. I'll show her that I'm eager for more assignments and possibly—*hopefully*—a long-awaited promotion.

It's a thirty-minute walk from the downtown district to the Puerto Plata cable car, where a long line of tourists waits to take the ten-minute journey up to the top of the mountain. I manage to make it in the last group for the day, and we get crammed into the cable car like sardines. I don't mind. Of the twelve of us, only two people speak English. I hear French rattled off quickly. Portuguese too. It would be stifling inside if not for the open windows. Everybody carves out spots at the sides as we rise over the city, lifted by a cable into the air along the side of the mountain. My stomach swoops with the ascent, and a little laugh of delight spills out of me. The woman to my left does the same, and we smile at each other, bonding over this unique, shared experience.

I know it's silly, but when we reach the very top of the mountain and I stand overlooking the entire city of Puerto Plata and the surrounding ocean, I can't help but tear up. It's more than I can take in all at once, not just the view itself, but also the stark difference between this day and all the ones that have come before it. Today, I'm standing on top of a freaking mountain. Last Thursday at this exact same time, I was sitting in a crappy hotel room, staring at the inside of a mostly empty minifridge, trying to decide which frozen dinner I wanted to cook (unsuccessfully) in the microwave.

I'm crying because of everything I've done wrong. I hate that I've wasted so much. I don't mean the years I spent taking care of my grandmother. No, I don't regret that one bit. But she died last year, and I've lived every day since her passing as if I'm dead too. How did I not see it before? The monotony of it? The sinking dead-end job?

I breathe in a sense of conviction, staring out over the city. I know I've done the right thing by submitting that article to Gwen. I've shaken free of it all. I've really put myself out there now. There's no going back.

Chapter Fourteen

PHILLIP

I'm pacing on my balcony, annoyed by the heat and the shitty signal I get out here. Already, I've tried and failed twice to connect with my team back in the States. Now, I have them on the phone for the third time, but I have no idea how long it'll last.

"Do they not have fucking cell towers in the Dominican Republic?"

To say I'm pissed would be an understatement. I'm on the phone with Angela Carew, my personal PR representative, and Gary Marshall, head of Woodmont's legal team.

Neither of them replies to my question, choosing to let it go. Wise, I think. I'm ready to chew someone's head off, and I don't really care who it is. It might as well be them.

"How do we kill it?" I ask, wanting to handle this problem quickly and efficiently. I want this off my plate so I can move on to more pressing matters, *like finding Casey Hughes*.

Neither of them responds right away. Gary clears his throat, only infuriating me further, before he replies with a weak tone. "I'm not sure we need to."

I didn't hear him right. Bad connection and all. "Excuse me?"

Angela speaks up now, sounding just as spineless as Gary. "Yes, actually, Phillip . . . I've read through it, and I had Laura take a look too. It's not *so* bad."

I squeeze my eyes closed and rub the bridge of my nose, trying to ease the tension headache forming there.

"I'm sorry. I thought I made myself perfectly clear here. I don't want this story to run. Casey Hughes took journalistic liberties that I don't agree with. Delving into my life. Bringing Vivienne into this, for Christ's sake—"

"You're looking at it from the wrong angle, taking it too personally."

No shit, Sherlock!

It's about *me*. What's more personal than *that?*

"Laura and I both think something like this has been a long time coming," Angela says, sounding more resolute in her recommendation now that Gary is on her side as well. "We've held off on taking interviews with larger publications, but *Forbes* or *Newsweek* would have eventually produced a story of a similar ilk. They've been contacting our offices off and on for months. Something would have eventually gone to print, with or without our backing, and I have no doubt their writers would have been a lot more ruthless about it. This piece from Ms. Hughes is soft, I assure you."

I open my mouth to protest, but Gary cuts in.

"I have to agree; you're getting off relatively easy with this, Phillip. I don't think it's worth coming down on the magazine and making a stink. Especially considering you were aware of the story. You did participate to some extent. So she fleshed out the rest of the interview . . ." His tone says *Big deal.* "You know they were going to discuss your relationships. It's just fodder. *Bon Voyage* is not the *New York Times.* This could have been much worse. In fact, I'm confident, in time, you'll come to appreciate the article for what it is—a puff piece, really."

"I think we should allow Angela to send approval and—"

His sentence gets cut short when the line goes dead. The connection's lost again.

My anger threatens to boil over.

I have half a mind to chuck my phone off the side of the balcony, but fortunately, I come to my senses. Since *Aurelia* is equipped with exceedingly good Wi-Fi, I pull up a new email on my phone and type quickly, responding to Angela and Gary.

> You do not have my approval. Do not reply to *Bon Voyage* yet.

There.

I've pumped the brakes for the time being. It feels good to regain the upper hand, exert control over my life again.

Casey's email surprised me when it popped up on my phone this afternoon. I was in a meeting with Tyson and the engineers. I wasn't even going to check my phone when it buzzed, but something compelled me to pull it out of my pocket. When I saw Casey's name flash across my screen, I excused myself and walked away from the group, opening the email to see she'd mimicked my style—no text in the body, just a lone attachment at the bottom.

I knew, no matter which way Casey sliced it, I wasn't going to like what she had to write about me. You're either someone who delights in seeing your name in print or you're not. I don't want to be the subject of public scrutiny. I don't want anyone prying into my life and poking around as if it's their right to do so just because I come from a prominent family.

Even still, I wasn't prepared to read Casey's personal take, and that's exactly what the article was—mostly Casey's opinion about me. Things she has no business discussing, namely my desperation for privacy and my struggle to connect with others. Casey doesn't understand what it's like to be a man in my position, to live life inside a fishbowl. When I first met her when we were young, we were able to escape that for a bit. She knew nothing about me or my past. As middle schoolers, we shared lunch together just like two normal kids. We saw and accepted each other for who we were, separate from any outside influence. In my world, that's a rare gift.

Keeping people at a distance has always been my preference. Money is so compelling, *too* compelling. I have a hard time trusting people, especially their motives. I've experienced enough moochers and leaches, sycophants and users to understand that most people are best kept at arm's length.

I never made it back to the meeting with Tyson. I took the stairs up to my suite and reread the article a second time, deciding I hated it even more than I first thought.

I was on the phone with my team ten minutes later. We've talked on and off for the better part of the afternoon, and now, after everything, I still don't really care what they have to say about it. So they have degrees in public relations and twenty years of experience in the field and a huge company backing them—*big whoop*. They're not the subject of the article; I am. If I don't want to give my consent, I won't. Simple as that. *Bon Voyage* will be slapped with every lawsuit I can throw at them.

Casey is the one who'll be fucked in all of this.

Casey.

My feelings for her are as complex as they come. I want to shield her from my wrath and unleash it on her, all at once. Freud would have a field day with me. My mother, too, would love to know that a woman has gotten under my skin in this way. She's always said it would happen eventually. I laughed her off. Now who's laughing?

Not me!

The morning after Casey and I slept together, I convinced myself of all the reasons to stay away from her for good, and yet as the hours ticked by, I felt more and more desperate to see her. I would have taken any measly excuse to talk to her, but she was off the boat most of yesterday and nowhere to be found today. She's been busy, apparently.

I should have pressed her last night, asked her what her plans were moving forward with the story, but I wasn't thinking about any of that when Tyson and I bumped into Sienna and her on the dock. Casey in her sundress, her long hair loose and a little tangled from the wind. Her lips plump and pink and tempting enough that I thought of kissing her in front of Tyson and Sienna, just laying one on her like a damn fool.

I'm no one's fool, though. Least of all *hers*.

Now, I have had a member of my staff hunt her down and issue a summons for her to come to my suite, and I feel a little like a dickhead dictator demanding she present herself for her royal beheading.

I pace on the carpet, trying to decide what punishment fits her crime. I dream up ludicrous ways to get back at her for what she's done, but none of them stick. It just feels good to imagine them for those few fleeting moments.

When I hear her knock, I flinch.

Then I close my eyes, inhale deeply. My goals and priorities haven't changed. I want this voyage to go smoothly. I want to go back to life the way I knew it before ever laying eyes on Casey Hughes in her adult form. Vivienne is my future. That's that.

Then I grab the door handle and whip it open to see Casey standing there, her bottom lip between her teeth, worry lines etched in her forehead, and all that shit flies right out the window.

I can't even speak to her, I'm *that* worked up.

I merely step back and wave my hand for her to come in like a pompous asshole.

"I'm surprised you wanted to talk to me today," she says, stepping forward with a healthy amount of reluctance.

"Are you?" I ask, my tone sharper than I intend.

She makes it into the living room, then turns around to face me. Already her worry is starting to melt away, her brow relaxing. When she speaks, she sounds mildly annoyed. "I take it you read the interview."

"*Yes*. I read it."

She doesn't give anything away. Those demure features—the ones I thought of as I jacked off in the shower this morning—stay perfectly stoic as she asks, "What did you think of it?"

"What did I think of it?" My head might explode, it really might. "I should let my lawyer tell you what I thought of it."

She hums, sounding bored. "So . . . you're not happy. That much is obvious. Is that why you called me here? Just to tell me off? Because when that attendant stopped me in the hall to tell me you wanted to see me, I was headed straight for the all-you-can-eat dessert buffet happening downstairs. That chocolate fountain is calling my name."

I step toward her. "You're not going to that buffet."

I've lost it, truly.

I'm forbidding her from a buffet? What next?

I never talked to Vivienne this way, not once. If there were ever any issues, we'd have proper sit-down discussions. She once invited me to a Google Calendar event titled Thermostat Temperature Meeting that she thought we should have at 8:45 p.m. the following Tuesday. I was so levelheaded with her, so even keeled. I barely recognize the man standing in front of Casey, blocking her from her chocolate fountain.

"Should I read you my favorite parts?" I slip my phone out of my pocket and proceed before she can argue. "Cantankerous. Rude. Stubborn. Prideful. Controlling." I take off my reading glasses and glare at her. Those were all words she used to describe me. Never mind that she also used *charming, handsome,* and *enigmatic*—I'm stuck on the negative adjectives at the moment. We'll get to the nice ones in due time.

Casey has the audacity to look proud of herself as she cocks her hip and crosses her arms. She's not scared of me, not even a little. She raises her brows as she asks, "Where's the lie?"

"I gave you answers. I played your little game."

She laughs like I'm completely delusional. "You never gave me answers! I never even got to ask you questions! Those were *your* questions, and they were absurd. You lobbed me softballs." Her tone is mocking and condescending as she continues, "*Who inspires you in business? What motivates you to work?* You really thought my editor would lap those up? Why'd you even send them to me?"

"I felt guilty."

Her eyes spark as her eyebrows shoot up. "There. Honesty. *For once.*"

My jaw ticks. "Yeah, that's right, Casey. I woke up the day after I slept with you, and I worried about how you were feeling. I didn't want you to think I was trying to take advantage of you."

She rears back, looking absolutely offended. "I wanted everything that happened."

"I was in a position of power over you," I press.

"You were in a lot of positions over me, true . . ."

God, she winds me up.

"Power?" She shrugs. "So what? I wanted it as much as you did. And I didn't try to use our night together against you. *You* did that all on your own."

We go silent for a spell, just long enough for me to acknowledge how heavily we're both breathing, how much tension fills the room right now.

"I felt blindsided," I say, wondering if I'm still talking about what she wrote or if I'm just talking about *her* in general.

She takes it in reference to her work. For the first time since she waltzed in, she looks contrite over what she's done. Her pride has fallen away, and she stares at me with sad eyes and a deep frown.

"What would you have done in my position? Let the chance of a lifetime pass you by because of one night with a man? A man, I should add, that you'll never see again as soon as this cruise ends? I don't feel bad for you."

A last vestige of anger bursts forth, and I spit venom. "I should kick you off this boat."

She meets my challenge head on, her chin lifting with the challenge. Her words are slow and precise. "So kick me off this boat."

I don't know who moved first. We'd have to review the tape to see whether I took a step forward or whether it was Casey who came toward me, but those were the last words uttered before I have Casey in my arms, my mouth claiming hers. There's no sharp slap. No. She *lets* me kiss her, and god, I enjoy it. Possession spreads through my veins, heating me from the inside. My hands go to her waist. She clutches the front of my shirt. I ache for her, and the feeling must be mutual. She leans into me as if needing more, to feel what I'm feeling, to take whatever I'm willing to give her.

Her lips part, and our tongues touch. Tangle. I shift even closer. Wanting to be as close to her as possible.

Her hands smooth down the front of my shirt, and then she impatiently untucks it from my pants.

I feed off her impatience as I grab the hem of her dress. "Take this off."

I step back and help her remove it and then toss it over to the couch. She's wearing a cream-colored bra, lavender panties. I don't know where to look. Everywhere. I want everything I see. I go to her and kiss her mouth, then her neck, her collarbone, her chest. I rain kisses all over her body as her fingers toy with my hair.

I kiss her sunshine tattoo, and then I stand back up, my hand finding its way between her thighs as I do it.

Her eyes are hooded and glazed when I meet them again.

I draw one of her nipples into my mouth, and she clutches the back of my head so tight it almost hurts. I move to her other breast and make her pant. She squeezes her eyes closed as if wanting to focus on just my mouth on her skin.

God, she's beautiful like this, with her skin on fire, her lips slightly swollen and red, her legs trembling.

I'm inexplicably drawn to her, so much so that I can't make it to the bedroom. Yet again, I use that couch, only this time, I lay her down on it and come up and over her. Her hair fans out around her face; her eyes are wide and innocent, looking up at me as I undress the rest of the way.

We don't say a word, scared to break this spell. Despite the day, despite her email, I want her with a fierceness that scares me.

A niggling voice in the back of my head wonders if I really had that much of an issue with the article or if it was all just an excuse to get her here, to demand she come and see me again. I know my anger was real, but its origin is murky. Loss of control has never sat well with me, but what exactly am I losing control over?

She smiles up at me, tiptoeing her fingers up my thigh. Apparently, I'm taking too long with the condom. She's impatient. I rip the foil open just as she reaches out to cup my hard length in her hand. She lifts up so she can take me in her mouth. I watch her lips glide over me, and I feel my heart beat like it's a separate creature inside me, fighting to get out. Oh fuck. I cup the back of her head. My fingers tangle in her hair. I want her so badly. I want her to lick and taste me, and she does, eagerly.

I don't have the willpower to stop her from sliding lower on the couch, angling herself so it's easier for her to keep me in her mouth. I rise up and tip my length past her lips, and she moans around me. I start to gently thrust my hips, and she matches my rhythm, taking me deeper. Shivers race over my skin, and she continues, making it so damn good I know I won't last. This is too perfect, too *everything*.

I can't let myself have it. I abruptly break away from her and reach for the condom again. Once I have it in place, I settle over her, trying to hold my weight off her as I part her thighs, but she pulls me down, wanting to feel me pinning her. Her nails bite into my skin as she clutches my back, and I sink into her with a guttural groan.

Her name falls from my lips in a hoarse exhale.

It's a handful of thrusts before she detonates—squeezing me so tightly I follow right after her.

Casey.

Chapter Fifteen

CASEY

"Keep your damn article."

Phillip's words surprise me. I didn't realize he was awake. I've been lying here in his bed, tucked up against him, naked. It's early in the morning—too early even for the sun to show its face—but I can't seem to go back to sleep. I've been studying various parts of Phillip. The blanket is tucked up around his hips, but above that, I can revel in his toned chest, the dusting of hair, the muscled arm bent up beside his head, that stark profile, his angular jaw.

When he speaks, my eyes fly up to his. He looks sleepy and soft compared to his usual austere persona. He hasn't donned his business-man mask yet.

"What do you mean?" I ask.

He sweeps my hair off my bare shoulder, and it makes me shiver. "I'll have my team approve it. It's done. Push it forward."

I frown as I try to keep up. Last night he was outraged by what I'd written. He called me to his suite to admonish me about it. *Now*, this morning, he's magically come to terms with it? *Approves* it, even?

My jaw tightens reflexively. I remember what he said last night about feeling guilty the morning after we first slept together. Is this more of the same?

"Is this because of what we did last night after our argument? It's not why I—I slept with you." I have a hard time pushing the words out. "It's not why I'm still lying here. You have to separate the two."

He swallows and shakes his head. His own expression has turned contemplative and moody, especially compared to the gentleness I saw in him a moment ago. "No, this has nothing to do with last night. I don't want to keep dragging this out. I want peace. So have your way and be done with it."

Belated excitement has me sitting up, clutching the sheet to my chest for some semblance of modesty.

"Are you serious?"

He smiles and reaches up to cup my jaw. He nods, studying my face reverently.

I have to fight the urge to lean into his touch. To give in to that feeling again. Last night was one time too many. A one-night stand is just that, one night. Though this was maybe necessary. One more romp in his bed to satisfy those lingering feelings. And the way I feel now, desperate for more of his touch? Well . . . I haven't had my coffee yet. Maybe I'm just a little tired.

This would be easier if I hadn't stayed the night, and some part of me wishes I hadn't. I didn't stay over the first time we slept together, and it felt easier to wake up the next day with that clean break. This—us lying naked in his bed together—introduces all sorts of complications.

"Did I fall asleep on the couch?" I ask, wondering now how we actually made it to his bed.

He smiles. "Yes. After the second time."

My cheeks flush, and I look away. "Right. *Whoops.*"

I'm starting to crawl out of his bed, my eyes already scanning his room for my abandoned clothes. Just my luck, I must have left everything in the living room. I'll have to scramble out of his bedroom naked or—

"Let me have this sheet," I say, tugging on it hard.

It doesn't budge. His body weighs it down.

He laughs. "Stop yanking it, would you? Just give me a second, and I'll hand it to you."

He sits up, and I'm treated with too much man for this early in the morning. All that tanned skin . . . all those muscles . . .

I momentarily lose track of what I was doing beyond checking him out like it's my life's greatest purpose. *God, look at him.*

He clears his throat, mocking me.

I think I hate him now more than ever.

"Here you go," he says, tugging the sheet free from the blanket and holding it out to me.

Of course, once he does, he turns and stands, not the *least* bit embarrassed by his nakedness.

I get a good look at his butt—consider it a parting gift—wrap the sheet around myself à la college toga-party attendee, and then book it out into the living room.

My panties and bra are strewn on the side of the couch like evidence of my poor decision-making. They taunt me as I approach. *Oh, girl, you're really in for it now.*

I slip them on like I'm being timed and then grab my dress, wrinkles and all, and tug it on. I feel much better once I'm fully clothed.

In all that time, Phillip has only managed to find himself a pair of low-slung pajama pants. They accentuate that tantalizing *V* men have that leads our eyes straight *down.* I avert my gaze before I fall victim to that *V.*

"Right, well, thank you for another—uh—lovely evening."

Phillip chuckles and shakes his head. "You're absurd. If you weren't racing off . . . we could continue. I could call breakfast up for us."

"Oh no. *No, no, no.*" I just keep repeating the word while I look for my shoes. One is underneath the coffee table, and one is near the television, which is to say it's wedged between the television and the wall. *Whoops.* I have to jiggle it for a moment, and even then, the heel leaves a scuff on the paint. I rub it, as if that will magically make it disappear. Then clear my throat. "Right. Send me the bill for that."

A quick peek at Phillip proves how much he's enjoying this, watching me squirm, that is.

I veer around him, taking the long way to the door. Even still, he meets me there, taking the handle so he can stall for a moment before he opens it.

"So that's it? You're off?"

I don't look at him. "I'm off. Yes. Work calls, after all. I'm sure my boss has sent a million emails by now. No time to delay."

He nods, his expression tightening ever so much. "Right. Okay."

There's no goodbye. The moment he opens that door, I duck under his arm and flee.

What a disaster!

What a perfectly confusing situation with a man who I can't even wrap my head around!

I have no intention of going down that road with him again. When he called me to his suite, I thought he wanted to have a discussion, sure, but sex? Never in a million years.

We just get under each other's skin. That argument . . . it felt like a boatload of foreplay, if you ask me. Like we were just wanting an excuse to pounce on each other again, and, boy, did we. I can't even think back on what I did to him on that couch or I'll die from embarrassment. I'm not that girl! I've never . . . probably *will* never . . . experience things like that again.

My next date with a man I meet back home, a man I procure through some dating app, will be such a letdown. I know it already. I'll just have to prepare myself for the disappointment and tell myself that not *every* man can be like Phillip. Sure, the sex is good, but his *personality*? Okay . . . also good. But his manners? Dammit, they're impeccable. There are other issues, though, like how he . . .

And when he . . .

Well, right.

One thing is certain; I know I'll never see Phillip again after this cruise. We live completely different lives, so if I'm looking for an excuse to push him away, I have it. This is nothing more than a fleeting, light-hearted cruise romance. A fling! How tropical! How worldly of me to go to bed with Phillip. There's no need to form attachments. I can be cool about the whole thing. Just watch.

When I arrive back at my suite, I yank off yesterday's clothes and shower. Already, I feel more like myself as I comb my long hair and let it start to air-dry. With comfy clothes in place, I take a seat at my desk and open my laptop. I can't wait to read Gwen's thoughts on what I sent her. I did everything she asked and more. I endured Phillip's wrath (er . . . well . . . whatever that was we did all night) to get her this story, so I'm expecting some kind of explosive email with a ton of emoji and effusive language.

It's why I sit dumbly staring at my screen for so long when I do finally pull up her email.

> Okay good. I've passed this on to our content editors. Now, those fact-checking assignments sent earlier in the week could wait until you get back home, but I don't see why they should. You'll have plenty of downtime over the coming days. Priority wise, Mark needs the Lancaster story back by tomorrow afternoon. The others can wait until next week.
>
> Thanks.

I blink at my screen, willing the letters to rearrange themselves into different, better words. Something like

Casey, this is wonderful! Just what we were looking
for. Let's discuss a new role for you when you get
back to the States. Maybe there's another assignment on the horizon for you . . . Congratulations,
Gwen

Am I a complete idiot?

A total, utter fool?

I thought this story would be the jump start to my career that I've
always been waiting for. I thought this was the start of something new
for me. Instead, Gwen gave me a veritable clap on the back, and now
it's back to life as normal. Fact-checking waits for no man! I cannot
believe she had the audacity to send me those assignments! *Our intern
just doesn't cut it, not compared to you!*

I see red.

Then I see maroon.

Then black.

I risked it all—Phillip's wrath, my journalistic integrity, my fucking
morals—for *this*?

With shaking hands, I click reply to Gwen's email.

I'm happy you are pushing forward with the story,
though I think there's been a bit of confusion on my
part. I saw this assignment as a stepping stone—a
transition of sorts. I'm hoping to be considered for
more writing assignments in the future. I feel as
though I've paid my dues with fact-checking over
the last few years and well . . . I thought maybe this
would be my way of proving how serious I am about
getting out in the field a little more. Could we discuss
this possibility when I get back to town?

Her reply is almost instantaneous. I picture her sitting at her glass-topped desk in her posh office in New York City, sipping her latte, unbothered by the world that exists thirty floors below her.

> Casey, yes, confusion most definitely. *Bon Voyage* doesn't have any open writing positions at the moment.
>
> Be sure to complete that Lancaster story for Mark, thanks.

Adrenaline courses through me; my world narrows down to that laptop screen, my body quaking as I type.

> And if I pressed you to consider a promotion now, rather than at some ambiguous time in the future, would you be willing to work with me? At least to meet with me about it? I've been with the company since college and I've been loyal to a fault. This is sort of a deal breaker for me . . .

I hit send and then sit there hoping her reply won't come as quickly this time, hoping she actually takes a moment to consider what I'm asking and how important this is to me.

Then my inbox pings, and my heart sinks.

> Right, Casey. I'm hearing you loud and clear and my advice is very simple: reconsider that ultimatum.
>
> You have a good thing going in your position and you, more than anybody, should realize how difficult it is to get your name on bylines. Gabriel interned with us for three years before he was ever given an

assignment! Now, I understand you're hungry and
I like to see your enthusiasm. That's just what *Bon
Voyage* needs! I might be able to chat with HR to see
about getting you a little bump in your salary. ;) No
promises, but I'll see what I can do.

Gabriel interned for three years . . .
Three years . . .
Is she serious right now?
Is she *fucking* serious!
I interned for four years—all through college, *all* unpaid. Then,
then, once I graduated, I took the lowliest position they would give me,
just to get my foot in the door. I was told there was a pecking order in
place, that if I was willing to stick it out for a year or two, they could
find a spot for me on the journalism team. Now, I realize that was never
going to happen. Years have slipped by. I've taken on the grunt work
as a fact-checker, and I've kept my head down. I've never asked for an
extension on a project. I've never slacked off. Hell, I've never even asked
for a raise!

I feel like I've been slapped across the face.

Time seems to stand still as I sit there letting tears roll down my
cheeks.

I'm surprised at how many come, at the well of anger and indig-
nation I feel over Gwen's brush-off. It's clear she has no intention of
promoting me, ever. I feel so completely used and led on. Worse, I
feel stupid, like this is somehow my fault. Maybe I should never have
accepted such a lowly position in the first place, maybe I should have
fought harder, forced a meeting with Gwen, really put myself out
there. Maybe as my grandmother was dying of cancer I should have
been caring more about my career and how to trample my way to the
top. Apparently, toiling away as a quiet worker bee gets you absolutely
nowhere.

I'm nothing to Gwen. I'm nothing to *anybody*, and that realization comes like a searing stab in the gut. I want to keel over and give in to the overwhelming anger.

It's not fair. This life is not fair.

I want to rage.

I want to fire off another email right away. I want the satisfaction that would come from telling her off. I could put in my two weeks' notice and revel in that power.

Instead, I sit numbly, letting my laptop fade to black as it goes to sleep. I see my reflection in the shiny screen. A lost, lonely girl, unsure of her future now more than ever.

Sometime later, there's a knock on my door.

Sienna's sweet voice. "Casey? You in there?"

I don't reply.

"Casey?" she asks again, knocking a little harder.

I listen to her footsteps as she walks away down the hall. Then I shoot to my feet and run for the door, flinging it open and calling out to her.

She turns, her smile shifting into a sympathetic frown once she gets a good look at me.

"Oh no. *Casey*. What's wrong?"

Chapter Sixteen
CASEY

I feel sedated by the calm blue water surrounding us. There's not a wave as far as I can see. Just deep ocean and sky that stretches on forever. It's late afternoon, and Sienna and I are lounging by the pool on board *Aurelia*. I'm lying on my stomach with my chin in my hands, staring at nothing, really.

"Are you thinking about it again?" Sienna asks me.

I've gone quiet on her, but I can't help it.

This morning, after a long discussion in my suite where I filled her in as best as I could on my job and why I've hit a wall, she convinced me to join her and a few others for a tour of Saint Thomas, culminating in a cocktail tasting on the beach. Apparently, the Virgin Islands are known for four cocktails in particular: the painkiller, the bushwhacker, the banana daiquiri, and the rum punch. The painkiller was my favorite and not just because the name was so fitting for my horrible day. It was a delicious blend of pineapple juice, orange juice, coconut cream, and dark rum that immediately slipped me right back into vacation mode. Well . . . at least for the length of time it took me to finish the fruity drink.

Then my pit of despair returned in full force.

It's helpful to have Sienna by my side, though, acting like a Band-Aid. I feel like I have to keep it together for her sake. I don't want to break down again here, poolside, while everyone else is having the time of their lives. There's a DJ playing fun dance music and waiters passing around drinks and complimentary snacks, trying to ensure everyone is well taken care of. The atmosphere is really fun, but I can't help but feel wholly apart from it all.

"I hate that you're not enjoying yourself," Sienna adds when I don't answer her.

"I am," I insist, rolling over to face her.

She sees right through my canned response.

With a shake of her head, she pushes up her sunglasses so they perch atop her blonde hair. I always think Sienna is stunning, but right now beside the pool, sun kissed in a bikini, she's something else. *Javier had better be somewhere nearby, eating his heart out,* I think.

"What did you think of the tour this morning?" she asks, smartly steering us back toward a safer topic than my impending doom. Talk of our tour won't bring tears to my eyes.

"It was really fun. I'm glad we'll be in Saint Thomas for another day. I want to go out and explore a bit more. I feel like we only got a taste of things this morning. And they mentioned that snorkeling excursion. That sounded really fun."

"Oh, I'll definitely join you for that. Swear you'll do it with me."

I nod in confirmation. "We can go off on our own afterward. I did that while we were in Puerto Plata."

She groans. "I'm jealous. I got talked into this walking tour, and it was *okay*—don't get me wrong—but the guide was just such a snooze! Sometimes they think they're really going to bowl us over with facts about bricks and mortar. Sir, unless Brad Pitt laid those bricks, I could give two shites."

I laugh. "Here, let me show you what I did. I actually made it to the top of the mountain there."

"*Stop!* You *did?* Oh, now I feel even worse. Let me see."

She sits up as I dig in my bag for my phone. I've been avoiding it all day—not wanting to stumble across another work email that would send me spiraling again. I haven't even begun to look at those assignments Gwen gave me. They can damn well wait. I worked my butt off getting her that story yesterday. I'm not going to hole up inside my suite for another day, toiling away at my computer.

"Here." I pass Sienna my phone and watch her scroll through the few photos I took when I was inside the cable car on the way up the mountain. As gorgeous as it looks, truly, the images hardly do the view justice.

I spent a few hours writing about my day in Puerto Plata as well. It's nothing to brag about, though, just a short piece highlighting my favorite parts of the city, with the most convenient route to get to and from the cable cars. It was a writing exercise more than anything, a pretend assignment, and I'm too shy to tell her about it.

"These are *good*, Casey." She looks up at me, eyes wide with excitement. "You should post them."

I laugh. "No social media, remember?"

She groans again as she hands me back my phone. "Right, ugh, how could I forget you're living in the Stone Age?"

"I will admit, being around you has *slightly* made me regret my social media stance, actually. You're so good about snapping photos and videos, posting, and then putting your phone away. It's not like you're on it twenty-four seven, even if it is your job."

She gets a strange look on her face as she starts to sit up. "Well, funny you should say that—"

"Sienna! Casey!"

Javier's voice surprises us both, but I'm the first to recover.

"Javier, hey!" I say with a welcoming wave. I peek at Sienna out of the corner of my eye to see she's ever so casually adjusting her position on her lounge chair, creating better angles, subtly arching her back to draw Javier's attention to her red bikini top. I can't help but smile to myself.

"How've you been? Did you recover from that jellyfish sting?"

God, my jellyfish sting? That feels like it was ages ago. I'm telling you, cruise ships are funny. I swear we're in a time warp, so an hour on board is like a week on land.

"All good," I say with a reassuring smile. "What have you been up to? Busy day?"

He looks even tanner than when I last saw him, like he's part of the sun now, so handsome with that thick dark hair and brilliant white smile. Sienna knows how to pick them, I'll just say that.

"Yeah, I went off on a hike that lasted much longer than I thought it would. I looked for you guys in the dining room when I got back, but lunch was pretty much over by then." He rocks back on his heels, stealing a glance at Sienna, who's yet to say a word to him, not even a greeting.

She doesn't look bitchy, per se, just aloof. Cool in a way I've never been able to affect. It's probably not in my DNA. You see, Sienna has these beautiful green eyes that seem to be ever so slightly hooded, giving the effect that she's perpetually bored with everything she's looking at. Now, for instance, she could be watching paint dry, for all the enthusiasm written across her face.

Poor Javier! He's really done himself no favors by waiting this long to approach her. She's been wanting this for *days*! Sure, she put up a good front with me today, trying hard to support me through my tears and self-indulgent wallowing. I'm sure she didn't want to seem selfish, shifting the focus back onto her and her dating problems, but she still slipped up and mentioned Javier a time or two. The first time, I remember, she asked out of the blue when I'd last seen him around the ship. The second time, a few hours later, she said—wholly unprompted, mind you—that she was perfectly fine with where things stood with Javier and she didn't really mind that he hadn't made a move or anything. "I prefer being single" were her exact words, which everyone knows is universally translated to *Please, god, send that man to my bed tonight!*

"Oh, a hike? That sounds fun! Sienna and I did a hike two days ago, and I'm still sore. What about you, Sienna?"

She hums and shrugs. "Not really anymore. I think I might go for a swim."

Her British accent seems more standoffish, prim, and proper than ever.

She stands, about to step around Javier and really take things up a notch, but he cuts in front of her.

Yes! Go Javier! I mostly resist the urge to throw my fist into the air, but it still lifts off my towel and hovers awkwardly near my shoulder.

"I was hoping you'd be free tonight? To go and have dinner off the ship? I made a reservation at this restaurant all the locals recommended."

Sienna thinks it over for an excruciatingly long time before replying casually, "A little late in the day for a dinner invite, don't you think?"

Sienna!

Javier's eyes narrow at the same time his smile widens. He likes this. He likes *her*. "I came to your suite. I knocked and knocked, trying to find you."

"We've been off the ship most of the day," I tell him since Sienna won't. "Then when we got back, we came straight here."

"See?" His brow rises. "I couldn't find you all day."

Sienna inspects her nails, really putting on a good show here. Even I'm starting to sweat, and I'm not even Javier!

"She'll go," I blurt out.

"Casey." Sienna levels me with an admonishing glare. "I will not. I can't leave you. Not with everything . . ." She shakes her head. "Not tonight."

While it's thoughtful of her to consider my feelings in all this, there is no way I'm letting her skip out on this dinner date with Javier. She helped me when I was at a low point earlier (never mind that I'm still very much there), and so now I'm going to help her.

"Javier, you have to take her. Poor Sienna has had such a rough day with me. She needs loads of wine, lots of good food, and maybe some dancing?"

Javier grins.

"Definitely dancing!" I amend.

"Case—"

I hold up my hand to stop her and push up from my lounger, already starting to wrap my towel around myself. "I've already made up my mind what I'll be doing tonight." I get my bag and stuff my paperback and phone inside. "I'm exhausted, and I'm going to shower and hit the hay early. So . . . there you have it. No choice. Enjoy dinner, you two!"

I walk away, feeling lighter than air, a maniacal cupid with too much power. The thrill of thrusting those two together carries me all the way to the bank of elevators and right back to my suite, but as that door opens, I realize reality has waited for me.

It's the quiet of the place that hits me where it hurts.

For so long after my grandmother passed away, I couldn't take the silence in her house. On days I didn't commute into the office, I'd take my laptop to a coffee shop (or more often, because it was free, the library) and only begrudgingly return to the house when it was close to dinnertime. Immediately upon my arrival, I'd walk around like a woman possessed, turning on the downstairs TV to the channel my grandmother always watched, the one with the news and *Wheel of Fortune* and *Jeopardy!* and a bunch of dumb game shows I never paid attention to but enjoyed hearing in the background of my life. Then I'd crank on the radio in the back hallway. I'd get the laundry going, and I'd open the windows to let the noise from the neighborhood trickle in, and all this together nearly worked. It almost made me feel as if my grandmother were still with me.

I never did get used to living there after she was gone. Her room stayed her room even though it was bigger and she had a queen bed, while I still resigned myself to a lumpy twin we never got around to replacing. I didn't touch her things, didn't pack anything until two weeks ago when her items were either going with me or getting sent to a landfill.

It made me sick to do it. Her smell was so pervasive in her room that I could barely stand to go in there, but once I did, I never wanted to leave. I thrust my face into the clothes in her closet, and I wept for the woman who raised me, the one I'd give anything to see again, even for one day.

I miss her more now than ever. I wish I had her here with me, telling me what to do.

Though that's laughable because I absolutely know what she'd tell me. She told me the same thing for years.

"Casey, you're wasting away in that job. That Genny—" Sidenote, she never could get Gwen's name right, or maybe she could, but it felt too good to say it wrong that she never wanted to correct herself. "She doesn't understand what she's got with an employee like you. You're doing them a service in that damn position. You hate it! And don't get it twisted. They need you; you don't need them. You're smart as a whip, and you've got looks to back it up. Don't roll your eyes at me. I'm telling you, you're more beautiful than any of the girls that come through working the beauty counter with me, and believe it when I say, I've seen some real lookers in my day. So I just don't get it, Sunshine. Why bother sticking it out? Why not chase that adventure you've always wanted?"

Our arguments played on a loop, never changing. I thought she was shortsighted and didn't understand the benefits of me slowly working my way up at a publication like *Bon Voyage*. Hello! No one makes editor in chief right off the bat! It felt like she was from a bygone era and couldn't comprehend the pressures I was dealing with. I couldn't just go and do something grand. I had college loans to pay for! A retirement account to contribute to! More importantly . . . a family member—my one and *only* family member—who needed me.

Now, standing in the doorway of my suite, regret pools inside me. I wonder if maybe I had things twisted, if I was so stubbornly rooted in my ways that I wasn't willing to see things from her perspective. She just wanted me to look over my options, to feel like I really had a say in my own future.

I know one thing for certain: she'd be spitting mad if she read the emails Gwen sent me this morning. When I recall them, though, the anger doesn't burn afresh. I'm just a mass of anxiety—overwhelmed and sad.

Suddenly, I don't want to go in. I step back and let the door slam closed.

I leave that quiet suite behind, not bothering to change out of my bathing suit or cover-up before I turn and head back down the hall. I move like a zombie, not fully aware of where I'm heading until I find myself outside Phillip's door.

I reach up and knock.

Nothing.

I knock again, slightly louder this time. My fist pounding more aggressively than I intend. I wince, but still, the door doesn't open. Phillip's not here.

God, I hate the fresh wave of sadness his absence brings.

It feels more telling than it is.

It's around dinnertime. It doesn't make sense that he would be here in his suite already. What did I expect?

I don't know exactly, but the tears come again. God, they just won't quit today. I've been a mess—taking this work thing harder than I should. *Pull yourself together,* I reprimand myself before sweeping my hands beneath my eyes, forcefully wiping away tears before they can really start to fall. I turn away from Phillip's door, once again wholly unsure of my destination as I start to slowly walk back down the hall. Even with all my internal protests, tears still gather, clouding my vision as I keep my head down, nervous that someone will walk out of their suite and see me like this. I don't want to deal with some stranger's questions.

Are you okay, dear?

Do you want to talk?

Is there someone you want me to call?

I hate every tear that falls, beating myself up for not staying strong. I've lived through harder days than today. Plenty of them.

Up ahead, I hear approaching footsteps and cringe.

Intentionally, I look down at the ground, moving to one side of the hallway so the person can sweep past me. Hopefully without getting too close of a look at my disheveled state.

"Casey."

Phillip's voice makes me freeze. My eyes pinch closed. My head stays down.

I clear my throat, trying to push past the tightness there as I speak, well, more like ramble. "Phillip, oh. Hi. I . . . um—" I look behind me as if wanting to check something down the hall.

"Were you trying to see me?" he asks, his voice gentle as if he already knows something isn't right.

The question makes my skin prickle. "*Oh.*" I shake my head adamantly, trying to sound surprised like the thought hadn't even occurred to me. Never once do I look at him, using my hair as a curtain to shield my splotchy cheeks. "No. No. I got turned around. Thought I was on a higher deck, but . . ."

I let the sentence dangle as I start to walk, intending to scurry past him, but his hand shoots out to stop me. He grips me right above my elbow, tightly enough that I can't slip away. My gut instinct is to wiggle free, but his grip doesn't waver.

Please don't. Please let go of me. I plead the words in my head while tears gather faster now than ever, as if my body realizes that here, with him, it's okay to finally let go.

"Sorry if you knocked. I was up with the captain. Just came down to change for dinner, actually."

His thumb rubs my arm soothingly as he speaks, and the gesture only makes things harder. My stomach is squeezed so tight, like it's twisted itself into a tangled knot.

"Okay. Yeah. Don't let me keep you."

I stare at the carpet—at a one-inch silver square in the pattern—willing him to leave.

"What's wrong?" he asks, edging closer.

I still haven't even looked at him. I really don't want him to see me like this. I'm not sure why I thought it was a good idea to come here. It just happened. My body made the decision before I could really think it through.

"What's wrong?" he asks again.

I shake my head, not wanting to confide in him. It's dangerous how much I already feel for him opening up to him the way I have—giving him more of myself is just too tempting.

"*Casey*," he pleads, his tone low as he reaches up to cup my face.

I look away, unwilling to meet his eyes as the tears fall down my cheeks until they reach his hand, pooling there.

I'm desperate for his comfort, I realize. I want to feel like there's someone in my corner. Sienna's been such a good friend today, keeping me distracted, tugging me along with her so I wouldn't have to wallow alone in my suite. Phillip is different, though. I want him to take away this pain, sweep me up in the feelings he's been so good at producing in the last few days.

"Could we go to your suite? Just one more time?"

He doesn't even hesitate. He lets go of my face, takes my hand—his grip warm and tight and assuring—and he pulls me down the hall to his suite. He's eager to get me behind the closed door, and I expect him to push me up against it and kiss me senseless like we've done the last two times we've been alone here. Instead, he brings me over to the couch, sitting me down before taking a chair opposite me.

"Tell me what's wrong. Is it us? Have I—?"

"*No!*" I say, rushing out the word so he knows I mean it. "Just, please. Could we . . . once more. That's all." It's easier if I talk without looking at him. It's partly cowardice, I realize, but there's nothing to be done. Phillip intimidates me on a good day when I have my full defenses up. Today, he'd simply undo me. "It feels silly to put myself in your path and then tell you that I'd rather not discuss why I'm obviously upset. It's . . . complicated, and it has nothing to do with you. Furthermore, you can't fix it, so in a way, there's no reason to discuss it at all. So let's do something *else*."

I'm hoping I'm making myself clear enough without having to actually spell it out.

"While I might not be able to fix the issue, I'd still like to know, Casey. You shouldn't have to carry—"

"I won't talk about it."

He doesn't understand. It's not *an issue*; it's my entire life in shambles here. There's no easy way to delve into it or I would! Well . . . maybe, I would.

"So you came here to use me, then? For comfort or a distraction or—"

I lift my chin, finally, *finally*, looking at him. My tone is bold and clear. "Yes. Both of those things, and I won't deny it. If that doesn't sit right with you, well, it doesn't really matter. I won't change my mind. I'll just leave."

His brow furrows as he looks me over. His voice sounds pained when he replies, "It doesn't have to be like this."

I laugh, and it rings out caustic and bitter. "It does, actually."

What would he know of my situation, anyway? He has a multitude of friends, family—*Vivienne*, even, would likely come running if only he asked it of her. Even without all of that, his money is his biggest safety net of all. There's no sense in trying to share with him how I'm feeling. He wouldn't understand. And more importantly, that's not what we are to each other. There are walls to keep up, lines we shouldn't cross.

I'm aware that I'm technically the one who first infringed upon them by showing up on his doorstep clearly distraught. I've put him in this difficult position and, well—

I stand up abruptly, deciding that now would be a good time to leave. Thoroughly embarrassed, I now have tons of material to torture myself with later in the confines of my quiet bedroom. I'll recall the fact that I damn near threw myself at him—while *crying*—and I'll cringe all over again.

Just as I take a step, Phillip speaks loudly and commandingly. "Sit."

I go still.

"*Sit down.*"

God, he almost sounds angry.

"You aren't going to show up here like this and then leave. Jesus, Casey. Do you think that little of me? That I would just let you wander out of here right now?"

"You have dinner," I say lamely.

Phillip sighs like I've pushed him to his limit, and maybe I have.

What an epic fail of a one-night stand. I've really managed to suck all the fun out of it. This is the sort of thing you have to deal with in long-term relationships and, even then, only because you *have to.*

Phillip stands and comes to me, his intensity radiating off him.

By the time he's in front of me, I've lost the willpower to meet his eyes. I stare at his chest as he holds his hands out to capture mine. Slowly, he weaves our fingers together, tightening his hold. What a simple, intimate act. Just our palms pressed together, nothing more, and it feels like he's reached inside my chest and stolen my heart.

Chapter Seventeen

PHILLIP

I feel a lot of things while staring down at Casey, our hands linked together—none of them good or easy. Though her current predicament takes precedence, I'm in a tricky position of my own, thanks to her. When she left my suite this morning with that quick send-off about needing to hurry off to work, I stood at my door and watched her walk down the hall, wondering about the pang in my chest, that niggling feeling I was too chicken to give a name to. It seemed best, and easiest, to make a clear goal for myself: I wasn't going to seek her out today. Not again, not after last night.

Now here she stands before me, like a wounded bird. She's never seemed smaller or more fragile than in her current state. Her brown hair hangs limp and damp from the pool. She's still wearing her bathing suit and cover-up. With so little to go on, I've looked for something physically wrong with her—bruising, scratches—and thankfully come away with nothing. That's not to say something physical didn't happen to her, but I just don't get the sense that's what's gone on here.

"Whatever it is, you can tell me."

She opens her mouth to protest again, but I speak first.

"If you'd rather not, I understand. But I feel left in the dark here, scared to make a misstep with you."

I've never been in this position before. I don't know what's right or wrong. Touching her, wanting to make her feel better seems natural, but then would that only make things worse in the long run? I don't know anymore.

Outside of this moment, I've been having a slight freak-out of my own. I've been confused, most certainly. I'd like nothing more than to go back to feeling totally in control of my life, to tidy up all these loose ends and refocus on what's important (or at least, what seemed important in the past), but Casey is all I can think about.

Tyson mentioned her at lunch earlier. It was only something simple. He asked if I'd had much more opportunity to see her around the ship, and I nearly chewed his head off.

"Why do you feel the need to pry into my life? That's none of your damn business."

He'd laughed it off. "Jesus. All right. I won't ask again."

Immediately after, I regretted how I responded. Getting my hackles up like that was clearly indicative of my state of mind. I've been worried about this . . . *fling* with Casey, and having him ask about her made it all seem so obvious, as if everyone could see the situation clearly except for me. It pissed me off.

"I know I shouldn't be here," Casey begins. "But I just feel like . . . I just want you for one more night. I swear it's done after this."

I close my eyes and stave off the urge to kiss her. God, I'm as desperate for the connection and intimacy as she is. I can no longer deny my full-blown attraction to her. The chemistry between us is explosive, but it feels so unnatural to give in to something I want, as if, surely, it's wrong or bad for me in some way. Love should come prepackaged with labels and clear instructions. Love. I choke on the word. We're not even close to that. Absolutely not.

This is just a fire between us—an inferno—and it will surely burn out.

So what's the harm in giving in like she wants?

I don't know. I can't think clearly when she stands and presses her body up against mine, seeking me out. She keeps my hands in hers and circles them behind her back, forcing me into a hug. Her cheek rests against my chest, and her eyes close. We stay there long enough so that my entire body turns languid. I know how she's feeling right now because I'm feeling it too. The touch of a lover—the soothing feel of being held in someone's arms. Someone who cares for you.

I lean down and kiss the top of her head, and then I unwind our arms and lead her into the bathroom.

She's still damp and probably cold. I crank the handle in the shower, letting the water run until it begins to steam and fog the glass. Caring for her seems right, so I don't question it when I walk over and catch the hem of her cover-up, dragging it over her hips and stomach and chest until she lifts her arms and lets me take it off over her head. I drop it on the floor and then reach behind her neck for the strings of her bikini. She shivers as I work the bow loose. The material slips down, and then I untie the second one behind her back, and it falls away completely. I take a moment to look over her, memorizing her body, tan and pink and perky and so sexy that I have a hard time not touching her.

I want to tiptoe my fingers up the center of her stomach, cup her breasts, kiss her—push her down to the ground . . .

Instead, I slip her bikini bottoms down so she can step out of them completely.

"Get in," I tell her, nodding toward the shower. The water should be perfect now, and I watch her step in and stand beneath the steady stream. Water sluices down her collarbone, her breasts, her ribs . . . stomach . . . I watch a droplet make its way inside the groove of her thigh, and when I look up again, Casey's watching me. Her face is red and splotchy—beautiful, always—but sad in a way that makes my breath hitch.

I want to know what's bothering her, but I know I can't keep pressing her, at least not right now.

She watches me undress. Originally, it wasn't my intention to get in with her, but I want that closeness again. She's a light I want to feed off of, *take from*, forever.

So far, she's only managed to get wet, not wash off, so when I step in and close the glass door behind me, I reach for the shampoo and lather some in my hands before circling my finger so she knows to turn around. I don't apply it masterfully—not like someone in a salon. But I pay careful attention to every bit of Casey's hair, massaging her scalp and working the shampoo suds into every strand before rinsing them clean.

"Conditioner?" I ask, unsure of her routine.

She smiles over her shoulder and nods. "I can do it, though."

Her voice is weak, not demanding, so I shake my head and continue. I'm enjoying it too much to give it up. After the conditioner, her hair is as smooth as silk. I gather it and twist, wrapping it around my fist like a rope, amazed by its softness. Casey releases a weak whimper, and I step toward her, pressing my front to her back, bending so my lips can graze the side of her neck.

"You're so sexy," I say, looking down the front of her body. God, the view is insane.

I want her all the fucking time, but right now, the need seems to churn viciously inside me.

She shimmies her hips, toying with me.

I release her hair and move my hands to the front of her body, sweeping my palms over her breasts, cupping her, teasing her. Her head tips back against my shoulder, and her lips fall open. My thumbs brush over the peaks of her breasts, and she moans, so I do it again, again, *again*. She's grinding back onto my hard length, her hands coming around to grip my thighs and hold me in place against her.

Water pours over us as the heat ratchets up. My aim is to touch her tenderly, but then she works her butt against me and my control shatters. My arms move lower, one bands around her stomach and the other slips between her thighs. She's so hot, so welcoming as my fingers glide across her. She bends one of her knees, spreading open for me so I can sink my middle finger into her.

"*Phillip*," she breathes with a heady sigh.

It's like she's so relieved to have me here touching her this way. Like she was worried she'd never experience it again. Tonight is it. She said so herself: "I swear it's done after this."

The thought makes me feel wild and desperate. The thought of never having this body pressed against mine . . .

No.

Don't go there.

I close my eyes to those thoughts and press another finger inside her, pumping and working her up until I feel her starting to shake. I want her to come just like this, from nothing more than my thumb gliding across her in slow circles, my fingers sweeping inside her. She starts matching my rhythm, rolling her hips against my hand, taking from me in such a bold, sexy way. It's the hottest thing I've ever watched. I want more but not until after I've wrung the first orgasm out of her, forced her to cry out in this confined space. Pride unfurls inside me as her breaths quicken and her nails bite into my forearm. She rises up onto her toes and . . . shatters.

"*God.*" She's shaking as she comes back down to reality, but when she turns and her eyes meet mine, they're dilated and wild.

"More" falls from her lips just before she hauls her body against mine and kisses me with so much passion I groan. I hold the back of her thighs so she has no choice but to wrap her arms around my neck and let me lift her up off the tiled floor. I hold her against me as our kiss deepens. Our tongues touch. Dance. I grip ahold of her thighs so tightly that I'm probably hurting her, but she doesn't protest. She mewls against me, sliding herself over me so that a few times, I accidentally slide inside her.

I don't have a fucking condom, and I need to feel her right now.

We should stop, but she keeps rocking against me, up and down, so that I can't form a coherent thought to save my life.

"I'm on birth control," she says, her words slipping out around her heavy breaths.

And that's all my brain needed.

A green light to sink into her to the hilt. We both sigh as she squeezes me tightly, wrapping her thighs around me as I press her up against the glass.

She winces against the chill, but then I distract her with my hand between her legs again. What follows is hot and heavy, unforgiving in a way that feels punishing for us both. I watch her body bounce on me, her breasts, her red lips, her wide blue eyes. I kiss her and feel that shift happening in her again, that unfurling. She lets me know she's close, and I slow my pace but keep my hand pressed between her legs. I look down, watching what I do to her, and she likes that—seems to enjoy everything about this because she's coming again, so tight it's like she has me in a vise.

Jesus, I barely manage to pull out before I fist my length and rub up and down, finishing myself off, spilling down the front of her body. I watch the water wash her clean.

Neither of us moves.

I peer up at her, hoping for a smile or some kind of lightness there, but her expression mirrors my own. Troubled and confused, if I had to guess.

"Let me finish cleaning you," I say, looking away.

I feel guilty for manhandling her like that. What started as soothing, controlled, and simple . . . just got away from me. She does that. She draws that out of me.

I take care of her now, finishing with soap, rubbing her arms and legs. She's quieter than ever. Passive and pliable. I cut the water and walk us out onto the heated tile floor. I wrap her up in a big towel, getting another for her hair.

She watches me in the mirror while I wring out her strands. I move, and she tracks me, lazy, sated, more at ease now than she was when I found her out in the hallway. It breaks my heart to think of her crying out there all alone.

"Do you feel like talking about it now?" I ask, my voice low.

She shakes her head, and I kiss her shoulder.

"All right. I'm going to order us some food. I'm starving. Let me get you some clothes to change into."

In my closet, I find a soft T-shirt and a pair of pajama pants for her. I smile thinking of how she'll look in them. *Amazing*, obviously, but cute too.

"You can tighten the drawstring," I say when I hand them over to her. "They should work."

She smiles and nods. "Thanks."

She retrieves her things from the bathroom—her damp bikini and cover-up—and then she goes out into the living room to change into my clothes. I order room service, using the phone on my bedside table, likely overdoing it with strawberry and chocolate milkshakes, pizza, french fries—anything that seems delicious and might offer her some comfort.

When I'm done, I walk into the living room. "I should have asked you what toppings you want on your piz—"

My sentence dies once I realize Casey isn't here, changing like I thought. I look around, searching briefly. The hallway bathroom is empty, and the light is off. The balcony is deserted too.

Holding out hope, I search the suite one more time, only to find my T-shirt and pants sitting neatly on the coffee table. Casey is gone.

Back in my bedroom, I go to check my phone—only realizing as I'm picking it up that Casey doesn't have my number.

There is a text waiting for me, though. From Vivienne.

Chapter Eighteen
CASEY

I'm not going to fall for a man in less than a week. I'm just . . . not going to accept that as my fate. How pathetic. How . . . wacky! I should be on one of those TLC shows called *Overnight Fiancée* or something equally cringeworthy. Those people are absolute loony tunes, and now I'm one of them.

It's why I booked it out of Phillip's suite just now. There is not going to be some cheesy dinner scene where we argue over the playlist, and he teases me about my love of Weezer and Red Hot Chili Peppers. Where we tuck into some pizza, and he goes "Oops, you have some sauce just there" and points to my lip and then leans in to kiss it off with a laugh and a giggle.

No to all of that.

Can you *imagine* what would happen if I were to admit to Phillip how I'm starting to feel about him?

Oh my god, he'd think. *The poor girl fell in love with me.* Not *poor* as in *sad*, but *poor* as in *lacking sufficient funds. LOL.*

This way is much better. He proved to be the distraction I needed, because now as I lie in bed back in my quiet suite, I'm not wallowing in self-pity about my job and bleak life prospects anymore; I'm laughing at myself for being dumb enough to actually develop feelings for Phillip.

I had literally *one* one-night stand, and look at me! I want him to propose! I want him to whisk me off and solve all my problems! I want him to be my Prince Charming!

Oh my god. It dawns on me suddenly like an anvil dropping straight onto my noggin. Maybe that's what this is really about. Maybe I'm a gold digger, and I never even realized it until now. The sex with Phillip is only mind blowing because of how many zeros are in his bank account. That must be it. I don't want him; I want what he can provide me. I'm after a Birkin. A Bentley. An all-expenses-paid trip to Bora Bora.

This theory makes me feel better for all of ten seconds, at which point I ask myself the obvious question, Would I still want Phillip if he were as destitute as me?

Yes.

The answer comes to me completely unbidden. Relentlessly fast, even.

Like a wimp, I try to scratch a line through it and try again. *No! Of course I wouldn't.* But the truth is already there, scaring me.

I pull the bedding over my head and try to hide. Of course it doesn't work. My breath is too hot, and though I would like a quick end to this evening, I'm not looking to suffocate beneath a down comforter, so I toss it back off my face and perk up as I hear Sienna's door slam. She's back from dinner! Muffled voices carry through the wall. Oh shit! She's not alone. I *think* that's Javier's accent, but I can't quite be sure. Then I hear a blunt object hit the wall, and I sit up.

What is happening over there?

But of course I already know.

Sienna releases a loud, throaty moan, and for the next thirty minutes, I'm treated to what could be considered free porn. I try shoving my pillow over my ears; then I turn on the TV and crank the volume up full blast. That only makes the people above me stomp on their floor, telling me to knock it off.

I wind up finding some earplugs in the bathroom, and that mostly does the trick. I mean, they can't go all night . . .

Cut to 3:00 a.m., my face is pressed against the wall as I shout "YOU GUYS HAVE TO STOP. *LITERALLY, GO TO SLEEP!*"

I mean, hello, some of us have had several mental breakdowns today, and we could really use some rest.

Sienna laughs and shouts back "*SORRY!*" in her singsong British accent, and I mostly forgive her, though I've already decided it's only fair that I rib her about this tomorrow for at least most of the morning. That's if I see her. She and Javier might be holed up in her bedroom all day. I smile at the thought, happy for her, somehow. I always thought misery loved company, but that's not how I feel. More like, at least someone's having a good day, you know?

Saturday is my seventh day on board *Aurelia*, and it brings with it the potential for a fresh start. When I pry my eyes open at a quarter past eight, I try not to immediately spiral back into the same funk I found myself in yesterday. I'm going to table the work situation for the time being.

Someone from the crew has slipped the day's itinerary under my door, and there's a whole slew of fun things lined up, from the looks of it:

Poolside Yoga—9:00 a.m.

Guided Historic Walking Tour—depart Aurelia at 9:00 a.m.; return by 12:00 p.m.

Snorkeling Excursion (Coki Point beach)—depart Aurelia at 10:00 a.m.; return by 2:00 p.m.

Culinary Arts Cooking Class with Executive Chef Thomas Keller (La Dame kitchen)—11:00 a.m.

Wine Tasting (Library)—3:30 p.m.

Sunset Cocktails (The bow—deck six)—6:30 p.m.

Jazz Band and Supper Club (La Dame)—8:30 p.m.

I would gladly do any of these activities, but Sienna and I talked about snorkeling, and though her plans might have changed now since Javier likely bent her into a pretzel several times throughout the night—I'd imagine she might need a little break from physical activities—I still have my heart set on being outside and in the water today. I need some good ole vitamin D.

I get dressed in a one-piece layered beneath jean shorts and a simple white blouse. I slip on sandals and grab a water bottle and stow a few snacks in my bag, just in case. I'm not sure what all the snorkeling excursion will entail, but I don't want to be out on a boat, starving because I didn't think to pack some mixed nuts.

On the threshold of my suite, I hesitate for a multitude of reasons.

I didn't crack open my laptop this morning. Should I at least check my email? *Absolutely not.*

Okay, well . . . should I be worried about bumping into Phillip immediately upon walking out into the hallway? *Possibly.*

But I can't stay locked away all day just because I'm scared of what it will be like when I see him today. Leaving how I did, all cloak and daggers like I was a secret agent, was kind of dumb, I realize. It's too late to change it, though. To go back and offer a firm handshake and a curt goodbye.

If I see him, I'll be cool. I'll smile and pretend like it's any other day on any other boat.

I head toward the dining hall, not bothering to knock on Sienna's door first. I don't want to accidentally see Javier's peen this morning, thank you very much. They can sleep in.

There's a breakfast buffet happening, though on a scale and magnitude I've never experienced before. This ain't your uncle's favorite Golden Corral. There's a bevy of French pastries set out on a table, the length of which could rival a football field. Fruit has been arranged in delicate little crystal glasses, presliced and perfectly proportioned. A chef whips up omelets. Another folds Nutella and strawberry cream inside delicate crepes.

I head toward the end of the line, not surprised that we're trudging forward at a snail's pace. Everyone wants to take their time perusing the options, including me. There are so many things to choose from. I don't have the biggest appetite, shocking considering I skipped dinner last night, but even *I'm* tempted by the cute French toast bites up ahead.

"Morning," a chipper voice says behind me.

I turn to see Tyson pick up a tray and plate of his own, then scoot into line behind me. It's always nice to see him, though obviously, my first instinct is to check to see if he's alone. It seems that Phillip is never far off. This morning, though, there's no Phillip in sight. A funny mixture of relief and disappointment washes over me, but I try not to let it show.

Instead, I smile brightly at Tyson, forcing the expression in the hope that I will actually start to feel happier than I am. "Hi, Tyson."

"Big morning so far?" he asks.

I laugh a little. "Oh . . . I sort of just rolled out of bed. Is that embarrassing? I do plan on snorkeling in a bit, though."

"Awesome. That should be really fun. I haven't snorkeled in Saint Thomas, but I hear it's great. Where are they taking you guys, again?"

I rearrange my tray, pushing it onto my left hand so I can dig into my purse for my itinerary. "Coki Point beach. Not sure I've pronounced that right . . ."

"You did. *Co-key*. It's a beautiful beach. Great areas for swimming, and you should see plenty of fish."

The line moves, and I tuck my itinerary away and shuffle forward. "What about you? Big plans today?"

"I'm actually departing this afternoon. Heading back to the States."

I'm surprised to hear this. "But we still have a few more destinations."

He nods. "Yes, but it was always the plan for me to leave early. I try to keep my travel to a minimum. It just gets to be too much, and I don't like to be away from my girlfriend, Samara, for too long."

"Phillip doesn't mind it? The travel?"

It feels almost strange to bring him up like this, as if my motives are overtly obvious. I hate that I want to know so much about him. It doesn't exactly help matters.

He shrugs. "Oh, Phillip's always loved the travel aspect of his job. I doubt he could ever stay in one place for long. Kind of like you travel journalists."

It stings to hear him call me a travel journalist when I'm truly *anything* but that at this point.

"Right, yes. I do love that part of my job . . . ," I lie, glad to see we're finally inching closer to the crepe station. "Where is he this morning?" I inquire mildly. "Phillip, I mean."

Tyson narrows his eyes in thought. "He's probably running around making sure the ship is ready to take on a few more passengers."

New passengers?

"I didn't realize there were others joining us midcruise?"

"I think it's a bit of a surprise thing." He smiles conspiratorially and leans in. "Vivienne and her friend flew in to see Phillip. Wanted to congratulate him on *Aurelia's* maiden voyage and everything. They definitely pulled it off. I didn't even know about it."

My chest constricts with this news, and it takes me an awfully long time to comprehend what he's saying.

Vivienne is here?

In Saint Thomas?

On board Aurelia?

"That—that must have been some surprise." My voice hitches, but he doesn't seem to notice.

"I can't imagine. I'm sure Phillip was glad to see her."

Tyson doesn't mean to wound me with his words. He's not being intentionally cruel, after all. It's only . . . I guess Phillip hasn't mentioned any of the things that have transpired between us. I'm not offended by it. That's okay. I told Sienna but only because it felt necessary to bring her in on it. Phillip has proved to be an extremely private person, so why would he go running to Tyson about our . . . our *whatever it was*.

Was being the operative word. If Vivienne is here, it's absolutely, conclusively finished between Phillip and me.

"I'm so happy for him."

Tyson sighs with relief. "God, me too." With a shake of his head, he adds, "You know, he bought a ring. Back in January, I think it was, before they broke it off. It really devastated him when things ended."

I touch his arm as I ask quickly, "So she ended it? Not him?"

Tyson looks at me curiously, and I realize this must seem odd. My eagerness, that is.

"This is absolutely off the record," I say solemnly, in case that's what he's worried about. "I'm not digging for an article or anything. I'm only just . . . wondering."

"Ma'am—"

The person in line behind Tyson waves for me to move ahead. It's about to be my turn to order a crepe.

"Oh, sorry," I say, rushing forward.

Tyson follows, and I'm aware of his attention on me. He studies my profile until I gain the courage to look up at him. His brow is furrowed. Whatever he's thinking, it looks like it's important.

"I've been wondering something myself actually. About you and Phillip."

"About us?" I nearly croak.

"Yes, it's just . . . it seemed like maybe there was something happening there."

"A friendship, that's all," I say, smiling, trying to cover our tracks. I'm not ashamed of what I've done with Phillip. I just don't want to ruin anything for him. If Vivienne has suddenly come back into his life and they're planning to work things out, I won't stand in the way of that. I don't want him to land in hot water just because of a few careless nights with me, ones he's likely already put behind him.

Suddenly, I can't do this.

"You know what?" I thunk my forehead with the heel of my hand. "What was I thinking? I have to be off. I can't stand in this line, not if I want to make it in time for snorkeling."

"Casey—"

"I'll see you later, okay?" I scurry to set my tray back with the others and then take the quickest route toward the dining room exit.

I don't mind really that I won't get to eat. Whatever tiny appetite I had was snuffed out by Tyson's mention of Vivienne. Now all I want to do is get off this boat as quickly as possible. Never mind that we aren't meant to meet for snorkeling for another hour. I walk off the ship and continue out onto Crown Bay pier, squinting beneath the blazing sun.

Beyond the gates of the port, there's a small shopping mall and a welcome center. But when I inquire, I'm told walking from Crown Bay to downtown is very difficult.

Just great.

I don't want to dish out the money it'll cost me to take a taxi, so I just start walking through the parking lot with no real objective. I have hopes that the people in the welcome center were lying about the distance to downtown just to give the taxi drivers business or something, but no, it's . . . actually very far. I make it to Waterfront Highway and then decide that walking forty minutes on a sidewalk while inhaling exhaust fumes doesn't sound all that appealing. So I turn back and aimlessly walk around the pier until I find a little concrete ledge right on the water. It's nice with the breeze.

Eventually, I reach for my trail mix, glad now more than ever that I thought to pack it considering it will be serving as my breakfast *and* lunch.

I'm proud of myself for keeping it together on the pier.

Given the gravity of the situation, I would have assumed that Tyson's news about Vivienne would rock my world, but it's had the exact opposite effect, actually. I feel totally numb. Like my emotions took one look at the pit of despair awaiting me and thought, *Hell, nah*, packed it up, and called it quits for the day.

I think, too, there's the benefit of not having seen Vivienne with my own two eyes, to confirm everything Tyson told me. It's not that I don't trust his word, but maybe he has it twisted or maybe Vivienne is only here to, I don't know, give Phillip his old sweatshirt that she accidentally kept after their breakup. That seems like as good an excuse as any to make a quick trip to a tropical island.

"You know, he bought a ring. Back in January" replays through my mind like a song I can't get out of my head.

A ring.

He bought Vivienne a ring.

Was it like . . . a little gemstone thing from James Avery? Or are we talking about *a ring*? *The* ring? Some whopping eight-carat diamond from Tiffany & Co. that requires a full-time bodyguard.

I had sexual relations with this man last night, and then sometime between my leaving his suite and my trying to get a measly little crepe for breakfast, his ex-girlfriend showed up!

I mean . . . can't a girl have *one* relaxing day on board this ship?

I think this just as a cruise ship blares its horn so loudly that I jump a mile in the air while emitting a high-pitched scream.

Jesus!

Eventually, it's time for me to go snorkeling, because, *yay*, let's go have a fun adventure as if my life isn't crumbling around me!

I'm zero percent surprised to find that Sienna is not in the group departing from the cruise ship. I don't even mind; it's better, actually, because then I don't have to explain myself to her. I can just be the quiet, weird one in the group, and no one questions it.

Our snorkel guide is hot. I notice him, eventually, when we're out on the boat and he comes to sit down next to me.

"Do you need any help getting your wet suit on?"

"Oh."

I must have zoned out for a second. Everyone else is wiggling and jiggling their bodies into some kind of moisture-wicking spandex material, and I'm meant to be doing the same, but instead, I was just staring off into the distance, comatose.

"I think I can manage it," I say, really looking at him for the first time since I boarded the little snorkeling boat.

He has longish, floppy blond hair, stormy-gray eyes, a jagged scar near his left eyebrow. His smile is nice and straight and white, and the way he's looking at me proves that, on the outside at least, I'm still whole. None of the sadness has eked out of me to pool on the surface and turn my skin a pallid, sickly gray.

He looks at me with a sort of funny expression. "Are you okay?" he asks, likely now wondering just how far gone I really am. He's probably worried he'll have to call the coast guard on me.

"Totally fine." I stand and pick up my wetsuit. "Now, what's your advice for getting this thing on?"

I have a tiny bit of fun, at least while I'm out in the water, swimming above a coral reef. I spot a giant sea turtle and all sorts of tropical fish. Way off in the distance, there's a reef shark, but he leaves us alone, wanting nothing to do with a bunch of annoying tourists. Smart shark.

We get to go out twice, and when it's time to wrap it up, I'm the last one to get back on board. I don't want to leave the water, even though my biceps and calves burn from all the swimming I've done. It's a good ache—a physical reminder that I am alive and well, even if it doesn't feel like it at the moment.

Our guide tries again to engage with me on the way back in.

"Want to steer the boat?" he asks, all lopsided grin and boyish charm.

I'll bet that works really well for him. He's probably pulled dozens of tourists with that same exact line. I'm not in danger of falling for him, though, so I shrug and stand. "Sure, why not?"

Because I'll probably never get another chance to steer a boat through the crystal clear turquoise waters surrounding Saint Thomas, so I might as well go for it.

"You're a natural," he says, sidling up behind me, a little too close. "Do you have plans la—"

"Not interested," I say quickly, mildly, like I don't mind at all that he's asked, but I'm not willing to go down that road even a tiny bit.

He nods, unbothered. "Roger that. Would you mind letting me take over again, then?" he says, edging me away from the wheel. "You're steering us in circles, actually."

Chapter Nineteen

PHILLIP

On Sunday, the first day of this cruise, if you told me Vivienne was going to show up unannounced on Saint Thomas, I would have breathed a heavy sigh of relief. She's come to her senses. *Finally.* Vivienne and Phillip, together forever. We'd move back into my place in New York City. We would reunite our separated household items. I'd get my beloved air fryer back. Then we'd discuss how best to tell our friends and family that we were going to be mature and put the past behind us to begin anew, afresh, and better than ever.

Now, though?

Now?

It felt like I was having a heart attack when I read Vivienne's text last night.

It was simple and to the point.

Look out on the pier...

There she was, standing alongside her best friend. They saw me when I walked out onto the balcony, and they waved wildly.

I had no choice but to walk down to the gangway and retrieve them.

"What are you doing here?" was the first dumb thing out of my mouth, and I said it slightly accusatorially, as if I were annoyed to see Vivienne. As if she had no right to be here.

For a fleeting moment, shock and hurt flashed across her face, but then her expression cooled, tempered, eased as she tucked those ugly emotions deep under a mask of peaceful compliance. That's the thing about Vivienne. She's the most agreeable person I've ever met.

I'm not so far removed from our relationship that I don't remember the ease of having a partner like her. Nothing was ever important enough to warrant a real negative emotion. Crying? Screaming? Absolutely not. That was uncouth, simply not done.

I never had to worry if she'd be in a bad mood when I got home from work late or if she'd be annoyed when I wanted to get Italian takeout for the second time in one week. Whatever I wanted was what she wanted. I'd tried to bring up her military-like compliance with her once, gently, of course. How do you look someone squarely in the eye and ask them why they have no backbone? Why she seemed so eager to mirror the likes and desires of the people around her rather than promote her own?

I see clearly now what was so appealing about her.

For a man who enjoys simplicity and control—*holy shit*, Vivienne is a veritable gold mine! I doubt I ever would have worked up the courage to leave her.

It was a shocking revelation to have, especially as I stared at her then, on the pier in Saint Thomas, in front of her friend.

"I came to congratulate you in person!" Vivienne said, coming forward to kiss me once on each cheek with practiced precision. Thank god she chose that route. Had she gone in to kiss me on the mouth, I'm not sure I would have been able to think quickly enough to turn away. My brain seemed to still not be firing on all cylinders, not since Casey left my suite, oh . . . all of fifteen minutes before.

Talk about whiplash.

I frowned as Vivienne stepped back. "You could have just called and saved yourself the trip. You know they have these newfangled things called telephones."

She giggled and looked to her friend, Mira—the carbon copy of her in every way. In fact, in the early days of dating, I referred to her in my head as Vivienne Junior, and it stuck. It's eerie, actually, how similarly they dress and act. Both with their prim smiles and perfect postures, the same designer handbags slung over their shoulders. Matching Cartier watches. Chanel glasses perched on top of their shiny jet-black hair.

"Well, I thought this would be much better!" Vivienne added with a chipper shimmy to her shoulders. "I *really* wanted to show you how much I care."

I blinked and stared at her, wondering if I'd missed something.

Had there been a reconciliatory phone call I'd forgotten about? An email? *Fax?*

"Can we speak somewhere? Private?" she asked with a timid smile. She always was so good at seeming innocent, though I guess it's really no act. She's lived in a privileged bubble her whole life. "That is, *after* you find us a little cabin to stay in. Nothing big. I know it's a huge imposition to have us on board, and you're probably fully booked."

I blinked at her, truly dumbfounded. She expected me to find her a place to stay on board *Aurelia*? She was planning to *stay*?

I realized then that they also had accompanying luggage at their feet.

I took a step back. "Let's—let's go get a drink, and we can talk."

It felt like a good intermediary step. I couldn't just send her packing. She came all the way here—I had to at least humor her for a little while. She deserved that much.

"A drink, yes. We've been traveling all day. Oh, and I'd love a tour as well! I've never seen *Aurelia* in person! I'm *so* excited. I remember seeing the blueprints and sketches when I'd peer over your shoulder while you were working," she said with a sentimental smile.

I didn't share the same warm feelings. I was still in crisis-management mode. I grabbed their bags, and we headed back to the gangway where a crew member immediately ran forward to take their bags from me.

"Should I put them in your room, sir?"

God, no.

"Have them sent to the library, please. We'll be in there for the time being, and I'd hate for them to lose their luggage."

"Right away, sir."

In the end, I placated Vivienne and Mira with a quick tour of the ship, followed by exactly one drink in the library. I steered clear of any personal topics and tried to pry out information about how long they planned to stay and the motives behind their visit, but they were annoyingly elusive.

"We really don't have any open suites or cabins," I told them. "Not unless you want to bunk with the crew."

Vivienne laughed. "Oh, we won't be picky. I promise, any room will do. Put us with the crew, for all we care."

"*Viv—*" Mira cut in, clearly not in agreement on this.

Vivienne just shook her head. "It was slightly rude of us to show up here like this, unannounced. I can't demand the best room on the ship, now can I? Though of course that room is already taken. I'm sure it's yours, isn't it?"

Her eyes twinkled with mischief, and I reached for my drink and downed another sip. This whole thing felt wrong.

Like I was cheating somehow.

Casey and I . . . god, we were complicated.

I couldn't label us or dare to delve into my desire for her, not while I feigned polite conversation, but I knew I needed to consider her feelings here. I never would have started something with her if I'd known my ex-girlfriend was about to surprise me with an impromptu visit. I wasn't trying to play anyone here.

During my silence, Mira stood to excuse herself. "Ladies' room?" she asked.

"Down the hall on the left." I stood. "Here, I can show you."

"No need!" She held up her hand, looking pointedly at Vivienne as if this was all some preplanned routine they'd choreographed. Then she whisked out of the room, and I had a feeling she'd be gone a strategically long time.

Great.

"Vivienne," I said, my voice taking on a stern edge. "I'd like you to be honest with me now. Say whatever it is and—"

Vivienne stood suddenly and started to peruse the library, inspecting the books and all the little artifacts we'd amassed for the dark walnut shelves. There are more than enough interesting things in here to keep a person occupied for the entire duration of their cruise. It's probably my favorite room on the ship.

"Oh, Phillip. It's wonderful, all of it. What an achievement."

She almost looked wistful when she glanced over her shoulder at me.

Even with everything else going on, it felt good to hear her say it. She'd been by my side while I dreamed up this ship—it only feels right that she should get to experience it now.

"I'm glad you like it."

"*More* than like it." She turned fully and looked down at her wineglass, running her finger over the rim before glancing up again with a troubled expression in her dark-brown eyes. "I do feel like an idiot, you know. Dropping you the way I did."

I cleared my throat. "Viv—"

"No." She shook her head. "It took a lot of courage to come down here and face you. Mira's had to listen to me go over this speech a million and one times, and it's only fair that you should hear me out."

This was extremely assertive coming from Vivienne, so I nodded and waved for her to continue, giving her the floor out of respect for the time we'd shared together.

"I've missed you so much this last month. More than I thought possible."

She paused here, I think, to give me a moment to share the same sentiment, so when I stayed quiet, her brows tugged together in slight frustration. Only for an instant, though. Always, *always*, she goes back to her natural state: a placating Pollyanna.

"It's so lonely without you. It's only right that I should admit to you now . . . there was a man, at work." When I sat up a little straighter, she hastened to get out her next words. "Just a friend, nothing more. Though I will say, a part of me had thought of what it would be like if we were to develop romantic feelings for one another."

I could barely believe it. Vivienne thinking about *cheating*? It was as far fetched as anything I'd ever heard. So unlike her that I couldn't even feel jealousy, only astonishment.

"After things ended between us," she went on, "I sought him out and let it be known that I was single. He asked me out on a date; I accepted, and well . . ." She shivered thinking back on it. "I absolutely hated it. He was so forward, so absolutely brazen. He really thought we were going to"—she lowers her voice—"*have sex* after only going on a handful of dates!"

I had to tamp down a laugh, as if I had a tickle in my throat.

I didn't realize we were still playing the chastity game. Vivienne was hardly a virgin, though now I recall her being slightly prudish. To each their own, but I just don't think it's all that crazy for grown adults to have consensual sex. It's hardly something to clutch your chest about.

"Why not try it?" I asked casually, both because I wanted to see if maybe I could ease her suffering and because I couldn't help the urge to rattle her a little.

Her eyes widened. "*Sex with a veritable stranger?*" she hissed with disgust like I'd just told her to lick a New York City subway turnstile during rush hour.

I couldn't help it; I thought of Casey. I missed her with a force that made me feel sick. I could imagine her face as she listened to this conversation, a private smile fighting to break free on her lips.

"It could be fun," I said with a shrug.

Vivienne shook her head adamantly. "No, absolutely not."

"Okay," I said, rubbing the back of my neck. "So then what happened?"

Her spine straightened again, her pedigree showing in her tone and stance. "Well, I came to my senses, of course. I realized what you and I had, and I couldn't *believe* I'd just walked away from it willingly. I thought maybe I wanted a little something more. Oh, some flowery romance or something, but let me tell you." She waved her hand like her words were a nuisance, and her voice grew haughtier than ever. "It's a nightmare out there. These men have absolutely no respect!"

"Right."

My casual tone caught her off guard. Maybe she was expecting a little more sympathy, but so far, I hadn't heard anything worth sympathizing with. If anything, I was grateful for this moment. Real, honest closure was within our grasp.

It's so simple to see that our positions have reversed. Vivienne broke things off with me because she had the courage to try for something *more*, and in the process, she got hurt. Now suddenly, our old relationship—as comfortable, easy, and bland as it was—seems compelling because it's familiar and safe. But now *I've* found Casey, and I know what real passion feels like, and I'm not willing to settle anymore. Safe is no longer enough.

"Just because this guy didn't work out, don't give up on finding someone, Vivienne."

My solution didn't please her. She frowned. "Why would I go out searching when the man I want is sitting right in front of me."

I tilted my head, holding her gaze as I spoke the truth out loud to her for the first time. "Come on. You know we weren't good together. Not in the long run."

She reared back, her eyes widening in surprise.

"There were happy times," she insisted.

"Of course there were. I care for you; I do, Viv, but . . ."

My voice trailed off, and she nodded. I watched her swallow and look away, composing herself as best as possible. "It's not enough, is it?"

"We were so perfectly *perfect* together, but no, that's not enough."

She chuckled and turned back to me. I could see the emotion swimming in her eyes then, the tears about to fall. She understood that I was doing the hard thing here, forcing us both out of our comfort zones.

"It's scary, isn't it? Trying for something else? Going out on a limb . . ." Her voice was barely above a whisper.

I puffed out a breath. "It's *terrifying*."

She walked toward me then, taking my free hand and squeezing it, rubbing her thumb along my knuckles. Then she leaned down, preparing to say one last thing. "Promise me we'll stay in touch. I'll always be rooting for you—"

"Oh! Sorry." The accented words came from the hallway.

I turned to see Casey's friend, Sienna, standing in the library's doorway alongside Javier, one of the photographers we brought on for the cruise. They stood hand in hand, pressed close together, which wasn't all that surprising. Though they were technically here for work purposes, there had been plenty of time to mix and mingle; just ask Casey and me . . .

"We thought no one would be here," Sienna added just before she took in the full tableau she'd stumbled upon: Vivienne damn near sandwiched between my legs. My hand in hers. Her head bent toward me.

Sienna's eyes darkened, and her lips flattened into a thin angry line. When she spoke again, her voice was biting. "We didn't mean to *interrupt*."

Then she turned and started to pull Javier behind her. She only made it a few steps before shaking her head and spinning back around, a mock-friendly smile pinned in place. "Oh, actually, Phillip. I'm glad I bumped into you. I meant to ask, have you seen Casey tonight? It's only . . . I haven't been able to find her, and you two have just been *so* inseparable this cruise. I figured you would know where she's been . . ."

She anticipated that this bomb would create real carnage. Vivienne would gasp in outrage; I'd have to console her with lies and promises. *I don't know what she's talking about, babe!* But I don't want my hand in Vivienne's. I'd been trying to work out how to free myself without hurting her feelings. Vivienne's grip slackened, and I withdrew my hand before replying mildly, "I was just with her. She left a bit abruptly, though. If you see her, tell her I ordered her a milkshake."

Slowly, Sienna's anger shifted. Her lips parted; her brow furrowed. She looked almost disappointed by the lack of drama her comment had elicited.

"Right" was all she said before she looked at Javier and then turned to lead him back out into the hall.

Vivienne took a careful step away from me, her hands clasping together in front of her hips. She didn't look pissed—Vivienne never would—but her eyes were more guarded now.

"Who's Casey?"

Chapter Twenty
CASEY

"I saw him with Vivienne last night."

I don't look at Sienna because I'm worried what my face might reveal. She and I are standing together on the bow for sunset cocktails. I'm wearing a pale-pink dress that almost blends in with the sky over the horizon. My hair is combed back and neatly twisted at the base of my neck. I picked up even more color when I was out snorkeling today, so I didn't need to apply any foundation before I left my suite, just some blush, bronze eye shadow, a few swipes of mascara, and my favorite berry-colored lipstick. It's odd how good I look on the outside when inside, I feel worse now than ever. I think if Sienna hadn't insisted I come out here with her, I would have stayed back in my suite.

The numbness from earlier is starting to wear off, especially now with Sienna's new comment. I managed to somehow put Phillip and Vivienne out of my mind most of the day while I was out on the excursion. I wish so badly I could keep it that way. Unfortunately, I can't help but ask her for details, even though I know they'll hurt to hear. "Did you? Where?"

"They were alone together in the library. She was all over him!" she says with disgust. "I mean . . . they weren't kissing or anything, but it looked like they might have been headed in that direction if I hadn't stumbled upon them, you know? I really think he thought he was going to get away with it! Having you and her. You'd be really proud of me. I did this whole Oh-have-you-seen-Casey spiel just to get under his skin."

My eyes widen, and I finally turn to her. "Sienna, *you didn't.*"

She grins, as beautiful as ever in her pale-green dress that almost perfectly matches her eyes. "*Absolutely*, I did! You thought I was just going to let him get away with that? Stringing you along while he plays two women?"

It hurts to hear her perspective on things. Is that really what he's been doing? It didn't feel that way. He and Vivienne aren't together—at least that's what he told me, and despite all the mounting evidence to the contrary, I'm not ready to throw him under the bus. I hate how that looks. It's a weak stance to want to support him right now. If I were a third party looking in, like Sienna, I'd be shouting at myself to see reason too. *He's a rich powerful man. OF COURSE he was playing you, girl!*

"I can't believe you said that. I'm sure he looked appalled. And Vivienne, god, what did she think?"

"Who cares about Vivienne!"

I bristle at her steely tone. "She's not the bad guy in all of this."

She shrugs and gives a little apathetic eye roll. "Fine. Whatever. She's not the bad guy, but I also don't want to be in her corner. I care about your feelings, and whether you are willing to admit it or not, you clearly have been involved intimately with Phillip the entire time we've been on this cruise. How many times have you slept together?"

I swallow and shrug, looking down. "It doesn't matter."

"So more than once."

"It really doesn't matter."

"Oh my god, more than twice, then. Casey, I'm sorry."

It's those words "I'm sorry" said in that sympathetic, caring tone that finally chisel away the last of my resolve. When I look back up at her with a tight smile, tears rim my bottom lashes. "It's fine, Sienna. Really. You're making it into a bigger deal than it is. Now tell me, what happened after you said that comment to them, which, by the way, I *don't* condone. I'm sure it made the situation worse than it has to be."

She frowns, clearly irritated that I'm not as worked up about Phillip as she is. "I'm sorry if I put my foot in my mouth. I just . . . It's not right, Casey."

I nudge her shoulder with mine and offer her a timid smile. "It's all right. You were just trying to be a good friend. You are one, you know? I can't believe I've only known you a week and already you're going to bat for me against Phillip Woodmont, of all people."

"You're the one who started a fling with him! I still can't believe it. Did he tell you he was single?"

It's hard for me to swallow past the emotions tightening my throat. "Yes."

"Damn. Well, I'm not saying I know what was going on between them, only that it didn't look good. They were alone in the library. I mean, she came all the way here to see him. Do you think he invited her?"

"No. Tyson mentioned it to me this morning. Apparently, it was a big surprise."

Sienna hums like she doesn't like the sound of that. Then her eyes widen upon seeing something behind me. "Oh god, incoming."

I recognize Phillip's presence even before I turn around. The shift in the air, the subtle notes of his cologne, the tingles that race down my spine.

I'm shaking by the time he finally speaks. "Casey, can I have a moment?"

"Don't bother," Sienna says for me as she steps toward him. "I told her I saw you with Vivienne last night. You must know Casey could do much better than the likes of you. You should *see* how many men flirt with her on a daily basis. Anyone would be lucky to have her!"

I squeeze my eyes closed and shake my head in warning. "Sienna—"

"*What?* It's the truth. You're a total catch, and he should bloody well know it."

"I appreciate the intel." There's humor in Phillip's voice when he speaks. Thank god for that. I think Sienna has slightly forgotten her manners. Phillip is the man in charge on this ship. It's plausible for him to have the two of us removed from *Aurelia* for causing trouble.

Phillip's hand gently touches my bare shoulder. "Casey?"

I open my eyes to see Sienna looking at me, a silent question in her gaze. *Do you want me to stay?*

I shake my head, and she sighs, likely disappointed that I'm not about to turn around and let Phillip have it. She'd love a good righteous showdown, but I don't have the energy. I'm just trying to keep it together as best as possible.

When Sienna slinks away, I turn to face Phillip.

Oof.

There it is.

The punch to the gut I was expecting. Looking at him, it's like I've been plugged back into the mainframe. All the feelings that have been peculiarly absent all day come rushing in all at once so forcefully that I'm surprised I remain standing.

The golden hour looks so good on him.

If Phillip ever gets married, he should arrange the ceremony for this exact time so that his lucky bride can stand across from him and get the pleasure of looking at him just like this, bathed in all the sunset hues.

He's wearing a navy blue suit paired with a light-blue shirt, hydrangea blue to be exact. It takes some courage to raise my gaze up his neck and jaw, over those carved cheekbones, to finally meet his eyes.

Oh, Phillip. What have you done? Making me fall like this . . .

"Hi," I say gently.

He tips his head and studies me, almost like it hurts to look at me. "Did Sienna tell you I ordered you a milkshake last night? Before you left . . ."

I chuckle and shake my head. "No, she didn't. She did mention the other stuff, though . . . the conversation in the library." Suddenly, the question occurs to me, and I ask, "Is Vivienne here?"

I want to steel myself if she's about to waltz over here and perform some public claiming of her man. I can just picture it now—her pressed against him, her hand sliding around his shoulder, squeezing with possession as she aims a sugary smile my way.

Panic sets in just as Phillip replies, "No. Vivienne and her friend are staying in a hotel, I think. I'm not sure, exactly."

"Oh."

"Are you surprised?"

"Yes. I guess so. I thought . . ." I shake my head, letting my sentence dwindle. I don't want to make assumptions about his relationship, given how little I know about it, so I keep it simple. "I thought she was here visiting. I assumed she'd be by your side tonight."

He nods. "Yes, I think she assumed that as well." My brows shoot up, and he continues, "She came here with the goal of repairing our relationship."

"Is that what you want?" I ask hurriedly, needing to know.

Break my heart quickly, Phillip. Don't stretch this out into some painful confession about how you really love her, and you didn't mean for things to get so out of hand with us. Vivienne is your real future, the woman of your dreams.

God, I could throw up.

"No."

I blink and inhale slowly, savoring that word before I respond with a cool tone. "It must have been difficult, then, having that conversation. I'll be honest, Sienna did mention that you two looked close last night in the library, that maybe—"

"Nothing happened between Vivienne and me. She was honest with me. She took my hand in a particularly vulnerable moment, and Sienna saw that. We didn't kiss. Or do anything for that matter."

I believe him because Phillip has never given me a reason not to trust him. He's been honest to a fault, in fact.

"I'm sorry things didn't work out for you."

And wildly enough, I mean those words.

I hold no assumptions about what Phillip and I are to one another, but I do get the sense that he and Vivienne were a serious thing for quite some time. If she came all the way here to share her feelings with him, well . . . I wonder if things would be different if I weren't standing in the way. I can't help but ask.

"It's not . . . to say . . . you aren't letting me stand in the way of you two, are you? Because you and I—" I shake my head, feeling my throat start to tighten with emotion. I have to force out my next words, as painful as they are. "Obviously this isn't a serious thing."

His brow furrows, and I rush on, scared that this conviction will burn away before I've finished saying what I need to say. "You're not beholden to me. It would be perfectly fine for you to go back with Vivienne. God, Tyson told me you had a ring picked out and everything! You were really serious about her, Phillip."

"I was," he confirms with a hard set to his jaw.

"And now?" I ask, holding my breath.

"Things have changed."

"Because of me?" I ask shakily.

Is it presumptuous to ask that? Oh well.

"In part, yes. I won't deny that."

Oh god. I've really messed up here. "You didn't cheat on her. Right? You told me you two were broken up. That's what I saw online as well. So you could come clean to her, admit you had a fling—meaningless and all that—and I'm sure she'd—"

"You're not listening." I jolt at his tone. "You changed things, Casey."

I gulp. "I'm sorry."

He laughs. *Laughs*! "You're apologizing?"

"Yes?" I say with a wince.

He sighs and turns so he can lean down and prop his elbows on the railing. He tugs his hands through his hair and then asks, point blank, "Where did you see this going?"

What a complicated question. Does he want to know where I saw us going at the start or where I hoped it could go if things were different . . . less complicated.

He doesn't know the half of it. I've still not been honest with him about my tenuous position with *Bon Voyage*, the absolute mess of my life.

"Nowhere, right? That's what we agreed."

We said it over and over again. We kept tight parameters on this relationship, and while, yes, the lines kept getting pushed little by little to accommodate our growing feelings, we cannot let this get so carried away that we've lost sight of how little this makes sense.

Phillip and me? Actually together? *In what world?*

"Right," he says stiffly.

"Is that . . . I thought we were on the same page, Phillip."

"We are."

He won't look at me, and it leads me to believe that perhaps, *maybe*, Phillip is feeling an ounce of what I'm feeling, this unexpected wild yearning, but I can't let him make this mistake. I won't be the one to lead him astray from a perfectly prearranged future. "If you walked away from Vivienne for me, please don't. Fix it. She's the woman for you. The woman you deserve to be with."

I don't know this, of course, since I've never met her, but I have my suspicions. The night I was rewriting my article about Phillip, I looked at photos of Phillip and Vivienne together online. Not the healthiest pastime by any means, but I was curious, and the internet proved fruitful.

It was relatively easy to find tidbits of information about Vivienne. She has a high-up job at Yves Saint Laurent. Her parents own a real estate empire. She went to the best schools and has all the right connections, and she's even received a humanitarian award from the National Charity League for her work with their organization. So she gives back! She's literally a saint! I mean, I cannot stack up against her in this life, or *any* life, for that matter. It's laughable.

"She would take you back . . . I'm sure."

"You're not understanding, Casey." He turns his head, staring at me, *showing* me if only I'd stop being so dumb. "She's not who I want."

I take a step back.

"No."

I say it firmly. Absolutely not.

He's not going to do this. Not going to admit he has feelings for me!

He is not going to make this harder by feeding me hope where there is none.

"You're wrong about your feelings for me. It's the sunset and the booze and this dress." I sweep my hand down my figure. "I don't normally wear pretty pink dresses while sipping mai tais on a fancy cruise ship! I'm the girl living out of dingy hotels, remember? The one with *no home*? I wear T-shirts and sweatpants *on the daily*. Sometimes I don't shower for three days, and I don't even feel bad about it! I am *not* someone you should like, Phillip Woodmont! Go to Vivienne. *Marry Vivienne.* Produce fancy, well-educated offspring. Forget. About. Me."

After this, I turn on my heel and hurriedly walk away before I can see his reaction to my words. I'm really good at this, I've found—leaving when the going gets tough is just so satisfying. Whoever said you have to stay and duke it out during moments of crisis was dead wrong. You can actually do whatever you want, and right now it feels so good to scurry back down to my suite—my one sanctuary on this godforsaken boat. I slam the door behind me; then I lock it for good measure, as if Phillip's going to be running after me. Laughable. After that diatribe, the man is probably thanking his lucky stars that things didn't go any further with us.

I look down at my half-empty mai tai and consider pouring it down the drain. Instead, I toss it back, swallowing all that sweet liquor down in one go. After, I stomp straight to my laptop and fling it open.

I'm ripping off Band-Aids left and right, might as well do one more . . .

I'm the villain in the movie who's finally completely unhinged. The Joker in that little nurse's outfit, about to light this place up.

There are emails waiting for me. Of course there are. I haven't so much as touched this computer since yesterday morning.

I open the latest one from Gwen's assistant. Sent only an hour ago. Never mind that it's a Saturday night. These people think work should take precedence, always.

> Hi Casey!
>
> Hope you're living it up in the Bahamas! Soo jealous. Any update on those assignments Gwen forwarded to you on Friday? We were hoping to have Mark's Lancaster story by this afternoon and I don't see it in my email? Can you send it again in case it bounced back for some reason? I've CC'd Gwen here for your convenience.

Without a moment's hesitation, I reply with one word.

> No.

A moment later, my phone rings. It startles me. My phone hasn't rung once since I've been on board *Aurelia*, both because the cell service is pretty spotty and because who needs to call me? Steve the tax man? He already got the house; he doesn't need anything else from me at this point.

The phone number belongs to none other than my boss, Gwen Levis.

I answer it with a cool and cheery, "Hello, Gwen!"

"Casey, hey," she says, sounding cheerful herself. "Sorry to call you on a Saturday evening. Not usually our style here, but we're in a pinch. Our intern quit earlier, actually. *So unprofessional.* Don't get me started. Anyway, we really need those assignments completed. Especially Mark's."

I lean back in my chair, reveling in the calm that's suddenly washed over me. For so long, I've cared so much about this job. In the past, I would have been stammering over every word if Gwen Levis deigned to call me. I don't think we've ever, *even once*, spoken on the phone before now. I'm not going to lie; it feels really good to have her coming to me for something. I think I'll revel in it for a moment.

"Oh *no*, sorry to hear you all are struggling."

Read, *No, I'm not.*

"Right. I saw your email. Maybe you accidentally sent it?"

"No." I chuckle. "I meant that email."

She doesn't say anything for a moment. Then asks, "What did you mean by 'no'? You haven't had time to get around to reviewing things? That's fine, but we need Mark's story to run by Tuesday, so how about you tackle it first thing—"

"No."

I'm really enjoying using that word as a whole sentence.

Gwen clears her throat. "Casey. If this is about those emails you sent yesterday, I said I'd think about giving you a raise, okay?" Her voice is high and tight now, like she's *this* close to losing it. "I can probably talk them into a two percent bump, maybe three percent, so let's just move forward and—"

Two percent? Two *fucking percent?*

Holy shit. She really doesn't get it. She never will.

I chuckle because this is actually pretty funny. "Sorry, you don't understand, Gwen. The answer is no; I won't be doing those assignments."

"Excuse me?"

She cannot comprehend this change in me. She only knows me as dutiful, quiet Casey. *Give Casey any assignment, and she'll do it. The grunt work? The boring stuff we can't even talk an intern into taking on? Casey will do it! Casey doesn't care. She's just glad to be here.*

It's pathetic, really, what I was willing to do just to say I worked at a publication like *Bon Voyage*. I can't believe I never saw it before now. The injustice of it all.

"Gwen, I quit. Active immediately."

"*What*? You can't quit," she shrieks so loudly that I have to hold the phone away from my ear. "Do you think this magazine is a *joke*? People are dying to fill your shoes. *Dying*."

"I thought you said the intern also quit today . . ."

"*You little brat*," she hisses through clenched teeth. "You listen here. You should be grateful for the job I gave you. You think you're going to go out and make it big? *Where*? I won't let you go to one of our competitors."

This is just a less cliché way of saying *You'll never work in this town again*, and I'm slightly annoyed she didn't just stick with the original.

She laughs shrilly. "After pulling this shit? You can kiss any sort of reference letter goodbye."

"Noted."

My calm response only rankles her more.

I know she wants to do more to me, but she really can't. The thing is, Gwen *barely* knows me. Like right now, if I asked her my last name, she'd go, *Uh, uh, uh—Hanes?* So it's not like she can dig deep into some arsenal of personal information to really take aim at me. I suppose she could poke fun at me for being the fact-check girl for as many years as I stuck it out, but like, okay, *ha ha ha!* I believed you when you hired me and told me I'd be able to work my way up in the company. What a dumbass, right?

She can't punish me like she wants. This isn't high school, and she's not the principal. There's no detention or suspension. There's not even any company property she can seize in a final fit of rage. My laptop is my own. I guess I might have left some knickknacks in my cubicle in New York. Enjoy my mostly dried up highlighters and bent-up Post-it Notes, Gwen . . .

"You want to quit? Fine. Good luck, Casey. *You'll need it*."

Then she hangs up, but not in that fun way where you can hear the receiver slam down on the other end of the line. How unsatisfying to have to just jab that little red *X*. Oh well.

There. I've done it.

I've left my dead-end job, freed myself from my heavy fact-checking shackles.

Only . . . now what?

Chapter Twenty-One
CASEY

I cannot believe that it's my seventh night of this cruise, and I'm only *now* finding out that the cool kids have been partying late into the night at La Dame this whole time! Apparently after their fancy French dinners, the place turns into a little nightclub. *Excuse me?* Left out much! (Never mind that I've been otherwise occupied, it still stings.)

Javier was the one to tell Sienna about it.

She let me in on the secret when she found me sitting in my desk chair, staring aimlessly at the wall. I told her about quitting *Bon Voyage*.

"*Yes*! Wonderful. About time, but"—she swirled her finger around my desk chair—"*this* is not what we're doing. We need to *celebrate*!"

I'm here in La Dame with Sienna now. It's the perfect setting for a bunch of rowdy folks because it's a compact restaurant with tons of booths and sexy low lighting. Around thirty or forty people are all clustered together while the DJ from the pool blares some of the best music of my life.

It really feels like the gang's all here. Bella, Jenna, and Avery are draped over a few of the *Nat Geo* guys. No shocker there. A few veterans from the *New Yorker* are breaking it down on the dance floor. A waiter, who's undone most of the buttons on his La Dame uniform to reveal a seriously buff chest that could fit right in with the *Magic Mike* cast, is passing around a tray of shots like a badass, and I take one gladly before downing it in one go.

"I think I'm drunk!" I shout into Sienna's face.

She laughs. "You're definitely drunk!"

"Oh my god, I love this song!"

It's a club remix of Whitney Houston's "I Wanna Dance with Somebody."

"You already said that!"

"Cool! I have no recollection of that! Maybe I have amnesia!"

Sienna holds up my hand with its empty shot glass. "I think it's just the alcohol!"

"Okay!" Then my eyes widen like I have a brilliant plan. "I think we should get more of it!"

"I think we should find a chair!"

"No! You pulled me *out* of a chair, remember? Back in my suite. I'm a free woman, Sienna. You can't stop me!"

At this point, I think it seems like a perfect idea to climb on top of the nearest table and start singing along to the song. Does it take me two attempts to hoist myself up? Sure! Do I still get resounding cheers from the crowd once I turn and start shimmying my hips and singing to them? Ab-so-fucking-lutely!

And just as I finish the chorus, giving it everything I've got, I see Phillip near the front door of the restaurant, encircled in the light from the hallway. He's just walked in, hands in his suit pockets, brow furrowed. Our eyes lock, and I can't help a huge sappy smile from spreading across my face. I brace myself for more of that angry scowl, but he doesn't seem annoyed that I'm up here, potentially damaging one of the tables in his fancy restaurant. He watches me dancing with humor in his gaze. Then he points to me and then points to the ground. The gesture is obvious: *get down.*

Instead, I beckon with my fingers, trying to draw him closer in time to the beat.

He shakes his head.

Phillip!

Fine.

I'll just have to keep singing to him. And I do. Oh yes. That chorus is building again. *Can you feel it, Phillip? The music? That longing I keep running from?*

I shake my hips and lift my arms and feel the summer anthem like it's a part of me. My eyes squeeze closed, and I smile, wishing Phillip would come away from the door and admonish me. Is he getting annoyed now? Wanting to drag me out of here?

But when I open my eyes again, he's left his post. Alarmed, I find he's weaving through the crowd, getting to me faster than I thought possible. His gaze never wavers. It's like he's on the hunt.

He slides past Sienna and Javier and the two guys standing directly in front of my table. I didn't even realize they were there, but Phillip steps in front of them without even a passing glance.

Oh, hello there, blue eyes. Come to get me?

"You're going to hurt yourself," he yells over the music, but still, that smile plays on his lips. He's having to war with himself. Punish me or . . .

I shimmy all the way down, lowering myself on the table until we're at eye level, and then I lean in for a moment, singing, as our lips *almost* graze. Phillip's eyes darken with dangerous intent as I peel back and stand again, spinning around.

I'm grinning; of course I am. It feels so good to play this silly game with him, to just be reckless and free and feel all those emotions you're supposed to feel when you're young, before the responsibilities of life weigh you down so heavily that you can't even remember what it is to be carefree and silly. To make mistakes and revel in the consequences.

Phillip's hand reaches out and grips my ankle, and then it slides higher so that I gasp and whip around. He can't touch me in public, right? Surely, he won't.

We're talking about the world's most private man! I doubt he's the PDA type. I can't even imagine him holding hands with a woman in a public setting, but he's quickly disproving my theory. His hand reaches up to grip my thigh, and he tugs until I'm tipping down and falling forward, off balance. That's his intent, of course, because he's there, catching me around the hips and sliding me down the front of his body.

"I was dancing," I say with a pouty bottom lip.

He keeps me pinned against him, not saying a word.

I peer to the left to see curious stares aimed in our direction. My cheeks flush with color.

"People are watching us," I warn him as his eyes fall to my mouth.

And then ignoring my warning, he leans forward and kisses me.

I give in to that kiss like it's the easiest thing I've ever done. Easier even than falling into bed at the end of a long day, sliding into the warmest bubble bath ever concocted, picking up your absolute favorite book.

His tongue slides into my mouth, and I press against him, giving him everything that my sober mind is too scared to relinquish. *Take it*, I seem to say now. *Have everything.*

My hands reach around to grab his butt, and he laughs and breaks away.

"*Casey.*"

"What?" I'm not the least bit contrite. "You have a great butt."

He takes my wrists and pulls me off him, keeping ahold of my hands.

"You should know . . . the editor of *Bon Voyage* contacted my assistant, wanting you kicked off this ship. She said you quit today?"

"She can't have me kicked off! I'm in international waters. *Try and get me!*"

He laughs and shakes his head. "How drunk are you?"

"Very. Excellently drunk." The song changes. "Oh my god, *more Whitney*! Is this some kind of fantasy come to life?"

"Did you quit, Casey?"

My eyes widen with excitement. "Yes! And you know what? Should we have drunken sex? Like really good, shameless sex?"

"That seems like what we've already been having . . ."

My shoulders sag. "Oh, true. Hey, hey—remember when I gave you that blow job?"

His eyes pinch closed. I think he's trying not to laugh.

When he looks at me again, I see a flicker of frustration. I'm not surprised. It was bound to show up eventually.

"I can't figure you out. You're all over the place, Casey. Is it the alcohol? I don't understand why you blew me off earlier."

"Oh, it's really simple." I speak loudly so he can hear me over the music, and then I point between us as I continue. "We can't date each other! I'm a lost person with no real future plan for myself, and you're like really put together and great!"

Seems like simple math to me. Two plus two equals Casey and Phillip are destined to be star-crossed lovers. The equation only balances out to tragedy.

He reaches up to smooth his hand around my neck so his thumb can glide over my pulse point. *Ooh la la.* That's heavenly.

"You didn't even give me a chance to explain how I feel about you," he says sadly.

Panic seizes my chest, sobering me slightly. We can't go here. "It's better if we don't discuss it. Like, obviously I'm attracted to you, and you're attracted to me; I can see it. God, even now, you look at me like you want to eat me up."

He smirks. "I do."

My heart starts to race, but I try to laugh him off. "Jesus, Phillip. You're so intense."

His hand on my neck tightens infinitesimally. "I'm not usually this way."

I puff out a disbelieving breath. "*Yeah, right.*"

He comes closer, brushing his hips against mine. "You do this, Casey. You make me feel like I'm finally fucking waking up, you know? I'm seeing what it's supposed to be like."

"Like *what's* supposed—*oh my god.*"

I layer my hands over his mouth. "Don't say another word! Are you absolutely out of your *mind?* We are not doing that! We are not going to have great sex in fun tropical places and mistake it for falling in love. That's like cruise ship–fling rule number one. I'm shocked you don't know this."

When I trust that he's not going to continue down the same road he was headed, I slip my hand away from his mouth.

"Can we go talk somewhere?" he asks, nodding past the crowd and toward the doorway.

"Yeah, I'm starting to get a headache anyway."

There actually is a finite amount of time a human brain can listen to Whitney Houston blaring at full blast, and I've reached it. I'm more than happy to let Phillip drag me out of La Dame. On my way, I blow a kiss and shoot a wink at Sienna, who's dancing hot and heavy with Javier. I haven't had the chance to ask her how serious they are. Have they set tight parameters around their relationship like we have? (Also, are they failing as miserably at upholding those parameters as we are?)

The thought drifts away with a new immediate need.

"Water."

I've never been so thirsty in my life.

Phillip has my hand, and he knows where to go, even if I'm suddenly feeling drunker than ever. "I'll take you back to your suite."

He calls the elevator, then leads me inside, watching me beneath his black lashes so that eventually, I'm forced to ask, "What?"

He shakes his head.

"You're hopeless, Phillip Woodmont."

"And you're—"

"Drunk," I insert, trying to cut the tension. I feel like I have to keep us in check. He's certainly not going to!

"Tell me why you quit your job."

I stare ahead, ignoring his attention. Counting those little glowing numbers changing as we ascend decks. "I'd rather not."

"Fine. Tell me, at least, if that's why you were upset yesterday?"

Ugh! "Yes. Partly." I rush the words out, hoping to get this over with fast. Now, in my current state, I can't exactly remember why I didn't want to bring Phillip in on everything. Because it's messy and chaotic? Oh well. He's not under some assumption that I'm a perfect Vivienne type. That ship has *sailed*. "Also, I was sad because it's been a hard few weeks. Moving out of my grandmother's house and having to put her things in storage . . ." I shake my head, hoping to push past the fresh wave of sadness. "In some ways, I feel like I'm experiencing her death all over again. It's been harder than I realized it would be. *And do not* get me started on work. Gwen Levis can go screw herself, for all I care. My exit from *Bon Voyage* was not exactly amicable, and I refuse to apologize for it."

He squeezes my hand, trying to reassure me.

No!

We're not doing this.

I turn to him. "Enough of that. Now tell me, what are the chances that we're about to get it on once we get to my suite? Fifty fifty? Seventy thirty?"

He tips his head, smiling. "Zero. I'm stone-cold sober."

"*Such* a disappointment," I say once the elevator reaches my floor. "So then why are you coming up here with me?" I ask, leading him down the hallway.

Outside my door, I present my key card to him like I'm Vanna White; then he swipes it and we're in.

"Can I interest you in a drink?"

"I thought you needed water."

My eyes go wide. "Yes! Water."

I forgot about my thirst, but now it's come back with a vengeance. I practically run toward my minibar and fill up a crystal glass, guzzle it down, and then have another.

Once I'm done, I turn to Phillip so I can ask something I've been wondering about. "So you have no idea where Vivienne is? She left last night?"

He's still near the door. He's been taking in the suite while I was quenching my thirst. Now, he looks at me. "She's probably back home by now. I'm not sure. We haven't been in contact since our breakup, beyond a few awkward texts, and after last night, I doubt she'll be calling me anytime soon."

"Was she upset when you didn't take her back?"

I bet she was. My heart hurts just thinking of being in her position. I could never imagine breaking up with Phillip. If I were lucky enough to trick him into dating me, that man would have a ring on his finger so fast. We'd be down the aisle ASAP. I'd be so scared to lose him that I wouldn't want to take any chances. And she just . . . *left him*?

"She was surprised, I think, by it. I assume she thought it would go differently. Sienna didn't really help things."

I wince before looking at him. I'm relieved he doesn't look annoyed.

"I don't think I would have turned Vivienne down *and* rubbed it in her face that I've already moved on, but it's better this way. Now, no one is under any assumptions that the relationship will be restored."

"Hold on." I put my hand out like a police officer directing traffic. "What do you mean about the *moving on* part?"

"Sienna brought you up, and Vivienne was curious."

My eyes practically bug out of my head. I knew Sienna brought me up in front of Vivienne. But I didn't know Phillip spoke about me! That's different! "What did you tell her?"

I must know, but Phillip doesn't answer. He kicks off his shoes by the door—a gentleman—and then starts to peel out of his jacket.

My mind immediately goes to the gutter. My eyes are on a slow descent down to his crotch. "I thought you said we weren't getting it on. Have my chances improved?"

I think my dancing eyebrows will surely win him over, so I'm shocked when he still shakes his head. "Not tonight. Come sit down with me, will you?"

"Can I change into my pajamas first?"

"Yeah. Go."

By the time I walk back into the living room in a cute matching pajama set (the only one I own and only because I found it on sale at Target, stuffed in a clearance bin), Phillip's sitting on my couch. Because someone gave him the exact script on how to make me fall in love with him, he has poured me a fresh glass of water and dug around in the snacks near the minibar. There's an assortment of candy and chips laid out on the table for us to share. All kinds of junk that immediately has my mouth watering.

I sit down to peruse my bevy of options and go for candy first. Wild, considering everyone knows that the snack pattern goes salty, then sweet, salty, then sweet ad infinitum. It almost feels sacrilegious to do it the other way around. I pop a few M&M's in my mouth, then hand the bag to Phillip. Then I go for chips. We swap the M&M's for the chips, then vice versa. And it's somehow accomplished without a single word until we finish both bags.

Then we reach for our waters in sync, meet eyes, and laugh.

"You're something else," I chide him, and boy, does that phrase have a hundred meanings. It lets me say so much with so little, and Phillip gets it. He understands what I'm withholding out of fear, and he's not scared of the magnitude of it. He welcomes it.

After I set my glass down, I settle back against him. I'm sick of the distance between us, even if it was only a few inches.

I lean my head against his shoulder, and the back of his pointer finger eases along the slope of my shoulder, ostensibly so he can brush my hair back, but all I feel are a thousand sparks lighting me up from the inside. He makes me feel this much anguish with a single touch. It's heart wrenching to feel this strongly for someone I know will exist in my life as a sentence, not a chapter.

"I told Vivienne"—his finger stills—"that in some ways, *important* ways, I feel for you in seven days what I never felt for her in two years."

I squeeze my eyes closed against his confession.

He turns me so we're chest to chest, my legs draped over his, as if he's trying to shield me. I bury my face against his chest, inhaling his scent, wishing he didn't feel like home. I haven't known that feeling in so long, not since my last big bear hug from my grandmother. To me, peace is a sensation more dangerous than lust.

"I didn't tell her that to belittle our relationship," Phillip continues, "or try to rewrite history. Vivienne was a wonderful partner and a good friend. I'd never want to hurt her, but I needed to explain to her why I was sticking to our breakup. I needed her to know the truth so that it'd be easier for her to walk away." He makes me look at him. "You have to understand the way we operated. You know my personality. Now imagine my dream partner."

I sit up (literally rising to the challenge) and smile as I tick personality traits off my fingers. "Easygoing, slow to anger, intelligent . . . hmm, you love being in charge, so I'd bet she needs to be deferential too."

He chuckles. "You just described Vivienne to a *T*."

A laugh bursts out of me. "And you're here with *me*? Oh my god, quick." I wave my hand frantically. "Get your phone and call her up right now because I will never, not in a million years, be that to you. Wait. *God.* I bet she's one of those women who would also gladly cook you dinner every night wearing high heels and a nightie. *Phillip!* I don't even own a nightie!"

During my rambling, he started toying with my hair, twisting the strands around his fingers, studying them as if he were musing over something. Now, he throws his head back and laughs, and I want to crawl into him and never leave.

Great, Casey.

That's a healthy thought.

I poke at him to get him to stop laughing, and he sobers, his features settling into something serious. I know he's about to devastate me one way or another. I brace myself as he begins. "I know this is just a fling, and it's crazy to think I can have you forever. You've made that perfectly clear. But I keep trying to stay away from you so we can pump the brakes and slow down, and instead, I find myself racing back to you as fast as I can each time we're apart. It's futile."

I squeeze my eyes closed and fall against his chest again.

"We're hopeless."

"Hopeless," he confirms.

"The cruise only lasts two more days," I say helpfully. "What if we just give in totally, like really play at this being a real relationship, and then at the end of the cruise when it's my time to depart the ship, I'll be on my way, and you will not, under any circumstances, come after me. It'll be a clean break. Something nice to look back on. Not something we overanalyze and stretch and ruin."

"Okay," he says, sounding relieved by the option.

It seems like the only way forward. There's no sense in trying to keep pulling ourselves apart while we're both still on board *Aurelia*. It's just going to be impossible. So we give in; we stop resisting our connection for the time being, and we revel in it. Then after . . . I don't know. We put a continent's worth of distance between us and hope for the best!

"Also, a basic ground rule," I start to add, and he nods for me to continue. "I'm not going to ask you what you're doing or where you're going after the cruise, and you won't ask me either. We don't exist to each other after this, okay?"

He cups my cheek, leaning down to kiss me.

"Okay."

Chapter Twenty-Two

CASEY

So apparently there's a difference between being on board *Aurelia* as an employee of *Bon Voyage* and being on board *Aurelia* as Phillip's invited guest. I thought I was already living in the lap of luxury, but the next morning when I wake up in my suite, utterly hungover, lamenting the idea of ever having to get up, I smell . . . breakfast.

I sit up and sniff, confused.

Out in the living room, someone has delivered (a) a dining table that wasn't there before, (b) four chairs to go around it, (c) a tablecloth, and (d) a dining table's worth of food for me—everything from croissants and *pain au chocolat* to bacon and sausage and three types of eggs. I lift the lids and find everything is still warm. I break off a bite of one of the croissants, and it practically melts in my mouth. I utter "oh my gawwwwd" while forcing more into my gullet as fast as possible.

In the center of the table, there's a floral arrangement with flowers I've never seen in my little corner of White Plains, New York, alongside a beautiful card with a gold leaf border and looping black cursive.

Phillip *would* have perfect handwriting . . .

I have a little work to get done this morning, but meet me at the pool around lunchtime.—P

PS I hope you enjoy your breakfast. If I've left something off, phone your butler, and he'll bring it up.

Right, of course. I'll just phone my butler.

Everyone, duh, if you need anything, *just phone your butlers!*

What is he even playing at? Are there people who would be dissatisfied with this insane breakfast spread? It's too much for me to eat all by myself; I have to share it.

I go knocking on Sienna's door, and Javier opens it.

"*Wah!*" I lift my hands. "You're not wearing any clothes!"

"A towel," he says, unfazed.

"A *hand* towel, from the looks of it." I peer through my parted fingers to see him standing there with his arms crossed, completely unbothered by his nakedness. "I can practically see your—*your*—"

"Casey . . . ," Sienna croaks, walking toward me with her head in her hands. "You'd better be over here for a bloody good reason, because my head is spinning after last night, and there's nothing I want more in the entire world than some tea and toast."

I drop my hands to my hips. "I have an entire *spread* in my suite, courtesy of Phillip. Tea included. I came over to invite you two to share it with me—and then I got distracted by Javier in this loincloth."

Her lips curl as she takes him in, pride shining in her eyes. "Yes, he *is* rather distracting . . . Javier, go change and meet us over in her suite. Casey, lead the way to that tea. I'm dying here."

"Hot and heavy stuff happening with you two, huh?" I ask once we're alone in my suite.

She waves away my statement. "Javier is merely someone to help me pass the time. Nothing serious. My god, look at all this! Oh, Twinings!" She says running toward the table where there's a tin of assorted teabags waiting for her. "Oh, I could cry."

"You two seemed serious last night in the club, dancing all over each other," I point out, going in for some bacon now that I've satisfied my initial carb craving.

She chuckles as she goes about making her cup of tea. "Oh, that?" Again, she's downplaying it. "It's nothing. Just . . . he's fun. That's all. What about you and Phillip, huh?"

"Oh. 'It's nothing. Just, he's fun.'" I throw her words back at her, and she sighs.

"We're both doomed then."

"Utterly."

She holds up a plate filled with pastries. "Here, have a Danish. It looks delicious, and maybe it'll distract us from these men."

All in all, we have a good morning. Javier has to jet off and work for a little while, but Sienna and I hit the gym and work out after breakfast. Then we slip down to the spa to get our nails done. I go to pay them (unsure of my place on board this ship), and the lady behind the counter chuckles at me!

"Mr. Woodmont would have my job if I accepted your payment, Ms. Hughes," she teases.

What in the world! How does she know? Did he send an all-staff email to them or something? Probably!

After Sienna and I part ways, it takes me a long time to figure out exactly what I want to wear to the pool. I have three bathing suits to choose from. I decide on the lavender one, which pairs nicely with a floral-patterned pareu that I knot at my waist. I braid my hair loosely enough that a few pieces slip free and frame my face. I draw the line at wearing wedges or heels to the pool deck. I will not break my ankle for the benefit of slightly elongated legs. Strappy sandals will have to do.

I reach for my laptop and phone to stow them in my pool bag, but on second thought, I leave them both behind instead. While it's tempting to immediately jump into strategizing about my future prospects, I want to take the next two days to decompress and settle into my current life. Scrolling through Indeed before I really know what I'm looking for will just lead me toward applying for another job I'll end up hating. While my savings aren't anything to brag about, they can keep me afloat for a little while if I'm careful with spending. It'll be hard to return to real life as I know it once I disembark from *Aurelia*. No more free food and beverages? No more complimentary laundry service and maid service and turndown service? You mean, I can't take my butler with me? What's a girl to do?

Maybe I'll shove as much food in my bag as I can before I leave the ship on Tuesday. Ha! Kidding. (*Mostly.*)

Instead of my laptop and phone, I take my paperback and my sunscreen.

I'm early, so I'm not surprised I beat Phillip to the pool area. I walk around, looking for free lounge chairs. Since we're cruising today to our last port in the Cayman Islands, everyone's on board the ship and making full use of its amenities. The pool is packed, and the loungers all have either warm bodies occupying them or are otherwise claimed with towels and bags. At first, I don't bother going toward the exclusive area that's cordoned off with red velvet rope. I've never been a VIP, exclusive, by-invite-only kind of gal. Then I remember who I'm quasi-dating for the remainder of this cruise, and I could thunk my forehead. Of course he'd ensure I have a place to sit. Or at least the people he *employs* would ensure it. There are two lounge chairs with a sign posted near them:

RESERVED FOR CASEY HUGHES

Well, isn't *that* convenient.

The moment—and I mean down to the *millisecond*—I touch my lounge chair, a champagne bucket is delivered, a fruit tray is brought, a snack basket is set out, and an umbrella is popped open.

Two attendants smile at me. "Can we get you anything else at the moment, Ms. Hughes?"

I get the feeling that if I asked for an elephant or even, hell, a *family* of elephants, they wouldn't bat an eye. *Right away. And would you prefer African or Asian?*

"I'm all set, thank you, both." I squint to read their name tags. "Elise and Danielle, you've both been very helpful. Thank you."

You know what's funny about all this? Playing at being rich is so stressful. Like, do I tip them? I don't have a single dollar on me. My wallet is back in my suite, and it's filled with cobwebs and spare buttons. Also, like, I know they set out the food and champagne, but do I open the champagne bottle, or do I ask them to do it?

Fortunately, they're back mere moments later with a cool wrap to drape across my shoulders and a glass of citrus-infused water from the spa.

"Would you like us to pop the champagne now or wait for Mr. Woodmont to join you?"

I smile. "We'll wait."

I don't want to seem rude. He's being incredibly generous, and also, after last night, I'm not dying to get going on more alcohol. The citrus water is perfect, though, hydrating and refreshing.

I've just finished my first glass, and they're pouring me a second when I see Phillip out of the corner of my eye. I turn as he rounds the edge of the pool. I don't know why it shocks me to see him wearing gray swimming trunks and a T-shirt. I guess I sort of thought he'd come out here to sunbathe in a suit. Hilarious mental image aside, I'm glad I have my sunglasses on so I can admire him at my leisure and still have plausible deniability.

I'm tempted to rearrange myself. I am sitting here, comfortable with one leg stretched out and one leg bent, people-watching and chatting with Elise and Danielle. Knowing that Phillip could be here at any moment, maybe I should have casually draped myself like an Aphrodite portrait or something. All seductive hips and curves. Alas, it's too late.

The moment he reaches me, he bends down to press a kiss on my cheek. With his lips near my ear, before he stands, he whispers, "Hi, gorgeous."

Damn all the butterflies fluttering in my stomach.

"Hi," I chirp like an excited tween.

He sits down on the lounger beside mine. I'm not surprised to see he has his laptop with him. It's Sunday, but I doubt work ever truly stops for him. But he said he would meet me at the pool, and he was right on time, so he gets kudos for that. I don't mind if he needs to get some things done. I want to read my book anyway.

"Have you eaten lunch?" he asks, tugging off his sunglasses so I get full access to those baby blues. Ugh. Does everything about him have to be both noteworthy and devastating?

I point to the table behind our lounge chairs where Elise and Danielle have laid out all the food.

"I told them I wasn't very hungry, but it's like they have a quota to meet or something."

He laughs. "It's my fault. I wanted to be sure you had everything you need."

I smile. "The breakfast spread was . . . decadent. I'll say that. I shared it with Sienna and Javier."

"Are they together officially?"

"I think the same way we are. Officially . . . *for the time being.*"

He studies me as I say this, his eyes narrowing a bit when he nods.

"I'm starved. Let me get a plate, and then you can tell me about your morning. Would you like anything?"

He stands up to get his food, and in doing so, he drapes a hand casually on my shoulder. It's nothing. And yet the brush of his fingers serves as yet another reminder of how casually he pulls my strings.

"I'm okay."

We settle in over the next half hour, reading and working and talking. I get the absolute pleasure of watching him take off his shirt and recline back in his chair. He works on his phone and his laptop—his concentration never wavering. He takes a call, and I close my eyes and listen to him. He has a way of speaking on the phone with a commanding, firm tone that sends tendrils of heat through my body.

Or maybe that's just the blazing sun.

Yes, that's it.

Phillip is busy, busy, busy, and that's okay. I'm hot, and I've just finished a chapter of my book. I want to go for a dip. I wish I could be in the ocean today, but this pool is a close second.

I push off my lounger and walk over to the pool so I can test the water. It's chilly, but I was hoping it would be. With the sun sitting straight overhead and temperatures rising by the second, I need to cool off. I walk down the stairs until my hips slip beneath the cool surface, and then I plunge under all at once, swimming the length of the pool before coming up on the other side. I take a breath and then do it again, swimming back and forth, carefully maneuvering around the other guests. Once, when I come up, Elise catches my attention and asks me if I need a drink.

"Could you send two piña coladas over to our lounge chairs, please?"

"Right away."

Phillip sees me pointing in his direction. He's not working anymore. His laptop is shut, and he's leaning back on his lounge chair, his knee propped up. Apparently, he's been watching me, though I'm not sure for how long. A funny little feeling trickles through me. I like his attention. It's intoxicating to know he can't take his eyes off me, and I'm not even trying to be sexy or seductive; I'm just swimming, just enjoying the water lapping over my body. I could stay in the water all day, but eventually, I see our drinks getting delivered, and I'm anxious to try mine.

Phillip watches me walk up the stairs. I'm aware of the image I present in my lavender bikini, water sluicing down my body. I can't seem to bother with feeling self-conscious. It's the sun and the setting and the heady knowledge that I'm probably driving Phillip insane. When I reach him, I take the towel off my lounge chair and pat my face and chest dry. Then I look at him with a smile.

"Working?" I ask, all charm.

"Not anymore." He pats his lounge chair near his hip so I'll take a seat beside him. I do because he asked nicely and because I want to give in to the simple pleasure of being near him. He wastes no time wrapping his arm around my waist and hauling me against him so that

I'm practically on his lap. I smell his cologne just before he kisses my shoulder.

"Thanks for the drink."

"Do you like fruity cocktails like that, or should I have sent over something else?"

"I like it all. A setting like this calls for a piña colada, and our poolside bartenders know just how to make them."

I retrieve them from the table and pass his over before we clink them together. "Cheers."

We hold eye contact as I take a sip. Creamy coconut blends with rum; then there's the kick of the pineapple juice. Yum! I think they've even added a hint of lime.

"It's delicious," I say, licking a bit of the frothy coconut cream off the corner of my mouth.

Phillip notices. I know because I see that muscle tick in his jaw.

"Is anybody watching us?" I ask, leaning toward him.

"I don't care" is his fervent reply before he meets me halfway and kisses me before I can kiss him. I smile against his lips, and he laughs before kissing me again. It's such a sudden shift—the teasing banter gives way to hot need in an instant. I lean into him and tilt my head while his hand comes up to tangle in my hair. Then we both realize how carried away we're getting, and we break apart. I laugh. Phillip clears his throat.

"Come swim with me," I say, standing.

"I'm embarrassed to admit I haven't been in our pool a single time."

"Phillip!" I reach for his hand and drag him after me. "We're fixing that right now. Come on."

Swimming is one of those activities that seems to cart you right back to your childhood. There's something so carefree about it, and I see Phillip relax as soon as we sink under the surface. He does what I did earlier, sliding under and getting his whole body wet, though he looks to be a much better swimmer than I am. I watch him cross the pool once and then swim back to me.

I smile and yelp as he picks me up in the water, and I wrap my legs around him. His hands grip my thighs, and he carries me around the pool like that, going fast so the water splashes around us. I laugh with glee until he backs me up to the bench along the perimeter and drops me down. I almost start to protest until his arms cage me in on the seat as he leans in for another kiss.

Just like before, it seems to go from zero to one hundred in a heartbeat.

"I know why you had to set me down," I taunt when he pulls back, looking me over with a desire-filled gaze. My hand moves under the water's surface, skimming down his chest and abs until I find the top of his swimming trunks.

He hisses and catches my hand. "Not wise, Casey."

But his tone isn't nearly admonishing enough. In fact, it's almost *challenging.*

"*Not wise?*" I tut, pushing my hand down farther so that I skim across the front of his trunks, right over his hard length.

He doesn't stop me. He lets me touch him in public, though where we are, the way we're angled, no one can see what we're doing. My hand is hidden beneath the surface of the water, and I won't take it too far, just . . . I'll continue doing this, teasing him gently, making him sweat . . .

"Casey," he groans through clenched teeth. "You're killing me here."

"Oops, sorry. Here, let's get out and go lounge some more."

I play like I'm going to get out, before his hands clamp down on my thighs. "Stay put, you menace. Give me a minute."

I'm wearing a gloating smirk. The power has already gone to my head.

I slip forward off the bench so that our bodies brush together. My stomach rubs over him, then my hips, and he squeezes his eyes closed for a second. When they open again, flames are lurking there. Maybe I've pushed too far, or maybe . . . I'm just enjoying the last few hours I have in this man's company. No sense in playing it safe now.

I lean forward until my lips barely brush his ear. "Should we go back to my suite *or yours?*"

Chapter Twenty-Three

PHILLIP

I wake up in Casey's bed and lean over to kiss her shoulder. She groans in protest, and I smile, stringing kisses down her arm.

"I'm sleeping," she moans into her pillow making the words come out garbled.

"*So?* Wake up," I tease, snaking my hand underneath the blanket until I can curve my hand around the base of her spine.

I don't want to acknowledge it, but already, sadness tinges the air. It's our last full day together. Overnight, we'll sail back to Fort Lauderdale, and all the guests, including Casey, will disembark from the ship starting at 10:00 a.m. tomorrow morning. I'll leave slightly before that.

We've established what we'll do. I've told Casey that I agree with her about keeping our relationship as it is: a lighthearted fling. I've promised her, and yet I can't seem to reconcile the decision. It feels like I'm doing the wrong thing. I might be respecting her wishes, but is it cowardly not to push her on it? Not to indulge these wild feelings?

I don't want to do it now. Not this morning when I have her pliant in my arms. She turns over, smiles sleepily up at me, and suggests that last night should have sated me enough.

She makes a good point. Yesterday afternoon, we ran from the pool to my suite, still sopping wet as we tumbled onto my bed together.

Then, even through dinner, we could barely eat.

"Stop," she said, biting down on her smile.

"I'm not doing anything," I replied.

She rolled her eyes. "You know exactly what you're doing."

We'd ended up in her suite after dinner. And now this morning, it's like I've never held her before, never kissed her. I want her with a fierceness that feels untamable. Scary, even. But I don't tell her. I turn her head, cradle her cheek, and kiss her as my hand slips up her thigh, bunching her pajama shorts. My fingers tease her panties, and then I tug them aside. I want to feel her there, but I touch everywhere else instead, torturing us both.

Finally, when I sink into her, my body pins her down; my hips thrust against hers, and she cries out loud enough that surely everyone can hear. We don't care, though. There's nothing outside these four walls.

"*Casey*," I say, my lips pressing against hers.

My heart races so fast, and I want to tell her how I'm feeling then, but I don't have the courage. I shake my head and push off her and go to the shower to cool off. There's nothing to be done.

The arrangement stands.

Later that morning, Casey talks me into going out on an excursion with her on Grand Cayman. It's a three-mile hike followed by a swim beneath a waterfall. I need to work, but Casey points out that I can work tomorrow and every day after that. After she's gone.

I hate that she says it so casually as if it's not as painful for her as it is for me.

I agree, though if I had the choice, Casey and I wouldn't leave her suite all day. Why bother?

Still, we go and join a small group.

Our guide is a little nervous because I'm tagging along. After a few comments like "Sir, if you'd prefer a different route" and "Mr.

Woodmont, is the pace okay?" I tell him to pretend like I'm not here, and we both seem more relaxed during the second portion of the hike.

Casey keeps up well, even though her tennis shoes aren't the best fit for the strenuous trail.

"I assure you, I'm fine. Sienna and I did a hike early on that had me wishing for death. *This* is a cakewalk in comparison, I promise."

Around lunchtime, we break through the last leg of the trail and find ourselves in a true tropical paradise. Centered in the clearing is a crystal clear swimming hole fed directly by a series of small waterfalls that flow down from the hilltops above us. A canopy of overgrown trees and foliage shades the scene. With how otherworldly it looks, it could be a secret meeting place for all kinds of magical creatures. Casey could be one. A nymph or a mermaid. She smiles as she slips out of her hiking gear. She's in a one-piece bathing suit, but it's very revealing. Her lush curves, every little dip and valley I've come to know so well. I walk over and spin her, leading us toward the water's edge.

My hand grips her waist, and I feel her shiver.

I hate that we're not alone. I'd take her right here on the grassy trail. Tugging her bathing suit down and . . .

"Should we jump in together?" Casey asks, drawing me out of my thoughts.

I smile and nod, letting her take my hand so we can leap into the cold water with gritted teeth. It has to be at least ten degrees colder than the pool on board *Aurelia*, and we both come up shivering. Casey laughs and swims over. Our feet tangle below the surface as we tread water.

"Let's go closer to the waterfall," she says just before she sets off like we're in a race.

I catch her easily, coming up alongside her as the water roars overhead. It's not a very large waterfall, but we still keep a careful distance from the deluge pouring into the swimming hole.

We spend the next hour swimming and eating our prepared lunches, our group spread out in small clusters. The air surrounding the swimming hole is so moist and hot that within seconds of pulling myself out of the cold water, I'm eager to go right back in.

Eventually, our guide calls out to everyone, letting us know it's time to head back.

I don't move, of course. A moment ago while Casey was sipping her water, I broke off and spoke with him. When Casey looks at me now, I shake my head.

"We're staying back for a moment."

It makes for a seamless transition as everyone gathers their gear and treks off down the trail, leaving the two of us alone in the forest.

Casey worries her bottom lip between her teeth before asking, "Shouldn't we head back? How are we going to know where to go?"

On the marked trails with a thousand signs? We'll manage.

I don't tell her that. I shrug and stand. "Let's swim."

I've been out of the water for too long. I'm hot and sweaty. And I need her.

Casey doesn't get in after me, though. I break through the surface and turn back to see her staring at the trail where everyone left. It's been long enough that we can't hear them anymore, but I think she's just making sure the coast is clear before she turns and walks over to a large rock that juts out over the shallow side of the swimming hole.

"I'm hot, but I don't think I can get back in that cold water again."

I swim toward her. "Suit yourself."

She lets her feet dangle over the edge, testing the cold water and recoiling back. "I just got warm again," she protests.

That's fine by me. I like her propped right there on the water's edge. The perfect height for what I envision.

Casey watches me swim closer, but she doesn't realize how nefarious my intentions are until I position myself beside her rock and I take ahold of her ankles to spread them apart.

Her eyes go wide. Her cheeks pink. "Phillip."

Even as she protests, she scoots her bottom closer for me. Giving herself over to the moment.

"Anyone could—"

"Let them."

I lower my face between her legs, kissing my way up her inner thigh, slowly easing her into the idea of letting me have her like this. Then her breathing picks up, and her body starts to relax. I press her thighs apart even more and hook my finger in the side of her bathing suit bottom and peel it back. For too long, I look at her. I know it makes her squirm being exposed like this, but that makes it all the more fun for me. Eventually, my head lowers, and I press a kiss to her inner thigh again, working closer to the final destination that will have her toes curling and her head tipping back. She angles her hips up for me, giving me all the access I need to taste her.

I feel her shaking. Her arms straining to hold herself up the longer I continue.

I reach an arm around her back, ensuring she won't go anywhere.

I love feeling her come apart strand by strand, unspooling before me until there's a sharp cry, a tense pause, and then a passionate groan of ecstasy. I take her there on the bank of the swimming hole, swapping positions with her so that I don't hurt her. She sits over me, straddling my hips. I tug the straps of her bathing suit down, freeing her breasts, and then my lips and mouth cover her, sucking and tasting as she slides down onto me, taking me deep as she rolls her hips, lifts, and sinks even lower still.

I scrape my teeth along the peak of her breast, and she fists her hands in my hair. Already, she's close to coming again, and I pick up my pace, unbothered by the hard rock beneath me. I'm numb to everything beyond her as I reach up to kiss her lips, holding her against me so our wet bodies are flush. It's so intimate that it almost hurts to have her like this. I feel her squeeze me, tightening, breaking with a passionate cry, and then I find my own release, seeing stars behind my closed lids, feeling as though the universe has condensed down to a single pinprick before it explodes back with blinding light. We stay there, catching our breath. Neither one of us says a word, even as we eventually stand and dress. Even as we start back up the trail, hand in hand. The truth is so obvious to us both that it's better just to stay silent.

Chapter Twenty-Four

CASEY

It's our last night on board *Aurelia*, and Sienna has claimed me. We've been getting ready in her suite and blasting music. She took a picture of me puckering my lips at her phone, and when she showed it to me, my jaw dropped. It looked so cool and professional, like an ad you'd see in *Vogue*. She has such a good eye for photography. Of course when I told her that, she barked out a laugh and said, "Uh, no, you're just a smokeshow!"

Now, I'm standing in her bathroom, leaning over the sink to carefully apply black winged liner just the way my grandmother taught me.

Sienna appears in the doorway and snorts. "*Good god*. It looks like you nicked everything they have at Chanel."

She's referring to my makeup spread. Les Beiges eye shadow palette, Noir Allure mascara, Les Chaînes de Chanel blush . . .

I smile down at it all. "My grandmother worked as a beauty consultant at the Chanel counter for over three decades. It's the only makeup I've ever used, and when I go into Saks to buy a replacement of something, the ladies my grandmother worked with always send me away with bags full of samples and gifts."

She walks in and toys with the row of lipsticks I have lined up, eventually twisting up *Rouge Coco* in the Mademoiselle shade, and I can hear my grandmother's description of it in my head: "A perfect neutral pink that pairs well with any skin tone."

"Is she the one who taught you how to do makeup? You're really good at it."

I nod and look at my reflection in the mirror, studying my favorite features—the ones I got from Jean Hughes. "Is it weird to feel connected to her this way? With eyeliner and lipstick?"

She shakes her head. "I think it's sweet. Makes me miss my gran too."

I bump my hip against her and offer a sympathetic smile. "Are we going to be down in the dumps, or should we kick things into gear for our last night?"

She grins, and I know I made the right choice in keeping my plans with her. I won't lie and say it was easy to leave Phillip. I mean, we've only been apart for an hour or two, and I'm already dying to see him. But I shove that feeling aside because I won't back out on Sienna now. She's really been there for me these last few days, and I feel like I've made a lifelong friend. We've promised we're going to stay in touch and visit each other—we're going to come up with some kind of concrete plan over dinner. We just have to finish getting ready and head out the door.

"Yes, right. Only . . ." She frowns and turns to me. "Are you *sure* about this? You absolutely can ditch me for dinner with your man."

I pause applying my makeup and scowl at her. "Sienna, I'm not ditching you!"

"Fine, fine," she says coolly. "Only I want you to know you *can* if you really want to. I'm not so desperate for company that I want to steal you away from him."

"I *want* to be here," I say. "Now, I think we should get as glitzy and glam as possible, okay? All the stuff we haven't had an excuse to wear yet."

Sienna's eyes alight with possibilities, and she's already hurrying to her closet. "I have this silver gown that's absurd and gorgeous, and I'm breaking it out! Oh! And you have to wear this red dress. It'll look heavenly on you. Want to see it?"

I agree to try it on, already knowing that if it's coming from her wardrobe, it'll be stylish and designer, no doubt.

She carries it into the bathroom, and it's the most vibrant shade of red. Already, I know I'll have to swap my lipstick to match it, which works well because I've kept the rest of my makeup neutral and relatively simple (for me, at least).

She hands it over. "And before you even start, I refuse to be sad about it."

She's talking about Javier.

He apparently broke things off with her this afternoon, saying it was better in the long run. "No need to drag out some long goodbye," he said, which I thought sounded a little bit cruel. Sienna disagreed with me, though I couldn't tell if she really believed it or if she was just trying to defend him.

"My only regret is that I didn't beat him to it! I mean, get real. It wasn't a breakup. We both knew the end was looming. And the thing is, I wasn't even tempted to keep it going. Don't get me wrong, he was bloody good looking. I mean, you saw him that time with his towel. I've never seen anything like him, but there's nothing beneath it, you know? No real chemistry with us. He seemed to like things one way—always wanting to go, go, go. Like today, I wanted to have a lazy day by the pool, but he insisted we book it into town for a horse ride. Turns out it was this really dodgy setup. They were trying to get away with putting us on a bunch of donkeys. I laughed and thought we'd turn right round, but Javier insisted it was fine. 'More authentic,'" she adds in a macho accent. "I told him I didn't want to go, and we had a little row about it. So ridiculous because the guides and everyone were just watching on! Anyway, it's done, and I'm glad for it. What about you and Phillip? God, I don't envy you still having to cut ties and all. There's no sense in making it this dramatic thing. Believe me, I regret getting carried away like that . . ."

"Right, yeah. We'll do it the simple way," I insist, feeling defensive.

"Will you even see each other again before you depart?"

He made me promise—swear, actually—that I would come to his suite once I was finished with Sienna, no matter the time.

"What if it's two a.m.?"

"I don't care," he said in a no-nonsense tone.

"Three a.m.?" I teased.

He leveled an unamused glower at me.

"*Three thirty?*"

I kept right on going until he sealed his lips to mine and then told me with a succinct, finite finish, "Come to me no matter the time, Casey. Swear it."

I smiled against his lips. "I swear it."

Now, as Sienna and I walk to dinner, my stomach squeezes tight again. It's ached all day. Maybe something was off with my breakfast . . . or maybe that picnic lunch by the waterfall was spoiled . . . *or maybe it's because you're leaving Phillip tomorrow, and the doom of it all is making your tummy hurt!*

I press the button for the elevator and rearrange my clutch.

Sienna glances toward me with a curious expression, and I force a smile.

"I'm starving," she groans. "I bet you are, too, after that hike."

Hike = waterfall = Phillip's face between my legs.

I gulp and nod, choosing to keep my mouth shut so she doesn't look over and notice the flush creeping up my neck. That's good, red dress, red lips, red skin. At least I match.

Tonight in the dining room, they're doing something special called the Flavors of *Aurelia*. All the chefs on board have banded together to work alongside Executive Chef Thomas Keller to create a multicourse tasting menu similar to what they offer at Michelin Star restaurants. Each course is paired with a wine offering, and as far as I know, the reservations for the evening booked up months ago. We only got in because Sienna sweet-talked the host, flirting shamelessly with him over the phone until he promised he'd work us into the schedule.

I'm sure I could have pulled strings with Phillip, but this seems to have worked out just fine. When we show up, our names are on the reservation list, and we're immediately whisked toward a table for two near the bank of floor-to-ceiling windows.

Almost as soon as I walk into the dining room, I feel tingles run the length of my spine, and I turn to look over my shoulder. Phillip sits at a secluded table in the far corner alongside Captain Neal and Devin, the chief engineer. As he reaches for his drink, he lifts his gaze, and our eyes meet across the crowded space.

We were just together, intimate only a few hours ago, and yet it feels all new again—tight, hot, heavy. It's like my lungs don't want to fully expand; my heart doesn't want to slow its pace; my hands can't seem to stop trembling.

It's adrenaline, nothing more.

Oh, really?

God, his eyes eat me alive. There's no smile or arched brow. Nothing too obvious, but his gaze still consumes me as I trek across the dining room behind Sienna and take my seat, my back to him.

It's hard to keep my attention focused straight ahead. I want to look back and see him again.

After I leave the ship tomorrow, I won't have another chance like this.

"Okay, you have to be honest with me. You're sad about Phillip, aren't you?"

I blink and shake my head, trying to push, push, push everything down. I don't want to be a shitty friend to Sienna. It's not fair to her.

"It's almost insulting if you try and cover it up, you know. Just tell me."

"Yes," I say hurriedly. "It's complicated between us. All the advice you gave earlier concerning Javier just doesn't seem to apply. You kept your wits about you, and I've apparently lost all of mine. I feel weird and strange, and I've been trying to ignore it, but well . . . I guess I'm not doing such a great job."

I peer up to find she's not annoyed with me. She has a soft smile and sympathetic eyes as she listens to me try and explain it. "You've really done it, haven't you? Broken all the cardinal rules. You weren't supposed to fall for him."

"I haven't!" I rush out, though at this point, maybe even *I* don't believe it.

She laughs with a shake of her head. "*Okay.*"

I look down, trying to ignore the sinking feeling in my stomach.

"What should we eat?" I say, quickly changing the subject.

"We don't get to choose, remember?" Sienna says with a laugh. "It's a tasting menu. They'll just start bringing the courses."

Right.

As a waiter comes around to give us wine, I ask Sienna about her family and friends back home. She tells me all about her gran. While she didn't raise Sienna, like my grandmother raised me, they're extremely close.

"She's the one who encouraged me to start taking my social media career seriously. Funny, considering she doesn't even have a smartphone, but yeah, she really believed in me when everyone else was telling me that it'd be much better in the long run if I just settled down and got a *normal* job, or better yet, married and changed nappies all day!"

I can't reconcile that mental image. Sienna working a desk job? Laughable.

"Where are you off to once you finish up here? You mentioned it was your gran's birthday?"

"Yes, her big eightieth shindig. I've been planning it for ages. I'm hosting it at a swanky nightclub in downtown Bristol. I've managed to book the whole place out. She'll love it."

"God, I want to be in a nightclub when I'm eighty."

Sienna winks. "Me too, babe. Me too."

"What about after that?"

She picks up her wine and takes a sip, mentally scrolling through her schedule. "I head to Sweden for a brand trip with Volvo, and then from there, I'm off to Dubai."

"For work?"

"For *pleasure*," she says with a coy smile.

"Amazing," I laugh. "I can't *wait* to see pictures."

"And what about you, Casey Hughes?" She hums. "What are *you* thinking you're going to do now?"

That's the million-dollar question, isn't it?

I study the side of my wineglass. "I thought at first that I might go back home just to get things sorted—"

Sienna makes a blaring sound like she's a game show buzzer, and I've just provided the wrong answer.

"*But* . . . ," I continue pointedly. "There's no real reason I have to do that."

"Right!"

"I mean, yes, it's practical and all. But being practical has not exactly served me well thus far."

Sienna grins. "So throw caution to the wind. Shake things up."

I can't help but smile as a zing of excitement has me sitting up straight and talking faster. "Well, I know I want to travel. I'm not *completely* opposed to working for another large-scale publication, but I'd expect it to be much of the same crap I dealt with at *Bon Voyage*. So, no, that's out for right now. I want to do something totally different."

"And if, perhaps . . . I already got the ball rolling for you on your new career, would you absolutely kill me?" she asks gently.

My eyes shoot up to meet hers. "What do you mean? You've called someone for me?"

I wouldn't be surprised. I'm sure she has a lot of contacts in the industry.

She winces. "No, not *exactly*. I just, I think I need you to promise that you won't kill me first before I tell you."

Excitement and dread comingle inside me—warring for the top spot. I force a laugh and shake my head. "I'm not going to kill you. Will you knock it off?"

That seems to settle it for her. She leans forward and props her elbows on the table. She no longer looks worried. Her face is pure delight. "You know all those pictures and videos of us I've been taking on the trip?" I nod, encouraging her to go on. "I ended up making a few day-in-the-life videos with all the footage, and you were in most of them, of course."

"Okay . . ."

"People have been curious about my *hot friend*, and well . . . it felt like such a waste to not be able to tag you."

I'm blinking fast, trying to keep pace with her. I've seen Sienna's Instagram account. She has *millions* of followers. She might seem normal, just any other friend sitting across from me at the dinner table, but she's far from it. On the internet, at least, she's a real celebrity.

"Oh, right," I say, not really sure where this is leading. She posted me on her account? So?

"*So*, I made you an Instagram account, and . . . you already have close to twenty-five thousand followers, and I bet if we check again, you'll have even more. You're growing by the second." She rushes the second half of her sentence out before wincing as if she expects an immediate freak-out, and well, I deliver right on cue.

"WHAT?"

"It's @TravelWithCaseyHughes," she rushes out. "I'm @TravelWithSiennaThompson, so it only seemed apropos to have our accounts match. And well, there you go, a popular Instagram account for the taking. I can connect you with my management team, or if you want to fly solo, that's fine too. I know loads of people who prefer that. Either way, it's up to you."

I still haven't said anything, and I think she's starting to get worried about me reneging on my promise not to kill her. She leans over the table and squeezes my hand.

"Are you upset with me?" she asks gently.

"*No.*"

I'm dumbfounded. Shocked. Utterly taken aback by her gesture.

Her tone gentles as she continues, "I think you could really do this, Casey. You could live out your dream of traveling and writing about it and make *real* money while you're at it. I won't sugarcoat it and say it's no work at all, but I've found it's different working for yourself. It sounds like you've slaved away at *Bon Voyage* for years now. Why not use that same amount of energy building your own brand instead? I mean, what do you have to lose?" She blanches. "No offense, but from what you've told me . . . there is absolutely *nothing* waiting for you at the end of this cruise. Not even your man, from the sounds of the arrangement you two have. Just think about it."

Without another thought, I'm up and out of my seat, launching myself at her. My arms go around her shoulders as I squeeze her. She makes a choking sound, but I don't let up. I can't. "Sienna, this is the nicest thing anyone has ever done for me."

When I pull back, she's blushing scarlet red. "Well . . . I mean, yeah. No. It's nothing. Just—"

She clears her throat and fixes her hair, clearly uncomfortable with my overt display of affection.

"Now, listen, sit down. God, just sit down, and I'll walk you through a real proper tutorial on what you'll need to do to get started, okay?"

"Okay, but one more hug."

She tenses like she's in agony. "Fine. One more."

I squeeze her again, offering up a million and one thank-yous, and then I wipe tears from my eyes and reclaim my seat. "All right. Fire away. I'm listening."

Chapter Twenty-Five
CASEY

I make it to Phillip's room a little after midnight. Sienna and I spent the last few hours walking through my new Instagram account. I felt like a grandpa asking her the silliest questions. I was truly starting from square one: "And what if I want to put one of those filters on it?"

By the time I finally felt like I had a handle on everything, it was later than I thought, but I wanted to keep my promise to Phillip, so I've come down to his suite—and as soon as I knock, he whisks open the door and drags me inside. It's like he was there, pacing frantically on the other side.

"Took you long enough," I tease.

"Took *you* long enough," he groans in mock annoyance.

"I've been really busy!"

He's already starting to draw up my dress as he leans in to kiss me with a frenzied passion. Apparently, the first item on his agenda is getting his hands all over me, and who am I to protest? Within minutes, I'm naked and pressed right up against the door of his suite. The cool wood holds me up as Phillip thrusts into me, stealing a kiss as I cry out for him.

Before getting here, I swore to myself that I would make the most of our night. I wouldn't bring up anything concerning our relationship or try to ruin our last few hours together. Phillip must have come to the same conclusion, or—as much as it hurts to consider—he's really not all that torn up about it, because neither one of us tries to delve into our future.

After we have sex against the door, we scurry into the bathroom to take a shower. We're so good about it, too, actually washing ourselves (go us!) and not getting distracted by each other. Okay, there is a moment when I just stare at him as he's soaping his chest and abs, a little slack jawed. To distract myself, I bring him in on the new development: the insanely generous thing Sienna's done for me. I'm bursting with excitement over it, and he's just as pleased as I am.

"Casey, this is just the thing for you."

"It really feels that way," I say, happiness brimming over. "And it's okay if it doesn't take off right away and all that. Not *everyone* can be Sienna Thompson. I might just not have the same general appeal as she does, you know? But that's okay because I'm not trying to be a duplicate of her. There's room for all of us, and really, I think my feed will be different. I want to really guide people through travel, and what Sienna does is way different. She uses these exotic destinations as more of accessories to her glamorous lifestyle, if that makes sense. And it's not a bad thing!" I hurry to amend. "I love it, I just think . . . my page would naturally be different than hers because, well, *I'm* different. I want to hone my voice and really create something unique."

Phillip's grinning at me. "I can tell how excited you are about it."

I worry my bottom lip between my teeth. "You'd tell me if it was silly, wouldn't you?"

There's no one else in my life to ask, no one to redirect me if I'm making a huge mistake. He steps forward, cradles my face, and tells me with absolute conviction, "It's genius, really. You'll work hard and make it successful; I know it."

I beam and lean in to kiss him, so relieved to have his approval.

Through the night, I barely manage a few hours of sleep. Phillip and I stay up late acting as if our sole mission in life is to try and memorize every curve and contour of each other's bodies. After I do finally crash, I wake up a few hours later with a bone-crushing weariness. I look at the clock on the bedside table and realize with panic that it's much later than I hoped. Morning is here. Our time together is officially drawing to a close, and though I try to press them down—*no, no, no, I repeat to myself. Don't be sad*—silent tears start to fall. As I lie there with a breaking heart, I never wake Phillip; I'm careful to gather myself before he stirs. With great care, I tidy up my feelings and stow them away, just like I've done the last few days.

When he finally looks at me with sleepy, sweet eyes, he leans over to kiss me. None the wiser. "I need to get ready, but stay in bed if you want. I know you must be tired."

So I do. I stay under the covers, listening to him move about the room, watching him pack—efficiently and quickly, of course—before he showers and dresses in a pressed navy suit. He's gorgeous and absolutely, positively devastating. This man can never be topped; I envy all the women who'll get the pleasure of crossing paths with him today. Tomorrow. God, how lucky someone would be to have this man *forever*.

Once he's nearly finished, I crawl out of bed (reluctantly, because, hello, not-too-hard-not-too-soft king mattress I'll never get to experience again in my life because I'm too poor), and I dress in my clothes from the night before. Phillip watches me as I do it, but I pretend not to notice because we're doing so well. I can't screw it up now.

He asks if I want breakfast, but I can't eat. Nothing's getting down into this stomach today. It's a vise.

"Still full from last night," I lie. "Besides, I need to go pack. My suite is a mess."

I'm not even exaggerating. I've been so busy the last few days that I haven't had a chance to begin getting my things together.

He checks his watch with a frown. "I leave here at nine."

"I think I depart an hour later."

It's already 8:05 a.m.

God, the minutes are slipping by like quicksand.

He looks up, meeting my eyes. My chest constricts. "I could stay, I think. I'd be cutting it close getting to—"

"No, no." I cut him off. "Let's say our goodbyes now."

I want to be helpful. It's so important for me to hold it together, to be strong in this. We really have the chance to keep things good between us. I think back on how Sienna described her fight with Javier, how she wished she'd just left while the getting was good. I want to make it so if we ever do cross paths again in the future, years down the line, we can smile and think back fondly of our time together. That wouldn't be such a bad thing. A happy farewell is within reach; I just have to ignore that ache of sadness and put on a brave face. I know I can do it. Especially if I rely on humor.

Once Phillip walks me to the door, I reach out my hand for him to formally shake, and I start to speak with a businesslike tone as if we've just ended a meeting together. "Phillip Woodmont, it's been an absolute pleasure. *My* pleasure, mostly." I throw in a teasing wink.

He laughs and accepts my hand. "Casey Hughes. It was good to see you, after all these years."

His gaze contradicts his words. Too serious. Too conflicted.

Heat springs from where we touch. His grip tightens, and my throat starts to tighten. The dam holding back all the unshed tears is starting to crack and splinter.

"You have yourself a fine cruise ship here. I loved every inch of it. Loved the whole trip, actually." A tear springs free even as I keep smiling. I laugh and brush it away like it's nothing. "Damn allergies."

Phillip frowns and tugs me close so he can envelop me in his arms. "*Casey*—"

I squeeze my eyes closed and shake my head so my forehead rolls back and forth against his sturdy chest. "Please don't make it harder."

"It doesn't have to be like this."

I can't consider otherwise. Hope can be such a terrible thing, and I've been so careful not to feed off it the last few days. I refuse to start now.

"You have somewhere to be, and so do I. I have a *whole new life* to be getting to, apparently! So stop delaying me, will you?" Only *I'm* the one hugging him for dear life, not letting go. "Just . . . okay. I'm going to step back; you're going to smile, and then I'm going to open the door and walk out. Are you ready?"

"No."

My heart sinks. "Phillip," I chide.

"Is this truly what you want?"

No. No. Absolutely not. It's the last thing I want, you fool, and yet I'm nodding. "Yes. It's the best way forward. I appreciate everything you've done. Your kindness . . ." I realize I'm veering far too close to a well of sentiment and sadness and feelings, so I stop short and let my sentence linger.

He bends to kiss the top of my head, and it seems like he's trying to absorb my scent for as long as he can. Despite everything, tears really start spilling down my cheeks. The dam is officially broken.

"Okay, here we go," I say, narrating my movements. "I'm stepping back. Look, I'm doing it. I'm waving. Now you wave to me."

He doesn't. His eyes are stormy, his brow deeply furrowed.

"Wave."

Still nothing.

I sigh. "Fine, we'll skip it. I'm going to kiss you one more time, and then that's it."

Without confirmation from him, I step forward, press up onto my toes, and plant a gentle, fleeting kiss on his lips, and when it's done, I turn for the door, wrench it open, and never look back.

Chapter Twenty-Six
CASEY

The shrill sound of the phone ringing on the nightstand pulls me out of my reverie. When I answer it, a sweet feminine voice tells me deck eight is now disembarking.

I thank her and then set the receiver back on its cradle before slowly turning to survey my suite. It's as neat and tidy as I found it, as if I didn't want the cleaning crew to judge me for an errant piece of trash or a throw pillow that has been left slightly askew. My luggage is already gone. An attendant came to retrieve it about an hour ago, and this time, I let the gentleman take it instead of arguing with him, because some things do change. Okay, I'm still slightly nervous that my laptop's about to get jacked, but oh well, it's too late to worry about it now.

The cruise is officially over.

We're back in Fort Lauderdale.

The worst of the goodbyes are over.

Sienna left a little while ago after giving me ten different ways to get in touch with her.

"And if I don't answer my mobile, which happens because I'm terrible at charging it, just keep trying, okay? You'll get through eventually. Also my email's there. You can always use that. I wrote to my manager last night, and he's supposed to phone you soon to see about bringing you on, only don't accept his terms right away. You really ought to make him sweat, but we can discuss that later. Oh god, look at me; I'm actually about to cry. This is utterly ridiculous! I've only just met you."

I hugged her, but she resisted, of course. "God, why do you Americans insist on all this touchy-feely nonsense?"

"Hug me back," I teased with an insistent tone.

Her hand barely touched my shoulder. "There, I've done it. Now release me before you accidentally wrinkle my Chloé blouse."

I stepped back and looked her over. "I think you and I were meant to be friends, Sienna Thompson. That's why you found me out on my balcony that first day."

She looked bored at her nails. "Oh, you mean when you were about to heave over the side of the ship?"

"Admit you love me."

She rolled her eyes. "Oh *lord.*"

"*Admit it.*"

"I'm fond of you. There. Okay? There's no one I'd rather have sailed around the Caribbean with, and though Javier proved to be a passing fancy, you, my dear, turned out to be the real deal."

I smile, thinking about the next time I'll see her. We've promised to meet up in a month or two in another exotic location. Sienna said it should work really nicely because if I sign on with her agency, it'll be easy for them to book us for the same brand trips. *If* I want to go down that route.

I still haven't come to grips with the fact that I'm doing this huge, monumental thing. It's a little scary and a lot exhilarating. I could fall on my face, oh, absolutely. I likely will at least once. There's no way it'll work out seamlessly for me, but I have the world spread out before me, and I can practically feel my grandmother at my back, pushing me forward.

Do it, Sunshine.

My first destination is the Fort Lauderdale international airport.

My second destination?

Well . . . it's up in the air. Literally.

"What's the next international flight out?"

Slowly, the woman behind the airline counter looks up from her computer, with one eyebrow raised like she hasn't heard me right.

"*Any* international flight?"

"Yes," I say, smiling. "*Any* flight. I'd like to book the next one out."

Yeah, she definitely thinks I have a few screws loose. Her mouth flattens with disapproval as her long neon-green nails tip-tap on her keyboard. Then she pauses and looks up at me.

"Serbia. Leaves in fifteen minutes."

"Oh . . ."

Now listen, would I hypothetically like to visit some lesser-traveled countries? Eventually, yes. Do I want to do it for my very first trip abroad? Eh . . .

It's probably best to enter at the shallow end.

"What's the next one after that?"

Her nails clatter some more, and when she speaks again, it's clear she's utterly bored by this process. "London, Heathrow, direct. Leaves in thirty minutes."

"I'll take it."

Her brown eyes widen. "You got your passport?" She's skeptical as I hand it over.

"Thirty minutes won't give you much time," she warns.

Well then, you better tip-tap-type those talons a little faster, I want to say. Instead, I smile. "I'll run."

Her brow furrows, and I don't miss the subtle shake of her head as she starts to book my ticket. The price is . . . painful, to say the least. I squeeze my eyes closed against the barrage of negative thoughts.

You can't afford this.

This is reckless!

Stupid!

Impulsive!

You have no place to stay! No one you know! What's your plan?

"Credit card," the lady says, waving her hand impatiently.

I blink my eyes open, conscious of the ever-growing line snaking into infinity behind me. Someone pointedly clears their throat. No one is patient in an airport; I get that. But, like, *hello*, some of us are making *major life decisions* here!

"*Card*," she prods again, shifting her weight and no doubt fighting an eye roll.

"Okay, um . . ." My hand shakes as I try and slip my card out of my wallet, stalling.

Then the line shifts to my left, and someone new steps up to the counter beside me. I catch a whiff of the person's perfume, and I immediately freeze. The scent is so familiar; of course it is—my grandmother wore it every day of my entire life.

Chanel N°5.

I look up quickly, expecting to see my grandmother standing there beside me, an affectionate smile on her face, but it's not her. It's a stranger. This woman is older than my grandmother, shorter—oh, and *alive*. A laugh bubbles out of me.

It's a sign, though, right? It has to be.

I grab my card and slide it across the counter. Then I hike my purse higher onto my shoulder and ask with a determined tone, "Which way is security?"

Chapter Twenty-Seven

CASEY

I know I've made the right decision, and here are my two foolproof reasons:

1. The flight attendant just announced our flight was less crowded than usual, and she invited us to spread out. (Uh, *score.*)

2. I snagged an aisle seat as planned, and the young woman who arrived to claim the window seat in my row was wearing headphones; she gave me a quick smile but then kept moving and otherwise made no attempt to engage with me.

This is meant to be. I feel good about my decision, which is a relief because there's no going back now. Not only has this airline snatched a thousand dollars from my bank account, but I'm also already on board the plane, buckling my seat belt, getting comfy. Soon, we'll all be skimming over the Atlantic.

I expect a wave of panic, something akin to my freak-out on my suite's balcony that first day aboard *Aurelia*. Any minute now, I'll have to drop my head between my knees and think happy thoughts, but . . . I feel oddly calm as I settle back against my seat and watch the last few stragglers trail down the aisle. I've already perused the in-flight menu and settled on a selection of the carb heavy hitters. My companion in the window seat has her neck pillow on, and she just popped a Xanax; she means business.

I want to ask her if this will be her first time in London, too, but I don't want to break this perfect, peaceful quiet we've created for ourselves, so instead, I turn to the screen mounted in front of me.

I'm just starting to flip through movie options when a flight attendant walks down the aisle, thoroughly inspecting passengers as she goes. I bet she's about to chide someone for not properly stowing their carry-on items. Just as a precaution, I kick my bag further under the seat in front of me. When I glance back up, she's looking at me with narrowed eyes. I go rigid, then slowly offer up a shy smile. She keeps studying me long enough that I look over my shoulder to see if maybe there's a rule breaker seated just *behind* me, but, no, it's me she's staring at. She continues walking, then stops just short of my seat and bends down.

Her eyes spark with something. Is that . . . excitement? *Why?*

Does she love reprimanding people? Maybe it's her favorite part of the job.

"Casey Hughes?" she asks.

I only now register her slightly strange smile.

"Uh . . . yes?" My reply is cautious, mostly because I'm scared I'm somehow in trouble. They can't kick me off the plane. I've already torn into my complimentary snack mix. "How did you know my name?"

Is that standard?

She shakes her head and laughs. "Oh . . . it's just—ma'am, I'm so excited to let you know that you've received an upgrade!"

"An upgrade?" I frown, taken aback. "There must be some mistake. Do you want to see my ticket?" I'm already bending down to dig in my purse for my boarding pass. "I'm not like a frequent flyer or anything. Maybe you have me confused with—"

Her smile widens. "Nope. I have it exactly right. If you'll collect your things and follow me, I'll lead you toward your new seat in first class."

I gulp. No doubt the blood drains from my face too. I lean in and lower my voice. "I can't afford that particular upgrade, so thank you, but no. I'm happy with the seat I have."

Her eyes widen in alarm. "No, this is completely complimentary. I apologize for not leading with that. This new seat is free of charge . . . just for you."

Okay . . .

Well, as weird as this is, I'm not going to just sit here and argue. I might as well see what this lady is offering me. This could be legit. I might be the beneficiary of some kind of exciting free upgrade. *That happens to people, right?*

It doesn't take me long to get my things. Just before I stand, I aim a sad smile at sleeping neck-pillow girl. She would have made a good airplane buddy.

The flight attendant offers to take my carry-on bag, so I'm left to just follow behind her, aware of everyone's eyes on me. No doubt they heard what she just said. They're wondering when *their* upgrade is coming. Because I feel so guilty, I can't look anyone in the eye before we slip through the partition dividing those grimy peasant seats from first class. I swear they scented the air. The lighting is better, softer, warmer. The aisle is wider. The seats themselves aren't seats at all; they're practically private cabins. The seats are arranged in a single-double-single configuration, and almost everyone who's already seated has drawn their curtains for privacy.

There looks to be a whole team of attendants, one or two for every guest.

Good god.

I assume I'm being led toward a solo spot, but then the flight attendant stops near a pair of seats right in the center of first class.

"You'll be right here. 3B."

I catch up to her and turn to check out my new digs. This is nothing compared to where I was previously parking my butt. This is luxury, dripping with class and refinement. My pale-blue seat is large enough to fold down into a bed. In my private cubicle, there's also a small cabinet, on top of which rests a Dior-branded Dopp kit and pajamas tied with a coordinating pale-blue ribbon. I'm already amazed, and that's before I look up to see the man sitting in 3C.

My heart plummets, then soars. My mouth drops open with astonishment, and when Phillip glances up from his book, he looks just as surprised as I am. He pulls his reading glasses off and just . . . stares.

Which doesn't make sense.

Why is *he* so surprised?

Didn't he know I was on board? Wasn't *he* the one to call me up here?

My free upgrade was obviously courtesy of him.

"Sir?" the flight attendant asks with hope laced in her question.

He nods with an astonished gaze. "Yes . . . it's her."

She looks at me, her eyes softening as she waves for me to take my seat. She stows my luggage in the cabinet beneath the mounted TV and then spends what feels like forty-five minutes going over every single feature imaginable: my massaging, ventilated, and cooling seat; the Bose headphones; a built-in beverage bar; snacks; magazines; eye mask . . . I half expect her to bring out a brand-new Jet Ski or something. By the time she steps back, I'm barely even registering everything at my disposal.

"Enjoy. I'll be back by in just a minute with a warm towel," she says before walking away.

My mouth opens and closes like a guppy as I half faint, half slide down into my seat. I glance over the short wall between Phillip and me. "What's happening?"

Phillip's forehead is furrowed so deeply that his eyebrows practically connect. "I'm not sure, actually . . ."

I'm annoyed that he seems to be as confused as I am.

I need answers!

"You clearly orchestrated this," I say, waving my hand around the plane like he was not only responsible for me being here but also everyone else on board too. "Phillip! You said you weren't going to come after me!"

He barks out a laugh and shakes his head in disbelief. He turns to face me, conviction in his gaze as he exclaims, "I didn't!"

When my expression doesn't ease, he goes on. "I swear to god this is not me coming after you. Though got to say I'm relieved . . . it just doesn't cut it. I *wanted* to come after you, Casey. Don't get me wrong. This morning, I was pacing in my suite trying to decide what to do. A thousand times, I almost came for you, to *insist* that we were making the wrong choice—that the arrangement we struck didn't take into account our unique circumstances."

"What unique circumstances?" I ask, sounding skeptical.

A beat passes, and I watch the way his expression eases and the tension in his shoulders lessons as his entire demeanor softens.

"I've fallen for you," he admits boldly.

His overwhelming confession barely seeps past my force field of shock.

If he didn't orchestrate this . . .

How did this happen?

"But you're here," I say dumbly.

It's like I've lost every last one of my brain cells. They got zapped when I went through the metal detectors at security.

"*I'm here* . . . exactly." He laughs with unabashed wonder. "By pure coincidence. You see, I finally came to a decision about contacting you. I decided I was going to give myself a little while to cool off. I was going to continue with my travel plans, fly to London for a week of meetings and then on to Belfast—"

"*Belfast?*"

"To check on a ship that's currently in production."

I want to go to Belfast! I want to go to Belfast *with him* . . .

He continues, "I told myself I could track you down once I got to London. I already knew I was going to make you see reason, beg you to give me a real chance."

"But—" I look behind me, trying to find the flight attendant, before I look back at Phillip with a furrowed brow. "I don't get what's going on."

"*Casey*," he stresses. "Don't you see what's happened? It was always my plan to fly out to London today. You can ask my assistant for proof. This ticket was booked weeks ago."

I shake my head. "I'm not accusing you of changing your flight last minute to follow me. I'm just . . . if you didn't know I was here, why did the flight attendant bring me up to you?"

This is when his smile turns a little wistful, his eyes so lovely and warm.

"When I first sat down here, I asked her to do a favor for me. I told her there was a woman I was hoping beyond hope would be on this flight and that I'd like her to check for me, just in case. I felt ridiculous asking her."

"You told her to *look for me*?"

"I was desperate! I told her what you looked like—" His eyes rove over my face like a gentle caress. "A gorgeous brunette with caramel highlights framing her face and expressive blue eyes. I told her your name, and then she walked away, and I laughed to myself because there was no way in hell you were on this flight, but I had to know. I'd prepared myself for her to walk back and shake her head and say, *I'm sorry, Mr. Woodmont, she's not here*, but instead, *you* walked up."

"Because I'm on this flight!"

"How?"

I shake my head. "I don't know exactly. I mean . . . I just booked the first—well, *second*—flight out of Fort Lauderdale once I got to the airport. I was going off of pure instinct."

He laughs. "This is insane."

"*Insane*," I repeat. "Did you upgrade my ticket?"

"Apparently," he says with a little smile.

"Thanks. I owe you."

I settle back against my seat and start fiddling with the remote control for the TV. I just need to figure this thing out. I want to watch a movie or, *or . . .*

"Casey."

My hand shakes as I press buttons. The TV doesn't start up, but that's because I haven't turned it on. Right.

"*Casey*," Phillip stresses my name, and I squeeze my eyes closed.

"How is this happening?" I ask myself out loud.

"Will you just look at me?"

I shake my head. "I can't. What were those complimentary drinks she listed off? I think I need something. A soda. *No*, a shot."

I'm leaning my head into the aisle, but all the flight attendants who were just here are now nowhere to be found!

Phillip says my name again, and I finally look at him. God, I can barely stand it. That face. Those terse eyebrows and intense blue eyes, those sharp cheekbones, and that perfect mouth.

"You don't understand how much it killed me to walk away from your suite this morning. I really thought that was the last time I was ever going to see you. And now you're just here, sitting beside me." Tears gather in the corners of my eyes, but they don't fall. "Phillip, I feel like I don't deserve it. It's too good."

He leans over the partition between us and scoops his hand beneath my hair, tilting my face so that I'm looking only at him.

"Please don't walk away from me out of fear. Not after this."

"You think this is fate?" I ask, trembling against his hand.

"It has to be."

He's right.

It has to be.

"I caught what you said earlier, about falling for me."

He pulls me closer to him so that I have to lean over the partition. "I meant it, Casey."

My stomach squeezes tightly, nerves and excitement blending and buzzing through me.

"Are we insane?" I ask with a little laugh.

His expression doesn't lighten. "If we are, I don't care."

I'm staring at his lips, waiting for him to kiss me. I want to feel his mouth pressed to mine. I want his solid body on me, physical confirmation that this is real and not an elaborate dream. He must sense my need because he closes the space between us and kisses me with tender affection. When he pulls back, he strings kisses along my cheek. And then he sighs, and his palpable relief washes over me, giving me comfort.

"I'm falling for you, too, Phillip."

I *have* fallen.

Hard.

My feelings are so obvious at this point that there's no sense in denying them to myself. I fell for Phillip despite every hope that I wouldn't. Every wall and every obstacle that I put in place proved utterly useless.

His responding smile threatens to upend me. Then he kisses me again, and that faint flame of desire curling through me, licking me from the inside out.

These curtains will have to be drawn ASAP. Phillip will have me over this partition and on his lap in no time.

The sound of footsteps carries down the aisle. No doubt it's the flight attendant with that warm towel she promised.

Phillip pulls back into his chair. "Wait. I didn't even get the chance to ask you yet. What are your plans? Where are you going once we land?"

"Oh, I didn't say? First, I'll be in London for a week . . . and then I guess I'm going to Belfast." I finish with a wink.

He laughs with wonderment.

"Ma'am," the flight attendant says from behind me. "Here's your warm towel. Is there anything else I can get you before we take off?"

I'm still looking at Phillip when I shake my head.

"No, thank you. I'm all set."

Everything I need is sitting in 3C.

"Wonderful. I'll be back around soon. For now, relax and enjoy your flight."

Oh, don't worry . . .

I plan to.

Epilogue
CASEY

Ahoy there! I'm Casey Hughes—novice travel influencer. I can't believe there are already so many of you following this account. I don't feel deserving of you all, and I will never stop thanking @TravelWithSiennaThompson for pushing me to take the leap and start this profile.

I suppose I should give you all a little context of who I am. I've seen some commenters wondering if I'm some heiress with money to burn, and, *boy, do I wish*! I'm actually a veritable nobody.

For the last few years, I've worked for a large travel magazine, doing a lot of unglamorous grunt work. My goal was to eventually become a travel writer, and I thought I was paying my dues and working my way toward that dream. Unfortunately . . . life doesn't always work that way.

To get where I am now, I had to say goodbye to the confines of my cubicle. I had to move on from an old career (that wasn't going anywhere) and leave the town I lived in my whole life. I had to take a leap of faith, and honestly . . . it was scary. It still is scary. I dove into the deep end with a laughable lack of savings and no real plan in place. There's been beauty in the chaos, though. And well . . . also a lot of unbeautiful chaos. I won't sugarcoat this. I'm flying by the seat of my pants. Rick Steves, I am not. But the world doesn't need another Rick Steves. He's the one and only. But here I am, Casey Hughes!

Any day might take me somewhere new, so follow along. I'll be sharing the good, the bad, and the ugly of what it looks like to explore the world. On my stories, I'll share little details of my day-to-day travels. On my feed, I'll post detailed itineraries for each destination so you all can easily reference them later.

Many of you have asked if I travel alone, and the short answer is *sometimes*. A few of you already noticed the man who occasionally pops up in my photos or on my stories. My boyfriend is the most deeply private person you'll ever meet, so for now, I won't be sharing too much about him on this account. But we'll be traveling together as much as his job allows. Other times, I'll be flying solo! For me, it's the best of both worlds.

Next up on our list? Tokyo!

Send me all of your Japan recs!

XO

Casey

Keep reading for a sneak peek at another irresistible romantic comedy by bestselling author R.S. Grey, *Enemies Abroad.*

Chapter One

I'm in my element this morning. Our principal called an all-staff meeting before school, so we all had to wake up at the crack of dawn to be here. My fellow teachers are dragging, but I'm not. I man the refreshment table—the one I voluntarily set up. I brought in a carafe of Starbucks coffee and a few dozen doughnuts. In the center of the spread, there's a tray of intricately iced sugar cookies replete with swirling designs and hand-rendered illustrations of the Lindale Middle School mascot. *Go Lizards!*

"Wow, Audrey, you've really outdone yourself."

I bask in the approval of my coworkers.

"Best cookies around," another one says, taking a second cookie with a wink.

My smile feels permanent.

But then it slips right off my face.

Noah Peterson walks into the room, and I'm shocked his arrival isn't accompanied by claps of thunder and billowing smoke. There should at least be some foreboding music.

He already has a thermos of coffee and a breakfast taco in hand. He has no reason to come over to my table. He should take a seat near the door and sit patiently for the meeting to start, but he just can't help himself.

I turn and busy myself by rearranging the napkins that were already layered in a neat fan.

He reaches me in no time at all because he's gargantuan and his strides eat up the distance.

I look up at him, donning a perfectly bored expression as if to say *Oh, it's just you. What a letdown.*

"Morning, Noah. What's in the thermos?" I ask. "Diesel fuel? Battery acid? Human blood?"

Okay. Apparently, I just can't help myself either.

Every day I wake up and think *Good morning to everyone except Noah Peterson.*

He points down at one of the sugar cookies.

"What's that supposed to be?"

He knows what it's supposed to be—I spent hours icing them to perfection—yet still, I find myself replying, "It's a lizard."

"Oh, gotcha."

My eyes are narrowed little slits. "It's . . . pretty obvious."

He tilts his head to the left, squints, and pretends to study it harder. "It kind of looks like a snake."

He picks one up and holds it out to another teacher for a second opinion.

"Oh, cute snake," the teacher says, innocently following Noah's lead.

My hands are tight fists. "Okay, you don't get any."

There's humor in his gaze now that he knows he's won. "I thought they were for everyone."

"Not you."

"I already touched this one."

I take it out of his hand and thunk it into the trash can beside the table, then walk away.

Just great.

Now I have to reset my mental days-without-incident tally back to zero. I was at an all-time record: two.

Still, I don't regret it. I didn't bake those cookies for Noah. He doesn't deserve to taste my delicious treats.

The meeting is due to start any minute, but the conference table is still relatively empty. Most of my coworkers choose to hover around the periphery of the room, lost in the masses so Principal O'Malley doesn't call on them to answer any questions.

I take a seat and carefully lay out my pens and personalized notepad. Property of Ms. Cohen.

I'm aware of Noah as he takes a seat on the opposite side of the table, a few chairs down.

Quickly, the seats fill around him.

He's everything I'm not. Easygoing and adored by all.

Every spring, his picture makes it into the yearbook beside the superlative title Lindale's Coolest Teacher. I never win any superlatives, not even the lame ones.

Apparently, I'm a *try hard*, as I once heard another teacher so lovingly put it when she didn't realize I was still in the lounge, nuking my Lean Cuisine. I'm the teacher who shows up obnoxiously early for meetings and volunteers to stay late for car pool. My classroom looks like the aftermath of a Michaels explosion. I have elaborate bulletin boards with layered decor, inspirational posters, reward charts. My students barely have room to sit.

When Noah first saw my classroom at the start of the school year, his eyebrows hit his hairline.

"Wow . . . this is a lot even for you, and that's not a compliment."

I chose to ignore his mocking tone and, instead, smiled as if he'd just said the nicest thing ever. Something like *Audrey, you're my hero. There's no one smarter or cooler than you.*

"Thank you."

"How long did this take you?"

"I bought most everything."

With that lie, I toed my trash can farther underneath my desk so he couldn't see the empty glue stick wrapper proclaiming *Now with 200 sticks!* Then I tucked my hand behind my back to hide the Band-Aid I was wearing on my right thumb. Cricut injury.

"Is that a papier-mâché replica of the Eiffel Tower?"

"Oh . . . yeah. You can find anything on Amazon these days."

The Eiffel Tower took me a whole week. It fills an entire corner of the classroom. Children can sit underneath it and read on soft pillows and blankets.

What do other people do on their summer breaks?

Now, Principal O'Malley walks into the conference room with a cup of gas station coffee and a rattling key ring. He's dressed in a faded gray suit and a patterned tie from the '90s. He's short and squat with a spare tire around his middle. The few wisps of hair left on the top of his head are desperately holding on for dear life.

When he calls an all-staff meeting, we know to buckle up for a long ride.

Like a drunk uncle given free rein of a mic at a wedding, Principal O'Malley knows how to fill time. He has the uncanny ability to stretch a brief announcement into an hour-long, rambling speech.

I zone out for a minute when we're discussing the efficiency of the lunch lines and find myself tuning in again to an entirely different topic.

"As you all go about your day, I want you to try to embody the acronym TEACHER. Terrific. Energetic. Awesome. Cheerful. Enthusiastic—"

"You missed *H*," someone calls out.

Principal O'Malley stops and starts to backtrack, ticking off the letters on his meaty fingers.

Oh dear god . . .

"Doesn't *H* stand for Hardworking?" someone else asks.

"I thought it was Helpful," Noah chimes in, knowing exactly what he's doing.

For ten minutes, the meeting gets derailed as Principal O'Malley takes a vote on whether we think *H* should stand for Helpful or Hardworking.

The tally comes out to an even split, and Vice Principal Trammell—the real brains behind the operation around here—steps in and politely suggests we move on to the next topic on the agenda.

"Ah yes." Principal O'Malley clears his throat and affects a whole new solemn tone when he continues. "I have some horrible news to report. Our beloved Mrs. Mann was in a motorcycle accident yesterday."

There's a collective gasp from around the room, and then everyone wants details.

"OMG!"

"Poor Mrs. Mann!"

"She was struck by a *motorcycle*?"

"She was *riding* on one," Principal O'Malley clarifies.

Not possible.

Mrs. Mann is a sixty-year-old social studies teacher who weighs eighty pounds soaking wet. Her wardrobe is purchased from an Amish catalog. She shouts at students for running through the hallways yet chides them for being late. She once scolded me for not having better posture.

"She's in a motorcycle club for ladies over sixty. Vests, patches—you name it. Anyway, yesterday, she had a little run-in with an ice cream truck and broke her wrist. Expecting a full recovery, but that means there's been a shake-up with the Rome trip this summer."

Every year, Mrs. Mann and her husband—a history professor at the local college—voluntarily take a group of ten middle school students to Italy for a three-week study-abroad program, and every year I think *Better them than me.* Who in their right mind would volunteer to use part of their summer break to chaperone thirteen-year-olds in a foreign country?

"The students have already been selected for this summer's trip, and you've probably seen them around the school, working hard to earn their fundraising dollars." He claps a hand on his belly. "They got me one too many times with the chocolate bars, but I tell you what . . .

they don't call them *World's Finest Chocolate* for nothing. I just can't resist 'em."

Having realized it might be best if she takes over, Vice Principal Trammell steps up, smiling politely. Without her, this place would unravel.

"We're looking for two teacher volunteers to take the place of Mrs. Mann and her husband for the trip, which will span three weeks in July. Are there any takers?"

Crickets.

Vice Principal Trammell's gaze sweeps the room, and we all look anywhere but at her.

"Mrs. Vincent?" Vice Principal Trammell asks, sounding hopeful.

Mrs. Vincent is the Spanish teacher, but she's one of those geniuses who speaks like eight languages, Italian being one of them.

She holds up her hands in defeat. "Oh *man*. I wish!" She doesn't wish. "It sounds so fun. Rome in the heat of summer—sign me up." She's barely masking her sarcasm. "But I'm due to deliver my baby at the end of August, so I doubt my OB wants me traveling overseas that late into my pregnancy."

Every pregnant teacher in the room breathes a heavy sigh of relief. What a perfect excuse.

If only I were pregnant.

Or married.

Or in a relationship of any kind.

My only commitment at the moment is with my dry cleaner. No one, and I mean *no one*, gets chocolate stains out of fabric like he does.

Vice Principal Trammell purses her lips. "Right. Well, if any of you has a change of heart, please let me know. We need to fill the two spots by Friday, or we'll have to inform the students that the trip is canceled. It'll really break their hearts."

She's digging deep with that one, trying to get us to bend.

For a moment, I start to give in. Maybe I *should* go. What a wonderful opportunity for these adolescents to explore the world and expand their minds.

Then I remember how Danny in my third period farted yesterday, and the smell was so nauseating I was forced to evacuate my entire classroom until a custodian could come open the windows and air it out. I bet the scent will still be there today.

My heart turns as cold as ice. If the trip is canceled, we'll just wheel in an old TV on a cart and have the students watch a grainy documentary about Rome. They'll be fine.

After the meeting, I stand and gather my things, neatly tearing off the top sheet of my notepad so I can trash it. Sensing early on that I wouldn't need to take notes during the meeting, I doodled in the margins instead. Just idyllic little scenes of Noah getting struck by lightning. Falling into the lion enclosure at the zoo. Crying as his check engine light comes on.

All the teachers filter out, joking and talking with each other. I look up as Noah passes by on the opposite side of the conference table. He makes like he's going to keep walking; then he suddenly stops midstride, rocks back on his heels, and looks over at me.

"Y'know, I'm surprised you didn't volunteer to go to Rome," he tells me. "*So* unlike you."

"I'm busy this summer."

Not wanting to encourage him, I head over to the refreshment table so I can start to pack up my extra cookies. He rounds the table and meets me there.

"I'll bet you are. Already planned your room decor for next year? I heard there's a shortage on construction paper across the city."

I go about my business as if I'm not the least bit bothered by him. It's not as easy as it seems, given his size. He's six feet something. He should be gangly and awkward, but he's not. He's broad shouldered and in my way.

I bat my eyelashes at him like I'm playing coy. "And what about you? What will *you* do all summer without children to terrorize?"

"My students love me."

It's true.

Noah is only one classroom over, and we share a wall. I hear every time he makes his class laugh.

Still, for good show, I grunt in disbelief and tilt my head so I can look into his breathtakingly hideous brown eyes.

"They only laugh at your jokes because they feel bad for you."

"I'm hilarious."

"You mispronounced *annoying*."

He doesn't want to smile, but he almost does. I lean forward, wanting it. Then realizing how close he is to giving me that pleasure, he restores his face to its factory setting.

After the meeting, I don't expect to hear anything more about Rome.

I put it out of my head completely until I get an email about it later that night. I'm in my apartment, alone, making enough dinner for five and calculating how many days I can get away with eating leftover mushroom risotto without feeling physically ill at the thought. My phone pings, and my heart leaps.

I want it to be a text from someone, *anyone*.

At twenty-seven, my single friends are starting to drop like flies. I can't go to a family function without a well-meaning relative feeling sorry for me.

"Your time will come, too, sweetie . . ."

Uh, thanks, Aunt Marge, but I'm sort of just trying to eat my pumpkin pie in peace if that's all right with you.

My friends are not only getting married, but also they're starting to reproduce.

Fun, boozy brunches have been replaced with playdates at the park and baby-yoga classes. I participate as much as I can. I throw myself into being the best *auntie* ever, but at the end of the day, my friends' lives are moving in a new direction, and mine isn't.

When I see that the notification on my phone is just an email from work, I almost don't read it. I already have a murder mystery cued up and a stack of assignments to grade, but the subject line catches my eye.

Bonus for Rome Chaperones!

Bonus?

I open the email and groan at how long it is. There are details about the trip: dates, expectations, guidelines. Yada yada. I only care about one thing, and I find it way at the bottom.

> Having conducted the trip every summer for the last fifteen years, Mr. and Mrs. Mann are very anxious to carry on the tradition and find two eager chaperones to fill their spots. Hearing that there was no initial interest, they have decided to generously establish an incentive fund. Each chaperone will be granted a $2,500 bonus on top of having their travel expenses covered.
>
> If interested, please stop by Principal O'Malley's office before May 20th.

Well now . . . that changes things.

I set down my phone and mull it over.

Twenty-five hundred dollars is nothing to scoff at. That amount of money doesn't regularly fall into my lap. My teacher salary affords me a one-bedroom apartment, meager living expenses, and a spare one hundred dollars a month to sock away into savings. I'm not exactly rolling in it.

At the same time, I'm not sure twenty-five hundred dollars is enough to convince me to spend three weeks abroad with a tagalong troop of middle schoolers.

Undecided, I take a bowl of risotto over to the couch and eat while I check my calendar.

Let's see, in July, I have my dad's birthday on the sixth and a routine dental cleaning on the thirteenth. There's also an event on the twentieth titled Beach Weekend with Jeff, but Jeff and I broke up a year ago, so I'm not sure what that's doing there.

I delete it, and my month clears up even more.

Some people would find this deeply depressing.

I only find it mildly depressing.

Look at all the days with no obligations. I could literally fall through an open manhole, and no one would report me missing for weeks!

I don't even need to consult my friends or family to know what their advice would be.

My mom would tell me *Do it! Shake things up! Get out of your comfort zone!*

My friends would say *Think of all the hot Italian men! You could find your soulmate!*

My dad would say *Rome! I just watched a HISTORY channel docu-series on Mount Vesuvius, and it's bound to blow any minute. You're better off staying in the States. Don't want to end up like those poor people in Pompeii.*

With a defeated sigh, I close my laptop.

It's decided, then. I'll go to Principal O'Malley's office first thing in the morning.

Apparently, I'm going to Rome.

ABOUT THE AUTHOR

R.S. Grey is the *USA Today* bestselling author of over thirty novels. She lives in Texas with her husband and two daughters.

Join Grey's mailing list to stay up to date on future releases at https://landing.mailerlite.com/webforms/landing/u9h5u7, and join the Little Reds Facebook group to connect with other readers at www.facebook.com/groups/1378399812435745/.

Stay connected with Grey on Facebook, Instagram (@AuthorRSGrey), and Goodreads (www.goodreads.com/rsgrey).

Find all Grey's books at https://rsgrey.com.